Southern Zion

DAVID R. WATERS

CONTENTS

ACKNOWLEDGMENTS

To the many great men and women, I've had the privilege to serve with for twenty years of law enforcement. Detective Chris Frosch, Lieutenant David Nabors, and Texas Rangers Richard Shing and J. Odom, to name a few. The endless hours of work, case prep, surveillance, and typing, forged respect and friendships never forgotten.

To Suz Korb, a creative genius and consummate professional. A talent I hope to one day reflect a fraction of. When writing, as difficult as it is to believe in yourself, it is even more difficult to have someone so respected believe in you as well. Her patience, her kindness, and honesty are much appreciated.

Lastly, to my wife, Marti. Her encouragement and support were a constant even when self-doubt was prevalent. The deafening silence she received after hard days was frustrating no doubt, but I wanted her smile to be pure, her hugs and kisses to be sincere, and her love unsullied by the malignant ghosts of reality. An 'I love you' is never enough, but I will continue to say it.

PROLOGUE

Texas Ranger Co. B-Garland, Texas

"Welcome to Company B Ranger Kidd," Major Hardy said smiling as he presented his hand for Kidd to shake. Kidd stood next to the Major. Next to Kidd's six foot two, two hundred and thirty-five-pound frame, the Major looked like Kidd's little brother.

The major's hand was smooth, but firm. Not at all like Kidd's journey to the Texas Rangers. It was a far cry from Albuquerque PD. Not a day went by where the death of his partner Keith Spearman didn't haunt his thoughts, but today was the official start of a new chapter in life. The hearings and inquiries into Spearman's death went from focusing on a corrupt administration and political system to a direct indictment of every action Kidd and the other detectives took during that last fateful investigation.

In the end, a good man was dead, the administration of the department was largely unaffected, and the politicians were still corrupt. The truth was a piece of Darren Kidd died that day as well. The strain was too much for Kidd and his wife, Michelle, who divorced him and promptly took their daughter Jillian and left for her childhood home in Corsicana, Texas. It was a new low point in the Detective's life and career, and he was for sure done with law enforcement, or so he thought.

It was Texas Ranger Sergeant Richard Flynt that came to Kidd's career rescue. He worked with Kidd on his last case and saw the investigative skills of the younger man. Flynt was also dear friends with Keith Spearman. So naturally, when the investigation into Spearman's death kept focusing on baseless rumors concerning Kidd and his colleagues' actions or inactions, Flynt decided to take some action. It didn't take much to convince Kidd he needed to leave Albuquerque PD. After all, he grew up in the Dallas area and he wanted to be near his daughter. There was nothing in Albuquerque to keep him.

Richard Flynt was a thirty-five-year career Texas Ranger. He stood six foot two inches, thin, and had a personality everyone loved. He was respected by every law enforcement entity in the state for his investigative prowess and made a lot of well-connected friends throughout the span of his career but despised by several of his own administrators. They viewed him as a prima donna that liked nothing more than to question their leadership and take every chance to make them look silly to his influential friends.

Truthfully, being personal friends with the Governor had its perks. Only Flynt could convince the sitting Governor to give an out of state, non-employee of the Texas Department of Public Safety a Texas Ranger Commission. That hadn't been done in decades. In the early days, the best investigators were appointed as Rangers by the state. That all changed in the thirties when the Rangers became a branch of the Texas Department of Public Safety.

Now Rangers were commissioned strictly from their ranks. Richard Flynt was not only able get Kidd commissioned, but he got him stationed in Garland with Company B as well. Flynt didn't necessarily like Garland, but it had the only Major that didn't want him fired. So, in the interest of maintaining harmony before his retirement, Flynt agreed to stay in Garland for the remainder of his career.

Kidd and Flynt recently cut their teeth on a Capital Murder case out of Kaufman, Texas. A local pizza parlor was robbed, and a clerk shot to death. It was Kidd's interrogation of an accomplice that broke the case. That got him noticed by the other Rangers of Company B, but his appointment wasn't exactly popular with the rest of The Department. Kidd knew that a target was on his back, he would have to continue to produce and prove himself, maybe for the rest of his career.

"What did you think of the speech?" Major Hardy joined Kidd at the table that contained the generic store-bought cake and punch that seem to accompany any get together at DPS. The room was very ordinary. The flat roofed, one-story office building off of Interstate 30 contained the drab brown or 'baby-shit' colored brick that seemed to dominate the administrative buildings constructed in North Texas in the seventies. The interior was plain as well with gray, berber carpet and neutral paint. There were only about twenty people that showed up for the celebration, a few Rangers in Company B, employees from the crime lab, and the intelligence unit that shared the building with the Rangers.

Kidd could actually tell who worked for each department because in a social setting the respective departments still mingled primarily with each other. It was a phenomenon he observed in every work setting he ever faced, but today he wondered if those work cliques were talking about him.

"It was good Sir, and I thank you for welcoming me to the unit," Kidd managed to irk out a smile, though so much more was on his mind. He couldn't help but survey the room and try to read the faces of his colleagues. He saw many actions and expressions that seemed genuinely accepting, but there were looks of jealousy and suspicion scattered in between. It was enough to cause Kidd some trepidation in the midst of a very satisfying moment. At the end of the speech, Kidd felt further removed from the unit, but that had been the mark of his career.

"That was a damn fine speech Major!" Flynt blurted as he joined the two men in the corner of the room. He put his arm around the Major as he stood beside him. Flynt's tall frame dressed impeccably in his white shirt, poly-denim slacks, and Lucchese boots towered over the Major. Flynt's thick, East Texas accent was deceptive. Yankees may have thought him to be some country bumpkin, but Flynt was one of the smartest men Kidd knew, his obvious sarcasm towards the major made Kidd chuckle inside.

In the speech, Major Hardy talked about the formation of the Texas Rangers in 1823 by Stephen F. Austin. Those ten men would form the basis of the oldest law enforcement organization in North America. The Major touched on famous Texas Ranger exploits such as Bonnie and Clyde and john Wesley Hardin, but concentrated mostly on the Governor 'Ma' Ferguson era, which saw the Rangers reorganized into six companies, A through F. Then there was a brief history about Company B. Kidd could see that Flynt took the information for granted, but he couldn't help but feel a little overwhelmed given his situation.

"Oh, shut the hell up smart-ass!" Hardy fired back. "I know when you're bull-shitting someone Richard."

"Nonsense Major! The history of the Rangers is never a mockin' subject. One riot, one Ranger Sir!" Flynt winked at Kidd. "But tell me something Major…what about the Mexican Revolution when we went out and killed all them folks in cold blood?" Hardy held his middle finger towards Flynt as he stepped away from the two men to answer his ringing cellular phone.

"Damn Richard, you're running out of Majors that will work with your stubborn ass," Kidd whispered. His expression gave away the concern he felt.

"Well why stop what works after thirty-five years?" Flynt looked at his new younger partner curiously. "You okay?"

Kidd smiled and was a bit impressed by Flynt's intuitiveness. "I really have never got a chance to thank you for…ya know…for setting me up here."

"Nice try but that's a bullshit answer."

Kidd nodded humbly, "A cake? I haven't done shit! And what's worse, I went ahead of God knows how many troopers that wanted my position? I just don't know that they'll ever accept me here."

It was Flynt's turn to laugh, "You know I been workin' here so long and I've learned a thing or two. First, you never give a shit what anyone else thinks, and second, when opportunities come, you take em'. All else be damned."

"Point taken."

"You'll have plenty of time to show up these bastards in the field. Believe me," Flynt said. The Major came up behind Flynt and tapped him on the shoulder.

"You and Kidd need to get down to Eagle Pass ASAP," Hardy said with a concerned look.

"Eagle Pass? That's D Company Major," Flynt replied in a puzzled voice.

"This is from the Deputy Director. He specifically asked for you Richard. He said something about a mass grave down there off the highway. They said the media hasn't got a hold of it just yet but it'll bust wide open. They got the highway closed for now, but they got to have it open in the morning. We got about twelve hours."

"I'm happy to go Major, but what about Eagle Pass PD?" Flynt interrupted. "That's Dan Gummit's outfit."

"Exactly," Major Hardy was smiling now.

"Who's Dan Gummit?" Kidd asked.

"Only the most worthless son of a bitch to ever don a uniform," Flynt answered. "He's a former Assistant Deputy Director of services…a real horse's ass." Flynt turned to Hardy and smiled, "Umm…no offense Major but Division has to know that me and Gummit hate each other, right?"

"Well that's what you get for having friends in high places," Hardy smiled. "Now get your asses down to Eagle Pass."

*

Eagle Pass, Texas

"I had to tell you first, you know…before it's announced in church," Amanda said with some apprehension in her voice. Sariah looked at her curiously. They stood in the barn on the far Northeast corner of the Johnson compound. Amanda Johnson and Sariah Larsen were the best of friends, but they couldn't be more different.

They were both daughters of polygamist fathers and mothers. Amanda's father was Bishop Thomas Johnson, the spiritual leader of the Texas Stake of The Inspired Church of Jesus Christ of Latter-day Saints. The Johnsons took a traditional approach to their religion and required their children to dress conservatively.

That meant the girls wore modest, ankle length dresses and were to tend the household chores in the compound under the direction of the sister-wives. "Ruth and I are going to move to Utah. We're being married off to the Smoot family." Amanda's voice was almost apologetic when she spoke. Sariah knew that Amanda was almost afraid of telling her of the engagement.

"Wow, I guess I should be falling all over you congratulating you for being an adolescent bride for a middle-aged pervert!" Sariah snapped. She wasn't mad at Amanda, but hurt she was about to lose her best friend, and angry about the circumstances.

"That's not fair Sariah!"

"It is the truth and you know it! You just can't leave the lifestyle or defy the brethren."

"And what about you?! You talk a big talk, but you can't leave either!" Amanda fumed at Sariah with her eyes tearing.

"At least I'm honest. You're a fake!"

Sariah pulled out a cigarette from her purse and lit it in disgust. She knew Amanda hated it when she smoked. Besides being against God's law, or The Word of Wisdom, the outward display of rebellion was maddening to the faithful.

Deep down Sariah knew Amanda was right about her being a fake, and it hurt. She consciously led her life to defy her upbringing and yet she couldn't leave the security of her home and culture. She wanted to be free of the brethren's grip and an oppressive religion, but she was only eighteen and she dearly loved her family.

They may be misguided, but they were hers. Besides, she only had a year of community college and work under her belt. Sariah's family was more modern than Amanda's. Sariah's father, Jeremiah, ran a small contracting business with Sariah's brothers.

Sariah had three mothers, Sara her natural mother, Susan, and Beth. Sara and Susan worked outside the home as nurses for a family doctor. They came home in the evening to assist Beth with the chores and child rearing. To her father's credit, he also helped with the household duties when he was not working.

Even her older brothers chipped in. As far as polygamist families are concerned, the Larsen's were as cosmopolitan as they come. Sariah stood and looked at Amanda, also tearing up. Her snug designer jeans and shirt stood in sharp contrast to Amanda's attire. Her brunette hair was straitened and highlighted, and her figure showed signs that her constant crossfit and zumba training was in fact paying off, minus the cigarette in her hand.

"You're right Amanda…I'm afraid of leaving, and I'm sorry for what I said." Both girls were crying and hugged. The barn was a simple steel structure on the Johnson's two-hundred-acre compound. The terrain on those acres was as diverse as South Texas itself, and seemed to contain every type of landscaping the region had to offer. From the rocky outcroppings to the brown dirt littered with brush, forbs, and trees.

The land surrounded the white walled, inner-compound where the temple was located and where the Johnson's actually lived. Sariah had to drive her car into the barn, outside the fenced compound, so that Amanda's mothers wouldn't see her arrive. It wasn't that she wasn't welcome at the Johnson's. After all, they were all members of God's true church.

But the Bishop and his wives thought Sariah, and the Larsen's in general, flirted too much with sin, with their worldly attitudes and lifestyle. She didn't worry about the Johnson children snitching her off. It was understood that as sons and daughters of polygamists, it was you against your parents. Since they always united in their parenting, the children had to be united in their behaviors.

That meant never spilling the secrets of your siblings, because they could always spill yours. Besides, she was very well liked by most of the Johnson kids. "How's Ruth doing?"

"You know her…she just wants to follow the prophet."

"So, President Josephs set the match?" Sariah inquired. Nephi Josephs was the President, Prophet, Seer, and Revelator of the Inspired Church of Jesus Christ of Latter-day Saints. Though he lived in Southern Utah, he occasionally visited the ward in Eagle Pass. His word was law to members of the church.

"That's what Father said," Amanda replied. She began to cry at that point. "I'm just scared!" Sariah held her best friend in her arms and sobbed with her. She stroked Amanda's silky, blonde hair. *She's only seventeen and Ruth is sixteen,* Sariah thought. Inside she boiled when she thought about this young, beautiful girl being violated by some nasty old pervert with scriptures as his justification. It just wasn't right. But what could she do?

CHAPTER ONE

Inferno

It was like hell on earth. The scene was chaotic and ugly, unlike the drive there. The El Indio Highway, well west of Ericka Street, looked like an invasion of emergency vehicles. Kidd counted three agencies, Eagle Pass PD, Maverick County SO, and Texas Department of Public Safety as well as ambulances and fire trucks as far as the eye could see.

It reminded Kidd of a human beehive. He looked at his partner who was cringing with disgust. Kidd knew what Flynt was thinking, the number of people in a crime scene is directly proportional to how pissed off the lead investigators would be. That meant someone must be really upset. Kidd started to count the bars and stars on some of the uniforms loitering around the scene. He laughed inside; some things never change.

The leadership, or brass, always showed up to the scene, and never helped. Everywhere they looked they saw badges and patches. There seemed to be a lot of talking but not much was being accomplished. Flynt and Kidd were waived to when they drove in the outer perimeter of the scene. Kidd sat silently and mentally prepared himself for the scene.

He could tell that Flynt was doing the same. The mark of a true investigator is his thought process before he even knows what he has. Normally, a series of plans and contingency plans will float around in his mind and that will ease the tension and anxiety of his soul. Today was different. Why did the soul need at ease? When witnessing the brutality of men, it's best to have the mind filled with purpose and the heart filled with something else.

It has been said that South Texas is like God's treadmill, the wonder and natural beauty is ever-present, but the drive can kill you. The map makes the distance look insignificant, but if one ever travelled from Dallas to Eagle Pass, they would swear you had crossed three latitude lines of the earth. It was like the earth couldn't make up its mind. Kidd had never been to this part of Texas. The only time that he ever drove south growing up was to go to the beach in Port Aransas. The south borderlands of Texas were never on the itinerary. Parts seemed to resemble the rugged hill country near San Antonio and Austin. Some resembled the rolling prairies of North Texas complete with the occasional tree lines and wooded areas that acted as natural boundaries to the scenery. Then there were pastures and farmland mixed in with the most beautiful and symmetrical grooves and lush vegetation and the ever-present desert seemed to creep and overtake the remaining space. The houses were as diverse as the land itself. Large, brick veneer ranch style houses sat in beautiful settings and immediately down the road, single-wide mobile homes would simply appear. All types live in the borderlands, Kidd was told by his partner, and Richard Flynt hasn't been wrong yet. They grabbed a bite at a little café outside Uvalde, before making their final decent to Eagle Pass. Maybe in the rest of the country cops went for doughnuts, but in Texas, it was meat.

"This is Eagle Pass City limits out here?" Kidd inquired looking at the vast, rural area.

"The city acquired this land from the county years ago. These border town populations are exploding so the city decided to prepare," Flynt answered. "You ready for this young buck?"

"Yep, it's like riding a bike, except nastier and a hell of a lot more tedious," Kidd grinned.

They parked about a quarter mile north of the scene on an unapproved section of the road. Kidd was glad Flynt parked so far away. Major crime scenes like this become a virtual law enforcement traffic jam once they cleared. They both got out of the blue, Crown Victoria almost on cue, like it was rehearsed. The crisp air was dusty from the efforts being expended at the scene. In the distance, Flynt could see a backhoe and about twenty unformed people with shovels. The two men walked toward the mayhem slowly and cast their eyes roundabout as if there was some valuable piece of evidence was going to pop up that was somehow missed by the virtual battalion of cops. In actuality, that happens more often than one would think. They approached the outer perimeter marked by the standard issue yellow, crime-scene tape. Kidd was handed a clipboard with a Major Incident Log attached which he signed willingly. The officer was from Eagle Pass, 'Martinez' the name plate showed. Martinez never even asked the Flynt and Kidd what their business was at the scene; another perk of a Texas Ranger. The uniform is universally recognized and respected throughout Texas.

"Damn could we get any more people in this crime scene?" Flynt asked sarcastically. Kidd and even Martinez laughed.

"It looks like dance, *no?*" Martinez observed causing the two Rangers to laugh. The three men stood back and looked, criticized and even made fun of the situation unfolding in front of them. To the west of their location, a bunch of highway workers mixed with a number of curious citizens stood and looked on as well. Martinez made a good observation, Kidd thought. The most common problem with murder scenes was being improperly secured. Whether there was two few officers to maintain control of the scene, or there be way too many people in the crime scene contaminating the area and any potential evidence. Crime Scene Investigation was a delicate science, there's only one opportunity to get it right.

"How long they been going at it?" Flynt inquired.

"Highway crew stumbled upon it about Zero Five-Thirty I'd say," Martinez replied. "They needed to grate the ground in this area and they turned up a grave. They called me from home and told me get up here ASAP…you know. So, I haul ass up here and they handed me the fucking case log!" Martinez grinned. "Anyway, I got twenty pages of names now."

Kidd stared at the names. Every person that sets foot inside that perimeter has to have their names on the sheet, and each sheet contained a hell of a lot of names. "Who is in charge of the scene?" Kidd spoke out.

"The big guy himself, Chief Gummit," Martinez said with his eyes semi-rolling. Kidd looked at Flynt who was obviously biting his tongue and wanting to say something. But the reality was you never spoke ill of an officer's chief, unless that officer says something.

"Is that a good thing?" Flynt asked.

"Hell, no man! It's a joke!" Martinez fumed. "He's got no business being there, but he took some FBI course that empowered his ass, so now if anybody farts in this town he feels he needs to be there."

"Who is on the crime scene?" Flynt spoke up.

"Nichols from DPS," Martinez replied.

"Where the hell is she?"

"Buried in all the damn brass I guess," Martinez giggled.

"Do me a favor, could you get on the radio and call for Nichols to come out here and meet us?" Flynt asked.

"Ten –four, Sergeant Flynt."

Kidd could here Martinez calling on the radio. He continued to watch the cop-beehive and listen to the rumble of the machinery and the distant voices. He still didn't comprehend what was in there. Although he had never felt more influential since he had become a Ranger, he still felt like a guest at every scene that he showed up to, much like the old horror movies that required the host to invite the vampire in. He was also a bit nervous to meet Nichols. As a new guy, you always worry about what your colleagues thought of you; this was especially true of Kidd given the peculiar circumstances surrounding his commission. As he looked around, he saw an attractive blonde walking towards him and Flynt. She wore navy blue 511cargo style pants and a black, nylon jacket with "DPS Crime Scene" prominently displayed in white letters across the back. As she approached the men, she took off her blue latex gloves and ran her hands through her thick, wavy hair. Kidd could see by her face that she had him by a few years, but it didn't matter, she was beautiful. It was then that he realized Nichols wasn't the stereotypical crime scene investigator he was used to.

"Well Richard Flynt! Where the hell they been keeping you?" Nichols smiled and threw her arms around Flynt and the two embraced in a less than professional manner. Kidd raised an eyebrow in suspicion.

"Well since you ran me off I been slumming over in

Garland," Flynt winked at her.

"You're so ornery, Sweetie!" She hugged Flynt again, further enhancing Kidd's suspicions.

Flynt turned to Kidd, "Partner, I'd like you to meet Deb Nichols, the best damn crime scene investigator in the department. Deb, this is Darren Kidd."

Kidd reached out his hand to shake, "Pleased to meet you…" Nichols promptly grabbed his hand and pulled him into her body for a hug. Kidd stiffened as if he were an adolescent touching a woman for the first time. His mind kept flashing back to all the sexual harassment classes he was forced to attend by the Marine Corps and the Albuquerque Police.

"I ain't gonna bite you hard Sweetie! We hug here in Texas," Nichols laughed, joined by a few chuckles from Flynt. Kidd blushed as he disengaged from the hug, noting that Nichols smelled really good for being a crime scene tech. She wasn't the overweight male patrol veterans he was used to working with.

"Now Deb, he's a little scared of sexual harassment," Flynt said in a patronizing tone.

"Doesn't he know that we don't support sexual harassment here in Texas, but we do grade it," Nichols chided and tapped Kidd on the butt to further add to his obvious embarrassment.

"Damn Deb he just got here!" Flynt laughed. "You're going to scare him off."

"You guys suck!" Kidd observed, laughing. They all caught up on small talk, ignoring the crime scene circus in their midst, as if there were an elephant in the room. Gradually, they began to come back around to the obvious.

"What do you got over there?" Flynt inquired.

"A cluster-fuck Richard," Nichols replied. "Looks like a mass grave, several bodies and parts, various stages of decomposition, some dismembered." Kidd was always amazed at the way crime scene techs could de-sensationalize the most horrific circumstances into a mundane work task.

"We talking, like, Mexican Cartels?" Kidd inquired. There were several documented mass graves in Chihuahua and Coahuila, but in the States, this was unheard of. Kidd knew that the press was going to have a field day. It would be the most sensational news in the country, and Americans morbid fascination with death would become ever present in this little corner of Texas. The world would soon recognize a corner of the world it had no idea existed. Flynt said he always loved coming to South Texas growing up, but most Texans had no use for the rough area and dismissed it as a crime ridden dessert that just so happened to be connected to the Lone Star State. The truth was, that the area was among the fastest growing areas in the United States and recognized for its rugged beauty as well as a sportsman's haven. The largest white-tailed deer in the country have been recorded in the area, which drew Flynt's father here when he was young. He shuttered at the thought of such a pristine land being stained by news crews and tabloid people.

"That's what I thought at first, Darren. But this one is strange."

"Why Deb?" Flynt inquired.

"The of the decedents appear to be female, and young. Last one put in was only there a couple months maybe. That's just a guess of course, but Doctor Sunjani from Fort Worth is coming out, he's bringing a forensic pathologist from Dallas named Richard Gent. I've heard of the guy, he's nationally known and published," Nichols responded. "The cartel graves across the border I've heard of are mostly dismembered men, usually buried at the same time. There's none of that here, and not near as brutal. It's almost like…nah I won't speculate."

"Speculate dammit!"

"Okay grumpy!" Nichols glared at Flynt for a brief moment. "Cartel graves are dug to dispose of a large amount of bodies for convenience sake. It's like the bastards kill so many they gotta have a place to put all of em', right? Whoever did this grave, buried these bodies at different times, like it's a central location. Very organized and stacked…yet chaotic because there's differing levels of decomposition throughout."

"But you said that they were dismembered", Kidd interrupted.

"Yes, but almost as an afterthought," Nichols replied. "It's just all random."

"You thinking our guys are home-grown Deb?" Flynt took a much lighter tone with that question.

"No, I won't go that far, I don't put anything past the Negras. Just sign the log and let's go under the tape." The Piedras Negras Cartel, or Negras as they were nicknamed, was known for their ruthlessness and fearless assassinations. They had earned their reputation by a fierce war against the Sinaloa Cartel and Los Zetas and gained a lot of territory in Coahuila. In the end however, they were pushed back to Piedras Negras where they held their ground against serious attacks from their rivals, a loose treaty was created. The Negras controlled the area and the routes into the states from Coahuila. It was assumed by most Americans that cartels do their dirty work in Mexico. Unfortunately, law enforcement knew better.

Both men signed the major log incident log that Martinez held and proceeded under the tape, towards the masses of emergency personnel. The scene was truly in a remote area, it was technically in the city limits of Eagle Pass, but far enough away from any civilization that the smell of decomposition, which was becoming more pronounced as they got closer to the scene, wouldn't be detected. There was an electric company access road they walked to get closer. The brush and mesquites that once thickened the landscape were torn aside by the contractor's heavy equipment. The signs of progress seemed not only to destroy the natural forbiddingness of the area but uncovered some secrets as well.

"You know Dan Gummit's on this don't you?" Nichols leaned in and spoke softly to Flynt. Kidd couldn't help but notice the way Flynt and Nichols acted towards one another. If he could sense the tension, anyone could.

"I heard," Flynt replied. "Hey Deb, ya'all still ain't datin' are you?" the comment drew a swift, but surprisingly hard punch in Flynt's shoulder that could be heard from a distance. Flynt even winced while he chuckled obviously at Nichols' expense.

"That was one damn date you asshole!" Nichols laughed with him. "Besides, I never figured you for the jealous type."

Kidd watched the exchange and knew he was going to pump Flynt for information later.

As they waded through the emergency workers, Kidd couldn't help but notice the unnecessary amount of people occupying the scene. As they approached they could see an artificially dug hole about ten by twenty feet. Kidd could see a small female torso, nude with the head missing, fully uncovered by dirt. Several bodies and parts that were still partially covered by the South Texas dirt lay right beside and underneath. The smell of human decomposition was particularly strong now. Kidd could see three officers there with cameras and at least four people taking notes. The hole was a good fifty feet from the access road. Given all of the people around, it would be difficult to determine what was not contaminated.

"Deb…what about footprints?" Flynt asked. Apparently, Kidd wasn't the only one thinking about the potential trace evidence.

"It was trampled when I got here. Hell. Dan had guys with shovels scooping every which way, and the earthmovers had their engines running," Nichols paused. "I got them to shut it down and wait for the pathologist, but it wasn't easy."

"Still a dumbass I see," Flynt shook his head. Kidd turned to see an older, portly man in a chief's uniform with two stars on his collar. He was accompanied by two other uniforms, lieutenants by the bars on their collars

"Speaking of the dumbass," Nichols muttered, smiling at Flynt as Dan Gummit approached.

"Richard Flynt?! How you been doing?" The chief extended his hand and Flynt took promptly.

"Dan this is Darren Kidd. He's new in Company B," Flynt managed a very tepid grin. Gummit reached for Kidd's hand to shake.

"Ah! You're the new Ranger with the special commission. You must be something to get one of those. Where'd ya come from son?" Kidd could hear the patronizing tone in his voice which was becoming irritating.

"Albuquerque PD," Kidd responded. He purposely did not say 'Sir' or 'Chief' just to see Gummit's reaction. He saw the suspicious looks and arrogance seen in so many supervisors. Kidd could see why Flynt and Gummit never got along.

"New Mexico? Ha! I thought you'd at least be from Texas. Old Richard here must have thought real highly of you."

"Nah… just a charity case," Flynt declared jokingly, but there was some shortness in his tone. "What do you got?"

"Mass grave… Mexican I think. Looks like them damn cartels again. Deb disagrees," Gummit replied almost disinterested. "She made us stop to wait for some doctor from Fort Worth. I think that we could've managed personally."

Nichols face was getting slightly red and her rolling eyes were a dead giveaway to anyone paying attention. "I never said it wasn't Mexican Dan! And we have to wait for the doctor. One is a nationally recognized medical examiner and the other is a world-renowned forensic pathologist and anthropologist. This isn't a run of the mill investigation."

"I think what she's saying, Dan, is that this investigation is going to look more like finding King Tut. Ya know…like letting the lab people dig with little bitty shovels and sifting the dirt through little screens," Flynt interjected. "This ain't your typical murder scene. By the way Dan, when was the last time you were at a murder scene? I mean doesn't that mess with your chief duties?"

"I go to several, Richard. It's called 'Servant-Leadership'."

"Holy shit Kidd a new catch phrase!" Flynt spurted, dripping with sarcasm. "Servant-Leadership…is that like 'Problem Orientated Policing' and 'Customer Service'? Damn, you all at the International Associations of Chiefs of Police sure are busy with all this horseshit?" Kidd had to turn his head to disguise his smile. In the last twenty years of law enforcement administrations were essentially trying to re-invent the wheel when it came to police work. Police Chiefs and politicians were convinced that the civil law suits and police misconduct were due to "old school" police tactics when in fact, police misconduct was a byproduct to the current hiring practices, behavioral screening, and lack of competent training; all due to policies that the current new crop of police chiefs actually put in place. Instead of patrol officers being encouraged to catch burglars and perform drug-interventions traffic stops, they were relegated to being door checkers and code enforcement officers, citing citizens for tall grass and leaning fences. They resembled campaign workers more than cops. Gum-shoe, beat police work was being replaced by a type of municipal big-brotherhood, that resembled an Orwellian existence rather that an American town or city. Policemen were being controlled by politicians and their hired lackeys all while the average citizen unknowingly suffered the unintended consequences. So while trying to create the perfect, politically correct, lawsuit proof community servant, they unwittingly began hiring individuals not suited for the job when the proverbial shit actually did hit the proverbial fan, a recipe for disaster in a modern, dangerous world. Even in the short time Kidd had been in law enforcement, he was constantly being barraged by catch phrases trying to coin a universal method or magic potion, not to cure crime, but rather to lawsuit proof the officers and protect the administrations. But the sad truth was that crime on earth would be present as long as man occupied it. That and if it wasn't broke, don't fix it. The level of frustration on the street was high, and it was guys like Gummit that created it. When frustration levels rise, some men can cope and handle it, others explode like a bomb. Nobody wanted the latter.

"You know…we ain't as big as you all at the State, but we ain't Podunk either. We can investigate our own damn crimes! We don't need you all 'Monday morning quarterbackin' us." Gummit snarled back in an obvious exaggerated accent. "The old way of police work is done…this is the new-normal. We're going to take them cartel boys down." Kidd could say something, but he chose to watch. The three people in front of him had an obvious history and he was kind of enjoying himself watching the drama unfold.

"Now come on Dan, I'm just funnin'. I didn't realize that the cartels were so afraid of servant-leadership?" Again, everyone covered their smiles. "But seriously Dan, they got to treat this like an archeological dig. It's meticulous and there needs to be an expert. We were called down here by Division to assist. We ain't takin' over anything, just here to help," Flynt said in a calming manner. "Have you heard any media rumbles yet?"

"They've been called. We're going to set up a media section about a quarter mile west."

"Who called em?"

"I did! You got to get out in front of these things Richard."

"I would think you'd want to hold them off a little longer, Dan?" Flynt was incensed, and Kidd could see it.

"It's my call."

"Okay? What do you all need done?"

"I think we got it covered, Richard," Gummit replied. It was obvious the chief was disgusted with all three of them, Kidd observed. Arrogance was such a destructive force in law enforcement. "If you all excuse me, I need to meet the press." Gummit turned and walked away from the group.

"Well that went well you two," Kidd said smiling at Nichols and Flynt. "I assume you all worked with one another before?" Both Nichols and Flynt looked at each other and sighed. It was as if it was going to be a chore to explain their associations to the chief.

"Dan was a Major over in McAllen when I was down there…before he went to Division" Flynt finally said. "Biggest asshole in three counties. I can't count the number of times he tried to screw me. But I guess I just was a little smarter."

The Rangers walked around the hole very deliberately and carefully. The stench from the grave seemed come on in spurts, lessening with the breeze and overpowering in the stagnant air. "The dismemberment does look haphazard," Kidd observed. There's gotta be different instruments and methods. The cuts aren't uniform." Kidd could see the ripped, rotted flesh and jagged edges of the visible bones. It reminded Kidd of the industrial accident films his middle school shop teacher used to show. It didn't resemble the uniformity and precision of the cartel graves shown on the Department of Justice intelligence bulletins. "And what kind of guy can continue to dig up the same grave? They have to be some disciplined sons of bitches."

"I told you, this just doesn't look like your typical cartel grave… it's brutal" Deb said. "This is going to be a mess to work. Plus…these look like teenagers."

"Well, no one ever accused the Negras of being gentle and meek." Flynt paused and took another look at the scene. "So, we got a hole that has been dug and re-dug adding victims with each. Do we even have a clue how many Deb?" Flynt inquired.

"I saw the ground penetrating radar readings. I'd estimate fourteen to sixteen."

"And realistically we have one way in?"

"Unless you try and come from the South, but there are no trails. We marked a grid square around the area. We didn't find any tracks from all-terrain vehicles, but there are horse tracks scattered about. But my money is on the access road."

Kidd looked around at the brown dirt and could see the tracks Deb was talking about. He took his cell phone from the belt clip and snapped a few shots of the terrain. He fought back the heaves as the wind shifted and the putrid sweet smell of the dirt covered gore blew his way. He concentrated on the task at hand and couldn't think about the horror in front of him. "There any county units or troopers that frequent over here? Seems like they may patrol it more than the city."

"Doubt it," Flynt answered. "Gummit doesn't like all the company in his area. My guess he's told Division and Maverick County to stay out. But now he's happy to get their help now, as long as the credit goes to him."

"He's that much of an asshole?"

Deb laughed at the comment. "Let's put it this way, he'll never get hemorrhoids he's such a perfect asshole." Kidd and Flynt chuckled at that.

"We have to do the victimology on this Richard, this is big. We need to do the follow up with Sunjani and the anthropologist." Kidd had never seen anything like this in his career. But what was sad was that he was okay with a cartel grave, but this was different. The news and the job had conditioned him be prepared to believe that he would see a number of men dismembered. Kidd knew the reputation of the Negras. In Kidd's mind, though brutal and evil, their crimes were at least understandable; money and drugs. But, what he was looking at now was horrifying. Not because of the gruesomeness of dismembered corpses, but because the scenario now could not be explained. Now he had young girls dead in a South Texas hole, and he couldn't reconcile it in his mind. But what was scarier was that there may not even be a good reason why, and these girls died in vain. That was the harsh reality of the job.

"Negative! It's Dan Gummit's baby now."

"You know he's just gonna screw it up Richard," Deb interjected.

"Well hell yes he will!"

"Well goddammit Richard, we just going to sit back and watch him dick this thing up?!" Kidd exclaimed. "Division sent us here to do something!"

"No Darren they didn't. They sent us here just to be here, just to say that the Department of Public Safety was there. They ain't gonna stand behind us in a pissing match with Dan Gummit. Hell, he used to be one of them."

"So that's it?"

"I didn't say that," Flynt took out his notebook. "If I know Dan, he hasn't even locked down who owns the land. Technically, he's performing an ill-advised search, but no Texas Judge is gonna throw any evidence out. We need to start with that."

"And just how are you going to get him to agree to let you help in his baby?" Deb asked.

"Let me handle that my dear. I said Dan was a difficult bastard, but that doesn't mean he can't be tamed. I worked with him for years, he can budge. You just have to speak his language…Asshole to be precise…and persuade him that all brilliant ideas are his. Ya'all are about to be dazzled." Flynt smiled.

"You want to talk with him now?" Kidd inquired.

"We got to Kidd. In a half a day this place will be filled with press. This story's gonna have some teeth and they're gonna flood this valley," Flynt paused. "Deb, can you do us a huge favor?"

"That's what I do."

The three took another look at the torn bodies lying in the

dirt. It was left unsaid that they all felt a loss, like the families of the unidentified. "Take control of this crime scene until Sunjani gets here. Once that little fella gets here, he'll keep Gummit's boys in line. Shit, he may from India, but he acts like a damn Nazi."

"I will Richard. Just don't give up on this, Sweetheart."

*

"Okay it's time for bed kids," Jeremiah Larsen called out while sitting next to his wives Sara, Susan and Beth at the end of their family home evening. The twelve children began to slowly get up from their resting places in the large living room. Their ages ranged from three years to twenty, with Sariah being the third oldest at seventeen, and the oldest girl. As the children moved, it resembled a herd of slow cattle with the constant murmuring of the smaller children complaining of their early bed time. Sara, Susan, and Beth were hugging each of the children as if they were running for political office and on a campaign trail. As in any polygamist household, the line between natural mother and sister-wife is skewed due to the closeness of the family and the blurred nurturing ties of motherhood. By all accounts it was a happy family, just not a lifestyle that appealed to Sariah. Like her brothers and sisters, she began to slowly move toward her room, which she shared with two of her sisters. "Sariah we need to speak with you." Sariah stopped at the sound of her father's voice. As liberated as she was, when her father spoke, she listened.

"About what?" she replied, sounding frighteningly like a Gentile teenager.

"Don't be cross my dear, we need to talk, and I think you know what about." Jeremiah was joined by Sariah's mother Sara. Susan and Beth stood in the large kitchen that adjoined the family room. The house was built like a city fourplex with four distinct living areas and a common kitchen and family room. Basically, the house could be divided into four apartments, but the Larsen's chose to live openly. The surrounding fifty acres provided an additional security for their faith in an ever more uncertain world.

"I don't know what this is about Dad."

"Bishop Johnson called and said that you were seen smoking again."

Sariah let out an audible sigh and rolled her eyes. She knew that Section Eighty-nine of the Doctrine and Covenants was going to be used against her. She couldn't count the number of times she heard that the commandment not to smoke came directly from God, through the prophet Joseph Smith. "Seriously Dad? We've been over this."

"Sariah watch your tone," Sara said sternly. Sariah listened to her mother above anyone else. She knew her mother made a choice to live the lifestyle, but she also knew her mother understood her objections to the polygamy, but smoking on the other hand; she knew she was going to hear it. "Smoking Sariah? Do I even have to say anything?" Sariah could see her mom was upset.

"Who cares what Bishop Johnson says?" Sariah said. "It's between me and God anyway."

"Sariah you know it does matter what Bishop Johnson says," Jeremiah interjected. "He is God's leader for this area, called by the Prophet Nephi Josephs, Sariah, you know this."

"Once again…"

"It's not just about you, it's about the family. It's about our standing in the sect," Beth chimed in from the kitchen.

"Umm…excuse me, Beth…this is a family talk, and besides, Dad should be the bishop," Sariah's voice was dripping with teenage disrespect.

"That's enough young lady! Apologize right now!" Sariah could see her mom, Sara fuming now.

"I'm sorry Beth." Sariah gave her mother the broken heart and contrite spirit look. Sara glared back; Sariah knew she wasn't out of trouble yet.

"I know you're struggling with faith. But just because you're struggling doesn't mean that your faith isn't true," Jeremiah said. "You're a beautiful girl, Sariah. And you remind me a lot of me when I was younger."

"I doubt that…"

"I went off to war Sariah…I thought I knew it all." He wasn't kidding. Jeremiah ran away from the sect at eighteen and joined the Army. He joined the 75th Ranger Regiment and was assigned to the 1st Battalion. Jeremiah saw action in Desert Storm. The realities of war seemed to exterminate any rebellious nature inside of him. He came back to the states and immediately returned to his father who accepted him back with a celebration that would rival the biblical story of the prodigal son. Days later, he was sealed to Sara, his true love. Beth and Susan were sealed to Jeremiah and Sara a few years later. It wasn't hard to figure out that Jeremiah wanted the same type of epiphany for Sariah that he had, but Sariah couldn't see that coming, not even with all the horrors life had to offer.

"Dad I'm not you. I do have faith, but I don't want the lifestyle. You and mom have always told us that we will have the ability to decide our own future, but every time I turn around you guys are trying to force me deeper into the church and shove it down my throat."

"I hardly think us encouraging you to be faithful is shoving something down your throat."

"Well I do."

"You're a young lady Sariah, your life is changing," Jeremiah looked at Sara for support. He was clearly uncomfortable with the subject matter that was about to come up.

"Have you thought about Bishop Johnson's talk?" Sara stepped in saving Jeremiah from obvious embarrassment. "You know…the talk he gave at church?"

"Umm I guess I wasn't paying attention," Sariah replied getting more and more nervous about the future questions. She watched as Beth and Susan came into the living area, from the kitchen and sat down. "What was his talk about?"

"Sariah? He said the prophet wants you to be his wife," Sara managed to utter. The tension in the air was so thick that it could almost be cut. Sariah's stomach sank to her toes rendering her unable to speak for what seemed to be an eternity. It was inevitable this day would come. Her being asked by the brethren to marry someone was part of life and culture, but she was floored that the prophet himself would request she marry of all people, Bishop Johnson. Everyone knew Sariah didn't like Bishop Johnson, she didn't even think that her father liked him. "Sariah, you have been called. This is from the prophet, Nephi Josephs according to the Bishop."

"You can take time to decide your ready Sariah, that's perfectly normal," Susan said. She was always the peacekeeper of the family.

"The answer is no!" Sariah growled almost sick to her stomach.

"You can't just make a decision in haste Sariah. You have to think it over," Jeremiah observed.

"There's nothing to think about...no!" Sariah could feel her eyes tearing up and she didn't want to cry in front of her parents. Sara approached Sariah and put her arms around her. She was the only person that Sariah would allow to do this, not even Jeremiah was allowed hugs so freely. Sariah watched as Jeremiah, Susan and Beth kneeled down on the floor beside them. They all began to pray. Jeremiah pled to the Lord that he would send his spirit to soften Sariah's heart and let her accept the faith of her fathers. He prayed that she would humble herself before God and the prophet. Sariah heard the words of her father, but she couldn't help think about the awful position she found herself in. No prayer in heaven could ease the sickening feeling. The religion of her fathers was becoming a nightmare of her own innocence. Sariah knew that she could never submit the madness, she had to take action.

CHAPTER TWO

Consecrated Ground

"You know canvassing is about a lost art," Flynt said as the two Rangers walked the long dirt pathway to the older farm house. It was the closest house to the crime scene and a potential gold mine in information. Kidd liked that Flynt was an old school cop. It was easy to forget the bare essentials of an investigation in the new technological laden world of law enforcement.

It seemed that more investigations were being done analytically from behind a desk instead of out on the streets with the people. The truth was that law enforcement, from the beginnings of modern police work in London till today, has never changed. Canvassing, questioning, and humping the beat are essential.

As often as administrations and political organizations try to update their image and sell a glamorized media-style portrayal of police work, real cops stuck to the basics. "This is police work, boy. You can have your damn computers and wi-fi."

"Yeah, yeah old man…so how did you get Gummit to agree to even let us assist in the investigation?" Kid asked as the two men kept walking the partially graded residential drive.

"You got to know how to work old Dan." Flynt smiled. "See, he thinks that this is all leg work, so he'll just let us do it to shut up Austin. What he doesn't realize is that you got to start somewhere."

"So, let the dumbass Rangers walk in the middle of nowhere on a rabbit trail?"

"Welcome to Texas, dumbass!" Flynt smirked. "But speaking of dumbasses, Dan told me he was getting an FBI profile."

"A profile? They don't even know how the victim's died yet?"

"Well, Dan made some friends at the FBI National Academy

and he wants to show off. Hell, when ya don't know shit about real police work it makes all the goddamn sense in the world." It was a running joke to line officers that the National Academy the FBI puts on for police administrators was nothing but a resume-padding waste of taxpayers' money. "Thank God for that damn FBI I tell ya."

Kidd laughed as they approached the white, ranch-style pier and beam house. The siding was unpainted and worn, and the flashings throughout the property gave the impression that the house was leaning. As they approached, out of instinct, they walked in a wedge formation and put their hands on their weapons. Kidd scanned the east side of the house, including the windows and crawl spaces. He turned to see Flynt doing the same. Though no words were spoken, the two exchanged the 'all clear' look and proceeded to the front door covered by an old-fashioned storm door. The wood deck creaked, and dust could be seen blowing from its cracks as the pressure of the Rangers footsteps fell upon it. The musty smell with a hint of mothballs reminded Kidd of his grandparents' house. If the floor could speak, the stories it could probably tell. Flynt knocked seven times, a superstition observed with a lot of old timers, but strangely still practiced by the Ranger.

"Can I help you?" said an older woman from the other side of the screen. She was in her mid-seventies with long gray hair. Her thin, frail arms were exposed from her short-sleeved, flower print dress she wore. She smiled, and the wrinkles on her face formed that look that reminded all men of their mothers, warm and welcoming. The men relaxed and remembered their manners.

"Good evening ma'am, I'm Sergeant Richard Flynt, and this here's Darren Kidd, with the Texas Rangers? And you are?"

"I'm Emma Merrit."

"Well Emma, we'd like to talk to you about the land over yonder," Flynt smiled at the woman who seemed very pleased at the recent company.

"Do ya' all want some coffee?" Emma asked.

"Well ma'am that's about the nicest damn thing we heard all day, but you sure you want us hunky men comin' in your house?

What will the neighbors say?" Kidd chimed in as he winked at Emma Merrit.

"Well Honey I sure hope so!" Emma laughed out loud. "I'd be the most popular gal at the community center sweetheart." The Rangers walked into the old house. Emma pinched Kidd's derriere as he walked by and she winked, "Sides, I could teach you two a thing or two."

"I bet you could," Flynt laughed and sat in a velour Queen Anne style chair in a living room with a hard wood floor. Kidd sat on an adjacent one. Emma disappeared into the kitchen and reappeared with two full coffee mugs surprisingly quickly. She sat immediately across from the men on a love seat with a grin. It was obvious Emma was ecstatic for the company. Kidd felt like he warped back in time to the thirties. This was an antique hunter's dream, the clean, old furniture in pristine condition. "We came to inquire about your neighbors."

"Neighbors? I ain't had any neighbors since about Seventy-Two. They bulldozed the houses since. Now they just use it for pastures."

"Who owns it now, Ma'am?"

"Well my husband bought up most of it after the housing went away, but I sold it after he died in about Ninety-one."

"Who'd you sell it too Ma'am?" Kidd asked.

"Them fellas with all the wives. You know…those religious people."

"Ahh, you mean the polygamists?"

"Yes, like those on the television," Emma remembered. "I don't got nothing against em'. Just hope God gives em' good spot in Hell for takin all them young wives." Emma's sarcasm brought the two Rangers to laughter.

"You know any names Ma'am," Flynt inquired.

"Well the man that leases the land is named Larsen…umm, Jeremiah Larsen. But he don't own it," Emma paused for a brief moment to reflect while Kidd and Flynt sipped their coffee.

"You happen to know who does Ma'am."

"I guess I don't. Those folks are secretive. Fact is they don't show their face…ever." Emma sat back in her chair and began to get reflective as most elderly people seem to do. "They sent their lawyer to deal with all the paperwork, real nice Mexican gal. Never actually met the buyer."

"Hmm…You ever actually see this Larsen character?"

"I met him once or twice…nice fellow. His herd makes their way out here now and again. They've hooked into my water before, left cash with me to pay for it. They live up the highway. Can't say much more though, like I said…they keep to themselves."

"You don't happen to have Larsen's information, do you?"

"Sure, it'll take me a minute to fetch it."

"Thank you, Ma'am," Flynt smiled and sat back in his chair. The men watched as Emma excused herself and made her way into the study of the residence. Kidd could see the old bookshelves covered in leather bound editions. Both Rangers enjoyed their coffee while they waited for Emma to return. She did so surprisingly quickly. It seemed that being old had no effect on the woman's organizational skills.

"Here you go, this is all I could find," Emma actually handed the paperwork to Kidd who promptly took out his notebook and started to copy pertinent information that he saw.

"Well Ma'am I think we've taken up too much of your time, but I certainly appreciate your kindness and helpfulness," Flynt said just as Emma got settled in her love seat.

"Anytime you handsome gentlemen need anything, just call…especially you cutie." Emma winked at Kidd causing a smile and a blush as he and Flynt made their way to the door. They stepped onto the porch and re-entered the reality of the investigation. Flynt picked up his cell phone dialed DPS Intelligence. Kidd could hear the other party answer the phone because his partner chose to keep his volume at an ungodly level.

"Give me everything you got on a Jeremiah Larsen."

*

It was a surprisingly chilly day at the Johnson compound, the Stake party was a success. Practically the entire sect was enjoying themselves in the lush green grass that grew within the compound walls. It was as if an oasis sprang up in the South Texas landscape and only a select, faithful people could enjoy the fruits of it. Sariah sneezed. Probably because of the lush, year-round, non-indigenous vegetation that was craftily planted in a region filled with sage, mesquite, and scrub brush. Sariah watched the kids run on the St. Augustine grass and act as if there was no care in the world. They didn't think about the fact that they were outcasts beyond the walls of the compound, or that they live under a religion that had absolute control over their very lives. Sariah sighed and smiled as Amanda came and sat by her in the grass.

"Hey Gentile Girl!" she exclaimed as she plopped down, smoothing her prairie dress as she stretched her legs. Sariah knew Amanda referred to her clothes which consisted of tight, hip-hugging jeans and a current, fashionable blouse. It was an outfit that was frowned upon by members of the Inspired Church of Jesus Christ of Latter-day Saints. Perception in the sect was everything. It was the very thing that motivated members' thoughts and actions and was a powerful tool for the brethren. While it may be true that the people governed themselves, the brethren sure suggested the methods. That was why defying them empowered Sariah and she didn't mind the digs from her best friend.

"Please bitch…you look like you should be selling pies to pioneers!" Sariah retorted and the two laughed. Sariah did wish that Amanda wore more fashionable clothing; Amanda lifted her skirt in a provocative manner to annoy Sariah even further. She had platinum blonde hair and a voluptuous, curvy figure. She reminded Sariah of a younger Marilyn Monroe, only restrained by her beliefs. Sariah flipped Amanda the bird as she sat.

"You're terrible Sariah!" The two girls sat and talked about the people and the food at the picnic, topics ranged from how obese certain sister-wives were to the fact that polygamists just couldn't cook barbeque like true Texans. Though the religious bonds were with them at birth, they were typical teenage girls, complete with dreams and silliness. There laughter and antics seem to mask the entire world around them as they sat in the corner of the lawn, so much so that they didn't even notice Amanda's father, Bishop Thomas Johnson sneak up behind them. He was a tall man, in his sixties, and had the paunchy look of a soon to retire businessmen. His horn-rimmed glasses and bad comb-over covering a freckled scalp was both imposing and disgusting all at once to Sariah.

"Hello girls…how are you enjoying the picnic?" He said with an inquisitive and curious tone.

"I'm having fun father," Amanda replied, silencing all of her teenage dialect in favor of a more formal tone. Sariah hated that Amanda always did that, spoke to her father like she was speaking to a professor, or a teacher. There was no love, tenderness, or playfulness in their communications. It was as if being a Bishop, the leader of the entire Stake and sect in the region made Johnson unapproachable as a father.

"It's pretty cool, Bishop," Sariah said with a smirk. Bishop Johnson looked at the girls, smiled, then turned to Amanda.

"Amanda…would you please excuse us, I would like to talk to Sariah for a few minutes?" Bishop Johnson smiled and watched as Amanda silently obeyed her father's wishes. Amanda gave a look to Sariah as she walked away, one of concern and curiosity. Sariah shot a similar look back to Amanda. She didn't know what the Bishop was going to say, but she was quite sure that she didn't want to hear it. "My dear do you know the origin of your name?"

"Umm…isn't it a name from the scriptures?" Sariah replied.

"The Book of Mormon actually."

"Oh…ok," her nervousness was a bit transparent by now.

"It was the name of the prophet Lehi's wife," Bishop Johnson smiled at Sariah, which made Sariah more uncomfortable. Sariah was familiar with the prophet Lehi, The Book of Mormon asserts that Lehi was warned by God to take him and his family, build a ship, and sail to the new world. Once there, the Lord once again established his church and the society that was created survived for a thousand years before its eventual destruction from war. The descendants of that society are todays American Indians according to Latter-day Saint beliefs. However, Sariah knew that science did not necessarily back that assertion.

"Oh, now I remember."

"She also had trials of her faith, just like you."

"What? I'm not following Bishop."

"Sariah, it's the Lord's plan that we suffer trials of faith. Lehi's wife Sariah had to endure many changes and hardships because of the Lord's commandment for them to flee Jerusalem. So, although you don't have the physical challenges, you have equally difficult spiritual challenges."

"I still don't follow Bishop."

"Sariah…you are trying to make a statement with your clothes and attitude."

"My clothes? My attitude? I really don't understand?" Sariah was beginning to feel the warm sensation of anger start to work its way to her mouth. She hated to be told with what she was feeling or doing by someone else, correct or not, and she certainly didn't want to hear it from Bishop Johnson of all people.

"Sariah it's a natural thing to question one's beliefs, but that doesn't mean they are not true. God speaks to the prophets and the prophets speak to man. Now sometimes, God tells us things that we don't necessarily want to hear. And I, Sariah, have been chosen by God, and the Prophet Nephi Josephs, to be the mouthpiece for him in this area."

"Wait…you're the mouthpiece for God or Nephi Josephs?" Sariah asked in a quasi-sarcastic tone. She was becoming really upset now. The only thing that channeled her rage was her mother's constant teaching that you never are disrespectful to the brethren.

"'And this is a decree, which I have sent forth in the beginning of the world, from my own mouth, from the foundation thereof, and by the mouths of my servants, thy fathers, have I decreed it, even as it shall be sent forth in the world, unto the ends thereof.' God spoke that verse to Enoch, Sariah."

"I know the verse…Moses Chapter Six verse Thirty in The Pearl of Great Price. I still don't see where it applies to me, Bishop?"

"It means that my voice *is* God's voice, Sariah, it's really that simple."

"Nothing is that simple," Sariah exclaimed, her stomach tightening in anticipation.

"Oh, but it is…and you, Sariah Larsen, need to choose ye this day whom you will serve!" Bishop Thompson looked at Sariah with a dark and a piercing stare.

"Bishop but you're making no sense!"

"You need to become my wife, Sariah…it is God's will."

The statement hit Sariah in the gut, a sick feeling that made her feel awkward, not to mention it put her on the spot. "Bishop…I…"

"You would have your own wing in the house, and you never would have to worry about finances," Johnson smiled which chilled Sariah to the core. He was right about that and she knew it. Bishop Johnson owned an aircraft metal fabrication plant. The six thousand square foot home on the two-hundred-acre parcel of land was only the tip of Johnson's wealth. The factory, and the other acreage spread throughout the Lone Star State had to be worth millions. His workers were all sect and family members. He was the final religious and financial word for The Inspired Church of Jesus Christ of Latter-day Saint members in Texas. Only Sariah's father and two other sect families were too proud to work for Bishop Johnson and ventured out on their own. Sariah's dad had a thriving general contracting business he shared with the Gant family and a small gentleman's farm with about a hundred head of cattle. Sariah's two older brothers handled the farm duties with a little help from her younger siblings and she worked as an administrative assistant at her father's office. She had to apply for the job and was paid like a normal employee, complete with taxes and deductions. That freedom allowed her to pay for her car and have money to pay for her gentile clothing.

"Bishop I can't think about this now…I can't …"

"Abraham had a trial of faith when he was told to sacrifice Isaac…this Sariah will be yours," Johnson reached over and laid his hand on her knee and slightly squeezed. He got up and walked back over to where the congregation gathered. Sariah could feel herself dry heave at the thought of being groped and pawed by this man. She couldn't fathom being his wife.

*

"Chuco, juan…*Sienta se por favor*," Carlos Estancia said as he greeted the two men as they sat down at a corner booth in the La Palma Restaurant. Not as nice as the restaurants in Dallas or San Antonio, but a nice spot for the area. Carlos liked the spot off of the El Indio Highway; it was being discreet in plain view. Eagle Pass had long been a city that two cultures have co-existed. To most of America the mixing of cultures was a threat to the autonomy of the people, but not in Texas, and especially not in the Borderlands. Mexican nationals doing business in America and small international agreements were made all the time and little to no thought was given as to the who the players were. Carlos was just getting to know the two men before him, but they were highly recommended

"*Gracias* Carlos, but…eh, we're short on cash *ese'*," Chuco said in a concerned manner. Carlos could see that his new friends were hungry for money, and that was a great benefit to him. La Palma wasn't exactly a four-star restaurant, but for two ex-cons with no money, it might as well have been.

"*Orale' guey*, this is on me. You guys are my friends," Carlos replied, and laughed at Chuco and Juan's humility. "Now let me answer the questions you have."

"Who told you about us?" Juan asked. He was the more skeptical of the two. But it wasn't like the boy had a reason to trust anyone, Carlos thought. The two boys had been in and out of lock-up practically since they could walk. The fact they would end up in prison was a forgone conclusion, an unfortunate reality for many kids that grow up in the valley. McAllen, Texas may be one of the fastest growing metro areas in the United States and have one of the fastest expanding middle classes, but there were still the seedy areas that spawned kids like Chuco and Juan.

"You're Tangos *no*?" Carlos inquired. Each of the men showed their '956" tattoos with star accents on their hands and neck.

"*Vallucos puro, ese'*," Juan answered. Carlos smiled to humor the two men, kids really, but the sight of the numerous skin art with the useless logos was actually sad. It was a mere testament that these two were doomed to a life of servitude, not to society, but to guys like him. Thank god there were people like Chuco and Juan, he thought, they were virtual slaves to illegal activity. No legitimate business would hire them.

"Let's just say my employers have an arrangement with Tango Blas."

"The Negras huh?" Juan inquired.

"Exactly, among others," Carlos replied. Juan appeared to be smarter than most, he thought. "The Negras made a deal with the Tangos inside. They take care of the enforcement in the states. It's been a good relationship so far."

"So how does it work? I mean, how do they operate? You know...the Negras?"

"That's a good question," Carlos laughed. "It's like this, I am only a middle man...a transporter. I move what they say to move."

"Who is your boss?" Chuco asked.

"We all got our bosses, *ese'*, all you got to know is I'm the *patron* here, *entiendes?*

"*Si, mon,*" both men nodded in the affirmative.

"My boss is none of your concern," Carlos stared at the two men before continuing. He had to make sure that they understood everything they were saying. "I get word what needs to be moved. We move it, that simple."

"What are we moving?" Juan interrupted.

"Crank, coke, kush, tar, you name it. We got about seven stops usually. Thing is, we don't know what we're hauling, and the dealers may not get what they ordered."

"I don't understand."

"Simple, the Negras send it and the dealers push it. If they send weed, dealers push it. Crank? They push it. If they send Bluebell Ice Cream, the *pinche cabrons* better become ice cream men *ese'!*"

"Damn, that's harsh!"

"*Plata o ploma, ese'*...silver or lead."

"Silver it is, *Patron'!*" Chuco chortled causing all three men to laugh and to pause to eat the food feverishly that was finally brought to them.

"Look, the Negras run the streets. They run the prison gangs that run the Latino gangs on the outside. You fuck with them, you'll most likely be killed by your own *vatos*. And if the Negras decide to come after you, your head and your torso are gonna be in two different states *ese'*."

"So what do we gotta do for this lick?"

Carlos handed Juan and Chuco a two identification cards. "I trust you can drive a truck now that my boy Jesus trained you?"

"*Si*, but we don't have our commercial," Juan answered.

"Yes, you do," Carlos smiled and passed a book across the table. "That is a logbook for a truck in Piedras Negras. Those are Mexican Licenses in your hands. They were provided by friends and are accepted at the port of entry. The GPS will take you to the spot. I don't know where it is." Carlos watched the two men inspect the items. The licenses were legitimately printed on official Mexican documentation with the men's pictures and operator license numbers registered in NCIC. Good enough to pass through the I.C.E. checkpoint at the border. "Just get in and drive to the checkpoint. Be cool or the *pinche migra* gets jumpy and will search your ass."

"Where do we take it?" Chuco inquired.

"There's gonna be a GPS in the truck. You take it to wherever it says. But listen up…if you get stopped…destroy that fucking GPS. The cops can't get that."

"What about us?" Chuco asked.

"What about you?" Carlos answered abruptly. He liked Juan, but he was still not entirely sure about his partner.

"I mean, if we get stopped?"

"Then you deal with it."

"Shit, like jail time?"

"Fuck yeah *ese!'*" Carlos almost couldn't believe the question. Even Juan was rolling his eyes, obviously embarrassed by his friend's naivety. "Either that, or you can have your *mamacita* bury you if they can find more than your torso under a fucking bridge." As much as he wanted to slap Chuco, he didn't want to scare the kid. He received word that Chuco was a tough *valluco* from the street, but he was about to get mixed in with the most violent people the earth has seen. Chuco and Juan just made a contract with the Negras. If there is anything that resembled modern day slavery, it was working for the Negras. They were now owned by the cartel, and membership was for life. The Negras did not give second chances, you either accomplish the task, or you die. There was no reasoning with these men and Carlos had never seen any group so brutal. Death, dismemberment, and evisceration were standard operating procedures. He witnessed their brutality on several occasions, even watched another business associate get his testicles fed to him just prior to having his head removed crudely with an old, rusting machete. That treatment was because the man skimmed five thousand dollars from the cartel. Chuco and Juan may be tough, but God has yet to create a more evil entity than the Negras. Their only redeeming value was the money. If you did what they said, they would pay, and pay well. Maybe it was his conscious or a bit of clarity, but he felt he had to try to impress on the two men the veracity of their commitment he was asking of them. "Look, if you all want to back out now, *esta bien*…it's okay…I can clear it."

"We're in," Juan said with a face like stone.

*

The hall was barely a third full when Mayor called the session to order. Eagle Pass City Hall was the same drab brick with flat roofs and metal trim that graced many smaller cities in Texas; even some larger ones. The design was a typical homage to every day USA, and not South Texas. It seemed diametrically opposed to the historic buildings in the area like the Maverick County Courthouse, with its timeless function and classic feel, but relegated to museum status. Such was life in South Texas; tradition had to make way for progression in all its mediocre forms.

"Let's get this meeting started, shall we?" Mayor Quintanilla said taking his official spot in the center of the chambers. All four council persons were present and accounted for; Jaime Soto sat on the right of Mayor Quintanilla and Michael Cordova to the right. Ted Benavidez and Sonia Nava each sat on the other end of the cherry wood table. Each seat place was equipped with a microphone and the sessions also were viewed on a state-of-the-art overhead projector complete with Power Point software. The gallery, though mostly empty was buzzing. It was a special session called in lieu of the grisly discovery off the El Indio Highway. The construction crew that made that discovery while constructing the new Coahuila Expressway that connected the El Indio Highway to Bulevar Centenario in Piedras Negras. The project was a huge undertaking that has been planned since 1998. The Federal Government finally produced all of the funding for a new Port of Entry in Eagle Pass but required the State and local governments to make the necessary improvements to the roads themselves. The State of Texas agreed to fund the actual Coahuila Expressway from the Port of entry to the El Indio Highway if the City of Eagle Pass paid for the improvements of El Indio Highway as well as the interchange between the roads. The fight has been going on for years. The proponents were the Chamber of Commerce and the local businesses, but landowners and environmentalist groups initially fought successfully to block the project only to see their efforts fall by the wayside as conservative political agendas eventually overcame them, as was always the case in Texas. Another victim to economic development, as evidenced in the scarce showing in the gallery, was public interest in stopping the project; it was almost non-existent. Still the political bloggers and junkies from all across the spectrum had to show their face and get their voices on record even if it was all for not. "This is a special emergency work session of the city council called by Councilman Soto. Mr. Soto you have the floor."

"Thank you, Mr. Mayor, members of the council, and ladies and gentlemen. As you all are aware, the Eagle Pass Police Department, along with several other police agencies are investigating what is an apparent mass grave that was uncovered by the road crews working on the new Coahuila Expressway," Jaime Soto paused and took a drink of water that was provided. "I am calling a petition the council to approve an environmental impact study on the land before we proceed with construction…"

"Mr. Mayor I object to Councilman Soto's thin veiled attempt to halt construction to the project…it's so transparent!" Michael Cordova hissed from his chair, almost with venom. It was no secret that he carried the torch for the Chamber of Commerce and local business.

"I don't know what's so transparent? I didn't even finish my statement."

"Let's have some order," the Mayor said wrapping a ceremonial gavel that sat by his side. Normally it sat by his side as a decoration piece, but whenever the Coahuila Expressway was discussed, that gavel saw action.

"I simply think we owe it to ourselves to perform the environmental impact study. It's important to my constituents," Soto said matter of factly.

"What are the costs?" Cordova asked.

"I have received two estimates so far from consultant groups out of Austin and Houston. They both can do it for five hundred thousand. Now that's pretty good considering the size of the area."

"That's five hundred thousand dollars we don't need to spend. It's a ridiculous and unnecessary cost, to satisfy some extremist constituents." Cordova had battled Soto and his environmentalist groupies for nine years. He wasn't going to scrap a billion-dollar project with limitless economic ramifications for the whims of a few squeaky wheels.

"Mr. Cordova…I take offense that you characterize my constituents that happen to care for the environment as 'extremist.' That is both wrong, and bigoted. You need to alter your tone so that we may have a rational debate."

"There is no rational debate with you, Jaime. I understand that you and your constituents do not like the project, but the people of Eagle Pass and Maverick County have spoken. They want the project to go through. And after years of fighting with

39

the State and Federal Governments to fork over the cash they promised…they delivered. Now you want us not only to cheat our citizens, but go back on the deals we made," Cordova observed. "I can tell you I'm not ready to go back on my promises to my voters."

"Stop making this sound like a pious quest for you Michael Cordova...this is only about the bottom line to you! The Feds and the State tell us to go to hell all the time. I'm saying that we can tell them that once in a while. Besides, they found a mass grave in the land…God only knows what else is floating around in that land."

"People die and are buried in the ground all the time Councilman Soto…just admit that you want to stall this project because you think it will be some shallow political victory. The investigation is ongoing and most likely won't be completed for several days. There have been no warnings or signs of danger to the general public and certainly nothing to prevent the construction of this interchange…"

"Once again you are way off base and wrong!"

"I move we put this to an immediate vote," Cordova interrupted. Soto looked obviously annoyed but stopped his speaking just the same.

The Mayor took his cue and called for the vote of each member of the council. Cordova, and Benavidez were both votes to reject the environmental impact study, while Sonia Nava and Jaime Soto were to the affirmative. The city's charter specified that the Mayor was the deciding vote in such situations. Mayor Quintanilla, in true political fashion, began speaking to all sides of the issue.

The first part of the speech was about how horrified he was about the discovery of the mass grave and how thankful he was for the public servants such and police and crime scene workers that make everyone safe on a daily basis. Then he started to argue that economic progress should not replace respect and reverence for the environment. The Mayor then ended with a strong, semi-rehearsed, state of the city address where he lauded his administration's accomplishments. In the end, his vote to reject Councilman Soto's proposal couldn't have shocked anyone in the gallery. A chapter was closed in city politics, but new ones always open.

CHAPTER THREE

Bridges

"So how does it work?" Sariah asked. "I mean…do you and the other wives take turns having sex with the husband, or do you guys all get freaky together?"

Sariah laughed as she and Amanda sat in the barn, drinking Cokes on the Johnson property. Once again, they found themselves in the solace of the old wooden structure with the corrugated steel for a roof.

They shared a strict religion, but they were teenage girls and some things were just universal. The barn gave them a sanctuary from the prying eyes of the sect, and especially the brethren. Amanda smiled and appeared somewhat embarrassed but chuckled.

"Apparently God only wants you to have sex one at a time…or at least that's what mother says," Amanda said with a red face.

"What about like…blow jobs?"

"Sariah!"

"What? Don't act like the subject will never come up, I'm not the one getting married in a week! You're gonna have to deal with the saggy old man balls."

"You are terrible Sariah!" The girls continued to giggle, but as the laughter began to fade, their smiles took a more serious tone and the realization that the best friends were about to split became more poignant.

Both had so many things they wanted to say to the other, but they couldn't manage to speak the words. It seemed if Sariah even started to tell Amanda how she felt that time would go faster, and her friend would leave her even sooner. It was hard enough that the one person she adored for as long as she remembered was leaving. Though their fathers didn't see eye to eye, or get along at all for that matter, they had a bond of sisterhood as strong as any blood tie. In their world, they only had each other; they were outcasts to the rest of the world.

"Are you guys flying up to Utah or driving? Sariah finally asked breaking the silence.

"Driving…I think. I don't know, maybe the bus."

"They're not going to pick you up?"

"I don't really know."

"Well why not?"

"They don't let me in their grand planning meetings, Sariah. I just have to obey."

"Well you're the one getting married! I should hope you should at least know the details?"

"Well you should know you don't question the brethren."

"That's just bullshit!"

"Sariah! Stop being so crude," Amanda said with a half giggle. "We are women, Sariah. The rules are different for us."

"That's why I don't want any part of this whole lifestyle."

"But you are part of the lifestyle."

"Yeah…don't remind me," Sariah leaned back against a square bale of hay and sighed. "So, do you have to like…shave his back?" the question evoked another huge outburst of laughter between the two girls, to the point they nearly doubled over. "You're gonna have old balls in your face!" Sariah cackled with Amanda's hearty laughter behind her. They laughed until their eyes teared, but the jubilation was only a precursor to eventual reality that Amanda was leaving. She wasn't coming back either. She was taking a step that Sariah was not willing to. On the one hand Sariah wanted to smack Amanda in the head in hopes that she would snap out of her trance, but on the other, Amanda had a faith that Sariah couldn't help but admire. It was the purest belief she had seen. Surely Amanda was able to see the contradictions in her belief and lifestyle, but she chose to press on and follow. There would be those that would think her weak, but they would be wrong. "So, what now?"

"I follow the prophet's commandments and be a good wife…What else is there?"

"The fact you even say that breaks my heart. You don't

43

think God has something else in store for you?"

"I just have to trust his will, Sariah," Amanda smiled at her friend. At the very least, Sariah knew she was loved, and she knew that Amanda prayed for her, but it was tough to see such a good friend doomed to a life of quiet servitude. The only solace that could be taken was that Amanda would be oblivious to her own misery due to a hopeless, irrational faith. The two sat quietly as they thought about the upcoming changes

"I'm going to miss you," Sariah finally said after an awkward silence.

"I'm going to miss you too."

"Have you spoken to Brother Smoot?"

"No…that's the weird thing. I don't even know what he sounds like."

"I'm sure that he would want to call you first, right?"

"I hope so. But Sariah… I'm really scared," Amanda's tears were real, and plentiful. "Part of me just wants to just jump into it…like a cold pool… and just get it over with. I mean it will sting, but it has to get better…right?" Sariah began to cry along with her friend. She fought back the urge to insult her lifestyle and the religion of her fathers to comfort a friend. She learned that Amanda's faith was so strong that it helped her overcome her very real fears; something to be admired.

"Sweetheart, of course it will get better. God would never be cruel to you," Sariah was trying to smile as convincingly as possible. "The Smoot's are nice people."

"Will you come and visit me?"

"Of course, you're my only friend," Sariah's smile brightened slightly. "Besides, whose gonna give you shit up there in Utah?"

*

"I got to admit to you I'm a bit nervous partner," Flynt told his partner as they drove outside the city limits of Eagle Pass. The houses became more and more scare and unique in design.

"Scared huh?" Kidd was intrigued by his partner's admission.

"It's not every day you get to meet a damn militant polygamist."

"Where the hell you get militant?"

"Eagle Pass PD intel," Flynt shoved some papers over to Kidd in the passenger's seat. Highway Kidd glanced at the intelligence bulletins. "Says Larsen here was a staunch opponent of that new Coahilla Highway."

"That doesn't make him a militant?"

"Well it damn sure doesn't make him our friend."

"So, we treat him like every other hook we talk to. He's not the only one that voted against that highway I'm sure."

"That's my point…I worked a case back in Nacadoches where a guy chained his ass to a tree that was marked to be cut. One of these guys that ain't worth a shit in life so they protest. We told him he had twenty-four hours to move or we was gonna move him."

"How were you going to move him?"

"Son…that is by God East Texas…police tell you to move…you gonna move," Flynt stared at Kidd to make sure he understood that point. "Anyhow…we come back and the boy's bare ass naked humpin' that tree in front of God and everyone!" The story made Kidd laugh out loud.

"First off…I'm about to call bullshit on that one and second…what the hell does this story have to do with anything?"

"Point is, some guys have nothing to live for but a cause and they're the most dangerous. Do you know that guy got a settlement from the road contractor?"

"What?"

"Damn sure did, sued the contractor and the insurance company settled."

"Alright, I get your story about people and their unpredictability, but call me an old soul…I want to see evidence," Kidd observed. "We ain't got dick on this guy. As far as we know, he should get a key to the city."

"He's a polygtamist!" Flynt said sounding somewhat annoyed. "Goddammit he's breaking the law." The tone of voice made Kidd chuckle a bit, almost under his breath. Flynt looked at Kidd furiously, "What the hell are you laughing at!?"

"Admit it, you're afraid of Mormons!" Kidd said in jest, still giggling.

"That's horseshit!"

"You think they're weird cultists just like every other Baptist in this state."

"First off, these ain't regular Mormons, they're polygamists and polygamists are goddamn weird! You weren't at that damn YFZ compound in Eldorado...I was." Flynt referred to the infamous April 2008 raid of the Fundamental Church of Jesus Christ of Latter-day Saints that lay four miles Northeast of Eldorado, Texas. Texas Child Protective Services received a tip from a girl who identified herself as a sixteen-year-old named "Sarah" who made allegations of widespread child sexual abuse, specifically, young girls being made into sister-wives for older men. Stories of young girls being raped and sodomized in the compound temple fueled a furious, yet somewhat inept investigation into the actions of the compound. The investigation was hamstrung by the fact that FLDS members refused to divulge their actions to outsiders; therefore, caseworkers had to rely on Sarah's descriptions of abuse in good faith. Law enforcement entered the compound complete with SWAT entry teams, snipers, and a battalion of troopers all on search warrants based on those sexual abuse allegations. Television cameras showed throngs of children being pried away from their crying mothers onto buses bound for only God knew. It was reminiscent of Native American kids in the 1800's forced to leave their homelands and go to school in Pennsylvania to unlearn their savage ways. In the end, a handful of men were prosecuted for Sexual Assault, including the group's charismatic leader, Warren Jeffs, but civilly it was a disaster. The legal team of the sister-wives, along with ACLU were able to force the State of Texas to return the children to their mothers. The case was even upheld by the Texas Supreme Court. It turned out that "Sarah" was actually a girl from Colorado that had never been on the compound. The state had no evidentiary basis to even enter the compound, even though a sex alter and audio tapes depicting Jeffs consummating several underage marriages were discovered inside the temple. The State decided to let the matter die down, and in true Texas form, the public lost interest in the renegade Mormons. But the stain of that event stuck with Flynt.

"I don't have to go in the compound. I know these people and you're just like everybody else. You freak out about their beliefs…Joseph Smith, magic underwear, everybody becoming gods…all that shit. Hell, they are weird! Fact is, you laugh at their beliefs while maintaining some pretty weird and screwed up beliefs of your own."

"The hell you say!" Flynt said annoyed. "That son of a bitch, Jeffs recorded his sex sessions with them girls. If that were a goddamn Baptist he'd be hung by now!

"But listen…you believe that God, Jesus, and the Holy Spirit are one and that when Jesus was baptized, he threw his voice, calling himself his own son all the while flying like a dove…Yep, that's much more believable," Kidd giggled.

"You going to hell for saying shit like that! How come you're defending them anyway?"

"I'm already going to hell, but I know these people better than you'd think."

"I know Michelle was Mormon, and you went to church with her and all…"

"I was baptized a Mormon, Richard," Kidd interjected almost shamefully. "Turns out ya marry one and the whole damn crew comes after you to convert you to the real God. I finally gave in…I thought that would make her happy."

"So, what now?"

"The hell you mean what now?"

"Well, I mean you wear them magic pajamas and do all that secret shit in the temple."

"Damnit Richard, I wear boxers for hell's sake!" Kidd's exasperation was replaced by humor. "We both know I don't belong in a church. I joined the church because I figured it wouldn't hurt nothin'. I didn't realize I'd be the world's worst Mormon."

"Well now I'd be the world's worst Mormon. Hell, I've heard of worse things a guy's done for a girl," Flynt smiled. "So

47

where do you go to church now?"

"Let's just say me and church don't mix."

"Me either. Welcome to law enforcement, Boy."

The Larsen house was off the highway about a quarter mile. The Italian Evergreens that lined the driveway contrasted the rough, brown West Texas earth. It was nothing like the photos kid saw of polygamist compounds or the images on television. The house was a modest ranch-style home that looked as it belonged in every-town USA. Two small children could be seen from a distance on a four wheeled all-terrain vehicle in a modest pasture to the north of the house. Flynt drove the Ford Crown Victoria up the paved driveway and parked near a Tan Chevrolet Suburban. Kidd saw a white male figure exit the front door, appeared in his forties, sturdy yet clean cut. His hair was a medium-reg military cut and his shirt was neatly tucked in. While he showed certain bodily signs of middle age, he seemed in pretty good shape. They recognized the man from his driver's license photo as Jeremiah Larsen. Kidd could see that Flynt saw the man too and placed his hand on his nickel plated, Colt .45 ACP as he exited the vehicle.

"Nine O'clock," Flynt said casually, practically under his breath to Kidd as he exited the vehicle, meaning that the threat was to their left. Kidd too stepped out of the vehicle with his hand on his stainless Kimber that he was given when he became a Ranger, yet never abandoning his trusty Heckler & Koch .40 Caliber tucked into the small of his back; a fact which got him ribbed by his new colleagues in Texas.

"Got em'," Flynt answered scanning his environment. He and Kidd began to walk toward with smiles on their faces and hands on their weapons. They operated by the old police adage to be kind to everyone but have a plan to kill them. As soon as they were within earshot of the front door, Flynt waived his hand and waited a response from Larsen which came a few seconds later accompanied by a suspicious stare.

"What can I do for you Officers?" Larsen called to Kidd and Flynt. Kidd watched Larsen; he was unique. When police walk onto most peoples' property, they become anxious as to why they are there, but not Larsen. He seemed calm, almost as if he was expecting the officers to visit. Kidd knew he had to keep an eye on him.

"We're lookin' for Jeremiah Larsen, Sir?" Flynt called back.

"I'm Jeremiah Larsen."

"Larsen…is that English?" Flynt inquired.

"Well, I'm French actually."

"I'm Sergeant Flynt and this is Darren Kidd with the Texas Rangers. We were hopin' to ask you a few questions bout some land you lease out by the highway."

"Is there a problem I need to know about?"

"Yes sir, two Texas Rangers show up at your house, I'd say there's a problem," Kidd smirked.

"Did I do something wrong, friend?"

"According to the United Sates Supreme Court… yes. But I tell you what...we'll let that slide since we ain't the Feds! Now do you want to skip the bullshit and talk?" Kidd watched Larsen grit his teeth.

"Whoa now, what my partner is trying to say is we want to talk," Flynt interjected trying to somewhat calm the situation.

"Pardon me but we don't trust the Department of Public Safety too much."

"Well pardon us, but we don't trust ya'all that much either…"

"We're here about a murder…matter of fact, several. We heard you were a religious man? So, I would think you would want to help, unless of course you had something to do with it?" Kidd chimed in. Though an outsider would think that Kidd was just being a jerk, few would ever realize the verbal tactics being employed. He was seeing how far Larsen could be pushed before breaking.

"I do respect the law, and I'm not a not a murderer. If you're here to talk, then let's talk," Larsen smiled and motioned for the Rangers to come inside. Kidd could see that Larsen was no hot head. Any normal person would have told Kidd to go to hell. Larsen however was clearly annoyed but smiled it off. That meant he had self-control and did not give in to anger. Kidd and Flynt followed Larsen into a large, spacious living room full of windows. The furniture and carpets were immaculate, nothing like Kidd expected with a household full of children. Larsen motioned the Rangers to sit on an oversized, microfiber sectional that looked as if it was picked directly out of a home magazine. Larsen sat across from the Rangers on a leather loveseat. Kidd saw two women that appeared in the thirties and forties in the kitchen. They pretended to be uninterested, but Kidd could see their concern. "Now what do you need to know officers?"

"What, ya ain't gonna offer us a cold beer?" Flynt asked mockingly.

"I'm afraid not" Larsen replied smiling. "I have cold water?"

"We kinda knew Mormons didn't drink," Kidd responded back immediately.

"Well good thing I'm not Mormon then huh?"

"Well what are you then?" Flynt asked.

"I belong to the Inspired Church of Jesus Christ of Latter-day Saints."

"There a difference?"

"Plenty."

"Like wives I suppose?" Kidd chimed in.

"Among other things. Mormons follow a corporate-like structure of suits that make up scriptures and laws of god as they go. We have a clearer understanding of the law," Larsen smiled again. "The laws of God never change…only our understanding."

"Well I'll be damned." Flynt finally relented on the subject. Kidd observed the room. A shadowbox caught his eye propped on a mantle.

"You a military man Mr. Larsen?" Kidd inquired knowing full well what the answer would be. He saw the Airborne wings and the service medals nicely arranged with a fighting eagle background.

"82nd Airborne," Larsen answered. "Did a little time in the sandbox, Desert Storm…you?"

"Did a little time with 1st Recon Battalion."

"Jarhead huh?

"Yup"

"Well…we never seem to have a shortage of wars in this country."

"Nope."

"I didn't know ya'all served in the military?" Flynt chimed in, directing his comments toward Larsen.

"Ya'all? I'm not sure I like that tone Sergeant Flynt."

"Well it's not meant to offend you, Mr. Larsen, I just didn't think you guys cared for the country, that's all."

"There are many things that upset me about this government, but don't ever think I don't love my country," Jeremiah replied with a serious tone. "Now what do you need officers?"

"Come to ask about that land out off the new El Indio Highway."

"The back forty?"

"If that's what you call it."

"We run a few heifers and steer out there. We put a round bale out there and the tank's always full. We rotate them out about every other month…my boys and I that is."

"What about that access road the electric company runs?" Kidd asked.

"I know the road, but it's too far west, the cattle don't make it out there. Too far away from the tanks I guess. That and there's no good pasture there and the cattle don't like that thick scrub brush," Larsen answered. "Is something going on out there?"

"Found a grave of sorts out there," Flynt said casually.

"Grave? Dear God!" Larsen was astonished. Kidd looked at him with intent. He seemed genuine, Kidd thought. But Larsen had to have some information they could use. Often times, it isn't the verbal answer that is important to the investigator, but the demeanor and reaction in which he says it. "Do you know who is buried there?"

"There's several," Kidd interjected. "It's a mass grave." Kidd watched Larsen's eyes widen as if he he's been told there was a death in his own family. Larsen looked down at the ground as if he was going to cry but composed himself in a true self-disciplined fashion. Kidd expected that from Larsen.

"I don't understand, I mean, I haven't seen any news or

anything?"

"You're about to," Flynt replied. "You own that land?"

"No, Thomas Johnson owns that land."

"And who is he?" Kidd inquired.

"He's the bishop of our sect. He owns a two hundred acre spread over in the county, but he's got tons of land all around here, including that back forty"

"He ever get out there?"

Larsen smiled as he looked away from the Rangers heightening their interest. "Bishop Johnson doesn't exactly get outdoors much. As far as his kids…I don't honestly know."

"How many kids does he have?"

"I really don't know that either...a bunch."

"You're pretty close to him? I mean, him being your bishop and all?" Flynt asked.

Kidd and Flynt watched as Jeremiah giggled again. "Yes, he is my bishop, but I wouldn't call us close necessarily."

"I can't help but sense you got something between you and this Johnson?"

"Yeah, we don't see eye to eye on a lot of things."

"Can you explain?" Kidd inquired.

"Well, he doesn't care for the way I run the family. I guess you could say I'm too liberal and modern for him."

"Yet you still support him as your spiritual leader?"

"The man is called of God. Who am I to question God?"

"What kind of a man is Johnson?" Flynt interrupted.

"I guess he could be described as traditional," Larsen smirked.

"So, if we talk to him is he going to offer us some wives or something?" Flynt's comments made all three men burst into laughter and served as a final relief to the once tension-filled room.

"Well…probably not. But he will try and convert both you guys."

"Well, I think once he meets us, he'll find out he don't want us in the church." Flynt's cell phone rang as he replied. "Flynt…yeah Deb." The look on his face changed and Kidd knew that it was serious. "Okay Deb, we're on our way." The two Rangers thanked Larsen and made their way to the car. As they made it to the front porch, Kidd turned to face Larsen.

"What do you think of the cartels, Mr. Larsen?

The question seemed to have shocked Jeremiah. He stared at Kidd for an awkward few seconds before finally answering. "I think they are a scourge on the land."

"What would you think if someone were to take money from them?" Another bait question from Kidd, some questions you want an answer, some you just want to see the person's reaction.

"In truth…they should be prosecuted."

"Fair enough Mr. Larsen," Kidd said as the two made their way to the Crown Vic parked in the front. Kidd was a little surprised with Larsen's answer to the question but couldn't argue with its directness. "What did Deb want?" Kidd finally asked when they sat down inside the vehicle.

"They have a dead councilman."

*

The Las Palmas Restaurant was nearing the end of the dinner rush when Carlos walked in the door. He smiled and winked at the hostess who looked over into the bar area. She gestured with her head that his appointment was waiting. Carlos blew her a kiss and walked toward the corner booth. An older woman sat in the booth with spreadsheets and schedules scattered in the makeshift work area. She was short, plump with graying hair that was in a neat, well done bob only disturbed by the reading glasses on her face. Though her age and traditional hair may not have been the trendiest, her clothes were classic and expensive. Marisella looked up and smiled at Carlos as he sat down. It clearly wasn't sexual, but motherly as she shoved the paperwork and removed her glasses from her face. Her wrinkles were hardly visible with her salon makeover and full lips. *"Ah, Carlos…sientase, por favor,"* Marisella said patting the seat as if Carlos were a boy.

"Well hello beautiful, *como estas?*" Carlos smiled at Marisella as he sat down brushing her hand. He could smell her expensive perfume and as always amazed how put together she was.

"Stop it," as she grabbed his hand and shook it as if she was punishing him, but the smile never really went away. "Do you want a drink?"

"*Si...Tequila por favor,*" Carlos answered. Over the years he had begun to recognize the tone of her voice, whether she was happy or sad, but today he had no clue. He did know however, when Marisella offered you a drink, it was not a request, but an order of sorts and the last thing Carlos wanted to do was disappoint her. He watched as she made a hand signal to the bartender who was cleaning glasses for the evening. The bartender responded by placing a double shot of their top shelf in front of Carlos, slouching in the rounded booth waiting to hear from Marisella. He took out a manila envelope filled with several thousand dollars and passed it to her across the table. Marisella took the envelope and placed it into her large, Gucci purse.

"Did you send the rest to the address I told you?"

"Chuco dropped it today, all is good."

"Those two new guys are working out for you I see?"

"Yeah they are good. They had no problems getting the trucks across the border. They were never stopped by the troopers."

"How did you get them trained on the trucks?"

"Got a guy in El Paso that owns a trucking company. They drove for him for two weeks and got pretty good with the trucks."

"*Bueno!* They know about our arrangement?" Marisella asked in a very serious nature.

"They know...believe me," Carlos replied. "I know you want to ask me something else."

Marisella smiled at Carlos. His perception was correct, but he didn't like the smile on her face. Whatever it was, she was serious. "Um, the girls never arrived?"

"What? When were they supposed to be there?"

"Saturday."

"No call?"

"Hell no! Why do you think I called you personally?"

Marisella said in an exasperated voice. "I think I need to meet with your boss."

"You know that can't happen...I don't know who he is? He got my information from the inside. He gives me orders over the net, I get it done. But this girl thing is bullshit Marisella, I hate it," Carlos replied quickly.

"So do I, entiendes?!" Marisella's voice became urgent. "But we don't make the rules, and Tio's unhappy!"

"Let me see what I can find out." A million thoughts went through his head as to why the job didn't get done. He went over the instructions and the details of the plan and couldn't find any flaws. After all, he's done it many times, always without a hitch.

"There are some people talking, Carlos, your boss ought to think about a sit down. I'd get the message to him if I were you."

It wasn't what he wanted to hear, and his boss wouldn't like it either. "Look Marisella, I know that things are bad, but I can fix it. Let me find out what happened," Carlos was practically pleading with her.

"You know I love you Carlos," Marisella paused and stared at the much younger man. "You know what? I will let you fix this. But just because I'm fond of you does not mean you will not be held accountable."

"You know I answer to people, just like you, Marisella," Carlos replied.

Marisella chuckled and gave Carlos a stern look. "I'm going to tell you something Carlos and you listen good. I answer to no man, *entiendes?*" She took a drink from her florally decorated coffee cup. "My colleagues trust me to do a job, and I do it well. You think I give a fuck about these girls?" Marisella stared at Carlos while he shook his head negative. "It's about the job Carlos, the money, but most of all to do what you say you are going to do. If you don't want the blame, send me to your boss..."

"I will take care of it Marisella...I just need time."

"You will get time, but not much," She said casually. "The offer is always open if you need help keeping your people in line," Marisella smirked.

"*Gracias* Marisella, but you know up here that Negras brutal shit don't fly," laughed Carlos.

She laughed out loud this time, shaking her head almost in unbelief. "Mijo, the Negras tactics work everywhere. Don't think for one minute that the cops in this country don't understand we are here. We operate quietly for business…but we still operate."

*

Flynt pulled the Crown Vic up directly behind a marked squad car about two car lengths from the yellow tape. From the looks of it, the responding officers cordoned off the entire residential block, alleyways and all. There were only four units at the scene along with the DPS Crime Scene Van which struck Kidd as odd. Usually, a small-town murder scene was overrun with police. Apparently, the mass grave took all of the department's resources and media attention leaving the dead councilman's murder to be solved with the same limited resources that most departments have to deal with. Flynt and Kidd signed the log carried by a young officer with a pressed uniform, biceps popping out of the short sleeves like dough from a can. The young officer motioned with his head, "Third house on the left. My sergeant should meet you." The Rangers thanked the officer and carefully stepped underneath tape, carefully walking towards the crime scene.

"Well I got to hand it to old Dan…at least they marked off a good chunk of real estate for this scene. Ain't nothing worse than one too small," Flynt advised as he moved his eyes in every direction, afraid that he would miss something.

"How do you know it was old Dan?" Kidd asked as he took out his small, Stinger flashlight. "Maybe it was a detective that just knows his job?"

"You never worked for Dan."

"I guess I'd better thank God for that." Kidd began flashing his light at every object and began to see numbered placards through the neighbor's yards. "Blood spatter maybe?"

"Yep...my guess is Deb got on the trail. Damn woman's like a vampire, I swear she can smell it," Flynt answered as he observed the directionality of the spatter. "Looks like they ran northbound out of the neighborhood."

"Hmmm...maybe a pickup vehicle out on the main road?"

"Probably so, but why risk the chance of being seen so early in the evening?"

"Not from the area I would guess? But you know most witnesses couldn't identify a ham sandwich."

"Maybe." They came up to the porch and carefully scanned the front of the residence. The numbered placards started from the front door. The Rangers looked up and saw Deb step out of the house in coveralls.

"Well hey handsomes! About damn time you two go to work. What the hell ya'all been doin'?"

"Pissin' off some polygamists I suppose," Flynt answered still looking around as if he was expecting to find the next piece of evidence. "How's the dig going with Sunjani?"

"We're making progress. I just didn't expect this though." Deb paused and let out a sigh. It reminded Kidd of all of an interviewee that was waiting to confess to relieve their soul. Kidd hadn't even stopped to think about the case's effect on Deb Nichols. He and Flynt had the luxury of interviewing people and investigating leads, all Deb had was a pile of bodies and misery. There was no 'why' for her, only death. "The final count was fourteen full corpses, but there were limbs unaccounted for. So, we guessed about sixteen in all, given the limbs were from two different people. Sunjani is still piecing some of the remains together. I mean...this could take months in the lab."

"Any idea how they died, Deb?" Kidd asked.

Deb let out a sigh and the two Rangers saw her eyes well up. "So far two were shot, three stabbed and five strangled. The others we have no idea, but we can safely assume homicide." Deb Nichols turned her head and looked at the floor as if it contained answers to all of life's questions. "Richard...I...I've never seen so much shit...I swear I could scream," Deb turned her head because she didn't want to show her emotions. Kidd knew why. Women in law enforcement already were behind the curve. Male cops were already suspicious of their emotional vulnerability, and if they did have any type of reaction it would only solidify the negative stereotypes. The truth was that women cops were just as emotionally strong as the men, maybe more so. Flynt put his arm around Deb and pulled her close to him.

"Don't let it get to you, Sweetheart. Don't let it win," Flynt whispered in her ear while she nodded and wiped her eyes with the handkerchief Flynt provided her from his pocket. A true renaissance man was his partner, Kidd thought. How many men still even carry handkerchiefs, much less have the chivalrous courtesy to know when to deploy them. The sad truth was the emotions of the professions were never talked about, by anyone. Flynt gave Deb a big hug before he released her. "Now what do we have inside?"

"Another fucked up scene that's what," Deb responded with a chuckle wiping her last tear. "His name is Jaime Soto, city councilman…and um," She paused.

"Good hell…what Deb? He's a Democrat or something?" Flynt inquired rather impatiently.

"Um…you gotta see this for yourself," Deb threw some rubber gloves to the Rangers while they signed the major incident log from the young officer posted in the front yard. The house was a modern, two-story brick, pitched roof home that seemed to dot the city neighborhoods like rashes. The neighborhood was definitely the richer section of Eagle Pass. They followed Deb through a long walkway covered in Austin Stone to a dark, solid oak door. The entry way was eighteen-inch tile, and a beautiful winding staircase stood in front of the men. Deb walked around the staircase to a large, open family room. Kidd observed the very clean, open, meticulously decorated room. It was sparsely furnished with custom furniture and clean, Indian area rugs which immediately signaled the victim had no children. As they entered into the room, the smell of burned flesh stung the senses in Kidd's nose. It was a smell that every cop eventually would experience. Kidd remembered his first burned victim on a traffic accident while he was a rookie in Albuquerque. It was an experience that led to him not eating meat for two weeks.

"Is that what I think it is Deb?" Flynt inquired, obviously bothered by the sudden aroma.

"Behind that wall, in the dining area…and yes," She answered.

The Rangers made their way to the source of the smell in a dining room that resembled a large nook off the main room. The top of the body was a male, nude and burned from the waist up. The victim appeared Hispanic given the tan color of his legs and black body hair. Black soot outlined the victim's upper body as if it was drawn on the floor. The victim laid face down with his legs spread. A large, black dildo was inserted into the victim's rectum. Blood seeped around the enormous sex toy indicating a forceful insertion while the deceased was alive. The Rangers moved closer for a better look with both flashlights furiously checking the immediate area, even though it had already been swept by Deb Nichols.

"How do we even know this is actually Soto?" Flynt inquired, referring to the fact the head and torso were badly burned making visual identification virtually impossible.

"Leg tattoo," Kidd pointed to a large, body-length portrait of Soto revealing a leg tattoo that spelled "Soto" down his calf. The investigators could see the matching tattoo on the victim's calf. *So why the burning?* Kidd thought as he stared at the victim and surroundings. Kidd could tell Deb and Flynt were puzzled as well. The hardest thing about a crime scene was getting into the mind of the one who created it. "So, what do we got…a bad date?" Kidd finally broke the silence as he made an obvious reference to the sex toy.

"Real bad, but that's not all. Check this out," Deb showed the Rangers a duffel bag full of sex toys and tools. The kit also contained industrial strength rubber bands and nipple clamps. Deb dumped the contents of the bag on the tile revealing handcuffs, dog collars, more sex toys, and chains in addition to paper diagrams explaining how to use the items, no doubt printed from a computer website. Both Flynt and Kidd looked at the torture kit and shuddered inside. They were typical reactions from those not associated with "the lifestyle", meaning bondage or 'BDSM.' To those in the lifestyle, sex was the means to the end. The abusing of the body and disregard for conventional 'vanilla' sex was the ultimate turn-on. It was a side of humanity that cops ran into on limited occasions, but it always left a scar on the psyche when the human body was tortured and abused for sexual pleasure.

"A guy really need all them dildos?" Flynt finally broke the awkward stunned silence from the discovery of the sexual torture implements and toys promoting chuckles from Kidd and Deb.

"Just one good one, Sweetheart," Deb replied with a smile.

"What are these diagrams of?" Kidd asked trying to move past the sexual awkwardness he felt.

"Apparently Mr. Soto was into autoerotic asphyxiation," Deb handed Kidd the papers showing diagrams of how to make safety releases on ligatures meant for people to essentially hang themselves while they masturbate. The theory is that the orgasms are more intense when a person's air supply is limited, but Kidd, like many officers, didn't want to experiment.

"So why the paper and not the internet like everybody else?"

"He's afraid of folks getting into his computer because of his position. My guess is that his hard drive is very clean," Flynt replied.

"Okay so we have a councilman into some sick shit lying burned with a dildo up his ass," Kidd paused, took off his hat and ran his finger through his hair. "What do we got?"

"Homicide?" Flynt smirked.

"Very funny Asshole! I mean what do we know about this guy?" Kidd looked around the room and went straight to the pictures. "Looks like he's got a boyfriend." Kidd stared at a small, thin gray-haired Hispanic man posing with Jaime Soto in the photos. Though there were no outward public displays of affection in the pictures, it was obvious the men had feelings for each other. Kidd barely had time for another thought when he heard a semi-familiar voice enter the room.

"He was a Liberal asshole member of the city council, Ranger Kidd," Dan Gummit said as he suddenly entered the scene.

"Well Dan, that's no way to speak of the dead and this makes two cases I've seen you come out to…what gives?" Flynt asked sarcastically.

"I run every investigation out here Richard," Gummit answered snidely.

"Is that the 'servant leadership' you was telling us about?"

"Something like that?" Gummit's stare kept becoming more intense at Flynt. Kidd was trying not to laugh. "I'd like for you two to work this one Richard."

"Are you serious Dan?" Flynt was shocked. He never would have expected those words from Dan Gummit. "We're here to help, but we don't want to take over…"

"Nonsense, Richard. All my detectives are tied up on this mass grave deal. I'll give Cahill a call and make it official." Kidd and Flynt were in disbelief as Gummit walked out of the room and left. They both marveled at the fact the chief never even mentioned the body lying directly in front of him and were downright stunned he gave a murder investigation away.

"What the hell just happened?" Kidd asked in a stunned, angry voice.

"You just got screwed by the biggest asshole to don a police uniform," Flynt answered matter of factly.

"No hemorrhoids huh?"

"Not a one."

CHAPTER FOUR

Interdiction

"Amanda?!" Sariah yelled after she pulled her car up into the barn area. Sariah opened the door and pulled the small, red sedan inside. It was an action she had done numerous times before. She looked forward with the weekly meeting with her best friend. Usually Amanda was out in the open waiting for her, but today she was strangely absent. She began to become uncomfortable and took out her cell phone, only to remember Amanda was forbidden to own any Gentile technology per her freak father. Sariah started to back up towards her vehicle when she saw a figure in the corner of her eye.

"Hey there, Sariah…what are you doing here?" Nathan Johnson appeared from the shadows as if he just materialized. The sound of his voice was even creepier that his father's, Sariah thought, and that wasn't easy. She also knew if Nathan was around, Josiah couldn't be that far behind.

"Hey there Gentile lover!" *Shit there he was*, she thought. Josiah stood about six foot, and was pretty skinny, though not weak. Nathan was just as tall, but a bit thicker. Both had that wiry strength that most likely came from working the outdoors and animals. But around the sect, they were feared. They were the boys that mothers and sister-wives warned the young ladies to stay away from. There were stories of immorality and perversion that circulated around the sect in silence, but they were like a protected species. They were the sons of the Bishop. Many of the wives even wished their daughters to be married to them, despite the horrible stories and reputations that went with them. They were Johnsons, and that name went a long way in the Inspired Church of Jesus Christ of Latter-day Saints. One more reason Sariah was getting out of the lifestyle.

"Hey guys, I…I was just here to see Amanda," she answered, her voice crackling just a bit. Instinctively, Sariah put her small purse, over her shoulder and folded her arms. She started to slowly back up towards her car.

"Amanda's not here, but we'd like to talk to you," Josiah said, almost giggling. Sariah's stomach was now queasy; she realized she was in a situation that could potentially get out of hand for her.

"Do you guys' know when she'll be back?" Sariah was trying to talk gently and divert a bad situation.

"Probably never," Josiah laughed, and Sariah could now feel her heart beating like a tribal drum. "She went off to Salt Lake."

"We are concerned about your salvation," Nathan said in a more reasonable tone of voice. Sariah decided she would have more luck talking and trying to reason with him.

"No need to be concerned, Nathan, I'm just fine," Sariah smiled, and used her natural beauty to try and persuade Nathan to control his brother and buy her enough time to leave gracefully.

"You haven't answered my father's call? That means you are disobeying the Lord."

"I'm just thinking about it…doesn't a girl have the right to consider her future?" Sariah smiled again.

"No, she don't, Bitch!" Josiah barked.

"Josiah! Enough! We are here to talk, not be rude," Nathan turned and smiled at Sariah. "We want to convince you to join the family."

"I'm flattered Nathan, but I truly am thinking about it…I promise," Sariah barely got the words out when she saw Josiah taking his clothes off in the background. "What…what is he doing, Nathan?" Sariah said with a genuine fear in her voice.

"Don't worry Sariah, it's a natural part of life," Nathan calmly walked over to Sariah's Mustang, opened the door and took the keys out of the ignition. He winked and started to take off his shirt. Josiah walked up to Sariah and stood a good six feet from her, fully nude, shaking his head as if Sariah was waiting her whole life for it. Sariah started looking for the door, or any other way out of the barn. "No one's going to hear you, Sariah…now take your clothes off!"

"Umm…if I marry you guys' father that would make me a

sister-wife…basically your mother. What would your father think?" Her mind was racing one hundred miles an hour, but it just wasn't fast enough.

"You think you're the only mother we fucked?" Josiah smiled an evil grin. Somehow the statement, as sickening as it sounded was probably true, Sariah thought.

"Okay, I'm officially creeped out now guys the joke is over," Sariah smiled and whispered in an effort to minimize the tension and avoid the obvious conclusion to the situation. She thought about her father and all of the advice and encouragement he gave her for dangerous situations. He was always scared for her, but she never worried a bit until now. He was right. There were evil people in the world that wanted to hurt her. And yet with all of her fear a switch flipped in her head. If she had to endure this evil she would do so on her terms. She stared at the two men now with the same amount of fear she had previously, but now she coupled it with anger. They may hurt her, but she would not make it easy. She reached into her purse covertly.

"This is no joke," Nathan said as he stood fully naked, and erect, in front of her.

"Yes, it is, ya'all remind me of school boys with those!" Sariah laughed referring to the Johnson's manhood. She suddenly felt the thud of Josiah's hand across her left cheek and the sting and burn that accompanied the punch. She fell to the ground on her back and saw Josiah coming for her. He grabbed her ankles and spread them apart. Sariah was startled with his strength, when she tried to close them, his naked body was in between them. Nathan kneeled to her side and was trying to rip her top off in the struggle. She rolled up on her back, like her father taught her in her Ju-Jitsu lessons and was able to get her legs up under Josiah's chest. She heaved her legs forward, like an inverted leg press as hard as she could, catapulting Josiah off of her and onto his back. She pulled the Smith and Wesson folding knife from her purse and gripped it like a fist pack. She threw a punch at Nathan's face that her father would be proud of and connected with his nose. It was a hard jolt to Nathan's nose as he rolled off in the dirt with his hands over his face. Sariah struggled to her feet and saw Josiah doing the same. The

64

dirt and loose hay from the floor of the barn stuck to his nude body like a candy sprinkles to ice cream. Sariah was to her feet quicker and landed a front kick to Josiah's chin stunning him and standing him up on the heels of his feet. She could hear and see from the corner of her eye Nathan getting up and getting ready to retaliate. She quickly unfolded her knife and grabbed Josiah's penis and testicles and gripped them with all her might forcing Josiah to scream in a horrifying frequency. She then stuck the knife blade up close to his pelvis, burying the tip of the blade in his scrotum causing it to bleed. "Don't you fucking move!" Josiah was gripped with fear and couldn't move. "Get your hands on top of your head!"

Sariah quickly turned and saw Nathan advancing towards her. She quickly turned Josiah to keep him between her and Nathan. "You better stop right there mother fucker or I'm gonna cut these pathetic balls from his body!!!" Sariah yelled forcefully at Nathan. Josiah kept screaming and whimpering when he saw the blood drip down to his inner thigh. His penis began to leak urine in fear. "Quit crying Bitch or you'll lose em!"

"Don't do anything stupid Sariah!" Nathan's voice turned from forceful to pleading. "Your keys are in my pants, just go."

"Shut up asshole! I say what I do next," Sariah snapped back. "I just might cut these little balls and keep them as a trophy! Albeit a small one," Sariah's tears instinctively began flowing. "Sit down right there and cross your legs Nathan or I swear the next set of nuts I cut off will be yours!"

"Sariah! Josiah! Nathan!" a voice called from the barn door. Sariah turned to see Bishop Johnson standing in the door way wearing his standard smoke gray suit. "What in the name of heaven is going on?!" Sariah turned to see Bishop Johnson, complete with white shirt and tie standing in the entryway of the barn. Nathan froze where he stood, and Josiah immediately stopped whimpering, it was as if the Bishop scared him more than the knife in his scrotum.

"Ask your rapist sons! Don't you come any closer!" Sariah said nervously. She began to back up while Josiah continued to sob.

"Sariah put down the knife and let's talk. I give you my word that these boys will be punished, and you will not be harmed in any way, not ever," Bishop Johnson spoke in a voice that she had never heard before. She didn't trust him, but maybe it was the years of religious training that taught her not to doubt the Lord's anointed, no matter how creepy they actually were. She lessened the grip on Josiah's testicles as he staggered away holding his scrotum in pain. "You two…get your clothes on and march straight to the temple…both of you! Now!" Johnson turned and looked at Sariah. "How can I convey to you how sorry I am?"

"I just want to go home!" Sariah began to tear again. She began to lose the vision of her left eye as it swelled.

"Sariah, you need to calm down," Johnson said almost tenderly.

"Where's Amanda?!"

"She's in Utah."

"I thought she wasn't leaving until next week?" Now the tears really started flowing. The attempted sexual assault was nothing compared to the loss of her best friend. "I didn't even get to say goodbye."

"There are never any endings, Sariah, only new beginnings. You will see Amanda soon enough. She was anxious to start the next phase of her mortal existence," Bishop Johnson said sounding pious as usual.

"Can't you just ever answer a direct question?! I mean…why does everything have to be a sermon?"

"Because everything we do, we do for our Heavenly Father. Life is a sermon."

"Goddamn! There you go again…"

"Don't take the Lord's name, Sariah, please…let's talk sensibly."

"So, talk fast I want to go home. My father's going to be pissed!"

"That's why we need to wait to tell him, Sariah," Bishop Johnson sounded nervous. "It's us against the world, Sariah. If we divide, the Gentiles will destroy us."

"Maybe they'll just destroy those two bastards…"

"Mark my words…they will pay for their sins. The brethren will see to that. But a house divided can't stand, Sariah, you know that," Bishop Johnson said quietly. "Let me speak with Jeremiah please…let me make this right for you and your family."

Sariah stared at the Bishop and knew he was right. She was afraid of what her father would do. The fact was that she didn't want any part of the lifestyle, but everyone she loved and cared for was part of it. She knew that the Gentiles were looking for any excuse to tear the sect apart. Personally, she didn't care for her sake, but she did care about her family and friends. "Okay Bishop, but keep them away from my family, or else!"

"Sariah, I can promise you that those two boys will never come near you again. As God is my witness, this incident will be atoned for and handled under the strict supervision of the church and the brethren," Bishop Johnson smiled slightly. "You are very mature for your age, and you are becoming more aware of your spirituality. As you grow older, the choices get harder, but today, you've shown the beginnings of womanhood. This family truly owes you a debt."

"No debt, Bishop. I just want to go home…I won't tell anyone."

✳

The two Rangers walked into the Border Café in downtown Eagle Pass. It was busy, but for some unknown reason they felt at home in this type of atmosphere. A thin, brunette middle-aged woman approached them with a smile, "Ya'all here for Don?" She was attractive and seemed to fancy Flynt.

"Yes Ma'am," Flynt replied tipping his Stetson while simultaneously winking at her as well. She smiled again at Flynt as he and Kidd followed her to a table next to the kitchen of the business. Kidd could hear his stomach growl as he passed by each table serving everything from Texas staples like chicken fried steak to border favorites like beef enchiladas. As they approached the booth, the pretty waitress had already set two iced teas for the men to drink. Already seated was a large man in his fifties, also wearing a cowboy hat with Wrangler jeans. The man had a thick, colored brown moustache and glasses. He stood up and greeted the two Rangers.

"Ranger Flynt and Ranger Kidd?" the man said as he extended his hand toward the two men.

"And you are the famed 'Texas Don'?" Flynt asked as the two men shook.

"The one and only," Texas had a small cult following throughout Texas and was well known to political leaders and cops alike. Between his numerous social media site, including a blog with several thousand followers, and his appearances at the legislature, he was a well-known staple in the cyber world, but no one knew much about the man. Flynt and Kidd were about to find out.

"Your message said you had a tip about the Soto murder?" Kidd asked curious about the fact a blogger had some tip about an actual murder intrigued him. Kidd saw Texas Don shake his head to the affirmative. "When did you find out about the murder? When Channel Four reported it?"

"C'mon Ranger Kidd, you know I got sources all around this place; Fire Department, Police Department, you name it."

"So, you knew before the news report…yes or no?"

"Well…yes I guess?"

"Look here Don…can I call you Don?" Flynt interrupted.

"Yes Sergeant."

"I don't give a damn about your little operation on the internet, when we ask you a question about a murder that you supposedly have knowledge about, we expect a straight answer. Is that understood?"

"Sergeant Flynt…I have made and broken a few careers in this state…"

"You think I give a good goddamn about you?" Flynt interrupted. Texas Don stopped his speech it its tracks staring in meekness at Kidd's partner. "I've been a Ranger for decades. I've served under countless Governors and Lieutenant Governors. I've been personally threatened by a Senator of the United States of America. Do you think I give any thought to a two-bit retired computer nerd with a goddamn superiority complex?" Flynt stared at Texas Don waiting for an answer that would never come. Texas Don sat at the table silent and humbled. "Now let's try this again…how did you find out about Soto's murder?"

"A contact of mine in the police department called me when it was dispatched."

"Why did they call you?" Kidd inquired.

"Cause he knew I was working on something," Texas Don answered.

"And what is that?" Kidd watched Texas Don reach into his brief case and pull out a stack of papers approximately four inches thick and plopped it on the table.

"There it is," Texas Don looked at the two Rangers.

"What the hell is that?" Flynt asked, obviously annoyed.

"All the evidence you need…ledgers, spreadsheets, purchase orders, it's all there."

"Um Don…this is a murder…not one of your damn political causes!"

"It's all connected, Sergeant Flynt," Texas Don swore. "These Liberals are all about corruption and my guess is that Soto was about to blow the whistle off this whole thing!"

"What whole thing?" Kidd inquired.

"The Coahuila Highway! The damn thing is nothing but an illegal slush fund for liberal, corrupt politicians."

"Damn I think I'm going to regret this," Flynt gave Kidd that sarcastic face. "How?" Flynt sounded exasperated as he asked the question. Kidd could tell he was going to have to step in and calm Flynt down. He knew his partner hated nothing more than time wasted on a murder investigation and Texas Don was a waste of time. Instead of offering the Rangers a valuable lead to solve the real murder of Jaime Soto, Texas Don offered nothing.

"It's all connected…what else could it be? A political situation and a murder of a politician…you don't see it's all connected? If you want my advice, I'd start with the Democratic Party of Maverick County. Those sons of bitches are the key to break this thing wide open."

"So, the Democrats murdered Soto?" Kidd asked

sarcastically. "Well that's that I guess."

"It's not that simple. I provided you a framework…you still got to investigate," Texas Don stated almost triumphantly.

"You seem like a reasonable man, Don. Can I level with you?" Flynt asked with a faux look of concern. "You didn't provide shit…okay? I'm being perfectly serious now. What I want you to do is get back into your truck or SUV, or whatever the hell else you drive and go back to your bunker or rock you crawled out of."

"You're just gonna let em' get away with all this corruption?"

"Yes…every goddamned bit of it. And if you want my advice, Don, I would stick to what you know."

"And what is that?" Texas Don asked in a more defiant tone.

"Spewing worthless bile across the internet to those too stupid, or lazy to do their own research and form their own opinions."

"That's what I'd expect from a government worker…"

"Don…our conversation's over and I wish you luck."

"Luck?"

"Yeah…if you're lucky enough to leave here with your head intact, I wish you the best."

"Maybe your director should hear about your tone…" The sentence wasn't completed before Kidd's fist slammed down on the table sending the tea glasses everywhere and startling Texas Don who reached for his beltline instinctively, only to have Kidd grab his hand and slam it down on the table while simultaneously pulling the Colt 1911 from Jim's waistband. Texas Don let out a groan from the impact of his hand on the hard table. Kidd calmly removed the magazine and locked the slide of the pistol. He gave the weapon a quick glance.

"You really didn't think I knew you were packing, Don?" Kidd's voice was an almost sadistic whisper. "How'd you like to go to jail for drawing a weapon on a Texas Ranger?" Texas Don went silent. "We are going to leave here now. Consider yourself lucky you're not in jail…or dead for that matter." Kidd smiled as he got up from the table. He tipped his hat to the restaurant patrons who waived back, partially out of fear perhaps. He tossed the 1911 pistol back to Don in parts and kept the magazine. "I'll mail these back to ya Don." Kidd finally said. Flynt grabbed Don's paperwork and followed Kidd out.

"Just think, Don…I gotta be a partner to that ornery sum bitch!"

*

Deb warmed her hands as she drank from her mug. The air conditioning in the new, Weslaco Department of Public Safety Crime Lab was always set to frigid she thought. The stainless-steel work stations and the tile only seemed to make the area even colder, stinging her skin anytime contact was made. She could hardly keep her eyes open. Between investigating the mass grave and now the councilman, if she wasn't knee deep in shit in the lab, she was traveling from McAllen to Eagle Pass. After her last divorce, she immersed herself in her work, but she had no idea this would be the result.

She had her own office and work station in the new lab, something she had never had in the past. She had her own research station, processing stations, and photo labs. She had a quick line to the DNA lab as well. She had lunch with the Head DNA Technician Susan Chapin every day she was not in the field so if there are ever results pending, she has the connection. She looked in her inbox and saw five profiles already in her inbox. She thanked Susan under her breath and began to thumb through them. Susan even matched the DNA profiles with Dr. Sunjani's Medical Examiner's report on each corpse. She sat down on her leather chair and began to recline. She took out her reading glasses and took another drink of coffee.

She opened the first profile and began to read. It was a fifteen-year-old girl, Mexican descent, just barely old enough to experience womanhood. Deb read the profile and shook her head. The body was mummified, and the Medical Examiner estimated the body has been buried at least a year. The report stated that the girl had been stabbed twenty times given the marks on her ribs and her arms removed upon burial. *Shit!* She thought to herself. She couldn't help but feel for the poor girl who probably didn't have the chances she had in life. Maybe this girl could've have been a doctor, or even a forensic scientist, but here she was a report and a number with the Texas Department of Public Safety. She threw the report down on her desk, there was no matches in any missing persons file out of the States or Mexico.

She opened the next file and her curiosity peaked. *Caucasian? What?* She reread the ethnicity and read on. The girl was sixteen years old, blonde hair, and probably died from asphyxiation, given the lack of trauma to her corpse. There was no match for her within the National Database for Missing and Exploited Children. The report stated that she was most likely in the ground for about six months which would explain the hair being found and analyzed. But the findings struck Deb as odd, because in the last twenty years, law enforcement officials have strived to keep meticulous documents concerning missing children. The non-reporting of any type of child crime has been criminalized so how could a blonde girl from United States end up in a hole and nobody have the foggiest clue as to who she is? *European maybe?* Deb thought to herself trying to come up with any observation that didn't involve sheer neglect or abuse on the part of the parents. Having never had any children of her own, she was very sensitive to crimes against children; they seem to affect her, unlike the run of the mill adult crimes she had grown accustomed to. Deb threw that one on the desk as well. There were no matches for her profile in CODIS, or Combined DNA Index System, either. She sighed and took another drink of coffee that was now lukewarm at best. She leaned back in her chair and rubbed her eyes with the well-manicured hands the other technicians made fun of. She never apologized for her femininity; it was her strength after all.

The third file she picked up was another Hispanic girl, most likely Mexican. Deb chuckled at the fact that on some profiles the Anthropologist can damn near tell you what the person had for lunch and others they're lucky to get the ethnic background of the victim at all. She silently wondered about just how scientific their work was…maybe it was just a SWAG, or 'sophisticated wild ass guess.' She giggled from sheer exhaustion as she entered the third victim's profile in CODIS. Her heart leaped as she saw the possible hit screen appear on her monitor…It is a crime scene tech's dream. Her hands shook from excitement and almost couldn't work the mouse. The computer seemed to just creep at a glacial pace as her much anticipated information loaded. Then it appeared, *Sandra Salazar*, Deb read across the screen. Sandra went missing from Laredo approximately four months ago. Deb picked up her cellular phone disregarding the hour. She had to get in touch with Flynt. For a brief second, she thought about calling Dan Gummit, but decided he could wait. She could at least fall asleep knowing that she contributed to the investigation…that was truly all she ever wanted. But there was one more thing. Deb took out her cell phone and dialed. It rang only two times before the deep, accented voice answered.

"Hello?"

"Richard…I need a big favor."

*

"Joshua…it's so good to hear from you!" Jeremiah Larsen was smiling when he got the call from his childhood friend who now lived with his four wives in Draper, Utah. When Jeremiah enlisted in the Army, his best friend, Joshua Gentry decided to stay at Brigham Young University and finish his degree. Though the Church of Jesus Christ of Latter-day Saints officially does not want their membership associated with the different polygamist sects, oftentimes the children of those polygamist families make it into the University. That was the case for Joshua. He blended in with the predominantly Mormon student body with surprising ease and followed the strict honor code with no problems whatsoever. Joshua graduated with honors with an engineering degree and was immediately hired by the Novell Corporation in Orem, Utah. The family moved outside of Draper, a more rural community between Provo and Salt Lake, to avoid any unwanted pressures from the communities and local law enforcement. For years, the Gentry family lived with no outside scrutiny from incensed citizens, and they liked it that way. That left Joshua plenty of time to focus on his calling within the Inspired Church of Jesus Christ of Latter-day Saints as a First Counselor to the bishop of the local ward. The sect was spread the Salt Lake and Utah Valley areas and west of Tooele, so Gentry's time was constantly spent visiting members in those areas.

"How are things in Southern Zion?" Gentry laughed as he spoke to his old friend. Jeremiah started to chuckle and shake his head.

"Good…when are you gonna get out of that Mormon-infested psycho-state?"

Gentry laughed, *"Well I got a good thing here. The Mormons are too busy with politics and trying to change so the Gentiles will like them. They don't pay us much attention."* It was true, and Jeremiah knew it. Mainstream Mormons sincerely cared what the rest of the world thought of them, Jeremiah and his sect didn't. Mormons changed their ordinances and beliefs to become more palatable to the public, Jeremiah's sect knew that God's law never changed for anyone. The Mormons despised his sect because they felt Jeremiah's people brought ridicule and shame to all people with Latter-day Saint beliefs. That hatred brought the members of the Inspired Church of Jesus Christ of Latter-day Saints closer together. That's why he and Joshua Gentry were so close. They spoke freely about the old days and acquaintances, Gentry was Jeremiah's only real contact to the outside world. Unlike Jeremiah, Gentry was dialed in with the leadership of the Inspired Church of Jesus Christ of Latter-day Saints. His next step would be a General Authority.

"So, what's the word from Zion?" Jeremiah chuckled as he asked.

"The church is growing. There are several weddings coming up."

"Well two Johnson girls just went down to be sealed to one of the Smoot's."

"Smoot huh? Well I didn't hear about that one. But like I said, the church is growing."

"But that is strange you haven't heard anything."

"Well the Smoots and Johnsons have always been close, so it really doesn't surprise me. Say, how are things with you and Bishop Johnson anyway?"

"Like oil and water," Jeremiah answered snidely. "I ask God for patience every night. I support his calling and I support the Prophet's decision, but that doesn't mean we have to be friends does it?"

"I suppose not, but you got to start playing nice with the brethren, Jeremiah. Like it or not, they are the voice of God. If you want to hold a position of authority, they have to approve, and right now Johnson is their man in Texas," Gentry pled. *"I just want you to succeed my friend."*

"They don't like my views or my family, Joshua...you know that!"

"Jeremiah, the LaFeys have nothing to do with this...you are Larsen now. You have done all you can to separate yourself. Besides, they're still in Colonia LaFey," Joshua Gentry was right. Even though Jeremiah was born a LaFey, he changed his name to Larsen. But the brethren knew his family, and the LaFey name was hard to distance yourself from.

"Sometimes I wonder if that was the right thing to do..."

"You had to...that is all," the conversation paused. Gentry finally broke the silence, *"What do you hear from Moroni anyway?"*

"We still talk once a month. Moroni is Moroni ya know? He has a big chip on his shoulder and he is itching to fight someone...anyone really."

"What about their activities?"

"Unapologetically the same."

CHAPTER FIVE

Politico

"Gentlemen…please come in and have a seat," Michael Cordova, the Mayor Pro-Temp of Eagle Pass was more than accommodating to the two Rangers as they made their way into his private office. The building was located in the historic district of Eagle Pass, near the Aztec Theatre, on Jefferson Street. Kidd could hear the deep echoing of he and Flynt's footprints and they trekked across the hollowed floor of the office. Cordova's office had vintage wood floors and leather furniture bundled around a large, cherry wood desk.

"I'm Sergeant Flynt…this is Sergeant Kidd of the Texas Rangers…"

"Yes…Chief Gummit told me you all were in town. I am so sorry to hear about Miguel…he was a good friend." Kidd observed Cordova. His courtesy was almost over the top and soupy-thick. It was as if his smile was surgically implanted and impossible to remove. These were the hardest interviews, Kidd thought. Politicians were always on their game and were used to cautiously answering any question given and they rarely make a mistake. It's how they get elected and stay in office so long. In order to get a real answer from Cordova, Kidd knew that he and Flynt would have to get under Cordova's skin. That was the fun part and they were well on their way.

"Well I'm sure that his family would appreciate that Mr. Cordova," Flynt briefly paused. "But isn't it true that you and Soto hated each other?"

"We were political rivals, but still very good friends," Cordova smiled uneasily.

"Really? Cause we heard ya'all weren't exactly friendly towards one another," Kidd asked studying the politician for any non-verbal behavioral clues.

"I don't know who you would hear that from?"

"It's all over the internet and local political blogs. I'm surprised that you haven't been paying attention."

"You're talking about Texas Don, Ranger Kidd?" Cordova laughed out loud. "You guys of all people should know that guy is a liar! He needs to get a real job, and a life."

"So, the reports of you and Soto getting into an argument that almost ended in an ass-whoopin' at the City Council work session are false?" Flynt inquired with an eyebrow raised. Kidd and Flynt did their homework. It was well documented that Cordova negotiated the city's terms for the highway and it was no secret Soto vigorously opposed it. During a work session, Soto and Cordova stepped outside and into each other's faces. Texas Don not only wrote about it on his blog, he posted an amateur cell phone video taken by a bystander. It was the talk of Eagle Pass for several weeks and polarized the politics ever further in Maverick County.

"That was an isolated, unfortunate incident Sergeant...I have already apologized."

"But you have to admit Mr. Cordova, it does appear that Soto being gone is one less pain in the ass, politically speaking of course," Kidd observed.

"Everyone's a pain in the ass politically, Ranger Kidd," Cordova's tone changed. "You guys think you know how to run a city? Well you guys don't know shit, pardon my language." Cordova eyeballed the two Rangers. Kidd could tell that the mere fact they dared to ask Cordova any questions upset him. They were police officers and he was an elected mayor pro temp. That meant he could answer the questions however he wanted, and they would like it.

"Well now what kind of language is that Mr. Mayor?"

"It's Mayor Pro-Temp," Cordova said in an indignant manner to the Rangers.

"I don't give a good goddamn what your title is," Kidd stared at Cordova with a calm, truly indifferent look that gave Cordova the impression that Kidd would just as soon shoot him as speak with him. That was exactly what Kidd wanted him to think. "This is a murder investigation you pompous pile of shit. Your position don't mean shit to us!"

Flynt laughed to attempt to break the ice in a burst of controlled laughter. It was obvious that Cordova went from a position of perceived domination to fear with just a few sentences. "What my partner means there, Councilman, or Pro Temp...or whatever the hell you are, is we aren't real intimidated by you politicians. I mean, our headquarters is in Austin. Ya'all couldn't scrape the shit off the bottom of their boots."

"I thought you had questions for me," Cordova asked in a more pleasant tone of voice, obviously taken back by the two men's indifference to his position of importance. "I have very important business to attend to."

"Who would want Soto dead?" Flynt inquired.

"A lot of people, Sergeant Flynt...I mean, take your pick,"

"Just for grins, where were you Thursday night?"

"Actually, my wife and I were in McAllen. We had tickets to the theater."

"When's the last time you heard from Soto?" Kidd interrupted.

"The work session on Tuesday night, I guess. He seemed as feisty as always."

"Anything particular discussed?"

"Same argument as always, he wants to do anything to stop the highway. But it can't be stopped now."

"That's a pretty hot topic still, huh?" Flynt smiled.

"More than ever. I am amazed how many hate progress."

"Well Mister Mayor, maybe one man's progress is another's hell. Who's to say any of us are right?"

"You sound like Jaime...always the idealist."

"He doesn't sound like a bad guy. After all, where would we be without idealism?"

"Able to get some things done," Cordova laughed. "I know you didn't come here to discuss political philosophy Sergeant?"

"Nope...I suppose that's all for now," Flynt smiled as he and Kidd slowly began to get up from the expensive office furniture simultaneously. Flynt turned and looked at the Mayor Pro-Temp, "By the way Mayor, could you get us a copy of this month's income receipts for the city?" The questioned seemed to render the politician speechless. He looked stunned as Flynt and Kidd slowly waited for a response.

"The city's budget is on the website, Sergeant?" Cordova's voice was noticeably less defiant and confident than previously.

"Well we've heard some things and just want to follow up. You know…for the sake of thoroughness," Kidd advised. "You know what they say, 'leave no stone unturned'."

"Well, I'm going to have to contact the City Attorney…"

"What on earth for?" Flynt asked with a puzzled look. "What do you have to hide Mayor Pro-Temp?" Kidd knew what his partner was doing. Flynt had no interest in seeing those receipts. Instead, he was studying Cordova's reactions to a question he didn't want to answer. Politicians don't mind showing their constituents the budget as a whole, but when it comes to the actual line-item expenditures they tend to raise more questions than answers. Cordova was getting uncomfortable with the Rangers, and they knew it.

"Well here's a card…have the lawyer call me," Flynt smiled as they walked out of the office. They made their way through the hallway to the parking lot. "What do you think?" Flynt asked his partner as they sat down in the Crown Vic.

"Crooked, not a killer," Kidd replied.

"Set up guy?"

"Wouldn't put it past him, but then again, I've never trusted those sons of bitches."

*

"I'm glad you guys came, *sienta se por favor,*" Carlos motioned for Chuco and Juan to come inside the little restaurant, *Mi Hermana's* located just outside the city limits of Eagle Pass. Carlos motioned the two men back into the bar area where a corner boot was waiting for them. The two Tangos looked around the place admiring the whole atmosphere.

"Smells good, *no?*" Chuco happily said as both he and Juan sat at the booth. "Is this place yours?"

"Hell no," Carlos responded with a snort and giggle. Carlos ordered a spread that included enchiladas and sopapillas. It was accompanied with the standard Tequila and beer. Each of them ate and drank as if it were his last. As the food and drink slowly began to disappear, the conversation slowly began to resume.

"I got something to discuss with you all," Carlos said as he put down his cerveza that washed down his traditional food. What he was to discuss with these two men was sensitive and he wasn't quite sure of their reaction.

"Another job, *no?*" Chuco asked.

"Not exactly, but yes."

"No entiendeo, ese," Juan joined the conversation.

"We are not just involved with dope… we sometimes take girls across the border for a boss in the Negras."

"Girls?"

"Yes, goddammit girls! You know *putas.*"

"That's some heavy shit Bro…dopes one thing, but girls…shit," Chuco chimed in, obviously uncomfortable with the subject.

"We don't work for saints, *ese!* What can I tell you?"

"I didn't know the Negras ran whores?" Juan inquired.

"They don't really…they just make money off them." Carlos again took interest in his dwindling meal but continued to speak to the men as if he was half interested. He expected reluctance, just as he was, but the reality was the job needed to get done. It really was that simple. "The Negras broker the transport to people all over Coahuila and the States who pay well. They throw us a transport fee and pocket the rest. They have done it for years." Carlos continued to eat. There wasn't much else to say. The Negras were who they are and they required much from those that worked for them.

"They don't run any whore houses themselves?"

"No," Carlos chuckled. "They're shadows, man. They don't operate businesses like that… it's too visible. They take from those people, but they themselves operate legitimate businesses in Mexico." Carlos observed Juan. He looked sort of puzzled by what he was being told, but Carlos could see the wheels turning in his head. He then looked around the restaurant that they sat in.

"Just in Mexico?"

Carlos smiled. "Sometimes in the States too." Juan knodded in acknowledgement. "We all take orders. If you want to get paid, you gotta play by their rules," Carlos said carefully looking at both Chuco and Juan to make sure they really understood what he was about to say. Too many people either didn't understand the Cartel, or they forgot the golden rule of dealing with the Cartel, they just didn't make the rules, they invented the game. "I need you guys to understand that. I've seen too many dead guys that forgot." Carlos watched as the men nodded in the affirmative. "We need girls."

"Fuck…doesn't everybody, *ese?"* Chuco said, causing the three men to laugh and lightening up the conversation as much as it could have.

"*No Cabron*, I'm serious," Carlos replied smiling. "Girls for the drop."

"Where do the girls come from?" Juan asked both concerned and curious.

"Relax Bro, these girls are pre-selected. They aren't normal like you sisters or *Madre'*. They got no families who care about them. In fact, they give up their own daughters."

"The Negras pay off the families?"

"Somebody does," Carlos sounded almost incredulous at his associate's naivety. "Nobody turns down the right offer." Carlos studied Chuco and Juan's reaction. Even as rough as their upbringing was in the valley, the thought of a parent selling their own child for the amusement of nameless men truly bothered the Tangos. It was a hard reality to for them. "As far as the Negras are concerned, they always pay for goods and services."

"Where do we need to go?" Chuco asked.

"I'll give you all the details," Carlos answered. Rule number one…stay away from the major ports of entry. It ain't like dope, the Human Trafficking Taskforce watches them hard. But we got their number."

*

Sariah found herself sitting outside of Bishop Johnson's office inside the temple. She kept looking at the white carpet that sat under her feet wondering if her shoes were somehow staining it. It was a lot like she felt about herself. She was raised in a religion that considered her and her family outsiders, sinners, even Gentiles. Maybe she was those things? Maybe her unworthiness as a member of the Inspired Church of Jesus Christ of Latter-day Saints caused her to stain the inside of the temple by her just being there. In any case, she didn't feel welcome in the religion of her fathers'. The waiting area in the temple was lavishly furnished with antique chairs and cherry wood tables. Just to get inside, there were brethren that acted as security. Only members of the church who met high standards could participate in the actual ordinances performed inside, but anybody could get an audience with the Bishop.

The door to Bishop Johnson's office opened and Kaye Johnson, Amanda and Ruth's mother, emerged with a solemn face. When she saw Sariah, she smiled and rushed to her and threw her arms around the young lady, squeezing her tight as if she hadn't seen her in years.

"Hi…hi Sister Johnson," Sariah managed to eek out as she was being squeezed.

"Hi Sariah…how is your family?"

"They're fine…how is Amanda and Ruth?"

Kaye Johnson looked concerned but smiled. "They are fine…and… really happy."

"You wanted to see me Sariah?" Bishop Johnson stepped into the doorway of his office. He wore a dark, smoke gray suit, white shirt, and a red tie. His smile seemed ever present and less sincere with every passing day. The Bishop motioned Sariah to come inside his office. Sariah waived goodbye to Kaye, who still had that awkward look. As she walked into the spatial office, the familiar knot appeared in her stomach again. That same feeling she got whenever she dealt with the Bishop; cold, dark, and empty. She wondered if she was the only one that was suspicious of his plastic smile and unrealistic piousness. "Please have a seat." As Bishop Johnson closed the door, Sariah instinctively began to look for an escape route, but there were none present. She still thought about her previous conversation with Kaye as well; something was off. She sat down carefully on the cloth seats directly in front of a large imposing oak desk that contrasted greatly with the shiny white carpet. "What can I do for you?"

Sariah fought for the words to say before she actually spoke them, "I've thought about the revelation Bishop."

"I am happy to hear that Sariah," Bishop Johnson's smile and eyes were piercing. "I hope you know that I am just the messenger. I simply act on what God tells me. I'm glad you've chosen to do what the Lord has commanded."

"Well Bishop, that's why I want to talk to you." Bishop Johnson's smile dulled and his countenanced darkened from its usual brightness.

"I'm not following."

"I'm not saying no, Bishop, I just need something…"

"I'm still not following."

"Well, you know my family is different than the others in the ward. I just need to spend time around your family before I can commit."

"That's not how the Lord works, Sariah. When God tells you to do something…you do it."

"God hasn't told me anything Bishop…you have."

"Whether it be my voice, or the voice of my servants it is the same."

"That may be, but I'm the one leaving my family!" Sariah stopped and began to tear up. She raised her head and mustered a smile for Bishop Johnson. "Look, just give me a job at the fabrication plant or something. Let me just get used to your family and that will help me fulfill the Lord's commandment," Sariah pled to the Bishop. She sincerely hoped that Bishop Johnson would take her seriously.

"Why can't you be humble like everyone else, Sariah?"

"You've met my family Bishop, humility isn't our strong suit."

"This has nothing to do with your family Sariah. Like Nephi in The Book of Mormon, you have the opportunity to influence your family for good and bring them back into the fold."

Sariah bit her lip. How could this man question the faithfulness of her family? While it was true that she didn't buy any of the dogma and ridiculous doctrine of the sect, her parents were the most faithful and genuine people she knew. She had to show restraint, but she couldn't let that comment go. "My parents are in the fold Bishop."

"Are they?" Bishop Johnson smiled again. "There would be no question that my daughters would follow each commandment of the Lord."

"My parents support the revelation, Bishop, but they allow me to use my agency and choose for myself. Isn't that what God commanded?" Sariah knew that mentioning 'agency', or 'free-agency' was a valid argument when dealing with any Latter-day Saint, polygamist or not. Agency represents the ability for man to choose for himself to accept God's plan. The LDS believe that a war in heaven occurred before mankind's existence. Satan, then Lucifer, presented a plan to God whereby all men could be saved and returned to God to live in celestial glory. So influential was Lucifer, almost as much as his spiritual brother, Jesus Christ, or Jehovah, that a third of the spirits in heaven supported Lucifer's plan. However, Lucifer's plan was in stark contrasts to God the Father's, or Elohim's plan. Lucifer became Satan and he and his minions were cast out of heaven and subjugated to a spiritual existence on earth tormenting the children of men on earth and trying to lead them to sin and spiritual death.

Bishop Johnson again smiled. "My Sariah, agency is for the Gentiles. The right to choose is only given to those in darkness. Once you accept the only true church, there is no more agency, only right and wrong. You were born under the covenant. You are the elect of God, Sariah. You don't have the luxury of agency, only obedience," Bishop Johnson arose from his seat and began walking behind Sariah carefully studying her. Sariah wasn't sure that she was convincing enough. The man may be a disgusting pedophile, but he wasn't stupid. She fought the fear inside to abandon her scheme, there was no turning back. "I tell you what Sariah, I will give you the chance to prove yourself faithful, but not by working at the plant." Sariah listened.

"Now I'm not following Bishop," she replied.

"You may work at the house, with the sister-wives," Bishop

Johnson said confidently. "If you want to learn obedience then you must surround yourself with the obedient."

"But don't you remember the last time I was on your property? I mean…I don't exactly get along with your sons," Sariah said with hesitancy. She would've much rather worked at the plant. She was taught hard work and she wouldn't be surrounded by sister-wives wearing clothes from the eighteen hundred's, and two of the creepiest males she ever met. But this wasn't about her, it was about something greater, and if there was one thing in life that was drilled into her by her parents, it was that some causes are greater than self. The only problem was she wasn't exactly sure she even had a cause; only a hunch she needed to look into.

"You need not worry about Nathan or Josiah. They have learned their lesson and will not be anywhere near you," Bishop Johnson's stare was intense. "That I can promise you."

"When would you like me to start?"

"Be at the house tomorrow morning at six."

"Okay…thank you Bishop."

"Glad to have you," Bishop Johnson's stare was even more intense now and that creepy smile returned.

*

U.S. Marshall John Lansford walked into the Maverick County crime scene. The scene was about five miles off the highway and barely accessible with a normal vehicle. The brown dirt was littered with green scrub and field grass and the trail appeared to be two brown parallel lines that unfortunately lead to death. His government Chevrolet Tahoe had quite a bit of trouble traversing the sparse trail. *Thank God there has been no rain*, he thought as he wound down the seemingly endless trail. As he approached, he saw a huge crime scene marked by yellow tape and surrounded by police squads with their flashing red and blue LED lights that hardly seemed necessary considering where they were, but cops were cops, and they loved their toys. He stepped out of the Tahoe and stretched his legs. In this part of the country, the former National Football

League linebacker stood out. He was African American, stood six foot five and weighed in at two hundred and seventy pounds, but there was no one that could find an ounce of fat on him. His lean, muscular arms stuck out of his Kevlar vest and were hard not to stare at. His hair was always in place and was even the butt of many of his colleague's jokes. They teased him that every time he caught a fugitive he'd have to catch a mirror for his hair. It was jealousy, he thought. The vest had no markings except for the 'U.S. Marshall' patched centered on the back. He walked toward the tape and through the deputies standing around the tape seemingly not busy.

"Marshall Lansford?" Lansford turned and saw the most attractive crime scene tech he had ever seen; blonde, lean, probably older than him, but somehow that was even a turn-on. "Hi, I'm Deborah Nichols from the DPS crime lab in McAllen, but you can call me Deb. They told me you were coming."

"I've heard of you Deb," he answered cordially, still admiring how a woman could look so good in a jumpsuit. "How can I help you guys?"

"Are you still heading the Human Trafficking Task Force?"

"Yep, our group covers all of the borderlands from El-Paso to McAllen."

"You may want to take a look at this then," Nichols handed him the crime scene log and he promptly signed it. They went under the tape and began to walk down a path towards a dry creek, cutting through trees and brush along the way. The terrain began to slope down into a canyon-like ravine. He still wasn't sure what exactly he is going to see, but he followed Deb anyway. He was promoted to GS-14 in April and put in charge of the Human Trafficking Task Force in South Texas. It wasn't a promotion that many people clamored for, but it did mean more money for Lansford, and it kept him in the action along the U.S./Mexico Border, at least to a degree. The fact was that human trafficking is an age-old problem that United Sates Law Enforcement was only beginning to understand. The Taskforce was a joint effort between federal agents, and state and local law enforcement. It was created as a political necessity, which wasn't bad in this case. Most of the task force's time and effort was spent teaching at local law enforcement agencies and spreading awareness of the problem. What was truly eye-opening to Lansford was there was such little awareness of a crime many consider worse than murder. Most of the cases the task force actually investigated were created by tips from citizens who may have caught the subject on their favorite television show. Whatever the case, the task force belonged to Lansford and he had the full cooperation of the Texas Department of Public Safety. He had to be made available to any request.

"Little ways back here, huh?" Lansford observed as he continued to descend down a seemingly endless trail which now resembled a crude path.

"Just up ahead," Deb responded as she ducked under a branch. Lansford looked ahead and saw a burned vehicle nose down in the ravine. The vehicle wasn't completely burned but it was more of a shell than a car and it appeared to be blue once.

"I don't suppose this is insurance fraud?"

"Afraid not."

Deb and Lansford approached the vehicle and the smell suddenly hit Lansford causing him to press his arm against his nose to cover the burned stench. Deb never even flinched. She simply carried on devoid of any emotion or sensitivity to the gruesome scene. Lansford could see two partially burned bodies in the back-seat area. The clothing that remained unburned appeared to be red silk with lace. The faces were completely charred and void of any identity and skin color was undetectable from their vantage point. However, both bodies appeared to have bullet defects in their skulls. Since they had to wait for the Medical Examiner to actually manipulate the bodies, the investigators carefully walked around the vehicle observing and recording every detail they could possibly see.

"What's with the clothes, Deb?" Lansford finally managed to ask.

"You see those heals?" she inquired. Lansford observed the clear plastic, partially burned platform heals on the victim directly behind the driver's seat of the vehicle. "Those are stripper shoes. These girls look like prostitutes."

"So not all human trafficking is prostitution, Deb. In fact, most of our cases deal with forced labor, not sexual slavery," Lansford responded. He was frustrated with the broad conception of the cases he worked. Movies and television depicted human trafficking in such a sensational manner that any father would lock up his daughter out of fear. In reality, those cases existed, but were the exception rather than the rule.

"I know, but from my guess looking at the bone and physical structure of these girls, my guess is they're only about fourteen to sixteen years old."

"Fourteen?"

"And the next obvious question is where the driver is?" Deb looked at Lansford who appeared to be still shocked at the attractive technician's assessment. "That's why I called you. I want your team to work this."

"I'm not a detective, Deb, but there are some on the task force," Lansford thought for just a moment. "I'll have them come out. I just catch em, I don't detect em."

"Look…each of these girls took bullets and then burned, they deserve something. Besides, I've got another idea for you," Deb was smiling.

"What's that?" Lansford smiled, obviously intrigued.

"You know Richard Flynt?"

"Yeah, the infamous Texas Ranger…I've heard nothing but great things...a cop's cop, not much for brass."

"Yeah, well he and his partner Darren Kidd got called down here to assist Eagle Pass with the mass grave. They came all the way up from Garland but got sidelined from that investigation by Eagle Pass Chief Dan Gummit."

"Now that guy's a tool!"

"Tell me about it. Then the bastard stuck them with the dead city councilman."

"So, what about them?"

Deb hands Lansford a business card. "That's Deputy Director Cahill's card."

"The Deputy Director?"

"*The* Deputy Director of the Department of Public Safety. I want you to call him and get those two to help you with this case."

"Shit, Deb, do they know about this?" Lansford balked at the suggestion. Today's investigators were so overloaded with cases that to increase their case load was the equivalent of punishment.

"Look…these guys are great investigators and know how operate down here."

"Yeah but…"

"Look, I'll make it up to them. If you get behind them with the task force it actually empowers them. Now they're going to be backed by DPS and the Task Force. Dan Gummit can't touch them," Deb pled. "You can tell them I did this, but I think this is right…I got a feeling."

"Alright, but I can't make any promises," Lansford replied. He again surveyed the scene. "What a fucking mess!"

*

Jeremiah checked to see if the coast was clear as he entered his office. He opened his cabinet and opened the small refrigerator located inside his work cabinet. He noticed the shadow but continued his task. He removed the Shiner Bock bottle from the small fridge and popped the top. He walked to the black leather recliner behind his work desk and plopped down. Only his first wife Sara knew he occasionally drank. It was a habit he picked up in a weak moment in the service and just sort of lingered. He was almost tired of asking the Lord for forgiveness. He now favored just showing up on judgment day and apologizing then.

"You know it's not polite to enter another man's house without knocking," Jeremiah directed his comment to Moroni LaFey sitting in the dark on Jeremiah's couch in the corner of the large room. "And it's downright creepy you just sitting there like that."

"It's not like I want to hide, Brother, but I'm not exactly welcome in your country," LaFey said in gest.

"That's your own fault you know."

"So, I'm told. You know you can go to hell for drinking?"

"So, I'm told," Jeremiah took another long pull from the bottle. "So why are you here?"

"Well that's no way to treat your favorite brother," Moroni took a drink from his own beer. "I've been hearing way too many rumblings from the Saints down here."

"Wait a minute, since when are you the 'Avenging Angel'?"

"I admit I am not a perfect Saint…or even man for that matter, but God has put me here for a purpose," Moroni paused. "It was your purpose too."

"No, it wasn't Moroni!" Jeremiah was visibly irritated. He loved his family and his heritage, but the name LaFey was almost like a millstone around his neck; unescapable. He moved to Texas and took the drastic measure of changing his name. His fellow members, even the average citizen could never understand the horrors that he was a part of in Colonia LaFey.

"I mean no disrespect, Mr. Larsen is it? I just want to talk." The 'Larsen' comment was obvious, but deserved Jeremiah thought. They spent their entire lives together, unseparated until Jeremiah joined the service. It was then that a lot of things changed for Jeremiah.

"Well, let's talk then."

"How are the wives?"

"Good, we have the normal problems, but nothing to complain about."

"Why haven't the brethren called you into leadership?"

"You know me and Bishop Johnson don't get along," Jerimiah drank again. "The only reason I'm still in the community is that I'm a good tithe payer and I'm from the colonies." He smiled and smiled at Moroni, "He's scared shitless of the LaFeys."

"Johnson is a hack, why doesn't Nephi Josephs remove him?"

"The Lord works in mysterious ways, Moroni."

"The Lord has nothing to do with that decision. Johnson is an earner for Josephs...that is all."

"Your jadedness is a real downer, Brother."

"Well, I come by it honestly," Moroni said. "I'm not the

Avenging Angel Jeremiah...but I won't stand by and let the Lord's Kingdom on Earth be destroyed by whores and apostates."

"You're implying a man that a prophet appointed is a whore and an apostate?"

Moroni laughed, "Jeremiah...the world is full of prophets. Some are better than others."

"I have a hard time speaking ill of the Lord's anointed."

"Sometimes the Lord's anointed need the hand of God to correct them. Even Joseph Smith wasn't above reproach," Moroni pointed out. Jeremiah was puzzled that his cousin would invoke the name of the Prophet Joseph, the historical founder of all Morminism. To the Latter-day Saint, the name of Joseph Smith is only second to Jesus Christ in sacredness, and even that was debatable on occasion.

"I think you need to strengthen your faith, Moroni."

"My faith is strong and God knows it."

"When do you plan on going back to Mexico?"

Moroni looked straight ahead with a chameleon's stare, "When the work is complete."

CHAPTER SIX

Patron

"So, tell me why we're going to Laredo again, Partner?" Kidd was curious.

"I told you, Deb needs a favor."

"Yeah I heard. We need to track down leads on Sandra Salazar, the DNA match Deb got in the lab."

"Well Hell, why'd ya ask if you already knew?" Flynt smiled.

"Well I thought this was Dan Gummit's case?"

"It is, but we're doing a favor for Deb."

"Right, but on Gummit's case?"

"Yep, now you're getting it."

"Won't Gummit be upset?"

"More than likely, but he won't find out for a while," Flynt smiled again a beaming grin. "He's kinda slow that way." The two men pulled into the La Mexicana Restaurant on Ursula Avenue in Laredo. By the looks of the parking lot, Kidd knew that the place must be popular with the locals. They were meeting Laredo PD Detective Jorge Garcia. Kidd had never met the man, but Flynt spoke very highly of him. That was enough for Kidd.

"How come we never meet these guys at their station?"

"You can't talk open in a station. You have to be on your best behavior there with the brass and all. When you dine with a man, you get to know him, not just what he does. That's what my Daddy always said anyway," Flynt replied honestly. "That and this place has some kick-ass enchiladas." Kidd saw a stalky, but athletic Hispanic male enter the restaurant. He was dressed in slacks and a dress shirt with a Glock Model 22 on the hip. He immediately saw Flynt and began to walk towards them. Almost on cue he approached the two men like an old friend.

"Well goddamn the Texas Rangers have invaded…*como estas, Richard?*" Detective Jorge Garcia shook hands and hugged Richard as he stood to greet his old friend.

"Well we gotta check on you 'border bastards' every now and again," Flynt responded. "Jorge Garcia…this here's Darren Kidd, my new partner." Kidd stood up for the greeting and extended his right hand to Garcia. The men exchanged a firm handshake and gave each other the cop once over look.

"Good to meet you," Kidd said smiling.

"I'm just sorry you have to work with this guy," Garcia said. "Let's sit down." The hostess approached Garcia who greeted her warmly. He muttered some phrases in Spanish and she led the three men to a quiet, large corner booth. They sat and situated themselves. The conversation was mostly catching up by Garcia and Flynt. Garcia quizzed Kidd a little on his surprise commission to the Rangers and his past work in Albuquerque, but nothing disrespectful. The food came surprisingly quick and the men ate heartily. Garcia treated the staff very well and they in turn pampered the men with great service. As the meal dwindled in size Flynt slid a manila envelope across to Garcia. He picked it up and read the contents with great interest, possibly some skepticism. "You found Sandra Salazar?" Garcia seemed relieved, yet still controlled.

"She was one of the girls received at the mass grave at Eagle Pass," Flynt replied. The subject seemed so mundane. "She have family?"

"Mom's doing a stretch at the Young Unit over in Galveston. She was never much of a mom. Sandra was looked after by her grandma, but she died a few years ago," Garcia looked at the profile again. "After her Grandma passed, it was just us cops who cared…no one else. That's was makes this so sad, really."

"Ya'all have any leads when she came up missing?" Kidd asked.

"We got an anonymous phone tip that a guy named Carlos was seen talking to Sandra before she was reported missing," Garcia paused. He saw the look on the Ranger's faces, "Yes I know that there are several Carlos's in Laredo, but this one was feared."

"Feared?"

"As in connected somehow with the Cartels. The Cartels

93

still have the power to touch these peoples' families, so they stay in line. They're like a boogeyman really. So this Carlos guy was somehow was connected, but no one was talking. Last we heard, he was in McAllen. We chased every Carlos who popped up"

"No descriptions or hard ID?"

"None…a ghost. Supposedly he was trying to 'recruit' girls from the Mall Del Norte."

"Recruit?"

"Sex trade most likely. Tough to tell whether the girls go to Mexico or the States, guess they got perverts on both sides of the border," Garcia again stared at the paperwork and turned to look at Flynt. "Can I get a copy of this? I need to close my file."

"It's yours my friend," Flynt shook hands with his old friend. "For what it's worth, we are sorry."

"Who's lead on the investigation?"

"Dan Gummit in Eagle Pass."

"You kidding? Shit, he can't handle that Richard. You guys need to step in."

"Why the hell you think we're here?" Flynt smiled. "I ain't gonna let that son of a bitch ruin this. I promise."

*

Trey Caldwell walked into Felipe's Hot Dogs in Eagle Pass. The location sat right on the El Indio Highway and was a popular local spot. Carlos watched as Trey seemed to strut to the seat instead of simply walking. His sandy blonde hair hid under his cap was in a military cut, but his neck tattoo simply screamed criminal. His sleeve tattoos on his muscular forearms exposed the Aryan Brotherhood symbols he picked up in prison. Trey had a lot of explaining to do and Carlos needed an explanation. After all, it wasn't Trey's ass in the grease with the Negras, it was his. He did his best to muster a smile given the public location.

"Sit down Trey," Carlos's smile seemed a bit dimmer as Trey got closer and actually sat down. Trey smirked and sat at the table.

"What…no food for me?" Trey smiled at Carlos, who was clearly in no mood for joking.

Carlos bit his tongue and lowered his voice almost to a whisper, "What the fuck is going on, Trey!" he whispered with intensity.

"There was a setback Carlos," Trey's demeanor was no longer the cocky thug he portrayed himself to be, but now started to humble himself once he saw his boss's anger. Trey wasn't a typical white boy that wanted to be bad boy. He was the bad boy. Trey was a fighter, but they were a dime a dozen. He had to make his mark on the streets differently; find some way to appease the Hispanic gangs and gain acceptance. The life he chose was a smuggler with a brutal side. While a White boy in South Texas had to watch his back on the streets, there were some distinct advantages. He was able to cross the border and make connections on the other side that proved very lucrative. It was mostly a small-time operation, one to two ounces at a time that he'd sell for a profit. Cocaine mostly, but Trey could get most anything. Heroin, Methamphetamine, and just about anything else Mexico had to offer were in his reach as well, someone merely had to have the money. His exploits ended in his extended stay in the Huntsville Unit and with his affiliations he made on the inside, it seemed he wore his welcome out in the valley. He became affiliated with the dangerous, White, Nazi Low-riders. It was mostly for survival, but it hardened his reputation when he eventually got out. So, he headed west to Eagle Pass and Laredo. It was there that Carlos heard about his smuggling talents and put him to work along the river.

"What the fuck do you mean setback? There's no setbacks, asshole!" Carlos collected himself and looked around the restaurant to ensure he wasn't making a scene. "What happened?" he managed to ask in a calm voice.

"Started getting followed, Man."

"Cops?"

"Yeah Dude…in slick cars."

"That's impossible…we got you the schedules. We fucking

know where they'll be!"

"I don't trust it!"

Carlos slammed his hand down on the table getting a few people's attention. He held his hands up in a surrender position and smiled to dis-alarm them. Carlos looked over at Trey and glared with an angry smile, "You're being paranoid…I told you to lay off the shit."

"No man I'm straight."

"You're not using?"

"Man, it's not about that, I swear."

"Then what?"

"Look I swear that I was straight. There's so much heat out there man. The Taskforce is all over the place. They got every cop in Texas sniffing out working girls. Shit ain't safe, Carlos, for real."

"Where are the girls right now, Trey? Carlos was getting more upset."

"It's just girl...and she's with the old lady. They're layin' low right now, that's all."

Holy fuck, Carlos thought. *What did this animal do?* "That girl belongs to Tio Muniz!" Carlos gritted his teeth as he spoke in that controlled whisper. Trey's face changed drastically now. It was amazing how just mentioning the name of a violent cartel could get a man's attention.

"Why didn't you tell me, Man?"

"I don't have to tell you, I pay your salary. Besides, who the fuck you think we work for?!"

"But you coulda said it was for the Negras, Carlos!"

"I don't say shit to you, Fucker! I give you a job and you do it…period! It don't matter if it's the Negras or Mickey Mouse!"

"That's fucking easy for you to say Carlos! You don't work the street," Trey barked back. "Besides, they'll come for you anyway."

"You think they won't come for you, Trey?" Carlos had an evil grin now. "How bout I just call Marisella now and give her your name, cause you know what motherfucker? I'm the only one that's kept you alive till now."

"Chill out, Carlos!" Now Trey found himself speaking in

that same intense whisper. "I can fix this." Trey looked around and finally looked Carlos in the eye. "I am going to need some more time. Can you hold them off for now?"

"Just deliver the girl, Trey!"

"That's what I'm trying to say, man. Some things got out of hand, but I will handle it. I just need some time."

"Hey...Fucker...listen to me," Carlos was seething at this point. He was careful that every new person he hired understood the demands of the bosses. Trey was given the same warning as all of them. Patience was not a virtue of the Cartel. If their money, merchandise, or product was late then it normally meant death. At the end of the day, Trey was right; Carlos was the one they would come after first. But make no mistake, Trey and his associates would end up in the same place eventually. "Get that girl delivered...now! These people are like elephants, they don't forget!" Carlos stared at Trey hoping that the urgency of his voice and gaze might propel his stubborn employee into action

"I'm going to Carlos! You know me? I just need some help, Man. I can't go down for human trafficking." Trey was no longer the cocky thug from the valley, but a humbled idiot about to incur the wrath of the most viscous cartel in Mexico.

"Prison will be the least of your worries if this delivery isn't made."

*

"So what was the big news you just had to give us Deb," Flynt asked as he and Kidd walked into her office in the DPS Crime Lab in McAllen. "Damn it's cold in here, too woman. What are ya hangin' meat?"

"Well hello to you too Richard and no there ain't no meat hanging," Deb threw her arms around Flynt who hugged her steadily in return. "Ya old man, you need some meat on your bones, so you don't get chilled." Deb then hugged Kidd, which was becoming more familiar and less awkward. "And you need a woman, son," Deb winked at Kidd.

"Yeah, I'm still paying for the last one," Kidd responded

without missing a beat.

"Ouch!" Deb laughed. "Well that's kind of an unwritten rule in law enforcement you need at least one divorce to be worth a damn!"

"I got two myself," Flynt smiled. "But I know you didn't want to talk about failed relationships. We'd be here all day with you girl," Flynt smiled as Deb promptly displayed her middle finger in his direction.

"Gummit's single I hear?" Kidd chimed in with the sounds of gasps and laughter in the background and the expense of Deb Nichols of course. She blushed, laughed and shook her head at him.

"Well I see you trained him well, Asshole!" she barked at Flynt. As they wound down their laughter and sat around Deb's desk, it had a lot of paperwork on it, but it was strangely organized. Flynt once told Kidd that Deb organized the dirt she scrubbed off her body. He was beginning to believe it. "I wanted to give you the reports back on the victims of the grave," Deb said as she began thumbing through the reports.

"What about clothing or personal items?" Kidd inquired.

"Some was recovered and sent to trace. It was in bad shape as you can imagine. Most the clothing is women's clothing. Silky material it looked like. Found a couple shoes as well."

"What kind of shoes?"

"Heels mostly."

"How old are these girls?"

They're all between fourteen and seventeen."

"Wait…what the hell are we looking at now, Deb?" Flynt asked suddenly alarmed.

"Look, this is only speculation, but you remember telling you about that scene I just worked out in Maverick County?"

"Yeah, the burned car with the two dead girls."

"Right, well what I didn't tell you is that I called in the Marshals and the Human trafficking Taskforce on the car case."

"Human Trafficking? That's a bit of a stretch don't you think?"

"What's a stretch Richard? They're young girls with provocative clothing and heels."

"Who came out from the Taskforce."

"Guy by the name of John Lansford of the Marshal's."

"Okay, I don't know him, but tell me two things. First, did ya ask this Lansford on a date, and two, what does he think?"

"First, fuck you, and second, he agrees with me."

Kidd felt it was a good time to join the conversation before it went from playful to ugly. "So, are you saying, Deb, that it is your opinion that the mass grave is a trafficker's grave?" The implications were huge. It was no secret that that the people who essentially enslave humans for others' sexual gratification were brutal, but this brought another level of depravity to the light. To discard a human after being subjected to sexual slavery was a new low that humanity was not ready to face, Kidd thought.

"That's my theory right now. But I'm not an investigator. Only you guys could prove it."

"Prove it? Shit, Deb, we'd have an easier time with the goddamned grassy knoll!? Flynt snarled.

"Now just calm down Grumpy, cause I'm afraid I got some more bad news."

"Oh, I can't wait for this either."

Deb looked almost embarrassed, even scared. It wasn't her normal strong face. "I kinda told Lansford you'd work with the task force while you're here." Flynt's eyes told the entire story. They rolled into the back of his head in such disgust Kidd questioned if they would ever normalize. Kidd knew that he and Deb had a close relationship, but it was about to be tested.

"I sure as hell hope you can un-tell him, girl."

"That's not going to be so easy. I kind of got Deputy Director Cahill involved," Deb almost shrieked as Flynt took his hat off, yelled a few obscenities and stared at the ceiling as if the answer was going to fall from heaven.

"So, what does that mean?" Kidd inquired.

"It means we're on the task force now," Flynt answered in a low, almost defeating voice. He let a few more breaths go and looked at Nichols. "Deb…did you think we didn't have enough shit piled up on our plates for a while?"

"Richard, if I'm right, these guys can help you. It will give

99

8

you guys more manpower. You're looking at it all wrong, Richard."

"I'm looking at it from thirty-plus goddamned years of doing this job, Deb. Now Dan Gummit will stick his nose in it…"

"That's what I'm trying to tell you Richard! Dan Gummit might be able to push around a couple Rangers, but there's no way he's pushing around the Human Trafficking Task Force."

"She's right Richard, we could use the bodies and the Deputy Director isn't a bad ally either," Kidd observed.

"You all are just missing one small point," Flynt stared at both Deb and Kidd as if he was about to expand on a lifelong lesson or proverb for their benefit. "We need evidence, or the Taskforce and the Director will both hang us out to dry when Dan Gummit calls his politician friends. No director stands up to an elected goddamned official…that's a universal truth."

*

"Tio…*Como estas,* it's good to see you!" Carlos called out as he again walked into the Los Palmas restaurant and sat at the dark booth reserved by Marisella. It was early in the afternoon and the bar was about half full, mostly the late afternoon crowd wanting to get an early start to their evening. Tio sat next to Marisella wearing jeans, a button shirt and a traditional, black cowboy hat, sharply flared up as seen in Mexico. Tio only looked up briefly and continued eating. Marisella motioned for Carlos to sit and he obliged. Tio never audibly answered Carlos, which disturbed him greatly. It meant that Tio was mad at him, which translated into the Negras being mad as well. That was never good for a man in Carlos' position.

"Are you hungry Carlos?" Marisella finally asked breaking the awkward silence between the parties.

"No but I can use a drink." Marisella motioned the waitress to bring the drink. Tio Muniz just kept silent and ate never even making any eye contact with either party. Marisella didn't seemed bothered, but Carlos became more fearful by the minute. Carlos watched Tio carefully for any sign of emotion or reaction, but there never seemed to be any. Though only mere moments of silence past, it was killing him. "Look...I talked to my guy. There were some complications with transporting the girls."

"I told you they would want to talk, Carlos, but you didn't listen!" Marisella was emphatic in her statement. Carlos suspected she was simply acting out for Tio, or sincere. Either way, it didn't matter.

"I did listen, but I didn't have an answer. I do now though."

"What were these transportation problems?" Tio finally said while wiping his face with the cloth napkin. "Delicioso, mi amor," Tio smiled at Marisella who in turn smiled back in thanks.

"My guy said the Human Trafficking Taskforce is swarming the border," Carlos advised. Tio started to chuckle followed by a smile from Marisella.

"The Taskforce?" Tio questioned, still chuckling from Carlos's answer. "That task force got nothing, *carbon!* Besides, you said you handled that?"

"They're a big deal, Tio...the U.S. Marshals, Texas DPS, and a lot of local investigators ain't no joke and I thought I had it handled." No sooner did Carlos get the words out of his mouth he regretted saying them. Tio glared at Carlos with a look of half disgust and the other anger. Carlos had that feeling of mistake and emptiness shoot from his stomach to his mouth. "Forgive me Tio, I...I am just as pissed as you. My guy, he...he is usually solid."

Tio smiled and slapped Carlos's shoulder in an overly friendly manor and laughed out loud. "It is a bitch to be the boss, *no?*" All three at the table laughed in agreement and drank as if there were no cares at all. They conversed for a bit, but Carlos never felt at peace. He kept waiting for the other shoe to drop. There were consequences for not coming through for these people. The question was how severe the consequences would be. Carlos looked on as Marisella started to waive at the wait staff. Carlos couldn't help but notice that the customers had thinned out dramatically in the bar of the restaurant and that the final few were making their way to the door. The only people that remained were some of Tio's men and Marisella's staff.

"Are you closing the bar, Marisella?"

"Si…till about Nine I would say," Marisella answered Carlos with a smile and motioned for more drinks. "I'll open it in time for the late crowd. Besides, now we can discuss what needs to be done in private." Tio sat silent in the booth as if he was disavowed of the whole business at hand.

"Look…Marisella and Tio, I got it covered. I got a lead on some other girls and I got the money…"

"Where is your boss Carlos?" Tio interrupted with a question that absolutely terrified Carlos. "Why does he not come himself?"

"Cause I can handle it…it's my job, Tio."

"But you haven't done your job and now what am I supposed to do with you right now?"

"I can fix this…I'll do anything."

"Are you a *joto*, Carlos?"

"Fuck no Tio! I swear," Somehow he knew the conversation was going South.

"I hear a lot of guys now a days are like that, *no?*"

"Maybe, Tio, but not me."

"I think you're gonna suck my *verga,*" Tio mentioned casually.

Carlos laughed nervously, "C'mon Tio, I get it…you can stop fucking with me now."

"But that is what bitches do, *no?*"

"I'm no bitch, Tio…I…"

"Perhaps I can make clarify myself, yes?" Tio smiled as Carlos felt the steel of the pistol next to his temple. He gasped in fear as Marisella and Tio giggled. "You're gonna show these people that you're my bitch, or I splatter your head all over this bar*, entiendes*?"

Now Carlos could see four of Tio's men laughing and watching from the bar as if it was a sick comedy sketch. He couldn't help but notice Marisella unzipping Tio's pants and pulling Tio's manhood out showing it to Carlos and laughing. "Well you better get started you little bitch!" she said, laughing at Carlos's horrified face. Carlos being hesitant began moving forward against his will, but Marisella became impatient. She grabbed Carlos by the back of his hair and forced him onto Tio causing Carlos to let out a very loud gagging noise that caused an eruption of laughter in the room. As he was being brutalized, he couldn't speak. Carlos managed to turn his eyes and looked at one of Marisella's waitresses mopping the floor. She couldn't help but keep glancing at him, her eyes were tearing and she looked so terrified and sad. He finally closed his eyes to the chorus of jeers. The noise in the room and began to fade. Carlos kept thinking about one thing as his humiliation and brutalization continued, at least he was alive.

CHAPTER SEVEN

Revelations & Enemies

Working in the compound wasn't all that bad Sariah thought as she continued her laundry duty. When the Bishop assigned her to that duty, she couldn't have known that a compound with over fifty sister wives, and children as far as the eye could see, would produce more laundry that she could have ever imagined. She used to complain about chores at her house, but this was a whole new level. She felt like running home and apologizing to her mother, maybe even the sister wives too. In fact, the task was so big that Bishop Johnson had to build a facility on the compound filled with industrial sized washing machines and dryers. They ran all day long every day of the week, and the piles replenished themselves almost magically.

Inside the laundry building, the dampness and moisture from the dryer vents combined with the Texas weather made summer working conditions unbearable. In the winter, they made up the sole form of heat in the large but hollow building. The Bishop's wives referred the facility as 'Satan's bedroom,' but none dared complain to the Bishop himself. That would be the equivalent of complaining against the Lord himself.

Sariah enjoyed the bond she and the Johnson sister wives had formed in her short time there in the compound. Though they still were fiercely loyal to their husband and Bishop, whom they firmly believed was called of God, they were able to figuratively let down their hair and let out comments and thoughts too controversial for the brethren's ears. She saw them smile and giggle, behavior not accepted in the Inspired Church of Jesus Christ of Latter-day Saints, especially from women.

As she shuffled laundry from the facilities to the main house, she noticed from the corner of her eye Kaye sat on the outside of the building. Sariah could see that she was sitting down. The sight of Amanda's mother, though not quite the same as having Amanda actually there, was comforting to Sariah and it made her happy, if only for memories. As she drew closer to Kaye she noticed Kaye had been crying. Kaye's eyes were puffy and red, in sharp contrast to her perfectly tight, braided hair. Crying wasn't abnormal for woman of the ILDS and the root cause generally always had something to with the brethren, but the ladies of the sect had only themselves to dry the tears. And the tears constantly flowed.

"Kaye?" Sariah spoke softly as she approached Kaye. She was an attractive woman, Sariah thought. Tall, blonde, and slender, Sariah knew where Amanda got her striking looks. She so wanted to yank Kaye's hair out of that ridiculous braid and give her a makeover. Kaye could get any man she wanted, certainly better ones than these old, suit wearing zombies, Sariah thought.

"Hey Sariah!" Kaye managed a smile as she stared at her daughter's best friend. Her smile could brighten any room, Sariah thought. She was certainly more than enough woman for one man.

"Are you okay, Kaye?"

Kaye managed to smile, "Yes dear, I'll be fine." She quick wiped the remaining tears from her face and smiled the all too familiar smile that Sariah grew up seeing from sister wives. "I'm just really missing my girls."

It was now Sariah's turn to smile to cover her sadness. "I miss them too." Kaye hugged Sariah and the two shared a brief moment. "Have you heard from them?"

"No...that's the thing, Sweetheart. The brethren do not want any contact between us." Kaye again managed a painful smile.

"But I...I don't understand?"

"Because the girls need time to adapt to their new families. The Lord has made it clear that contact with us may disrupt their new family situation."

"That doesn't make any sense..."

"The Lord's will sometimes doesn't."

"But how do we know it's the Lord's will, Kaye? I mean what if it's just the brethren..."

"Sariah!" Kaye said forcefully. It wasn't uncommon to hear the sister wives verbally correct the children. It was all the mothers of Zion's job to keep the children in line. The men of the sect were too busy exercising their priesthood authority and tending to the matters of the church. The women are expected to raise and tend to the children, even if they weren't their own. "You must not speak ill of the brethren. They speak for the Lord. You have to have faith in that."

"Well maybe I don't have it, and I never will."

"Then I am sad for you, and I will pray…"

"I don't want prayers! I want my friends!" Sariah snapped back expecting a stronger reaction from Kaye that never came. "I've been prayed for all my life and I'm still waiting for something to happen."

"Maybe it already has?"

"Then why do I hate the church? Why do I hate the brethren? Amanda kept me straight and sane," a few more tears lined her face. "Now I don't even have her." Kaye hugged Sariah again.

"Her life is different now and you need to start thinking about the future too."

"I don't want to get…"

"I know you don't want to get married my dear, did you honestly think I wanted to?" Sariah snapped her head from Kaye's shoulders. Now Kaye had her attention. "I was given to my husband by orders from the brethren."

"Why did you go then?"

"Cause I believe, Sariah!" Kaye said forcefully, suddenly realizing her tone of voice. "I believe in the brethren. This is the religion of my father, and I covenanted with the Lord to serve him always."

"I just can't Kaye."

"You can, dear. It's what we were born for."

*

"And who is this we are seeing?" Kidd asked as he and Flynt drove the narrow dirt road for what seemed like forever. The Crown Vic kept absorbing the bumps but Kidd had his doubts as the road kept winding and the ruts seemed to be getting deeper. The mesquites and brush kept getting thick and it seemed to be a path to nowhere.

"Jim Foster," Flynt replied smiling. The two men drove over a cattle guard surrounded by a crude, traditional barbed wire fence supported by wood posts. There were a few head of Hereford scattered across the field as they drove towards a modest home in the distance with a metal horse barn immediately to its South.

"*The* Jim Foster?"

Flynt looked at Kidd and smirked, "*The* Jim Foster." They drove closer to the house. "How do you know about Jim Foster?"

"The I-10 killings, the Texas Ten…every cop in the Southwest knows his work," Kidd answered without missing a beat. "He retired out here?"

"He was forced to retire," Flynt Muttered. "The Department don't have no use for guys like Jim no more…me either for that matter." A modest, but well-maintained ranch house was now visible and seemed oddly out of place in the rustic setting. The red bricks and steel roof seemed to clash with the weathered wood of the landscaping.

"How's he going to help us?"

"Just listen, you'll see."

They approached the front, wrap-around porch on foot. An older man, about six foot in poly denim and a Stetson straw stood waiting for them. No doubt the man was old, but not a hint of feebleness was observed. The man wasn't showing, but there was no doubt he was carrying, Kidd thought. He watched as Flynt approached the man and shook his hand, not with the casual indifference of the current generation, but with the respect and reverence not seen anymore. They whispered words to each other, but Kidd couldn't hear.

"Jim, this is Darren Kidd, my new partner."

The old man stared at Kidd to size him up. It was a feeling that Kidd was definitely getting used to since becoming the new kid in the Rangers. Foster never smiled, yet somehow you could tell he was not angry. He reached his hand to Kidd's, "It's good to meet you, son. I ain't seen a special commission since the late sixties, you must be okay."

"I think I know the right people."

"Richard? Shit! I ain't never seen a guy get suspended then golf with the goddamn Governor all in the same weekend," Foster laughed. "Well shit boy, maybe you do know the right people."

"I beat that son of a bitch that day, too!" Flynt added to the already lightened mood. "Next thing I know he's the goddamn President!" The room erupted in laughter.

"Hey there Darren…you ever ask Richard about that all-nighter with Lady Ann?" Kidd immediately saw some rare embarrassment in Flynt's face when Foster brought that up. "Old Richard here took good care of our lady Governor it seems." Foster no doubt was referring to a recent female governor. Kidd had heard the rumor, but Flynt would never confirm or deny.

"Now when are you just gonna die you ornery old asshole! Besides, that could be the only reason I even still got a damn job, but I'll never tell you sons a bitches."

The small talk continued for several minutes as the men sat down in Foster's living room with leather couches and cherry wood floors. The room was littered with pictures and memorabilia. Foster had a large family and several grandchildren, but it was easy to see that he preferred the solace and space that this country provided. As much as he may have loved to have his kids and grandkids near him, he preferred to be by himself as well. There was a loneliness to him, but it wasn't unwelcomed, and it seemed to fit.

"How you been holding up since Nita passed?" Flynt's question, though somber, didn't seem to faze Foster emotionally. Foster appeared to take the question in stride, as if it were a question about what he had for dinner. Though no man is that strong, Foster was the kind of man that would create some doubt.

"Fair to midland I suppose," Foster paused as he set three mugs down on the coffee table in the middle of the living room. He disappeared in the kitchen and returned with a steaming old-fashioned percolator. Three cups of coffee were poured, and the roasted flavor mixed with the scent of the hardwood filled the air. It was welcoming, and Kidd suddenly felt oddly more at ease. It was as if he was the one that was old friends with Foster, or maybe that's just how Foster made everyone feel. Foster picked up his mug and sat down on. "I don't spose' I'll ever find a woman that that again."

"She was special," Flynt said softly.

"Hell, I don't need a woman anymore," Foster took a long drink. "I know you ain't down here for small talk. I reckon you're on a case?"

"Ain't I always?"

"You're goddamn lucky to have a job."

"Well tell me something new, ya old fart," it was Flynt's turn to drink his coffee.

"You on the mass grave in Eagle Pass?"

"Not exactly."

"The hell does that mean?"

"That's Dan Gummit's case, but Deb Nichols keeps trying to drag us in."

"If Dan Gummit's runnin' things you need to be in."

"Well, let's just say we're keepin' an eye on things for now," Flynt set his mug down on the table. "We're on the dead councilman."

"Heard about that…any connection to the grave?"

"Don't rightly know. What do you know about the polygamists out here?"

"You mean the Super-Mormons?"

"If that's what you call em."

"Well what do you call em?"

"Old man…answer the goddamn question!"

Foster chuckled at the frustration of his former partner. He seemed to feel good being needed. It seemed to Kidd, he hadn't felt that way in quite some time. Foster took another casual sip of coffee, "Well you'll have to be a bit more specific. You want to know who leads em?"

"Nephi Josephs," Kidd interjected. "He was ordained Prophet, Seer, and Revelator of the Inspired Church of Jesus Christ of Latter-day Saints about ten years ago."

"Well look at the new guy!" Foster observed. "Locally it's Bishop Thomas Johnson, but he's nothin' to Josephs, cept a paycheck for the church."

"So where do these guys come from…Utah, like Warren Jeffs?" Flynt asked.

"Well they all got roots in Utah, but Jeffs is the Fundamentalist Church of Jesus Christ of Latter-day Saints. Josephs' group is the Inspired Church of Jesus Christ of Latter-day Saints. They mostly are renegade polygamists from the Mexican Colonies. Don't know if the two mix."

"Mexican Colonies?"

"Goddamn Boy! Didn't you ever study in school?" Foster growled at Flynt. "In the late 1880's some Mormons were commanded by the Prophet, John Taylor I think his name was, to colonize the area. That was because Congress passed the Edmonds Act in about 1882."

"Edmunds Act?"

Foster glared Flynt who smiled back like a five-year-old, "Basically Congress passed a law to stop Polygamy in the Utah Territories. Made polygamy a felony and they started seizing property, so Mormons had to hide their extra wives from the government."

"So, they went to Mexico?"

"Hell yeah, that a way they could practice without the Feds botherin' em'. Only problem was they had to dodge the Apaches and Poncho Villa. The Romney's went down their first."

"The politicians?"

"The same…there were several colonies set up. But now there's just Colonia Juarez, Colonia Dublan, and Colonia LaFey. Most left during the Mexican Revolution. When they came back to the states, they had to renounce polygamy, which they did. But then they just hid their wives again. Eventually, the church in Salt Lake finally got serious about polygamy and said if anyone is caught, they'd be excommunicated. But that wasn't till the early 1900's. Put some of them leaders they call "General Authorities" in jail even. This was all done so they could get statehood."

"But some didn't ever get outta polygamy?"

"Nope, that's why you got these folks scattered about," Jim took another drink of coffee. "Funny this is, when Joseph Smith introduced polygamy to Mormons in Nauvoo, Illinois, a lot of them didn't care for it. When Smith died, the folks that supported polygamy followed Brigham Young and the folks that didn't support Brigham Young stayed back east and formed other churches."

"I always thought it was Brigham Young who invented that polygamy mess?"

Foster laughed, "That's what the Mormons want you to believe, but it ain't true. Smith had anywhere from thirty-one to thirty-four wives they say. What's even more curious is that some of them wives were already married."

"Like...polyandry?"

"Yep...there's stories of husbands being sent on church missions just so that he could 'spiritually marry' the wives."

"Now what the hell does that mean?"

"Ain't a lot a people know, really. Most think it's so when they die they are married in heaven. Then they can make spirit babies to populate all the worlds they create."

"Okay...forget I asked," Flynt couldn't hide his bewilderment. Kidd knew the last part about Mormons still believing in plural marriage for the eternities, but he never knew the history behind the belief. "So where does this Johnson or Joseph's clan come from?"

"Don't rightly know for sure, some say Juarez, others Dublan. They're hard core, don't know one know too much about em'. They don't give interviews and they damn sure don't mess with the local law. They keep out of the spotlight and pay all their taxes. They pretty much keep to themselves"

"So how do they afford all them damn wives and kids? Hell, just one wife at a time made me go under,"

"Johnson operates an aircraft fabrication plant. A lot of folks in their local congregation work there. Well, men mostly. The women got to run the home and tend to the temple that sits in the compound."

"Like Eldorado?"

"Exactly, but the Inspired temple is a hell of a lot nicer than the Fundamentalist temple…bout twice the size. Anyhow, I guess old Johnson's company does quite well."

"How come you learn all this, Jim?" Kidd asked extremely curious that a good old Texas Baptist knew so much about polygamist sects and Mormon History. Kidd was baptized a Mormon and he didn't even know this stuff.

"2008 they called me in to assist in Eldorado. I tracked down Nephi Josephs then. I wanted to make sure these Inspired guys weren't affiliated with the Fundamentalists, Warren's group. Seems some in the Agency thought since they was all polygamists, Josephs might hide Warren. Turns out the two groups hate each other. Nephi Josephs sent word that no Inspired members were to help the Fundamentalists in any way, shape, or form." Foster sat back in his chair seemingly satisfied that he could provide the younger men with assistance. His forehead wrinkled as he looked the men over. "Say, what's all this polygamist talk got to do with ya'alls' case?"

"Don't know, really," Flynt replied honestly. "Names keep poppin' up in our heads I guess. The land the grave is on is owned by Johnson."

"Well, ain't like I haven't been there," Jim said referring to the investigation.

"You know a Jeremiah Larsen?" Kidd asked.

"Name don't ring a bell," Foster kept rocking in his recliner. "But if ya'all want to know someone that knows everything about those people, contact the Stake President of the Mormon Church there in McAllen…a fellow by the name a' Steve Kimball."

They sat with Jim Foster for another forty-five minutes talking cases and general life. Kidd couldn't help but think that the man that sat in front of him was such a vast resource of knowledge and experience. When he was gone, the world would lose all of it. It was a virtual race against the clock to learn from Foster. Once again, an example of the older generation's ingenuity and ethics would die soon with nothing more than a paragraph obituary in print. But the ripple effect left those that knew him would be everlasting. Before he even left his presence, Kidd couldn't wait for his next visit with Jim Foster.

"You still got it?" Jim asked as Flynt and Kidd started for the door. Flynt reached into his front pocket and pulled out a single .45 Caliber bullet. He showed it to Foster. The two men embraced and for a moment, both seemed teary eyed. Almost as if they would not see each other again. "May God bless you and keep you safe."

"Keep well my friend," Flynt and Kidd walk down the front steps toward the Crown Vic.

"What the hell's the bullet for?"

"Old Ranger tradition," Flynt replied as he continued to walk.

"And?"

"It's about honor."

"Honor?"

"You do everything to preserve your honor, son," Kidd emphasized to his younger partner. "Even save the last round for yourself."

*

"Thank you, Deputy Director Cahill for seeing me," U.S. Marshall John Lansford said coming into the Austin office. A dark, cherry wood desk with rather modern steel framed chairs sat before him. Cops were not decorators, that much was obvious to Lansford.

"Call me G.W.," the Deputy Director said motioning Lansford to sit down. Lansford did so and leaned back in a semi-formal posture. "That was a good press conference you gave. I appreciate the nice things you said about the agency." The press conference was something that law enforcement usually utilizes during catastrophes and major cases. Recently, more agencies began to use them for positive and proactive news for the public. What better fodder for the public than to know that multiple agencies, such as the U.S. Marshalls and Texas Department of Public Safety, formed a task force that was focused on stopping human trafficking. Even though Lansford described the horrific case involving people actually burned inside their vehicles, the idea that the authorities sent a task force to help is comforting to the public. Lansford's tall muscular frame and good looks didn't hurt as well the task force immediately put him in front of everyone. The Deputy Director looked like a typical old school administrator, short, slightly hefty and wearing a pristine uniform.

"We couldn't do this without DPS, Sir. I appreciate all of the agency's support and resources. Washington has tightened its belt as I'm sure you know."

"Well, the State of Texas ain't exactly shellin' out the dough either, but we do what we can," the Director sat back in his chair. "But what specifically can I help with?"

"You know Deb Nichols, Sir?"

The Director smiled and shook, his head in the affirmative, "Oh, Deb and I go way back." Lansford got the feeling there may have been something between the two, but he dare not ask.

"Well, she's working pretty hard on those cases down at Eagle Pass."

"Yep, talk about a shitstorm."

"No doubt, Sir. She also caught that case where the bodies were burned in the car."

"I heard about that one."

"Well, she has a theory about the two cases and how they're related."

"Well, Deb may suck for relationships, but you can bet your ass she knows her cases," Cahill blurted out. Lansford had a difficult time hiding his laughter and finally had to let out a chuckle. "What's her theory?"

"She thinks they're human trafficking related," Lansford said extremely serious. He noticed the Director's face suddenly peaked with interest and solemnity at the same time.

"How does she figure?"

"Clothing found, age of victims, the fact that most are female. I gotta admit, crime scene isn't my thing, but she sounds confident," Lansford answered.

"Sounds more like a theory and not facts."

"That's why I'm here...she wants us in."

"Us?"

"The Taskforce, I mean."

"I spoke to Deb about this," Cahill looked at the Marshal. "Ya'all know you're treading heavily into Dan Gummit's territory."

"That's what she said. I admit I only know the guy by reputation…and it's not that that great."

"Say it…he's an asshole. I used to work with the son of a bitch, he could fuck up a wet dream."

"What's his deal?"

"He's a highly motivated leader that just so happens to suck at being a cop. Problem is, he spent his entire career sucking up to every politician he could. He knows every bottom feeder from the panhandle down…and the bastard ain't afraid to use em' neither."

"So, our involvement is a no go?"

"I didn't say that…"

"Well how would we contribute?"

"You shadow the investigation and hit the leads he can't."

"Won't he see that?"

"Probably not, but leave that to me," Cahill leaned back in his chair. "He can't turn down a popular task force's help. It would look bad for him with his political buddies."

"Well that leads me to my next question."

"What's that?"

"The task force is light on homicide investigators. Deb Nichols said you got a couple Rangers in the area to help out? Deb said something about Richard Flynt and a new guy named Kidd were working there in Eagle Pass."

"I already assigned em to you, but I warn you…Richard's ornery as hell. The new guy, Kidd, just received a special commission. I've heard nothing, but I've heard nothing but good things. But I gotta warn you Marshal Lansford…Richard Flynt and Dan Gummit hate each other. Dan used to be Richard's boss and well…it ain't easy being Richard's boss."

"I met Richard in Dallas a ways back. He'd be a great help."

"Just do me a huge favor," Cahill looked Lansford square in the eye. He was smiling but his tone was as serious as could be.

115

"Keep Flynt away from Dan Gummit. I don't need the kinda shit he can drum up on my desk."

*

Sariah watched the press conference in secret on her cellular phone. Televisions were specifically outlawed on the Johnson Compound. Bishop Johnson made it abundantly clear that television chased the Spirit of God from sacred ground. Luckily for her, her father loved technology and she always had the latest and greatest smart phone. *Human Trafficking?* She had never even heard the term before, but thanks to the internet, she had a definition and examples in mere minutes. But even the internet couldn't filter the horror as she read about the topic at hand. She read about young girls being sold into sexual slavery and servitude. Sariah was appalled at the abuse and sheer horror these girls were subjected to, until she realized that her own religion wasn't much better. The press conference centered on the Human Trafficking Task Force being sent in to investigate the mass grave in Eagle Pass and the burned vehicle with bodies found in Maverick County. These were Gentile problems the brethren would probably say. They would use the whole incident as a scare tactic. If those girls had kept the commandments, they would be alive the brethren would preach, but somehow real life was far more complex Sariah thought.

The Johnson family was just odd, even for polygamists. Even more odd, was that she had been on the compound for several days and no word from Amanda. *What kind of family is this?* She thought. She at least hoped that if she were sentenced to a horrifying polygamist existence, at least her mother and father would make an effort to call her. Every day she witnessed the teary-eyed emotional mother of Amanda struggle to keep it together. Something had to be wrong. Amanda may not have made attempts to contact Sariah due to the counsel of the brethren, *but her own mother?* She knew she had to investigate the matter further, but she needed help. Her parents were out of the question though, their undying devotion to this barbaric lifestyle made them not trustable. For that matter, anyone associated with the sect was out. So, who was left, the Gentiles? *Maybe this U.S. Marshall Lansford could help?* She thought. If she went the Gentiles and the brethren found out, the consequences would be disastrous. She realized that all of the church thought she was already lost, but she didn't want her family affected by her actions. Apparently when you belong to God's church, God's people get a say-so in your life. So, whatever her decision, secrecy was paramount. Luckily, that was a skill taught to her since birth.

She continued to watch the coverage that was now focused on the burned bodies found in Maverick County. They began to flash pictures that police released to the media to help identify these poor souls. The pictures showed a badly burned vehicle hull, shoes, and the melted plastic of electronics. The images were no doubt used to shock the public, but Sariah was simply unfazed by them. As the images appeared and disappeared, her interest began to fade like any teenager with the power of multimedia at their disposal. Then one image appeared that caused her stomach to drop and shook her to the core. She saved the image on her phone and looked at it several times hoping it wasn't what she thought, but it was unmistakable. The picture was a ring shaped as a shield. Anyone associated with Mormon or Fundamentalist Mormon culture knew that was a 'CTR' ring. It stood for 'Choose the Right." Now she was certain she needed to talk to this Marshal.

*

"Please come in and take a seat officers," Latter-day Saint Stake President Steve Kimball. The West McAllen Stake Center was on North 29th Street in McAllen. Kidd marveled at what a beautiful city McAllen had become. Growing up, he thought the town was blue collar, slow paced, and dirty. However, with the dawn of a new century came business and industries that thrived and bloomed. What was once a simple border town became one of the fastest growing cities in the United States, and the envy of the two countries. "To what do I owe this pleasure?" The men all shook hands and exchanged introductions before finally settling down in the plain wood, padded office furniture.

"My name is Richard Flynt, and this is Darren Kidd with the Texas Rangers," Flynt and Kidd both shook hands with the Mormon leader. "Well...we were kind of hoping to get some information. Got your name from Jim Foster," Flynt said cheerfully. Kidd stared down the man in front of them. His thoughts returned to when he was a practicing Mormon and was going through a divorce. When his wife heard about his affair, she told her Bishop who reported it directly to the Stake President. Kidd remembered sitting across from his Stake President being quizzed about his indiscretions and personal life. It wasn't as if Kidd didn't already know he did wrong, but he didn't expect the 'loving' chastisement and counsel from a man who lived a life in a bubble religion. A man that Kidd knew hadn't seen half the shit in life that he had. Instead of admiring the man for his job, Kidd decided to do a little more research into The Church of Jesus Christ of Latter-day Saints and was appalled at what he found out. It turned out the church's real history was a far cry from the whitewashed version spoon fed to him by missionaries.

"How is Jim?" Kimball asked with a fair amount of sincerity.

"Ornery as hell…uh…oops, I apologize there, President. Is that what you want to be called…President?" Flynt's tone made Kimball's responses a little off balance. Kidd could tell it was not a place that Kimball liked to be. In Mormonism, Kimball was the highest local authority and not used to a challenge at all.

"Steve is fine. How can I be of service to the Texas Rangers?"

"We're interested in The Inspired Church of Jesus Christ of Latter-day Saints," Kidd said still staring at Kimball suspiciously. He waited with anticipation for what he knew would be an interesting answer.

"Ah, Nephi Joseph's group," Kimball responded in a snarky tone. "They originally come from Southern Utah and the Mexican Colonies…just like the Fundamentalists."

"Well pardon me President, wasn't it your church that

created them?

"I'm sorry Ranger Kidd, I'm not sure what you're asking?"

"What I'm saying is that all of you guys come from the same doctrine, so why the animosity now?"

"They give our church a bad name."

"But see that's my point, President. I understand why say Baptists would hate the polygamists, but ya' all should be a little more sympathetic being that you come from the same place."

"I'm not sure what you mean by the same place?"

"I mean polygamy."

"Polygamy is not a doctrine of the Church of Jesus Christ of Latter-day Saints. But to the Inspireds' it is known as 'The Principle'."

"But ya'all used to practice 'The Principle' just the same though?"

"The practice ended in 1890."

Kidd smiled, but inside he was holding back years of research and study, not to mention anger. *Do these guys ever deviate from the script?* He thought as he prepared to choose his words. "Now President Kimball, you and I both know that polygamy continued to be practiced into the 1900's. In fact, the main reason for establishing the Mormon colonies was so that polygamy could be practiced without worrying about the U.S. Government looking over your shoulder."

It was President Kimball's turn to sit back in his chair, smile, and study the Texas Ranger that sat before him. For Kidd, he had Kimball where he wanted him. Kimball now knew that he had to be honest with these cops. "Very good Ranger Kidd," Kimball's head continued to nod. "You obviously have done your homework. I would love to know your experience with the church, but that is not why you're here." Kimball looked at the two Rangers very sincerely. "I'm honestly trying to help."

"And I do appreciate it," Kidd winked at Kimball. "But if we are to trust any answers you give, you got to be honest…warts and all. Now tell me about these Inspired guys?"

"They believe that the main stream church has been taken over by apostates, or people who do not believe in the true doctrine of Mormonism. It's mainly because we don't practice

119

'The Principle.' They have openly criticized the Prophet, but they remain in the shadows…outside the spotlight."

"What about this Joseph's character?" Flynt finally chimed in. "Have you met him?"

"I have," Kimball responded. "He is a cousin of mine. He runs the sect from St. George, Utah."

"And he openly practices polygamy there?"

"I wouldn't say 'openly' necessarily. But let's just say that everyone knows who he is and what he believes."

"How does he run his church?"

"With an iron fist. He knows everything and everyone and nothing occurs in Utah without his blessing."

"What about here in Texas?" Kidd asked.

Kimball laughed at the question. "Texas is a little different. The Bishop out here is Thomas Johnson."

"And this Johnson doesn't have to answer to Josephs?"

"Johnson owns a very lucrative aircraft fabrication plant West of Eagle Pass," Kimball acknowledged. "Since the ILDS only has about five thousand members, Johnson is very important to the sect's finances."

"So, Joseph makes Johnson a bishop and leaves him alone cause he's the golden goose?" Flynt inquired.

"Exactly…let's put it this way, Johnson *is* the prophet here in Texas. Josephs relies on his tithing money to keep the whole sect afloat." Kimball's comments didn't necessarily surprise Kidd as he sat back and listened. It wasn't unheard of in religion that money brings certain privileges. Though all the churches preach equality directly from Jesus himself, even the most pious parishioners admit that generous offerings seem to bring extra benefits. It would figure that polygamists would follow suit.

"How many wives does Johnson have?"

Kimball sat back in his chair and though. "Last I heard was over fifty, but you got to understand these guys can increase and decrease their wives in mere days. So that question is not an easy one to answer."

"How do we get to meet this Johnson character?" Flynt inquired.

"It won't be easy. Johnson hates law enforcement and will

probably want a lawyer present."

"Will he let us on the compound?"

"Not without a warrant. I have a phone number for his secretary. He'll probably want to meet at a neutral site if at all. He won't go near a police station voluntarily."

"How does the money work?"

Kimball stalled his answer. It seemed to Kidd that even though he obviously hated the polygamists maybe there was some feeling of unity in the two churches beliefs. It was just speculation. Kimball cleared his throat before finally answering Flynt's question. "It's called the UCF. It stands for the United Consecration Fund."

"Is it a corporate entity like your church?" Kidd had found out long ago that the Mormon Church was actually a cooperate entity.

"More kudos to your investigative skills, Sergeant Flynt. The UCF is a shell corporation funded by the Inspireds. As a member of the sect, you deed your business, financials, even your property to God...meaning the sect. All of that is transferred over to the UCF. Nephi Josephs oversees those funds and the deeds associated with them. The sect then distributes money according to each family's need. Let's put it this way, if you can control the UCF, then you control everyone in the sect. Basically, Nephi Josephs owns the sect."

"How's that?"

"He's the prophet. He has complete control over the UCF."

"Like you Mormons?" Kidd blurted out, remembering going through the temple and promising his assets and increase to the church. It was a principle Joseph Smith taught referred to as 'The Law of Consecration.' But to the church's credit, they never came to collect, they merely asked for ten percent.

"Yes, but ours is a theoretical promise made in the temple. The ILDS actually forces its members to sign contracts and turn their wealth over to the sect. So the sect literally owns their wealth."

"What about Johnson?" Flynt inquired.

"Easily the biggest contributor I'm sure."

"You got an idea of what kind of assets they're pushing?"

"No idea. But like I said, it's the high millions. I wouldn't be surprised if they've passed a billion."

"Do you know Jeremiah Larsen?" Kidd chimed in almost interrupting their exchange.

Kimball smiled at the two Rangers, a smile that was obvious he had some information they would especially value. "You mean Jeremiah LaFey?"

"I'm not following." Kidd studied the Stake President. It was curious this man knew so much about the polygamists, but not necessarily surprising. When he was active in the LDS Church, he observed a nepotism he had never seen before. Much of the hierarchy and local leadership all came from the same source, descendants of the early founders of the church. That fact alone sometimes made the fifteen million strong organization seem small and cliquish. "I've heard of the LaBarons…"

"Alright…alright…ya'all are talking over this old man's head. Who are the La Feys, LeBarons or whatever?" Flynt asked in an obvious disgusted manner. Kidd didn't blame him. During his time in the Mormon Church he often felt talked over and oblivious to many conversations. The church was rich in tradition and oral history that was ingrained in those born into the church, or 'under the covenant.' But to an outsider looking in, it was confusing and oftentimes strange and off-putting.

"I'm sorry, that was rude Sergeant Flynt," Kimball opened his computer tablet and showed Flynt a picture of the famous murderer. The LeBaron family, a polygamist group, moved to Mexico in the early 1920's to escape the watchful eye of the United States Federal Government as well as the leadership of the Church of Jesus Christ of Latter-day Saints. The infamous family founded 'Colonia LeBaron' in Galeana, Chihuahua as well as the Church of the Firstborn of the Fullness of times. "Ervil LeBaron ordered the killings of over twenty-five people, mostly rival polygamist leaders in addition to a lot of his immediate family, like his brother Joel. They've written several books about him."

"And Larsen is one of them?"

"No, Larsen's a LaFey."

"And who are they?"

"They are even more feared than the LeBarons," Kimball again used his computer tablet to illustrate some of his points. He pulled up a map of Northern Mexico. "Colonia LaFey is right in here," Kimball pointed to an are in the South Sierra Madre mountains.

"I don't see it written anywhere?" Kidd observed.

"And you won't," Kimball replied immediately.

"I thought the only colonies left were Juarez and Dublan?"

"I don't think that Colonia LaFey is recognized by the Mexican Government but trust me…it's there."

"What did the LaFey's do?"

"When most of the colonies were being abandoned during the Mexican Revolution, the LaFey's decided to stay and fight. When they were attacked by the revolutionaries, they would retaliate by covertly sneaking into Mexican towns and literally slaughtering families in the most gruesome ways possible. That included decapitations and the impaling of heads, skinning of infants, nothing was off limits. They believed that it was the hand of God that strengthened them, and they were fearless fighters. They even held off a full-frontal assault from the Mexicans."

"So, what happened to them?" Flynt inquired.

"An uneasy truce developed and eventually the fighting just stopped. But when the Cartels rose to power, they made an alliance with the LaFeys because of their connection with the states."

"What's in the states?"

"Guns…the LaFeys have supplied the guns to the cartels for years."

"Who are supplying them the guns?" Kidd inquired.

"No idea, neither does the ATF or *Federales*. And they don't even know how they are getting into Mexico. They don't even know where their guns come from, much less who is helping them in the U.S."

"Do they have any connection to the Inspired Church of Jesus Christ of Latter-day Saints?"

"The ILDS have officially distanced themselves from the

LaFeys. But there is a connection. Jeremiah's brother, Moroni, is the leader of the group. They resemble a militia more than a church. They're entrenched in those mountains and only God knows what kind of weaponry they have, or what they are capable of. Rumors about their underground defenses have circulated in LDS culture for years."

"Is Jeremiah dangerous?"

"I've only heard that Jeremiah is a man of honor. But he is a LaFey. So that makes him dangerous."

"What about your church? Do they have any interactions with the LaFeys?"

"Every few years the church receives a warning letter from the LaFeys."

"A warning letter?"

"They warn that if the church assists either the U.S. or Mexican Governments in attempting to go after them, they will kill every member they can, basically."

"And ya'all think they're serious?" Flynt asked in a far more somber tone than he began the initial conversation with.

"Ranger Flynt, I've seen firsthand what these people have done," Kimball stared at the two Rangers. "I'll give this to the LaFey's, they are more concerned with survival than they seem to be about religion. So, unlike the LeBaron's kooky religious executions, the LaFeys simply want to be left alone. But make no mistake…I know they are serious."

CHAPTER EIGHT

Alliances

John Lansford's office inside of Laredo PD was sparsely decorated with awards and accommodations, mostly for his work with the Human Trafficking Task Force. Sariah nearly begged the officers for an audience with Lansford. They told her she would have to wait, but at least they let her inside his office. She interacted with social media on her phone, but she couldn't hide her fear. She was raised to fear the police. She was taught that they represented forces that sought to destroy her relationship with the one true God. She knew if anyone in her sect found out, she would be ostracized more so than she already was, but her family would suffer the most. Lansford walked through the door causing a chill to her body. She couldn't help but notice his large biceps that seem to stretch the black, U.S. Marshall's shirt on his back. She returned his smile while she sat on the cut rate office furniture that looked donated.

"Hi…I'm John Lansford, can I help you?" Lansford stated in a puzzled voice looking at the beautiful young lady that sat before him. Sariah could tell that he was as uncomfortable with her as she was with him. He took a seat behind the modest desk and looked at the young girl. Sariah didn't have much experience with Black people. She was taught that Black people were cursed with their dark skin due to the unrighteousness of their forefathers, namely Cain and Ham from The Old Testament. Mormon sects even carried that belief further. Bruce R. McKonkie, a famous Latter-day Saint Apostle wrote that Black people were less valiant spirits in the pre-existence and war in heaven, even referring to them as "fence-sitters." Sariah stared at the man that sat before her, she was not getting the impression that this physically imposing man sat on any fences.

"I think I want to report a missing person," Sariah said in a timid voice that must've sounded incredibly juvenile to anyone within earshot.

"Um…okay…the police department takes those reports," Lansford was still puzzled. "I work for the Human Trafficking Task Force. Let's start with your name?"

"My name is Sariah Larsen and I know who you are and what you do, Marshal Lansford. I saw you on T.V." Sariah was nervous and obviously struggling with words. "I think my friend was abducted."

"What makes you think she was abducted?"

"I don't know…I just do," Sariah's eyes were shimmering with moisture as she swelled with emotion. She watched as Lansford, almost on cue, walked from behind the desk and sat down in the adjoining officer chair. He handed the woman a tissue from the box on his desk. He kept a plentiful supply considering his job description.

"What happened?" Lansford asked in a truly sincere tone and put his hand on her shoulder. That was the first time that Sariah was ever touched by an older gentile, a Black man at that. She didn't know what to think about it, but she did feel surprisingly comforted.

Sariah began crying. "They told me my friend was married off to a man in Utah, but I can't talk to her. I…"

"Wait…married? How old is your friend?" Lansford was really confused now.

"She's seventeen, and her sister is sixteen," Sariah replied with surprising ease. She knew it must've sounded strange to Lansford, but she was so used to the fact young girls married it was effortless for her.

"Kind of young?"

"Mr. Lansford, if I tell you something secret…do you promise not to get me or my family in trouble?"

"I guess that depends…"

"Please, Mr. Lansford!" Sariah pled with the man, streaming tears and all. She could tell Lansford looked at her and could only see someone's daughter or niece. She could see he was about to make one of those decisions that all law enforcement officers have to make. The one in which the right thing isn't necessarily the most legal or prudent thing.

"Okay, okay Sariah…you're not in trouble," Lansford

replied, almost regretting it immediately.

"And my family too...swear it!"

"You're family too, now what's the problem?" Lansford said in a semi-exasperated tone.

"My family is not normal. We are polygamists," Sariah said in an apologetic tone.

"Wait...you mean like Mormons?"

"Not exactly, but close."

"Were you all part of that group that The Department of Public Safety raided a few years back?"

"A little closer, but that wasn't us. We're the Inspired Church of Jesus Christ of Latter-day Saints. We live out in Eagle Pass. Those people in Eldorado were the Fundamentalist Church of Jesus Christ of Latter-day Saints."

"So that was your big secret?"

"It's illegal ya know."

"Yeah, but I don't work polygamy cases. Hell, I don't even understand it," Lansford sounded very matter of fact. "That and I really don't give a damn. Now you want to tell me about your friend now?"

"Her name is Amanda Johnson," Sariah wiped her eyes. "And her sister is Ruth. They're the daughters of Bishop Johnson over in Eagle Pass."

"And Bishop Johnson is?"

"The leader of the ILDS...well not the real leader, he's not the prophet or anything."

"Wait...prophet?"

"The prophet lives in Utah; Bishop Johnson runs things here in Texas."

"What does a prophet do?"

"He leads the church. He's the one with the authority to grant husbands additional wives."

"But I thought you said Bishop Johnson runs things here?"

"He does, but the prophet has the final word."

"Damn! This is confusing," Lansford stated in frustration. "I still don't get this whole prophet...bishop thing Sariah."

"Come on, you can keep up! You seem pretty sharp for a cop," Sariah smiled at the Marshal causing a slight grin in return. She was beginning to warm up to Lansford. All her life she was taught that Gentiles wanted nothing more than to hurt her and destroy the church. But Lansford hasn't even asked about her family and seems unconcerned about the fact that they were polygamists. She took a few moments to explain to the Marshal church hierarchy.

"So tell me about Amanda and Ruth. You said before they were getting married?"

"They were given to a man in Utah…or so I was told,"

"Given?"

"Yep, to some old guy that probably already has like five wives."

"Damn! How old is this guy?"

"Probably like fifty or something, trouble is, I don't know who he is," Sariah watched as Lansford was trying to comprehend the whole thing. She could see by his reaction that he could never understand such a lifestyle. His face was part horror, part concern, and part unbelief. He worked tirelessly every day to help others, mostly younger women, to break away from slavery, whether sexual or not. Sariah knew she must have dropped a bombshell on him. "I know it's fucked up, huh?"

"You got that right," Lansford acknowledged. "Now watch your mouth, little girl!" Lansford smiled which elicited a smile from the teenager. "Did they want to get married?"

Sariah was initially silent for a few moments after the question. How could she explain this answer without making her sound as crazy as her people? It was truly a leap of faith to speak with this man, yet it had to be so. "Well…yes and no," she finally uttered apologetically creating a truly confused look on the Marshal's face.

"What does that mean?"

"In our religion, being a wife and mother is everything. They begin to teach us that as little girls. So yes…they wanted to get married, but I don't think they wanted to marry that man right now."

"Who gives these brethren the right to choose who marries who?"

"God and the brethren."

SOUTHERN ZION

"God?" Lansford shook his head. "Well…it's original, I'll give em' that." Lansford looked at the young girl that sat before him. "What about you?"

"What about me?"

"Well?" Lansford replied casually yet curiously. The question made Sariah's heart sink. "You're about seventeen, right?"

"Eighteen."

"Who does God and the brethren want you to marry?" Lansford inquired. Sariah's head went into her hands in an embarrassing downward stare. She couldn't answer the man without divulging everything. She already stepped over the line displeasing her family, the brethren, and possibly God. Did she really want to pass the point of no return? She couldn't bring herself to answer, but that strong hand once again was felt on her shoulder and she was beginning to feel more at ease. Lansford again began to speak. "I work every day to help girls, about your age. I deal with sexual slavery, slave labor, shit that's worse than death. Not to mention you just told me that girls are being given away to older men for marriage because God said so? And even worse, they accept it. Now I have to know about you. I made a promise to you, now you gotta tell me everything or this relationship won't work."

Sariah again wiped the tears from her eyes. "Bishop Johnson told me God wanted me to marry him." She watched Lansford's face again as he struggled with this whole concept.

"You said no?"

"Yes…a ton of times, but God is apparently very persistent," Sariah and Lansford couldn't help but laugh at the statement. Sariah could feel that this man cared about her situation. "My parents always told me it was my choice to stay in the religion."

"So why don't you leave?"

"Because I love my family and it's a great dishonor to them for a child to leave the sect entirely…especially a girl. My Dad is already unpopular with the brethren for the way we live."

"How are you guy's different?"

"I can dress how I want, think how I want, and I drive."

"What did Amanda and Ruth think about the brethren?"

129

"They truly believe, Marshal Lansford. They believe if they disobey the brethren, they disobey God."

"Well if they went voluntarily, why do you think they're in danger?" The question really was the obvious one to ask, Sariah thought. It was fair, and she hoped her answer would spark the interest of this gentile cop.

"We're a small community, Marshal Lansford...word spreads. No one has heard from them...not even their own mother. Amanda was my best friend."

"Would she call you?"

"Well, the brethren don't like younger girls to stay in contact with their friends. They think it takes away from their wifely duties I guess. But not calling her mother? That's really suspicious."

"And you've spoken with her mother?"

"Yes, I got a job on their compound under the guise I was considering marriage. But I have no intention to get married. I only want to find Amanda," Sariah said with conviction. She watched as Lansford looked at her. He appeared to somewhat admire her for her determination. He shook his head in the affirmative.

"Look, I gotta be straight with you, Sariah. I don't know if I can help you. I mean, you said yourself this is your culture and the girls left voluntarily? I can make some calls, but..."

"Before you say no...there's one more thing I forgot to mention," Sariah said without hesitation. "That ring that was shown by the news...it's a CTR ring."

"CTR ring?"

"Yes...that means your victims are connected to Mormonism in some fashion."

"Are you sure?"

"Positive. That symbol has been used forever."

"By polygamists too?"

"By some...yes."

Lansford stared at the girl very curiously. "Are you thinking these are you're friends?"

"I am praying that's not the case. Amanda never wore any rings, but her sister did," Sariah replied. "I just want your help.

130

Now I just gave you some help…I need yours."

The Marshal stared at the girl again and exhaled a long breath. This little girl was beautiful and smart. Not only did she capture Lansford's attention, she managed to send him on an investigation he was sure to be a 'rabbit trail.' "I'm going to need the husband's information in Utah…" Lansford couldn't even get out the sentence before Sariah handed her piece of paper.

"Way ahead of you Marshal," Sariah beamed with a smile. Sariah knew that she had him, and Lansford smiled. "These are the names and addresses of the Smoots' I know in Utah."

"I need you to do something for me now."

"Anything," She replied anxiously.

"Next time you're in the compound, get something that belongs to the girls that has their DNA," Lansford said casually. "I know that sounds bad, but it's actually standard procedure." Sariah was amazed that Lansford could ask that question so effortlessly when it implied that her dear friend could be deceased. She understood that it had to be done, but she did not want to face that scenario. The young girl was able to gasp out her response.

"Okay…I will."

*

"Hey Richard…You ever met a prophet before?" Kidd smiled as they pulled in the parking lot of the Gonzalez & Nava Law Firm. The, single story brown brick building was new, well landscaped, and adorned with expensive cars in the parking lot. This obviously wasn't the typical defense hack, or ambulance chasers the Rangers were used to. This office appeared more like a corporate defense firm.

"I never knew we had prophets in Texas," Flynt answered in a confused manner. "And I'll be damned if this prophet don't have himself a lawyer!"

"Did Moses have a lawyer?"

"Guess he coulda used one with them pesky Israelites, but quit yer blashemin'!" Flynt replied as he stepped out of the

Crown Vic.

"So, what do we know about this lawyer, Sonia Nava?"

"She represents several wealthy clients, but made her bones in immigration law. She's also on the Eagle Pass City Council," Flynt replied. With his connections in the Bar Association, Flynt could get the story on any lawyer. Just as lawyers tried to get information on police officers they may confront, cops did the same thing.

"Well goddamn, polygamists and illegal aliens, that's a hell of a clientele. Just out of curiosity, where'd she land on the highway vote? For or against?"

Flynt smiled. "Against. Seems her and Soto had a bit in common," Flynt eyeballed his younger partner. "Funny you should ask that question."

"Wouldn't you?" Kidd smiled at his partner. He already knew the answer to his question. The two entered the office and were guided by young, attractive blonde into a conference room with a large oak table surrounded by leather high-backed chairs. Sonia Nava stood up from the far side of the table and greeted the two Rangers as they walked in. She was pushing fifty but looked more towards forty. Her long brown hair shined with its meticulous loose curls. Her makeup and skin were as perfect as her outfit. Definitely beautiful, and the dating type, but the attorney in her made her a little less desirable in the Rangers' minds.

"Please come in officers, I'm Sonia Nava and this is my client, Thomas Johnson," Nava pointed to the man who remained seated and stoic during the introductions. Johnson appeared smug and smiled pretentiously as if the world actually did revolve around him. He had a look that Kidd could recognize from anywhere. It was the look of a church person, the people that seemed to gaze on you with pity and contempt. Kidd could see that Johnson was such a man. To Johnson, he and Flynt were civil servants, or suckers that worked for a mere wage and lacked the knowledge or skill set to earn a decent living. On the other hand, Johnson believed himself so righteous, that his mere presence could benefit the poor, lost Rangers. The story was not unique to Johnson. They saw this attitude many times before.

"Well hey there, Tom, or Tommy, or Bishop. Shit…what do we call you, Sir?" Flynt inquired jovially as he shook Johnson's hand. "I'm Sergeant Richard Flynt and this is Darren Kidd with the Texas Rangers."

"Bishop Thomas Johnson…Bishop Johnson is fine," Johnson's smile was less cordial which only fueled the desire to push his limits. This would be a fun interview, Kidd thought.

"Well Bishop, I need to talk to you about your property."

Sonia Nava immediately interrupted, "We are well aware of the police activity on Bishop Johnson's land, though we haven't been informed of specifics."

"Somehow I doubt that," Kidd scoffed causing a look of anger from Nava.

"Is there a question sometime in the future?"

"Wow, objection Counselor!" Kidd's sarcastic outburst caused a flurry of laughter between him and Flynt. Nava and Johnson were not amused.

"Now, now, there Bishop and Ms. Nava…or is it Mrs. Nava?" Flynt's grin caused Kidd to laugh out loud again.

"It's Ms. and if you both want to waste more of our time, then this interview is over!"

"Alright, alright, alright," Flynt composed himself while Kidd observed the religious man and the lawyer. "Look, Ms. Nava," Flynt's emphasis on the Ms. caused Kidd to almost lose his composure again. "There's a mass grave found on the Bishop here's property. Now we got a lot of questions."

"Pardon me, but I was under the impression that the investigation was being conducted by Eagle Pass PD?" Nava observed, sounding as condescending as ever.

"Ms. Nava, were the Texas Rangers," Kidd interrupted. "Jurisdiction, pardon my language, don't mean shit to us." Nava appeared slightly taken back by Kidd's tone. But then again, the last thing you want from a lawyer is the impression you could be pushed around.

"So back to the questions, Bishop, when's the last time you were on the back forty?" Flynt continued.

Johnson looked at Nava for approval. She simply gave a nod

to the affirmative. "I don't go out there. The land is cared for by Brother Larsen."

"Yeah, we met Jeremiah," Flynt smiled at the two. "But that wasn't our question was it?"

"I was out there about two years ago."

"Any family a' yours go out there?"

"No…as I said, Brother Larsen takes care of the property."

"You realize sixteen bodies were found on your property, Bishop?" Kidd's emphasis on the word Bishop was obvious to both Johnson and Nava.

"I'm not sure I like…" Nava couldn't even get out her concern before Kidd continued.

"Seventeen people killed and buried on your client's land and you don't like our questions? You know what I don't like? I don't like finding sixteen dead fucking bodies!"

"Sir, my client has been nothing but cooperative…"

"So, he needs a goddamn attorney to answer some simple questions? That's cooperation?!" Kidd directed the outburst at Nava who was getting visibly upset. Her red face was still surprisingly attractive. He could tell she was about to pull her client from the interview.

"Alright now," Flynt said in a surprisingly soothing voice. He had a gift for calming hostile feelings. If the partnership was good cop, bad cop, then it was obvious the respective rolls. "Sonia…may I call you Sonia?" Nava shook her head in the affirmative. Johnson sat motionless and extremely disengaged. "Be honest…are you here because the fact your client is a polygamist?" Nava's eyes became just a bit wider and Johnson all of a sudden became quite interested. "Let me see if I can put you at ease then. We know, and we don't care about the wives and religion. We are trying to solve crime. That is all."

"You'll have to pardon me if I'm a bit nervous around the Texas Department of Public Safety." Johnson's voice was like hearing a deaf man speak for the first time. Both Flynt and Kidd were now paying attention. "You guys don't seem to like us all that much."

"Ah come on Bishop, it wasn't ya'all out there in El Dorado?"

"Yes, but our people have endured years of persecution…"

"The Fundamentalists are your people?"

"No, but we do have similarity in our beliefs…"

"You mean like Joseph Smith and the <u>Book of Mormon</u>?"

"To name a few."

"But you yourself have never been the target of police activity?"

Johnson smiled smugly, "Not that I am aware."

"Touché," Flynt smiled right back. "What do you actually know about the grave?"

"Only what I've seen in the news."

"So, is it only Larsen's family that goes out on that property?" Kidd got back into the conversation.

"My sons occasionally are on the property, not for work I assure you," Johnson giggled pretentiously. He was obviously becoming more comfortable, at least with Flynt. "They ride horses and other such things."

"Well, when can we talk to them?"

"I'm afraid that would be impossible," Johnson said abruptly, obviously rattled by the question. "I don't want my family bothered."

"Okay, so sixteen dead bodies but the kiddies can't be bothered…" Kidd again interrupted.

"Ranger Kidd that is enough!" Nava snapped.

"Well now that is a reasonable request Sonia…is it not?" Flynt inquired, once again attempting to lighten the mood. "We want to know if the boys saw something."

"I assure you they haven't. If they had, they would have told me," Johnson replied.

"You think your children tell you everything?" Kidd asked, somewhat amused by Johnson's response.

"I am not only their father…I am their spiritual leader as well. We have a close relationship. Believe me, they would tell me."

"You know Bishop, that's got to be the dumbest thing I've ever heard. I guarantee those boys keep a ton of shit from you."

Nava finally had enough. "The interview is over, gentlemen!"

"Good cause ya'all are boring the shit out of me!" Kidd barked back. "I just pray to God I don't find your client knows more than he's saying counsellor, I'm gonna stick my size twelve foot up his ass and neither you, or all the fucking prophets in Texas are gonna save him!"

"Well then, you all can leave my office and don't contact my client without notifying me first," Nava was fuming. "I also understand that you all spoke with my client, Michael Cordova? Do not contact him as well."

"Why certainly counsellor," Flynt winked. "But you know if or when we arrest them, we ain't gonna tell you right?" Nava and Johnson left the conference room and walked down the hall. The two Rangers casually got up to leave towards the exit. Flynt looked at Kidd and laughed. "We got to work on your people skills."

*

The Crown Victoria screeched to a halt in front of the Soto crime scene. Flynt and Kidd jump out of the vehicle and approach the officer guarding the scene. In some cases, investigators re-open crime scenes for another look, though it's rare. The Soto crime scene was such a scene. Kidd and Flynt again signed the log. Deb Nichols sounded so excited on the phone, but behind the voice of excitement was sheer exhaustion. It was the side of law enforcement seldom seen. Deb met them as they walked toward the house. Her eyes told the story of her commitment and exhaustion. As they walked to the entry way of the house, Flynt gently put his arms around the tired investigator and sweetly kissed her head, placing his lips in her flowing hair. Deb Nichols closed her eyes and embraced the elder Ranger.

"When's the last time you slept my Dear?" Flynt whispered in her ear.

"When have you last slept?" She retorted causing a giggle and one last squeeze before the two separated.

"Two questions…why'd you re-open the crime scene? And what's so important that we needed to get here right away?"

Deb smiled at Flynt's question. She motioned them to follow her inside.

"I was looking over the photo graphs and realized something was missed," Deb said as she guided the men through the house toward a rear sliding glass door with a large dog door built in. Flynt and Kidd immediately realized what she was talking about.

"How did you get another warrant?" Kidd asked curiously. If a crime scene is initially released, then an additional search warrant is required to enter the property. Usually, a detective or district attorney handles those matters, not a crime scene investigator.

"You are so cute!" Deb hugged Kidd and squeezed his cheeks as if he were her nephew. "Let's just say ya'all ain't the only ones who know folks that can get things done."

"So did you get anything off of the doggie door," Flynt asked still smiling from her display with his younger partner.

"I got several latents," she beamed. "Good ridge detail, two sets, both with a whorl pattern, the other a loop. But they have very distinct points."

"Obvious question," Kidd interrupted. "Where's the dog?"

"Never found one," Deb replied.

"That's a goddamn big dog to lose," Kidd observed as he showed the picture of a large Rottweiler to Flynt and Deb. The two never replied but added that to the literally millions of thoughts running through their heads.

"Are you thinking this is the entry point?" Flynt finally asked.

"That's what I thought at first, but follow me," Deb walked toward the windowsill at the West side of the house that led to a formal dining room. "If you recall, I got some latent prints on this area where the victim was found."

"Yeah, I follow."

"Now I'm no expert in Ridgeology, but I think the two sets of prints I lifted from the doggie door are a match to these I lifted from in here."

Flynt looked around the room seemingly observing everything he stared at. "Deb…do you still have that bag of sex

137

toys?"

"Every single anal intruder," she replied again causing a short burst of laughter from the group.

"We need that stuff swabbed and see if we can get profiles on them."

"Shit Richard…you know the girls at the lab hate swabbing dildos! I'm going to have to buy them a hell of a lot of beer."

"Do it Deb! You want the damn case solved don't ya?"

"We also need the computer forensics to kick it in the ass and get us that diagnostic report," Kidd knew what Flynt was thinking. Flynt looked over at the younger party and winked.

"So you all are the detectives, where's the entry point…the doggie door or the dining room window?"

"Neither…" Flynt could barely get the word out when he heard a distinct "Hey!" and some rustling coming from outside where the patrol officer was stationed outside the door. Kidd and Flynt ran outside to a pointing patrol officer outside the tape.

"I…I saw some motherfucker on the side of the house! He jumped the back fence you want me to get him?!" The officer was excited and panting.

"No!" Kidd barked. "Stay here and protect Nichols. Get on the radio and see if we can get a perimeter on this neighborhood!" He barely said the last word when he started for the fence and scaled it with relatively no problem but felt his aching knees when he stuck the landing. He noticed his partner running for the Crown Vic instead of following him. It was all Kidd now. *Fuck, I'm getting too old for this!*

Kidd jumped Soto's fence into the backyard in pursuit and could hear dogs barking in the yard behind the house, he sprinted to the back fence and jumped it. He could see a figure, but his lungs and muscles were starting their initial burn that comes with every foot pursuit. Kidd sprinted towards the figure praying to god there were no dogs in the back yard of the unknown residence. As he leaped the fences he could see the figure running up the road. *Thank God this guy's not fast*, he thought as he started behind the figure rapidly catching up. As he got closer, he could see that the figure appeared overweight, maybe even old.

"You better stop motherfucker!" Kidd yelled as he was getting tantalizingly closer to his target. He never even saw the Crown Vic screech to a halt in front of the running suspect, causing the suspect to turn and briefly face the oncoming Ranger Kidd. Kidd lowered his shoulder and planted it center mass. The force of Kidd's velocity, mass, and anger caused the suspect to topple with his head and torso slamming to the ground and his feet flying directly in the air. Kidd recovered from the hit and drew his fist back to strike the suspect, when the realization occurred. "Texas Don?! What the hell?! It was all he could do not to strike the man in his face.

"I'm sorry! I'm sorry!" Texas Don repeated as Kidd held his arms and Flynt cuffed him.

"Well now, Don. That's the truest goddamn thing I ever heard come out your mouth!"

*

"We've had a setback," Carlos approached and appeared nervous. Chuco and Juan were sitting in their car in front of Carlos's apartment. "I need you guys to scope an address after you make the pick-up."

"What are we looking for, *ese*?" Juan asked with curiosity. Carlos gave him a stern look, Juan was the smart one. Juan looked at his boss and nodded.

"The *guerro* didn't get the girls across," Carlos said apologetically. "I just need you to look, man. I ain't gonna make you transport them though…I ain't gonna bring that shit on you, but if we make the Negras upset, we all in some shit, *entiendes?*"

"Si," Juan replied and took the piece of paper from him.

"You just gotta look and see if you see any girls, *ese,*" Carlos instructed. "The Boss is gonna oversee any moves so just look."

"I say we find this fucking, gringo for bringin all this shit down on us!" Chuco spoke out. "We'll fucking take care of him like we do in the valley."

Carlos smiled and shook Chuco's hand as if they were

lifelong friends. "*Orale,*" he muttered as he slapped Chuco in the arm while reaching in the vehicle. "But you guys don't want any part of this gringo, *entiendes?* He's a brutal fucker, Nazi Lowrider AB." Carlos thought that might sound weird considering Carlos had connections with Tango Blas and Aryan Brotherhood. It simply showed that money transcended any allegiances in prison. Carlos knew Caldwell, he also knew he could kill Chuco and Juan without blinking. The Nazi Lowriders were the AB's brutal enforcement arm. They were the worst of the worst. While he liked their enthusiasm, they had no idea of just how dangerous Caldwell was. In fact, it was a Tango that recommended Caldwell in the first place.

"We tag those fuckers all day long, *ese!*"

"I know, *Carnal*, but this fucker is different. He shanked and cut the tongues out of his enemies on the inside. Rumor has it he ate em," Carlos looked at the two men with serious intent. "Serious…stay away. Besides, the bosses want to handle this. I just pity the fuckers that are gonna get him…he ain't gonna go easy."

"The Bosses know that?" Juan asked.

"Gonna find out I guess," Carlos shook the hands of the two men and watched them drive away.

CHAPTER NINE

Consistency

"You know when we spoke with your dumb ass before, Don, we figured you as an idiot, but not a murderer," Flynt said looking directly at Texas Don who sat helplessly in the Eagle Pass Police Department interview room. His jeans and boots were replaced with the orange jump suit that was skin tight next to the portly inmate's body. Texas Don was being charged with Interference with Public Duties, specifically for coming into the secured crime scene, but the real question needed to be answered. Why did the political blogger feel the need to come to the house of a dead man? "I don't think a White, fat-ass, Republican is going to do well in Huntsville."

"You got it all wrong Rangers...I'm trying to help you guys!" Don tried to squirm in his chair, his face bruised from when he was taken into custody.

"Then why did you run Don?" Kidd stood up as he addressed the blogger. Texas Don sank back into his chair, fearing the younger Ranger. "I may be getting old and tore down, but I can still catch your dumb ass all day long! You understand me fat boy?! Now start flapping those gums if you don't want a murder charge!"

Don was crying now. He put his head down into his lap to shield his embarrassment from the two lawmen he sat in front of. The Rangers gave him a minute to compose himself before he finally picked his head up. "I don't know how to make ya'all believe me. It's all connected. The graves, the killings, and the city council! Soto is dead...what more proof do you need?"

"Actually, we need a lot more proof ya jackass!" Kidd paced to the other side of the room leaving Flynt looking at Texas Don trying to figure out what to do with this man.

"Just what proof were you lookin' for? What are you expecting to find?" Flynt asked, almost halfway interested.

"Computers, ledgers, anything to expose these corrupt politicians. Soto knew what was going on, and they killed him for it," Texas Don replied.

"That is a wild accusation, Don. Besides, we got all of the computers."

"Well then you need to stop them, Ranger Flynt."

"You're still a suspect for a murder, Don."

"Well I told you I don't know shit and I didn't kill no one! And you ain't gonna find any evidence that says so neither!"

"Then I suppose you ain't got nothing to worry about then, besides this little misdemeanor."

"And I suppose I'm done talking. I want to see my lawyer."

*

The Chevrolet Malibu crept along the farm road that paralleled the Johnson's compound walls. There were a multitude of children playing outside the compound, but there were no girls that Chuco and Juan would want to report back to Carlos. Just inside their vehicle was a backpack with one hundred thousand dollars. The smuggling and the drops were easy for the men; it was what they lived for. This other side of the business they were being pulled into was not.

"This is some bullshit, *ese,*" Juan finally said as they cased the compound for girls. "These girls are babies."

"You heard Carlos. It ain't like we gotta grab them. That's their problem," Juan said.

"But don't you get it? We're spotting for them. They're gonna come get some girl and take her from her family, *Guey!* We're just as guilty as them."

"That's the life though. That's the way it is…some things we can't change."

"I didn't bargain for this shit, man."

"You heard Carlos, we gotta do what we gotta do. They'll kill us."

"They'll kill Carlos and his Boss…whoever the fuck that is!"

"And you don't think they'll come after us? You know how they are."

"Maybe we deserve it."

They circled the place another time. It was as if they were hunting for prey. They remained silent, perhaps as a protest to the despicable thing they were a part of. Perhaps it was because they simply had a job to do and did not want to suffer the consequences of not following orders. Whatever the reason, after the second pass, they decided to abandon the search and get the money back to Carlos. Both felt a sense of relief for abandoning the task, but a real sense of fear in not completing it.

*

It wouldn't have been a big deal to see a car circling the compound. It wasn't as if the compound was so out of the way that no cars ever came by, but the same car, a red Chevrolet Malibu, circling twice? That was unusual. Sariah did get a good look at the occupants though. Two Hispanic males with tattoos, she saw them through the fencing while she was gathering clothes. It wasn't the fact the two men were Hispanic, or even driving by the remote compound. This was South Texas, it could be argued the norm was Hispanic and tattooed, but these men seemed to be staring at the younger Johnson sisters in a way that could only be described as creepy by a teenage girl. It was true that Sariah led a very sheltered life, but even so, every woman was born with the instinct to spot a predator, especially when the predator is male. Something wasn't right. *Could this have something to do with Amanda?* It was a ridiculous assumption, she thought.

She quickly dropped the clothes off and ran to her car. She knew she could catch the car before it got out to the highway, she knew the roads and doubted those two men did. She really didn't care if anyone knew she was leaving. She tore onto the farm road and decided to take a shortcut to the highway down a dirt path she and Amanda used to drive to be alone, or meet up with boys. The path led right to the highway. She stopped underneath the tree line to remain out of sight. If the car was going back into Eagle Pass, she would definitely see it. Sure enough, the red Malibu turned onto the highway towards town and the occupants were unaware they were being observed. She let them pass for a spell then climbed onto the highway and eased behind the vehicle. She drove at a distance not to arouse suspicion, but close enough see all she needed. *DHK-4151,* she thought to herself as drove behind the vehicle. Sariah's adrenaline began to flow and she didn't even know why. In fact, she didn't really even know why she was following these two, her instincts simply kicked in. It was most unladylike considering her upbringing, she could hear the words of her mother and the sister-wives in her ears imploring her to be meek and avoid any unnecessary conflict. Let the men handle all of the conflict and concentrate on motherhood, her only equalizer to the masculine world. Yet here she was following two people that she didn't know, and most likely never would want to. Sariah's awareness was heightened, and her excitement levels were too high. In short, she liked how she felt.

As the vehicles came into town, Sariah followed red Malibu into a downtown neighborhood. She peered in the mirror and saw her hair in the nasty bun she's become accustomed to since working on the Johnson compound. She quickly pulled the bobby pins from her hair letting it fall over her face. She watched the car wind through all of the residential streets coming to a rest in the parking lot of an apartment complex. Though she couldn't remember how to get back here, Sariah looked at the surrounding area to familiarize herself at the location. Since Eagle Pass just didn't have that many apartment complexes, she should be able to recognize it again. The Malibu parked in a handicapped parking space close to the entrance of the courtyard of the complex, but no one got out of the vehicle. Sariah drove to a corner parking space that still got her close enough to see the Malibu. She slowly turned the engine of to her own vehicle and sunk into her chair. Not only had she ventured out into the Gentile's world, she was meddling in things she knew nothing about, but again, she was happy.

It was about fifteen minutes and a very handsome Hispanic male came out to the Malibu. He leaned into the passenger's side window and appeared to shake the men's hands. There was a smile on the man's face initially, but it quickly turned into a look of concern. The Hispanic man looked at the ground in a sad, almost desperate manner. Sariah was anxious, and wanted to get closer, but she was sure she'd be noticed. So, she stayed put, almost with a helpless feeling. The passenger then handed the handsome man a backpack. *I wonder what's in there?* She thought as she sat watching the men even more intently. It had to be drugs. Drugs were the evil sin of the Gentiles according to her church leaders, and parents, though the occasional weed smoke was not unheard of in the sect. Then as quickly as he appeared, the handsome, Hispanic male disappeared into the complex. The Malibu then drove out to the road winding its way into the neighborhood.

DHK-4151, she kept repeating in her mind.

*

"You got anything for me?" Lansford's sense of urgency over the phone was obvious. It was in his very DNA, it's why he became a U.S. Marshall. To him, seconds and minutes mattered. It could mean the very difference between success and failure. To say that it ruled his professional was a given. To say its effect on his personal life was another matter.

"Well, how are you, Deb? Or have you gotten more than two hours of sleep Deb?" Nichol's voice was tired and irritable. Lansford realized how uncaring he must have sounded by the tone her response.

"Wow, that was a bit insensitive, huh?"

"Umm, a little bit."

"Well now that we both know I'm an asshole and you're already mad at me, you got anything?" Both giggled at Lansford's attempt to lighten the mood.

"Well since you asked so nicely, I got something," There was a hint of excitement in Deb's voice that wasn't showered in exhaustion as her previous statements. *"I got a hit on a latent I lifted off the rearview mirror!"* That was good news to Lansford. Deb was able to explain anytime a driver gets in a vehicle invariably one of the first things they touch is the rearview mirror. *"I got fifteen matching points!"*

"So…"

"So, what?" Lansford could almost see Nichols smiling on the other end of the phone knowing how impatient he was. *"Okay…okay,"* Deb laughed, Lansford could hear her shuffle papers. *"His name is Trey Caldwell. I'm scanning his QH now to send it to you."*

"What's this guy's deal?"

"Aryan Brotherhood out of Huntsville. Finally got sent up on a distribution charge, but he's got a few arrests for Sexual Assault. Just got out last Fall."

"So, he's on parole?"

"Yep. Looks like his PO is Larry Smith out of Laredo, you better get on this one quick like."

"Shit, I've got press conferences in McAllen all week!"

"Is that all you Feds do is smile for the cameras?"

"You'd think. Say…you think those Rangers would track this lead for me?"

"I think that could happen, but you owe me."

"More and more it seems."

*

The number that appeared on the caller identification was unknown to Carlos, but he couldn't afford not to take calls. With the Negras on his ass, there could be no mistakes which meant he had to be available. His stomach dropped from the nervousness he felt. "Carlos?" he said as he answered the phone.

"I know it was you, Fucker!" the voice was low and intense, but unmistakably Caldwell's. *"I'm gonna fucking kill you! Believe that!"*

"Trey? What's wrong, man?" That was all he needed, Carlos thought, a pissed off associate that Carlos needed way more than Carlos needed Carlos.

"Don't you fucking play that! You sold me out…now you fucking die!" Caldwell's voice never cracked or stuttered. *"You got a dead spic on your hands too. I bet those Negras fuckers won't like that?"*

"What the fuck are you saying, Bro?" Carlos's head was

spinning now. He knew Caldwell was crazy, but he never heard him talk like this.

"Don't fuck with me! You brought those fucking Mexicans down on me! They tried to kill me, but I got one of them Fucker! I stuck him like a fucking pig and I'm gonna get you too, you wetback fuck!"

"Chad…listen…I didn't have a thing to do with whatever you're talking about! I never told anybody about you," Carlos was at a loss for words. He couldn't deny it any harder. It was anger and frustration, but mostly panic in his voice. "They were upset about the girls not being delivered…they must have figured out who you were. You gotta believe me…I didn't tell them shit!"

"Keep bullshitting me, Fucker. You know what? I ain't gonna kill you. I got something much worse in mind…"

"Listen, whatever it is…it can be fixed. Can you get me that girl?" Carlos was almost pleading at this point. It was a precarious position he found himself to be in. On the one hand, the Negras were not to be trifled with. If they were double-crossed, he would most assuredly die. On the other hand, Caldwell was crazy, and worse, unpredictable. A delivery of girls could get at least satisfy Tio Muniz. "I'll talk to Tio Muniz…I can fix this, just help me out."

"No more girls, Carlos. You're done," Caldwell's voice was calm as he uttered the ultimatum over the cellular phone. As for Carlos, he knew the reality of his situation and he wasn't going down because of a filthy racist like Caldwell. Besides, the whole reason he was in trouble with the Negras was because of Caldwell. Truth be told, Caldwell deserved to die and Carlos was quite confident the Negras would eventually get to him, despite his Aryan Brotherhood connections. It was all for the best, he thought. It was preservation time for him and Caldwell needed to go. Carlos couldn't worry about a man who had long ago outlived his usefulness.

"Sounds like you're done, *ese?* I ain't the one running from the *Negras.*"

"I knew you sold me out." Caldwell's voice lowered, Carlos already grew tired of the conversation. There was really

nothing more to say.

"No *cabron,* you sold us both out when you fucked up the drop!" Carlos said with confidence. "So, take your best shot, *guey*, cause I think the Negras will get your ass before you even get close to me." He smiled the smile of a man who had had endured a beating and lived, albeit scarred.

Caldwell was silent on the other end. But when his voice was heard again it was sharper than anything Carlos could have heard. *"I told you, Carlos, I ain't coming after you,"* Caldwell finally uttered through the airwaves. *"I'm going to the cops! Now the Negras will definitely get your ass."* Right then Carlos suddenly could not feel his own heart. Now there was definitely a problem and self-preservation was unlikely.

*

"So remind me why we're going to this trailer park again?" Kidd heard Flynt's initial explanation. It seemed like every time Deb Nichols called their work load increased and they had to chase down more shit. Kidd drove through town while Flynt sat uninterested reading the file. "Why don't you just admit that you still love Deb?"

"I told your dumb ass, she got a hit on AFIS from a print lifted on that burned car case," Flynt replied with a voice of playful disdain. "The hell you know about love?"

"Correct me if I'm wrong, that's a Human Trafficking Task Force Case, right?" Kidd knew that whatever his partner's reply would be, it couldn't justify their situation. The sad truth about law enforcement was that people constantly attempted to divert and delegate their duties, not because of laziness or indifference, but simply because of the massive workloads.

"You know that we've been assigned to help them. You and Deb thought this was such a damn good idea," Flynt smiled at his junior partner. "Guess what? Now we have grunt work. Now can we please find this son of a bitch and get this over with."

"But it doesn't piss you off that an entire task force needs us to find this guy?"

"Sure does…wait…that's right, it don't matter what I think."

"Sure, it matters ya grumpy old son of a bitch! That's a hell of an attitude."

"Worked for me thus far."

"Yeah, I can see that," Kidd was bored with the subject. "So what do we know about this guy?"

"Trey Caldwell, six foot, two hundred , two pen trips. Says here he was affiliated with the Nazi Lowriders on the inside."

"No shit? Sounds like he'd be good for something," Kidd thought. The Lowriders had quite a reputation in the Texas Department of Corrections. Anytime there was any interaction with the Aryan Brotherhood, the only thing that was constant was their unpredictability. Kidd pulled into a trailer park on the outskirts of town. He couldn't help but notice the eyes of the people, mostly children, glued to the vehicle as if they were a travelling side show. Kidd always thought that every trailer park looked the same, filled with dilapidated tin skirting and junk void of any type of order. Kidd smiled as the children innocently played seemingly unaware of society's disdain for them and their circumstances. He wondered if it ever crossed their minds that they were all but forgotten amongst the world around them, like a sideshow at a carnival that everyone passes to get to the rollercoaster. It was a lesson Kidd learned on the street, innocence must be protected. Kidd watched as the children ran through the piles of junk as though it were an expensive playground in the wealthiest of suburbs. Kidd's smile soon faded as he realized that the innocent faces he stared at would soon mature, and their outlook on life would most likely turn to despair.

The two Rangers continued to walk the park and scan their surroundings. They never walked the middle of the street but tried to 'hug' the buildings as to lower their physical profile. Kidd hated trailer parks for tactical reasons. Mostly because a trailer can't stop a bullet and he couldn't count the number of times he had to drag some asshole from underneath the skirting. That and the fact they are laid out in rows and never numbered correctly certainly didn't help.

"What number we looking for?" Kidd whispered.

"Seventeen," Flynt replied. "But I ain't seen a goddamn number yet."

"Hold up!" Kidd lifted his arm in a fist, the tactical sign to stop. He pointed silently to Flynt a singlewide trailer that appeared to have been pried open and freely swinging. It was definitely suspicious, and both men knew it needed to be investigated. Both Rangers drew their weapons and tactically approached the trailer. Flynt held his weapon towards the door while Kidd made a quick check around the back and under the trailer. When he was done searching, Kidd held up his thumb to let Flynt know he was okay and ready to go.

"Texas Rangers!" Flynt yelled as he pointed his .45 directly at the door. There appeared to be no answer or movement so Flynt carefully reached for the front door and pulled. The door came open with ease allowing Kidd to slip inside and begin clearing. The brown shag carpet of the entryway was red with blood and the body of a lifeless, Hispanic male lying just inside. Almost in a choreographed nature, Flynt and Kidd stepped over the body methodically searched the house, every room, closet, and cabinet ignoring the fact there was a dead man at their feet. It was simply muscle memory. As the completed their secondary search of the location Flynt calmly took out his phone and contacted County Dispatch. The two men then approached the body. "County is sending a couple deputies. They're about fifteen minutes out," Flynt finally uttered obviously still deep in thought.

"We sure screwed up this crime scene," Kidd said, partially disgusted with himself.

"Well it ain't like we had a choice," Flynt crouched at the body. "Well this sure as hell ain't Caldwell." The body was a Hispanic male, five foot five, one hundred and fifty-pounds lying face down on the floor. The man's throat literally had gouges of flesh and skin removed, as if attacked by a wild animal. "Looks like he got hit in the neck several times with a blade."

"Hit? I'd say more like carved," Kidd responded. "This is definitely Caldwell's place." Kidd showed Flynt a picture hanging on the wall that was clearly the man they were looking for. "What's your theory?"

"I used to see this stuff in the prisons. They strike several times at sensitive areas till the flesh simply disintegrates. This guy's artery's gone too."

"Well our boy's no stranger to prison fighting tactics."

"Nope," Flynt continued examining the victim and his eyes focused on a small tattoo on the victim's neck that was easily dismissible. "He's a Negras," Flynt finally observed out loud.

The two Rangers went silent for several moments. The fact that a dead member of the most violent Mexican cartel was lying here was only the first question. What were the implications? It was long ago accepted that cartels operated in the United States, but mostly through U.S. street gang allies. But this guy was a bona fide Negras. There were two realities that both of the Rangers realized. First, Caldwell was in serious danger. It wasn't as if Caldwell's death would be particularly troubling to either men, but he did potentially have information on a Murder case which made him valuable, so he must be found. But second and far more troubling was the fact that the Negras were operating in America.

"This blood doesn't appear to match the other," Kidd observed near the door pointing to a transfer pattern on the door knob. "What do you want to bet the blood is Caldwell's?"

"Safe bet."

"Okay so we all watch the news stories regularly. Why not do a typical cartel hit and spray the place with lead?"

"Negras make their name by killing. It's considered honorable and challenging to kill your opponent with your hands, not a gun. This guy was trying to make a name for himself."

"I don't get that, a kill's a kill, right?"

"You know what the average price for a professional hit is in Mexico?"

"I'm sure you'll tell me."

"Bout two hundred American dollars. So what I'm saying is, in order for these guys to make a living killing, they have to be kinda special."

"I guess this guy ain't that special?"

"Being special is hard when you pick the wrong motherfucker."

CHAPTER TEN

Reveal

Doing the daily chores at the Johnson compound was almost excruciatingly boring. Not only was it degrading to women, but Johnson had the younger children doing meaningless chores as well, male and female alike. Johnson was such a traditional bastard. Even though there were commercial dryers on the compound, he preferred the sheets hung dried from a clothes line. As usual, the morning chores on the compound resembled an ant hill with all of the workers going in seemingly all directions and yet the jobs were all being accomplished. Sariah performed her tasks seamlessly, but her mind kept thinking about Amanda and Ruth. She continued to wonder if those two Hispanics had anything to do with their disappearance and felt helpless that her only recourse was a Gentile U.S. Marshal she didn't even know or fully trust. She felt frustration that she seemed to be the only one concerned for these girls lives and that the Gospel that preached about the sacred majesty of woman was the first to disregard their actual worth. And yet as much as she hated her church, she looked over all of the Johnson family and felt nothing but love. Could she ever get over that such a cadre of sweet people was literally trapped in such a tyrannical existence in which a select group of men literally controlled every aspect of their lives? Could she ever let go of this mindset that the brethren speak for God and that all others may as well be silent? Sure it was easy to rebel, but even if she had the means to get away from all of them, would she? Would she forget all of the moralistic stories from the scriptures that seemed so contradictory but were drummed in her head for her entire life? It wasn't that simple and Sariah knew it. She knew of the young boys that were exiled from the sect simply because there were not enough women for the brethren to share. Those boys made their ways to the cities living with fact their God rejected them. Some were finally liberated, yet some were plagued with guilt and turned to the standard drugs and street crime; in the worst cases, suicide.

"Hi Sariah…I like your outfit," the sweet voice of Jill Johnson was unmistakable. Sariah turned to see the little girl's beautiful blonde hair and infectious smile. Sariah smiled right back and grabbed the little girl in her arms giving her a hug only a mother could top.

"How is my favorite girl!" Sariah said rubbing her nose against Jill's. The statement wasn't that much of an exaggeration. Whenever she visited Amanda she made it a point to find Jill. Jill was one of those children that could make anyone smile. It was as if her soul was a lightbulb and brightened the very spirits that came in contact with her. She was the innocent, young version of Amanda that Sariah adored. That's why it sickened Sariah to think this beautiful girl would end up in the hands of an old pervert who would convince her God commanded it. "What are you doing you crazy little puppy?" Sariah rubbed her nose again.

"I'm helping!" Jill giggled from al the nose rubbing.

"I can see that. You're such a big girl."

"Why don't you stay here with me?" Jill's eyes were so cute they literally cut right to Sariah's heart.

"Well I have to go home sometime, silly?"

"But I miss Manda, so you can be here now," Jill smiled and was obviously proud of her solution. Sariah almost teared up when she heard it but decided to be strong for her little angel.

"Well, Amanda's a big girl sweetie, and sometimes big girls have to go."

"But all my sisters go!" Jill's happy face wrinkled in anger. "Kathlyn, Linda, Sandra, now Ruth and Manda."

"It's all part of growing up baby…"

"But why won't they visit me! Don't they love me?" The statement took Sariah back. She didn't really know the other sisters very well, but never visit the family? Sariah found it odd that a religious sect that emphasized family would just cut off all communication like that.

"Well I know for a fact that Manda would never just leave

and not visit pumpkin," Sariah said trying to reassure the child. "She would die first."

"But that's what happens. So, would you think about moving here with me?"

"I will...now go help your Mama," Sariah thought for a moment. It was time to directly confront someone, but Bishop Johnson was out of the question. There was only one man she could implicitly trust.

*

"This place is seriously nasty!" Kidd finally exclaimed as they methodically searched Caldwell's trailer. With every step, the smell of mildew and filth tickled the noses of the Rangers. Normally, they would wait for the crime scene investigators to photograph and process the scene prior to their looking the place over, but these were extreme circumstances, they had to get to Caldwell. There was no question that the Negras would get to him, the only question was when.

"Old Caldwell's got him a girlfriend," Flynt said as he held up a pair of black, lace panties in the air with his gloved hands. "Nuthin says class like crotchless I always say."

"Give that to Deb for DNA," Kidd chucked eliciting a smirk from his senior partner. As he looked through the seeming endless stacks of paper strung across the floor, Kidd couldn't help but notice some notebook paper lying under some dirty clothes and trash. The bedroom had a bare, soiled mattress on the floor that acted as a centerpiece to the clothing, trash, and hypodermic needles that lay beneath the grime on the paneled walls and on top of the chunky carpet. The dirty stench didn't faze the Rangers anymore, their senses normalized to their surroundings as if they were used to such conditions. The fact was that most people couldn't be in such a place. But Kidd couldn't count the number of times he set foot in such filthy circumstances. "He does have a girlfriend, and she has a court date," Kidd said as he was holding up some hand-written notes."

"This girl got a name?"

"Nope, it just says, 'babe's court date'. He didn't even

capitalize the B."

"Fuckin scoundrel," Flynt smirked as he continued his search, digging through the trash like a possum foraging for tiny morsels. It wasn't until there was a quick shuffle of paperwork that Kidd raised his head.

"Holy Shit!" Flynt exclaimed. "Isn't this a Mormon trinket?" He held up a bracelet of the Angel Moroni playing the trumpet. Kidd immediately recognized the image which stands proudly atop every Mormon Temple. He was the prophet that buried the very golden plates that Joseph Smith claimed to translate that would become the Book of Mormon.

"We gotta find Caldwell and this girl now. I ain't buying the girl with the crotchless panties would where an Angel Moroni Necklace. This asshole thought he could pawn that."

"Now I don't know…the horniest girl I've ever been with was the minister's daughter," Flynt said smiling.

"Very goddamn funny, but I'm serious!" Kidd retorted almost laughing but still half disgusted. "Crime scene's going to be here any second, and we can't waste time like this. We need to get his Parole Officer to violate him, so we can get him into custody, then we need to find this girl!"

Flynt smiled as he watched his junior partner scrambled, forgetting that they still had to explain the dead cartel member to the responding officers. Police work was not about speed, it was about thoroughness. It seemed that was a secret reserved for the oldest cops. "Ya think we ought to tell the responders how we found the dead Mexican?" the question shot a look of impatience mixed with obviousness from the junior Ranger. Flynt picked up the phone and contacted his friend in Maverick County Probation. They talked for what seemed to be an eternity before Flynt finally ended the call. Kidd waited what seemed like a lifetime to get information out of his partner before he couldn't hold it any longer.

"So?"

"So, what?"

"Seriously, old man? What did the Parole Officer say?"

"He said Caldwell was already violated for popping dirty on his last drug test," Flynt said passively. "I know where to find

156

the boy too." Flynt sat thinking in silence. It was a habit that killed his junior partner who insisted on having the information at once.

"So, where's he at?"

"He turned himself in to the Maverick County Jail about an hour ago."

"That's good," Kidd replied.

"For who?" Kidd thought about Flynt's reply. Caldwell was as good as dead on the inside as well as on the outside of those walls. The Negras would hunt him mercilessly.

"Can we put him in isolation for now?"

"Way ahead of you," Flynt said as his phone once again came out of the holster.

*

"Come in and sit down, Sariah," Jeremiah smiled as he greeted his daughter. She stepped nervously into her father's office feeling his embrace as she passed him in the threshold. She even became more skittish when she observed a strange man, with a familiar face sitting on the couch smiling at her as she walked in. He had such a familiar face, but Sariah just couldn't place him. He smiled a warm smile at her and appeared as if he wanted to hug her, but it seemed as if he was constrained, whether it was insecurity or propriety, she couldn't tell. Strangely, she felt a connection to the man as well.

"You don't remember me do you, sweetheart?" the man questioned her.

"No...no, Sir."

"Sariah, this is your Uncle Moroni LaFey," Jeremiah said in an effort to jog her memory.

"Hi," she said smiling back at the man. Though Sariah didn't recognize the face, she did the name. Moroni LaFey was a notorious and infamous anti-hero to polygamist Latter-day Saints. The rumors and legends were extensive and wild. Moroni LaFey was even rumored to have killed the former Prophet of the Inspired Church of Jesus Christ of Latter-day Saints. What she did know was that her father told her and her siblings never to mention the name LaFey to anyone outside the family. Yet here he was inside of her home and her father referring to him as her uncle.

"You didn't know you had such an infamous family, did you?" Moroni smiled at the young, confused girl.

"I don't understand?" she stated to the two men.

"We've kept this from you for too long, Sariah. That was my decision. I am a LaFey, so that makes you one as well."

"But why hide it?" Sariah looked at Moroni and Jeremiah intensely.

"Because the name LaFey is a liability in Utah and Texas."

"But you taught us that our name is the most important thing we own!" Sariah's anger was turning to tears. "And now mine was a lie?!"

"It's more complicated than that, Sariah."

"Then tell me!"

"It's because of me, Sweetheart," Moroni's soft calm voice was calm, but cold. There was no tinge of emotion present, yet somehow he was captivating. "My reputation is such that there is fear that is associated with the LaFey name. Your Dad is only doing what he felt was best for his family. Now sit down, and I will answer all of your questions." His soft spoken, yet firm voice had her attention. His reputation preceded him, but although she feared the name Moroni LaFey she may never get the opportunity to ask these questions again. After all what else was being hid from her?

"I can ask anything I want?" Sariah's voice was that of a skeptical teenage girl.

"This is your chance, my dear," Moroni answered calmly. Jeremiah on the other hand sat nervously behind his desk obviously in fear of Sariah knowing the truth about her family.

"Do you work for the cartels in Mexico?"

"No, I do not. I do, however, conduct some business with them. It keeps our colony safe and prosperous."

"But don't the brethren object to it?" the question led to a chuckle from Moroni and a wry smile from Jeremiah.

"Sariah, my dear...sometimes the brethren are more interested in the bottom line than spiritual salvation. I guess what I'm trying to say is, they may disapprove of the means, but they have never turned away the money."

"What is your business with the cartels?"

"Guns and grain mostly. But they purchase our citrus fruit and cattle as well. They don't have the connections in the states that we do."

"How do you get the guns to them?"

"I'm afraid that is one question I cannot answer. But suffice it to say that your uncle has far more connections in the States that it may seem."

"Are you a prophet?" That question really drew laughter from Jeremiah and Moroni. Sariah thought it a valid question since she was raised to revere such men. Men who claimed they actually walked with God and received revelation directly from Jesus Christ. Her father and uncle's reaction was not faith promoting.

"I am not a prophet, my sweet niece, but I do consider myself a guardian of the faith. Many other do so as well, but I have never see God or even an angel. I have just been blessed with clarity of mind and purpose."

"What's a 'guardian'?"

"Someone who is able to keep the brethren straight."

"But isn't that sacrilegious?"

"Is it?" Moroni sat back in his chair.

"Have you killed before?" Sariah thought this would be another question that Moroni would artfully dodge, but she was shocked at his answer.

"Of course, it's part of my calling," Moroni answered with literally no shake or nerves in his voice. "Orin Josephs had to die. His son Nephi took his place. Orin was no prophet of God. He was a snake and a money launderer. There have been others, but you get the gist."

"This is blowing my mind!" Sariah just pondered what she had just heard. The life she led was no more and even her father could see it. It was finances that ruled everything. Maybe her religion was not as much about serving God as much as it was about preserving itself; *but what about truth?* It seemed that the brethren needed men like her father and uncle far more than her father and uncle needed them. It was enough to not only question your theology, but your lifestyle and heritage as well. *What was all this for?*

"Do you have any other questions, Sweetheart?"

"Just one," Sariah replied with a serious voice. "Why don't the cartels ever come after you?"

"Pardon?" Moroni was a bit taken back by the question and Sariah could see it. But she could also see that he knew exactly what Sariah was asking.

"I mean, all of the colonies were forced out by revolutionaries and drug lords. But now it's only the LaFeys and the LeBarons. Now the LaBarons are so isolated and insignificant I can understand why the cartels would leave them alone…"

"The LeBarons are pimps and pay the cartels off," Moroni interrupted.

"How did Colonia LaFey survive and prosper then?"

"Like I said, we provide a service…"

"I don't want the bullshit answer, Uncle Moroni! The truth!" Both Moroni and Jeremiah's eyes widened, and sly grins crossed their collective faces.

"Have you ever heard the name Juan Carlos Basilla?" Moroni smiled as mentioned the name.

"Um…it sounds familiar, but I really can't place it."

"He was the founder of the Negras, the most brutal drug lord Mexico had seen," Moroni replied. Sariah recalled hearing stories about this man. His name was infamous in the states. Men like Basilla struck a mysterious fear in most Americans. It was partly for fear of living in such a violent atmosphere and partly because an entirely different world lay just across a meager fence line and whether or not the American Public liked it or not, these men were woven into their current society.

"Okay, but like he died a long time ago, right?"

Moroni seemed oblivious to the girl's reply and kept telling the dark story. "He had the most beautiful green garden in front of his villa as I had ever seen. He grew all sorts of beautiful fruits and vegetables there. It was his pride," Moroni stared out of the window as if memories were streaming in his mind and the accompanying emotions followed. "When the Negras were formed, Basilla vowed to either chase our people out of Mexico, or simply kill us all. Our land was quite desirable to them, you see. But to simply leave Mexico was out of the question. Our people survived the Revolution and every cartel before and we were not going to bow to this man."

"But the Negras are ruthless…"

"Quite so, so I went with your uncle Hyrum to speak with this man. Jeremiah was too little, but really wanted to tag along. Your Grandpa was simply too sick. *Senor Basilla*, to his credit, allowed us inside of his hacienda and treated very cordial. Unfortunately, *Senor Basilla* felt that our beliefs were an abomination to God and insisted we leave at once. I explained we would leave his place, but not Mexico. He promised that we would regret the decision."

Sariah was enthralled with the story, as if it were a school girl listening to her first fairy tale. "What happened then?"

"A few nights later, we found Brother Nixon and his wives dead in their beds, throats slashed ear to ear. They knew of our temple ceremonies and were mocking us. All of their children were taken. We eventually found each of the children scattered amongst the fields. There were sixteen in all," Moroni's eyes welled with tears. "I remember little Racheal Nixon used to sit on my lap at church. I used to give her mints from my pocket. I found her little body mangled in a trash can."

Sariah could hardly contain hardly contain her emotions as well, but she needed to hear more of the story.

"After we buried Racheal, a few days later, me and your uncles paid Senor Basilla a visit…"

"What happened?!" Sariah practically shouted.

"Easy now my Dear," Moroni smiled. "We took positions on the ridges surrounding the compound. Your Dad was there. Each of the guards was executed by gunfire. When the shooting started, more of them started coming out of the hacienda and each of them cut down. While the shootout was going on I led some brothers into the house where we killed the rest of the guards." While the story was being told, Jeremiah laid a full glass of scotch before Moroni. Sariah was too involved in the story to acknowledge her father and uncle's obvious hypocrisy. Moroni's pull on the drink was a good indication that he had some experience drinking. "We took *Senor Basilla* and his family of course," He stared down at the floor, not as a guilty man, but someone with fierce resolve and belief.

"So what happened to *Senor Basilla?*"

"He was impaled alive in front of the compound. He lived a couple of hours. As members of the Negras came to get him, we continued to cut them down with long range fire from the hills."

"What about the family?"

"Their heads were put on steaks surrounding the compound and their bodies shredded and used as mulch for that beautiful garden," Moroni smiled, which didn't sit well with Sariah. "It was as red as the sunset."

"I don't understand the brutality," Sariah managed to get out now in full tears. "I don't understand…"

"Yes dear, but I assure you the Negras do," Moroni responded coldly. "That garden never looked so beautiful," Moroni paused again. "Well, I was then contacted by Basilla's second in command, *Senor Martinez*. A peace treaty, if you will, was made. It was *Senor Martinez* who realized that an alliance with us could be far more profitable than a war. As it turns out, the Negras and their associates are our chief customers of our guns and grain. They are now run by Martinez's nephew who they call '*El Patron*'."

Sariah could hardly process what she heard and remained silent for several awkward moments while her new-found uncle and father drank forbidden drinks. She sat and looked at the two men in front of her and realized she had a choice to make. Either she condemned these men as killers and hypocrites or she embraced them as men willing to take all necessary action to protect their family and faith. As she grew older, the lines between faithful and psychotic grew even dimmer. History was written by the winners and the definition of greatness was often skewed by those who told the story and the number of listeners that subscribed to it. But often the other side had a story as well and, if given the right context, was just as valid with its own listeners. It wasn't that she had nothing to say concerning the matter, she just couldn't.

"Are you okay, Sweetheart?"

Sariah took a moment to truly think about the question and all of its implications, but the answer was decisive and surprisingly simple. "Yes Daddy, I'm okay."

"Your Father seems to think you have some concerns over Bishop Johnson," Moroni said with a smile. "I would very much like to hear them."

CHAPTER ELEVEN

The Turn

"I'm glad you came to me first, Carlos," Tio Muniz said softly. Carlos sat across the same booth where Muniz sexually assaulted and humiliated him. But this time there was no audience and no Marisella to facilitate anything. "It is good to come together when there is a problem, *no?*"

"Absolutely, Tio," He humbly responded. Just because he was alone with Muniz didn't make Carlos feel any less danger. The fact was that a problem arose from his handling of a situation, and the Negras despised problems. "Caldwell called me and told me he killed one of your guys. I'm sorry, Tio. How can I fix this?"

Muniz giggled a little bit and smiled. Carlos felt a little more at ease. "I must apologize to you, Carlos." Muniz's statement hit Carlos like a ton of bricks, he could hardly believe a man with such an ego could say such a thing. "I am not an unreasonable man. I sent that *cabron* to solve both our problems. He fucking made it worse! *Chinga!*" Tio spouted the profanity with vitriol. "I cannot hold you responsible for my mistake, but I must fix this myself."

"Word is he's in Maverick County Jail. He's gonna talk to the cops...I fucked up, Tio."

"Why Carlos...how you say...kick a dead horse? Yes, you fucked up, but you paid for it, yes?" It was at this point that Carlos was undecided whether or not to answer Muniz. The memories of being brutalized were so prevalent in his mind that he could never forget, but Muniz was a man capable of unspeakable horror. There were stories of his exploits in killing rivals. Carlos decided to agree with Muniz and simply nodded his head looking squarely at the floor. "Then we don't need to revisit such nonsense. Let us simply solve the problem," Muniz was almost jovial, which didn't necessarily make Carlos feel better.

"But how, *Tio?* He may have already ratted us out."

"S*i*, but what can he say? He can drop our names, but he's a murderer, *entiendes?* Let him ramble."

"But how do we shut him up?

"That's already been taken care of. Now stop worrying Carlos," Muniz grinned. The smile set Carlos at ease. At least he wouldn't die tonight. As for Caldwell, even Carlos knew his days were numbered. "But I need to remind you of something, my friend."

"Of course, Tio," Carlos's swallowed and felt his stomach drop as if he were on a roller coaster.

"Do not mistake my kindness today as a pass on your responsibilities," Tio replied coldly. "Some of my associates are very displeased with you and your boss and they are ready to take action."

"Tio, I promise I can fix this, we've got a plan," Carlos had become accustom to pleading at this point and it seemed Muniz was used to being pled to.

"You know exactly what needs to happen, Carlos," Tio's evil grin returned. "I suggest you hurry, my associates have many virtues, but patience is not one."

"I understand."

"Go and wait for my call. I will send instructions for a pick up to satisfy my clients, *entiendes?*" Tio smiled. "Tell your boss, this one's on me."

"Si, Tio."

*

It only took a phone call to an old friend who happened to be a deputy at the Maverick County Jail to secure an interview with Caldwell. Flynt just happened to have the connections to make it happen quickly. When they arrived at the jail, their room was set up with three chairs and no audio/video recording equipment, this interview would be off the record. This wasn't the official interview standard among criminal cases. This was a special case and the most vital thing that Caldwell could provide was not a confession, but information. As the Rangers arrived, Caldwell sat in a chair, staring at the bland walls smugly while his orange jumpsuit would provide the only color in the room. A good investigator can generally tell how difficult a subject will be before any word is uttered; Kidd could tell by Trey Caldwell's demeanor that this would be a long interview. Even in a jumpsuit, sitting on a steel chair on a concrete floor, Caldwell's arrogance showed through. He was comfortable with incarceration and it showed, but for the investigator, it meant that further incarceration wasn't a threat so alternative strategies had to be employed. In essence, Caldwell was a man at home behind bars.

"I wasn't expecting the Rangers, I asked for the U.S. Marshals," Caldwell said smugly as he sat back in the metal seat, still handcuffed with his hands out front.

"Well, we all can't get what we want, now can we? Besides, it's too damn close to the weekend for any Fed to give a shit," Flynt replied.

"Well, looks like you all ain't getting shit from me…"

"Oh I think we will," Flynt said calmly and smiled big. "Hey look at me a second…you got something on your face." Flynt leaned in to his face, appearing to examine the man's features intently. He continued to look at Caldwell face.

"What is it?" Caldwell replied with concern. He barely got the words out of his mouth when Flynt's crushing right fist connected squarely with his nose. Caldwell's head snapped back violently causing his plastic chair to fall backwards sending Caldwell to the ground with a thud. The blood began to poor out of the prisoner's nose onto the freshly mopped concrete. On cue, Kidd grabbed the prisoner, picked him and the chair up off the floor. Caldwell's hands were covering his nose and trying to stop the bleeding, which resembled a red stream at this point.

"What the fuck!" Caldwell screamed at the top of his lungs. "You motherfuckers can't do this!" He turned and looked at Kidd. "You just gonna sit there and watch?!"

"No…I laughed at first," Kidd smiled.

"Then get that spic guard in here!" Caldwell snarled. Kidd

smiled and opened the door revealing Deputy Romero standing directly outside the door. Caldwell made eye contact with the deputy, "These motherfuckers are beating me!" pleading with the man to intervene.

"No entiendo, cabron," Romero smiled and politely closed the door again. Kidd could see the mounting frustration in the man's eyes. He thought he was under control and could manipulate the system, but he had never met Richard Flynt.

"Oh now relax Trey," Flynt said in a calming manner as he put rubber gloved on his hands and took two wooden handled, sterile swabs from his coat pocket. He covered the cotton tips with distilled water from a small vial also contained in his pocket. He squatted to the floor and rubbed the swabs in the various drops of Caldwell's blood. He then set them inside cardboard swab boxes and set them on the small table to dry. "Ain't you never heard of a Texas Search Warrant?"

"A what?!"

"A Texas Search Warrant…Stupid," Kidd casually added sitting back in his chair carefully watching the prisoner.

"That's some bullshit!"

"Well it's a reality, son. Now if I were you, I'd start talking."

"I still ain't got no deal."

Kidd listened to the arrogance of this man and could no longer hold his contempt. He spent his entire law enforcement career listening to criminals who commit the most heinous crimes then expect the system to accommodate them when they are caught. It was no wonder other criminals hate snitches. "Listen here, Adolf, you got one choice. We are your only hope right now."

"I don't follow," Caldwell replied.

"You see, Trey, the man you killed was a *Negras*. That means they ain't gonna quit till you're dead, son," Flynt added. It was so simple to for everyone to realize the danger Caldwell was in. Caldwell's time on earth was limited. Kidd even doubted the department and all of their resources could save him. So why couldn't this man face reality.

"I got my brothers in here. Ain't no Mexican gonna get near me."

Flynt chuckled, "I don't know whether you're just a dumbass or really believe the shit coming out of your mouth. Unless I'm very wrong, your 'brothers' have already sold you down the river. You see, Trey, green has a hell of a lot more loyalty than white." Caldwell remained defiant, but Flynt's mention of money seemed to shake the prisoner a bit. He uncomfortable sat back in his chair and exhaled, wanting to portray an image of toughness, but Kidd could see that he was irked. Even he had to know that the Negras could buy the entire Aryan Brotherhood.

"You guys don't know my brothers…"

"Wrong you ignorant, Nazi son of a bitch, I know you better than you know yourself. I wiped my ass with you peckerwoods for fifteen plus in Nacogdoches. I couldn't get ahead, ya'all were so damn active. I've heard all of your bullshit and seen all ya'all got to offer and I ain't impressed. So, let this sink in…your little prison club ain't shit compared to the Negras, and your 'brothers' know it. They can wipe ya'all out in a few strokes. So, you got a few minutes to tell us what we need to hear. Cause when we're gone, you're going back to general pop."

"That's bullshit, I need to be in confinement till this thing blows over…"

"You got shit between your ears? Did you not hear a goddamn thing that was just said? This thing ain't blowing over. We are all you got," Kidd reaffirmed.

"Okay, okay!" Caldwell said almost pleading as he lifted his defined, sleeved arms over his head and covered his face with his hands. "All I know is that his name is Carlos. I used to meet him at the hot dog place in town."

"Oh wow, a fucking cartel guy named, 'Carlos.' I'm good, what about you Sarge?" Kidd snapped sarcastically looking at his senior partner.

"He's not in the cartel, he's their fucking dupe. He's a bitch, he takes orders."

"From who?"

"I don't know! I used to meet him at the hot dog place in town."

"You better give us more than that."

"Like the girls in the car, Trey," Flynt interrupted. Caldwell turned silent and looked at the ceiling and exhaled.

"I need a deal."

"Those girls didn't deserve that."

"Please, I will talk, but I need the deal."

"Carlos and a hot dog stand ain't gonna get nobody a deal."

"I didn't mean it to go down like that," Caldwell said in a quiet, intense voice causing both Rangers to nearly come out of their seats.

"Listen to me Trey, you need to tell me everything now," It was Flynt who appeared to be interested now. "I mean everything!"

"I'm gonna take my chance with my brothers. I ain't saying anymore till I get immunity."

*

She was so thankful her parents had WiFi in the house. Many families in the sect thought the internet was a gateway to Satan's invasion in their very lives. Sariah could see their point. After all, any type of filth that you could conceive could be found there. But there was so much more that it had to offer. So, Sariah decided to look for her mysterious car and license plate online. As it turned out, it took only ten minutes of searching and the care, license plate, and owner were located.

The registration returned to Elizida Garcia, 1624 Washington St., Eagle Pass, Texas. It was the same area where she followed the two Hispanic men, so she knew she had the right vehicle and place. The only question she had was why those men were around the Johnson Compound? Did they have anything to do with her friend's disappearance, or maybe her sister's? It was a question that would have to be answered. Her father and uncle made her promise to not to take any action herself and to be careful of Bishop Johnson. She was about to deliberately disobey them. Maybe she was a LaFey after all?

*

"You ain't going back to your cell until you tell us a little more, Trey," Kidd was getting tired of this racist bastard stalling. The bodies of his victims lay dead and burned and this disgrace for a human wanted immunity. "Besides, the more time you're in your cell the better chance the *Negras* have to get you."

"I'll do some time, but I…"

"You're goddamn right you'll do some time!"

"Easy, easy, now," Flynt said in a calming tone. "My partner is right, son. When you kill little girls in Texas ain't no DA in any county going to give immunity. Best you can hope for is a plea. But you won't even get that until I hear some talk outta you."

"Look, I know he's got some new guy, a couple of new spics named Puco or Chuco and Juan, I think. They live down on Washington Street. Those are Carlos's guys."

"So, what's Carlos' last name?"

"Shit, I really don't know. But if you find those guys, they'll lead you to him."

"Why are you protecting this Carlos guy?"

"I'm not protecting him!" Caldwell snapped back. "That son of a bitch sent the Negras after me and it was his fault them girls had to die. I never wanted no part of them girls, I just wanted to move dope. Then that bastard makes me move girls for those fucking perverts! I hope the bastard dies! I would kill him myself if I could…"

"Wo, wo, why'd those girls need to die?" Kidd interrupted Caldwell's rant. It didn't bother Kidd or Flynt that the Negras had a beef with this man. The bloodshed over drugs and money was so common that not even your typical, privileged American even batted an eyelash when it was mentioned. Even cops and the justice system won't pursue narcotics related deaths as hard. It is human nature to look at a tragedy and condemn the victim for bad choices, in fact it's easy. But when the victims are children, especially young girls, there were no obstacles for swift and harsh justice, especially in Texas.

"They just had to…I saved them."

CHAPTER TWELVE

The Alliance

"So, we're looking for a Chuco and Juan that lives down in this neighborhood?" Kidd was obviously being sarcastic given that the neighborhood was all Hispanic. He also enjoyed getting under the skin of his senior partner. With enough goading, Kidd could always get Flynt to flare up.

"I'll give you the Juan, dumbass, but how many goddamn Chucos can there be?" Flynt said rolling his eyes as he drove the Crown Vic through the neighborhood. Though they were anxious to get something done, often times when you enter an investigation blind, it takes time to develop any material relevant to the investigation. So, they essentially were riding blind not even knowing if Chuco and Juan even existed. As they rolled down the street, a smaller, red sedan with a noticeably teenaged white girl driving passed them grabbing Kidd's attention. This was the type of thing that grabbed a cop's attention, glimpses of things out of place. It wasn't profiling, it was observing things that didn't fit. That was a concept that civilians just could not grasp, but cops could.

"You see that?" Kidd's head snapped as he watched the vehicle drive by slowly registering the license plate. He immediately called DPS Headquarters to run the plate through NCIC.

"Sure as hell did," Flynt replied whipping the Crown Vic into a stealthy u-turn. Flynt accelerated so they could get within following distance to the vehicle, yet not crowd the car and make the driver suspicious. This was a delicate skill that sometimes worked and sometimes failed, depending on the alertness of the person being followed. "Pretty young girl in this area?"

"Don't lie, you meant White girl in an all Mexican neighborhood, right?" Kidd smirked. He couldn't foresee the day when the whole race issue could be removed from police work as a whole. Racism was the new McCarthyism, cops tried in vain to avoid the stigma of being labeled racist. But it was the obvious elephant in the room when it came to policing; people are different shades and colors. They also tend to live among other people with similar shades and colors. In reality, people live more to a comfort standard than to a diverse one, but that was society's cross to bear. In this case, this girl did not belong in this neighborhood and the one thing that shows up rarely in police work is coincidence.

"Goddamn, you young ones are gonna kill this profession with you your political correctness."

"Well, I ain't exactly young, and you'll never guess who that car returns to?" Kidd advised his partner regarding the information received back from headquarters.

"Who's that?"

"Jeremiah Larsen."

"Guess we need to practice our traffic stops."

*

Sariah drove the neighborhood over and over, but she couldn't find the car or the two men. It was a shady neighborhood, she thought. Her upbringing in a sheltered, rural environment mad it difficult to relate to city folks. That coupled with the brethren's teaching that cities are nothing more that breeding grounds for evil made her doubly anxious as she drove the streets. It wasn't until the dark blue Crown Vic, obviously police, approached in her rear-view mirror that her mind quickly snapped back into the moment.

Shit, I wasn't speeding, she thought as she glanced at her speedometer and the road slowly tightening her grip on the steering wheel. She still didn't trust law enforcement and why should she? The brethren talk about them being puppets for an oppressive government under direct control of Satan. Even though the two sects hated one another, the brethren preached that the cops made up lies about Warren Jeffs and the Fundamentalists and it was only a matter of time before the Inspired Church was under attack. It was true that Sariah hated her religion, but she didn't want to see her people suffer. That was the only reason she hadn't run away yet. She did acknowledge to herself that Marshal Lansford seemed like an honorable man, but she couldn't take chances on the rest of them. Her only choice was to keep quiet and say nothing; something she was taught to do from birth.

Sariah watched as the grill lights from the Ford activated and the LED red and blues blinded her rear-view mirrors even before dusk. She pulled to the side of the road and calmly reached into her purse to get her license and her glove box to retrieve her insurance information eyeballing her cellular phone. Does she call her father or uncle? If she did, she would have to explain why she was in the area and following this lead, both explanations would land her in a world of shit, she thought. She looked in the rear view mirror expecting a uniform traffic cop from Eagle Pass. She knew they drove around in plain police cars, with no light bars, trying to be stealthier. But the two men that emerged were Texas Rangers. *Shit!* Sariah's pulse just quickened. The Rangers were especially feared by Texas polygamist sects. They single handedly took down the priesthood leaders at the Yearning-For-Zion Ranch, and now they were stopping her on the street. They weren't traffic cops, so what the hell did they want? She kept staring at the phone and her hand inched ever so slowly to call for help, but she stopped. She got herself into the mess and she would get herself out of it. She said a quick prayer which seemed a bit hypocritical, even for her, and rolled the window down.

An older, tall dark, and somewhat handsome, considering his age, man leaned closer to her window obviously to speak. He was dressed extremely nice and she couldn't help but notice the stainless steel .45 ACP at his hip. "Excuse me ma'am, my name is Sergeant Flynt, and this here is Ranger Kidd from the Texas Rangers. Can we have a word with you?" The man smiled and had a very soothing voice, with an inviting Texas accent. His partner, a bigger, younger man stood silent at the passenger side of her vehicle. He looked a little more tactical. If she had to guess, he was the 'bad cop.'

"I'm sorry...was...was I speeding?" Sariah managed to smile in a flirty way, but it didn't seem to faze these men.

Almost as a natural response, she handed the Ranger her license and observed him looking it over intently.

"Well no ma'am, but we couldn't help but notice you in this neighborhood and wanted to see if you were okay," Flynt continued to smile at her making her even more nervous.

"I'm sorry…you want to know if I'm okay cause I'm driving in a neighborhood?"

"Well yes, you see we don't see many girls from the Inspired Church of Jesus Christ of Latter-day Saints in this neighborhood."

Her stomach sank when he said those words. She knew this had nothing to do with a traffic stop, they must have read her father's information from the registration. "Well…my aunt lives right over there," *Shit! He's gonna see right through that one*, she thought. She looked into his eyes and could tell he was not moved at all.

"Oh, really…what's her name?"

Sariah looked down at her feet. *This is pointless*, she thought. She looked up at the tall Ranger and smiled, "I don't have an aunt here in this neighborhood. What do you want from me?" Her tone was serious and almost angry.

"Sariah, we just want to talk. That is all, I promise."

The Ranger using her first name really threw her for a second, but she quickly snapped back into reality and reality was, the Rangers were the enemy. "I really have nothing to say and I don't feel comfortable talking with you all. So, if I haven't broken any law, I'm going to be on my way."

"Oh, but you did break the law, Sariah," she turned her head and observed Ranger Kidd with his head up to her passenger window, "Didn't look like ya came to a complete stop back at the sign."

"Are you serious?"

"Oh, hell yes we're serious! What if a kid were to be walking across the street when you so recklessly barreled through that intersection," Flynt added. Sariah wasn't sure what was going on, but something gnawed at her and she began to slowly realize these Rangers weren't taking 'no' for an answer.

"Well what does that mean?' She reluctantly inquired.

"Means you're going with us to Jail," Kidd stated coldly with a seeming dark purpose. He stared at Sariah, smiled and tipped his hat. "Now get out of the car...slowly."

*

Texas Don looked over his work and smiled. He laughed at the notion that 'real' writers couldn't stoop to blogging as a means for news and commentary. Who were they kidding, he thought as he finished the paragraph. It was no secret that newspapers were declining in sales and more people were turning to the internet and why wouldn't they? Even the big newspapers themselves had online sites though they clung to the dead trees as tightly as possible. How ironic that the very industry that prides itself on being on the cutting edge of society clings to a technology credited to Ancient Egypt. He was the progressive. It would be him that would expose the world to the corrupt, leftists that have spread throughout even his remote corner of Texas. The once proud, red Lone Star State that stood as a beacon for conservative ideals was now subject to the whims of the progressives that wanted government control of everything. Thank God for the rural counties, he thought as he uploaded the stats and figures he received from his anonymous source at the city.

The city worker was an underpaid, often overlooked segment of society, but they were a wealth of information, especially when it comes to city finances. Don knew the politicians couldn't wipe their own ass without assistance and they had to use city workers to do their deeds. He also knew that there wasn't a more resentful person of the politician's demands than the actual person carrying them out. On the one hand, politicians praised the hard work and dedication of the employee, but then would turn around and fire them at the whims of their finicky constituents. So, who better to double-cross a crook than a beat down, underpaid indentured servant?

Don smiled and waked to the kitchen. He opened the refrigerator door to an assortment of pre-packaged, processed foods and light beer. The latter was an attempt to show the doctor that he was in fact serious about losing weight, although he had no actual pounds or inches lost to show for it. He twisted the lid off of the bottle and lit a cigarette. He opened the kitchen window to let the smoke escape with little residual. He may be divorced and single, but he was no slob and took pride in his clean house. He took a few pulls and drags in quiet celebration.

Don walked back to his computer, still running, and decided to plug his cellular phone into the computer. Yes, it was a bit of paranoia, he thought, but in today's information society you could never have too many sources. If by some chance his computers were seized by a corrupt government, he would have a backup. After all, the law works for the politicians and if the right one orders a chief of police to take down a disruptive citizen, that chief will do it. His subordinates will follow orders blindly because they have families to take care of, this was simply reality. But if he goes down, he'll take a few with him. He felt pretty smart and even invincible when the doorbell rang snapping him back into the moment. He took a few more drinks before casually gliding towards the door in a triumphant manner, putting his cellular phone in his pocket. A smile even graced his face, as he flung the door opened not at all curious as to whom it could be.

The burn and sting in his chest caused his knees to buckle under him, but he never felt them hit the ground and never heard the shot. He stared straight ahead hoping to see his attacker, but his eyesight slowly drifted into a snowy haze. He did see a figure disappear into the darkness and he was powerless to even protest. The thud of his face to the bare floor was heard, but the burning of his wounds was now coupled with his shortness of breath. He was able to reach into his pocket and get his cellular phone. With agonal breathing, he was able to scan his contacts and attach the files he just loaded. With his last bit of strength, his thumb pressed the touch screen 'send' button. On that quiet Texas night, Don's body fell numb as his life slipped away.

*

"I don't know what you guys want from me?" Sariah's eyes

were annoyed, but began to moisten as she found herself in the uncomfortable chair in that interview room at Eagle Pass PD. Kidd could see she did not want to be there, but there was no option but to question her. There are no such things as coincidences in police work, only facts that deserve to be looked into and other facts that deserved to be looked into even more. The use of the interview room was courtesy of Detective Hamilton, Eagle Pass PD. Kidd met him at the mass grave. Hamilton seemed sharp and intuitive with a healthy distrust for brass, much like Kidd and his partner. Hamilton told the two Rangers that if they ever needed anything, to call. In law enforcement, those words are seldom uttered if the person saying them is not sincere. It is an unofficial rule that you help your fellow officers above yourself.

"We just want you to talk to us, Sariah. We know you got something to say. We need your trust," Kidd pled with the teenager and was a bit dismayed when she sighed and gave a sarcastic chuckle.

"You think I'm gonna trust the Texas Department of Public Safety?" She asked in an almost defiant tone. "We all know what you did to the Fundamentalist Church, and we know we have a target on our back!" Kidd could see her point about the distrust for police, so he decided to take the conversation in a different direction.

"By 'we' you mean the Inspired Church of Jesus Christ of Latter-day Saints?" Kidd asked.

"Yes…the others call us 'the Inspireds' but I really don't know why, there's nothing inspired about us really," Sariah answered in a melancholy voice. Kidd was shocked at her answer. She just got defending the church now her tone took a sudden turn. It was time to steer the interview to keep her talking.

"Now why would you say your church isn't inspired, Sariah?" The secret to an interview is to keep someone talking. It is an art, and one that very few law enforcement officers can master.

"Let's cut the bullshit, I know you know my family, well…we are polygamists. That's why I'm here!"

"Yes, we know your family practices 'the principle,' but that isn't why you're here. Besides, we don't care about polygamy, we chase murderers, rapists, and all kinds of scum. What someone does in the privacy of their homes don't bother us," Kidd smiled. Actually, the thought of polygamy disgusted him, but he had to keep Sariah talking. He had to diffuse her anger and convince her that he and his partner actually wanted and needed her help. But it was also about convincing her that the Rangers could help her. When you are born and raised in a counter culture that feared authorities and distrusted all governmental power, the word of any official is useless. Kidd knew this girl; she was no different than all the other disaffected children living in abusive communities that still choose to defend their own abuse. The trick for Kidd was getting her to open up. To do that, she had to feel welcome in the Rangers presence. Strangely it wasn't so hard to like Sariah. Both men could see this young woman was a fighter.

Sariah laughed as she looked at the floor, "Come on Ranger Kidd…everybody hates polygamy, including half the people who practice it!"

"Tell us why you hate it so bad, Sariah?" Flynt joined the conversation from across the room in the corner. "What's it like to live like that?"

The question struck a nerve in the young lady. Sariah's sarcastic laugh turned to a look of seriousness and concern. It was as if she was told horrible news. "I wake up every day dreading what God may say," her eyes began to glaze; Kidd knew they may be having a breakthrough with her. "A few months ago, Bishop Johnson told me that God commanded that he take me for a wife." Sariah could hardly choke out the words and looked down to the floor in shame and embarrassment. Her fingers and body were twitching so hard, she gave the appearance of a Tourette's patient. She appeared almost ill, with a look of disgust saved for only the most extreme occasion.

"What did you say?" Kidd asked the young girl in a genuine concerned voice.

"I didn't say yes…and I didn't say no," The tears were now beginning to stream. She put her face in her hands only removing them to accept the tissue handed to her by Flynt. Sariah suddenly snapped her head up and growled with a voice of anger, "I couldn't just tell him to fuck off because this fucking religion is everything to our family!" She stared at the Rangers alternating her angered glances between both men. "All I could do was stall him until I could figure a way out of this."

"You figure a way?"

"Not a clue."

"What about your folks? What do they think?" Kidd inquired.

"They never argue with God, even though I'm pretty sure Dad hates Bishop Johnson."

"Wait, now I'm confused," Flynt blurted out. "So, your Dad don't like Johnson, but he would still go along with him because he thinks he speaks for God?"

"Exactly," Sariah exclaimed. "How fucked up is that?"

"Young lady…normally I'd scold you for using such language, but you're absolutely right…that is fucked up."

"What are you going to do?" Kidd asked, now truly concerned.

"Keep stalling," she said wiping the tears from her eyes and sounding far more composed. The brightness from the daylight thru the window turned to night several hours ago. It was getting late. "Do I have to stay in jail?"

"No Sariah go home to your house tonight."

"I haven't been completely honest with you all either," Sariah's statement shocked both men beyond belief causing all attention to be placed on the young lady. Sariah pulled Marshal John Lansford's card from her oversized purse. She explained to the men in great detail that she believed something terrible happened to Amanda and Ruth, but she couldn't figure out what. She explained living on the compound with Bishop Johnson in order to investigate the matter. She told them about the wedding in Utah and how nobody could confirm anything. She explained herself in great detail down to why she was in that neighborhood attempting to locate two suspicious Hispanic males. She even handed the paper containing the license plate to Kidd who passed it to Flynt. Flynt immediately took out his phone and began checking the tag. Sariah opened up to the very men that just minutes before had no trust from her. Kidd couldn't figure out why she trusted the Rangers now? Perhaps she was she just desperate to find her friend and would accept any help she could find, even if it came from the Devil himself. After explaining her dilemma, she looked at the two men sitting across from her, "What should I do?" Sariah stared at the two Rangers for some type of guidance, seemingly pleading with her glance.

"Do you have any personal belongings of your friends?" Kidd asked the morbid question rather hoping Sariah didn't understand exactly what he was implying. It was a known fact that young ladies didn't live long if in fact what Sariah feared happened actually took place. Sariah reached into her purse and pulled out a paper lunch bag. The bag had 'Amanda' written in marker on the outside. Inside the bag was a hair brush complete with several follicles ripe for DNA analysis. "Damn, you're prepared."

"Marshal Lansford asked me to get this. Ranger Kidd…I may come from a bunch of crazy polygamists, but don't think I'm as naïve as they are," Sariah smirked sarcastically at the Ranger solidifying the fact that Kidd liked this spunky girl. She looked at Kidd and Flynt, the latter was still busy on the phone. "So, what now?"

"You let us look into this for you," Kidd replied matter of factly.

"I want to be a part of this!"

"You are a part of this."

"No, I want to help…"

"That's a fine idea," Flynt said butting into the circular argument of his partner. Both Kidd and Sariah looked at him in somewhat disbelief. "But for now, I want you to go home and not to Johnson's place."

"I can't just go home? Bishop Johnson will get suspicious."

"You're a big girl, but I don't trust that man, ya hear? Any man that takes a little girl for a bride ain't a man, which makes him dangerous and a bit nutty."

"I get it Ranger Flynt, but what will I tell my Dad?"

"The truth…and here is my card. I will welcome the phone call," Flynt smiled and escorted the young lady to the door. "Your vehicle is waiting right outside.

"When will I hear from you guys?"

"Soon," Flynt said hurrying the girl out the door. The two watched from a distance and Sariah walked to the front of the station escorted by a female detention officer.

"Well that was kind of sudden?" Kidd observed. "We were having a breakthrough there." Kidd saw that his partner was on the phone. His partner also had that concerned look that he learned to recognize so well. Flynt hung up the phone with a loud sigh.

"That was headquarters," Flynt replied.

"And?"

"Texas Don was shot through the chest…he's dead."

"What the…"

"Dan Gummit's keeping it quiet. He's not even planning a press release," Flynt stood up, staring at the corner of the room as if it were a window. "But what's weird is I just checked my email…"

"What the hell is so weird about that?"

"I got an email from Texas Don bout an hour ago."

"Let's get over there," Kidd exclaimed getting up from his chair hastily.

"We been cold trailing this whole thing," Flynt said in a serious tone.

"What do you mean?"

"Ever since we been here it's been smoke and mirrors." He was right, Kidd thought. Often times the investigation focuses on the 'who' and 'what', often making the 'why' irrelevant. But every so often, it is the 'why' that answers everything.

"What do you suggest?"

"Let's break a couple mirrors," Flynt took out his cellular phone and dialed.

"*Hello?*"

"Marshal John Lansford?"

"*Yes?*"

"I'm Sergeant Flynt with the Texas Rangers…it's about time we met, huh?"

CHAPTER THIRTEEN

The Course

"Orale," Carlos smiled, shaking Chuco and Juan's hands in tight grips accompanied by one armed hugs. It was a sign respect on the street. They went inside Carlos's tiny apartment and sat down on the couch. The apartment was scarcely decorated, due to the fact Carlos was never there, but it was neatly kept and comfortable for just him. "Drink?" It was less a question than an affirmation. Both men were handed a cold beer from the refrigerator.

"What did *Tio* say about that *pendejo?*" Chuco asked.

"They said they would take care of him. Said it was their problem, so they would fix it," Carlos replied. "He's in County, but not in general population..."

"You know the Fucker ratted you out!" Juan interrupted.

"Relax," Carlos smiled. "He don't know shit about us. He don't know me, my boss, you guys…nothing. The fuck's he gonna say? 'Hey, this cat named Carlos is a drug dealer'." Carlos smiled. He had to make the two men feel at ease, or it would affect their work. The truth was Carlos was terrified. He woke up to the single prayer that Tio Muniz was a man of honor and wouldn't kill him in an instant. Tio already brutalized him for fun to prove a point and Carlos was sure Tio was not above just killing him just because. It was the business he chose. Whatever the problems, you never passed it on to your employees, Carlos thought. If there were any actions to be taken, they would be taken against himself. Chuco and Juan should be safe, they were small time. He turned and smiled at his companions, "Don't worry, things are taken care of."

"So why are we here? What need to move?" Juan inquired. He was still the smart one, Carlos thought.

"We ain't out of the woods yet," Carlos smiled. "We gotta fix what the *Guerro* fucked up." Carlos could see that statement was not popular with his associates so it was time he became the salesman. "It's just one time…Tio will find a replacement."

"Fuck man, I don't like this sorta shit, man," Chuco complained. "This shit's bad."

"Tell me something I don't know motherfucker!" Carlos caught himself before he lost his temper. It was his ass on the line, not theirs. "Look…all I know is that we just need to pick up and drop them off. I was assured there was no rough stuff. They promised." Carlos was lying through his teeth, and he was fairly sure his associates knew it, but he had to say something.

"Seriously *ese?*" Juan smiled. "The Negras and no rough stuff? That's like trying to swim without getting wet."

"Yeah, Yeah, fuck you…but serious, let's just get this drop out of the way. I will make sure Tio will take this assignment from us and let us run the dope like we should."

"So where do we go get these girls?"

"Tio has it all planned out. He's gonna shoot me the coordinates in a few. I'll let you guys know."

*

The two Rangers walked to up to the tape at Texas Don's house. They were greeted by Eagle Pass Detective Hamilton. He was about forty, decent shape, trim with graying hair and extremely intense about his job, Kidd could see. Flynt seemed to know him pretty well. As his partner approached the Detective, Hamilton reached his hand out his hand to shake Flynt's, Kidd could see there was a micro SD card in his palm. As the two men shook, the card was transferred to Flynt's.

"Checked the phone, looks like old Don already sent you this," Hamilton smiled. "Just thought you'd need a hard copy."

"Chief Gummit may take exception?" Flynt smiled back.

"He's loving his press time on this mass grave…he won't get another fifteen minutes before he retires or is fired."

"Yep, that's Gummit alright. Who called it in?"

"One of those door to door perfume salesman, you know, the ones that got all the brand names for half the price? Anyway, old boy sees Don here and runs away cause he's on parole. I at

184

least got to respect he called it in…said he didn't hear the shot though."

"What happened here," Kidd interrupted politely. The two Rangers could see Don lying lifeless in the doorway. It was strange to think that they had just spoken with the man seemingly hours ago, and he was now dead. As a cop, Kidd faced several circumstances where witnesses or suspects were killed, and it was difficult to determine whether his involvement in the case contributed to the death, or was strictly coincidental. Either way, a man was dead that Kidd was involved with. It was reason enough for a good, corn mash Kentucky Bourbon.

"Looks like Don was having a beer, goes to get the door, opens it and takes one to the chest. Looks like maybe a nine mill…good shot placement."

"Witnesses?" Flynt asked.

"Nah, you know…we're in the burbs so unless you speed down the street nobody hears shit. We're lookin' though."

"Prints?" Kidd inquired.

"They're dusting the door bell, then we're going to swab for some touch DNA. Right now, the techs don't see any ridge detail for prints. We could get lucky on the touch DNA, but there's no way to tell. DPS is backed up six months on DNA, so we really need someone to come forward."

Fuck! Kidd thought. Hamilton was right, they needed some information. "What about video cameras in the neighborhood?"

"Glad you asked. About three houses west of here is a guy we popped for dope three years ago. He did a year stretch and when he came home, he put some cameras up. There was a white truck and a black car that drove by about the time we think Don got shot. The resolution sucks, but at least it's something."

"We'll keep our eyes open," Flynt smiled at Hamilton as he extended his hand again to shake. "Keep us informed?"

"You owe me a beer," Hamilton replied firmly taking Flynt's hand again. He gave a friendly nod to Kidd who returned the gesture. Kidd and Flynt walked back to the Ford slowly and very deep in thought. Flynt finally broke his silence.

"You want to get a head of this case?"

"I'd take any answer to this bitch right now?"

185

"Then let's go shopping," Flynt smiled as the two got into the Crown Vic.

*

Sariah walked into the barn on the Johnson Compound after she parked her outside. She needed a minute to gather her thoughts and courage before entering that house. It was like she had to motivate herself like an athlete getting ready for the game. Her stomach churned at the thought of running into Bishop Johnson, or even worse, those nasty offspring sons of his. She pulled a cigarette from her purse and lit it. A long drag followed with an even healthier exhale. She sat down on a hay bale and carefully leaned back. She learned to love the smell of barns, the horses, the hay, and the implements; there was nothing better. She and Amanda would play in that very barn for hours at a time as girls; a time before worrying about marriage and upsetting God. She stretched her legs out and continued to smoke.

"I cannot give you a temple recommend if you smoke, Sariah…you know that?"

Sariah's head snapped forward and the fleeting tranquility was gone at the sound of Bishop Johnson's voice. "B…Bishop Johnson?" Sariah managed the fakest of smiles while trying to sound sincere. She quickly put the cigarette out on the ground and tucked the butt into her purse. He stood erect, still in his black suit and white shirt from the day. The light behind him made him appear as a silhouette in the night, very dark and imposing.

"Kaye told me you just left all of a sudden and haven't been back," Johnson's smirk was even creepy. Sariah even wondered how he could keep all the names of the wives and kids straight. She was even more concerned that he was keeping track of her movements.

"There were some family things I had to take care of," Sariah knew she wasn't a very convincing liar and hoped Bishop Johnson would be none the wiser. But as he stared at her, she could see that he wasn't convinced of her story. "But I'm back now."

"Has your issue been taken care of?"

"Yes, Bishop, I was thinking about taking a trip to Utah, you know to visit." Bishop Johnson again smiled at her deviously.

"You know, if I didn't know any better, I'd say you were conversing with Gentiles?" Bishop smiled and sat down next to Sariah. The smell of his cologne brought Sariah to the verge of dry heaving, but she managed to maintain her composure. "Bishop, I…I don't know what you mean? I don't talk to Gentiles." Bishop Johnson stared at the young girl with such a blank look, Sariah could almost feel it. She chose to stare at his severely receded hairline rather than gaze into those maniacal eyes.

"The eyes of man are weak, Sariah, but the eyes of God see perfectly," Johnson's voice revealed a sinister tinge, the same tinge he got when he preached on Sundays. She knew he was about to expound some deep doctrine from the scriptures in order to coerce her into making a decision she didn't want to. But she lived in Bishop Johnson's world, the world of the Inspired Church, and the Inspireds did not value the opinion, or life for that matter, of a young woman. Whenever she looked into his eyes she felt degraded and minimalized. "I think you need to tell what you have been up to."

"Bishop, I swear…"

"Now careful child, you only swear when you're ready to die for something," Johnson was smiling now, but not in a jovial way. Sariah's skin was covered in goose-bumps because of fear. She could feel her legs start to shake as she struggled maintain her composure and not make this madman anymore suspicious. "It isn't enough that we not deceive our leaders, Sariah, we need to uphold them and open up to them completely."

Sariah closed her eyes in brief thought. The Bishop was on the warpath and she wasn't going to escape his query. He absolutely couldn't find out about her speaking with the U.S. Marshalls or Texas Rangers. She realized she should have listened to Ranger Kidd and just stayed away from the Johnson Compound, but she didn't. At best, finding out she was working with the law enforcement meant the Bishop would shut her father out of the religion all together, breaking his ever-faithful heart. At worst, it could mean her life. Although most the world thought of Mormons and Mormon Fundamentalist Sects as harmless, God-fearing people that focused all of their attention on their families. In reality, Mormon history was fraught with violence, misogyny, and racism. And though the majority of members don't reflect that seedy history, or even know about it, still it remained. Polygamists were even more dangerous. Sariah knew of several women who met horrible fates, all for disobeying the brethren. Sadly, it was at that moment that Sariah realized there was really only one way to diffuse Bishop Johnson's suspicion. "Bishop, how can I convince you I don't talk to the Gentiles?" Her voice became soft; her fear became determination and adrenaline.

"You can take your calling from God and your spirituality more seriously. You can start to heed to God's eternal plan of salvation," Bishop Johnson words were stern and direct. He was a man used to people following his counsel.

Sariah smiled and playfully tapped the Bishop on his arm, "I know about the plan, but I'm just a teenager, I want to have some fun." With her touch, the Bishop's tense posture turned more relaxed. He even managed to eek out a sly grin. "Can't I just be young for a little bit before I follow God's law?" She inched closer to the Bishop.

"Youth is no excuse for disobedience…"

"But it is for fun. Haven't you ever done anything crazy?"

"Of course, Sariah, but…" Bishop Johnson laughed and sat back, his stare even more relaxed. "Have you even thought about God's order for us to be married?"

Sariah's stomach dropped momentarily, but she was able to recover. "Of course, it's all I think about. Can't we just have a little fun before its official?" Sariah almost gasped as she reached over and put her hand on the Bishop's thigh and started rubbing lightly. "I mean, if God says I belong to you then that's that." She could hear the Bishop's breathing start to intensify and sweat beads form on his forehead. She rubbed higher and could feel he had an erection. She nearly heaved at the thought, but there was no turning back; this was the only way.

"Sariah, God would have it so that we're married…" Before Bishop could finish, Sariah lunged close to his face and grabbed his inner thigh.

"If God already gave me to you, then there is no problem, right?" she whispered as she got down on her knees in front of the older Bishop. His pants unzipped surprisingly easy. She reached into his underwear, known as garments, to expose his erect penis. As she went down to perform, tears began to form in her youthful eyes. Johnson couldn't see because his eyes were closed, and head was back resting against the wall of the barn. What made her the most upset was that performing such a disgusting act was easier than she had thought it would be. She had been brutalized all of her life in this sect, both mentally and socially, sexual abuse was simply a progression. She continued to pleasure the Bishop until he let off several grunts and finished. Sariah wiped her eyes and her mouth as she gazed up at the Bishop who was now smiling from ear to ear. Somehow, his pleasure at her expense began to sink into her mind and her thoughts began to grow dark with shame and rage. The next words out of the man's mouth really sickened Sariah.

"Now that's a good girl."

*

"This is getting outrageous," Kidd sighed laying his head on the passenger head rest of the Crown Vic. "This whole situation is spinning out of control and I'm just along for the fucking ride!"

Flynt smiled as he drove, as if he had information only privileged people could know. Kidd wondered how the man could smile with the death and confusion that surrounded them. What did his partner see that he couldn't? Texas Don's death was merely the icing on such a macabre and horrific set of murderous circumstances. It was as if South Texas was on fire, and there was no quenching it. "Had an old Ranger out in East Texas, went by D.R. Puckett," Flynt continued to drive, and his voice appeared unremarkable, as if it was a bore to explain himself to Kidd. "It was said he even palled around with Frank Hamer, but I don't know." Kidd was now interested because of his partner's mention of the legendary name of Frank Hamer. Hamer was the famous Texas Ranger that put an end to Clyde Barrow and Bonnie Parker's murderous rampage in the Thirties. Flynt's stories always had a point, Kidd thought, but it was getting to the point that was fun for Flynt, but hell on everyone else. "He had a case that finally did him in. Swore he'd solve it and then retire."

"I know there's a point somewhere...do I even ask when you can get to the goddamn thing?"

"Now calm down, I'm getting there...indulge me," Flynt again smiled at his obviously agitated partner. "They had a string of kid molestations and murders around Tyler. He told me that he'd never seen such brutality." Flynt suddenly turned serious as he discussed the particulars of the case. "He told me that Docs' told him they couldn't imagine the pain these girls experienced before their deaths and he even cried when he told me. Now you got to understand, Puckett was a man with five kills under his belt. I ain't never seen that man shaken up to that point."

"But that happens to every cop sooner or later..."

"Not to the old Rangers. They were something else," The senior partner corrected Kidd. "The final victim was a girl named Katrina Spicer. She was nine, beautiful blonde..." Flynt stopped talking momentarily to compose himself. No matter how hard the cop, child deaths were not easy. "Doc said she was so brutalized they left out two thirds of her internal injuries off of the autopsy report... mostly vaginal related."

"Jesus..."

"The rub to this little girl's death is that her mother's boyfriend, Johnny Ray West, was who Puckett thought was good for the murders. But it wasn't till Katrina's death until he could make the arrest."

"So how many were killed before her?"

"Six, I believe. But Puckett swore she was the primary victim and that the other girls were warm ups."

"He couldn't have known that..."

"Swears he did…but he couldn't save her. She had to die before he could get to the monster."

"So, what happened?"

"Puckett tracked Johnny Ray to Gun Barrel City and shot him dead… that was his sixth."

"So, Texas Don…what is he?"

"A necessary tragedy and our first break," Flynt responded answering his ringing cell phone seamlessly by driving. His face changed, but Kidd could not hear the other side of the conversation. Flynt slowed the vehicle down and made a u-turn and drove toward Highway 131.

"Where are we going?"

"Maverick County Jail."

"Can I ask why?"

"The second break."

CHAPTER FOURTEEN

Dish Served Cold

Caldwell was brought into the interview room again and sat down in the same plastic chair. He smiled as smugly as their first interview as he leaned back in his seat. He stretched his legs out prominently featuring the orange rubber flip flops issued by the jail. Flynt and Kidd were standing as the grand entrance commenced. "I didn't think I'd see ya'all so soon." Kidd walked with a distinct purpose, across the room over to the seated prisoner. Caldwell grinned as Kidd approached. Kidd bent his knees, drew back, and punched the man square between the nose and mouth. Caldwell's head snapped back and traces of blood spatter could be seen with the naked eye. Caldwell again found himself on the cold, concrete floor of that room. "Fuck!!!" Caldwell yelled as he staggered to pick himself up. "What the fuck was that...another Texas Search Warrant?!"

"No," Kidd smiled from ear to ear. "Just felt like it."

"You mother fuckers..."

"Shut your goddamn mouth for a second," Flynt strategically interrupted Caldwell. "Let's talk about your phone privileges, Trey."

"My phone what?"

"Privileges ya dumbass," Kidd added.

"You know they record all of your phone calls, right?" Flynt thought he was asking a rhetorical question, but he apparently underestimated Caldwell.

"I got fucking rights!"

"You're in jail...wow, you really are a dumbass!" Kidd smiled.

"We want to know about this call," Flynt took out his cellular phone and pressed play on an mp3 file:

Caldwell: How is she?

Unknown woman: She's weak, she needs help.

Caldwell: You can't take her anywhere! Just get her some fucking food.

Unknown woman: With what fucking money! I gotta get the fuck outta this shitty motel…

Flynt pressed stop on the phone. "First of all…who is she?"

"I don't have to tell…"

"I was afraid you'd say that, so in my hand is your transfer to McAllen."

"McAllen?"

"Yep, McAllen…that's Gulf Cartel territory or 'Golfos' if you will. Hey partner, who are the Golfos affiliated with?" Flynt asked with extreme sarcasm.

"Why that would be the Negras, Sergeant Flynt," Kidd smiled and looked at Caldwell who attempted to look stoic but was failing miserably. Caldwell knew the alliance between the two organizations. "Damn, I bet they could just shank you in front of the warden in that rat hole."

"Shit they may eat him while they're at it," Flynt said causing him and Kidd to laugh again. Caldwell was squirming in his chair. "You've got only one choice to even have any hope to live."

It was Caldwell's turn to laugh, but it was chuckles of joy, "You all think I'm any safer here?"

"I actually do. Now I ain't saying they won't shank your ass here, but I know for a fact the cartels are better represented there. Now give us a name!" Flynt was extremely serious now and he had no time for this criminal. There was a young woman in need, that was hurt, scared, and this monster held that information in. It was inexcusable, he needed to talk.

"I'm scared…"

"You're fucking scared?!" Kidd was seeing red. "There's a fucking girl who needs help, Trey! Goddamnit for once in your pathetic life do the right thing!" Kidd's words must have hit some type of nerve in the hardened criminal. Or perhaps it was Caldwell's contemplation of his own mortality.

"Her name is Lena Davis," Caldwell said in a broken voice.

"She's a girl I fuck from Laredo."

"Where at?"

"I met her at the motel off of I-35…just past Webb."

"Where did you see her last?"

"That fucking same motel!" Caldwell's answer was only overshadowed by Flynt's sudden exit from the room to use the phone.

"Now listen to me Trey," Kidd moved in close to Caldwell in an effort to make him uncomfortable and remain on edge and it was obviously working. "You need to tell me exactly what went happened with those girls." Caldwell's face turned white as if he had seen a ghost. "Where did they come from?"

"Look, I get an address sent to me, GPS coordinates. I drive down to the location…"

"Where is the location?"

"It's just right off the road, near Laredo. I have no idea where these girls come from or who brought them there."

"What happened?"

"I made the pickup in the middle of the night, three girls. Carlos was there. The girls are knocked out and taped up… all that shit. I got em loaded in the car. But something wasn't right, man."

"What do you mean?"

"The whole thing was fucked up! There was heat I know it. They start to wake up, so I un-taped their mouths and told em if they screamed or did anything stupid, I'd kill them. There were two White girls and one Mexican, I take em' back to the motel." Caldwell glanced at the floor when he spoke about the girls. He was ashamed. He only looked up to glance at Kidd's reaction, and Kidd knew that Caldwell could never be led to believe he was ever being judgmental. People don't talk to judgmental people. That was rule number one for interrogators. "Anyway, the night I'm supposed to make the drop, I drive towards the border. This vehicle comes behind me, gets right on my ass…I'm thinking it's the fucking Taskforce."

"Why?"

"Late model Tahoe, middle of the night…who else could it be?"

Goddamn this guy was dumb. "Don't you think Chevy made more than one Tahoe?"

"They were driving like Feds, man!"

Kidd had no doubt Caldwell believed he was being followed. "Okay, you thought they were Feds, go on."

"So, I do a heat run to see what they're going to do, ya know," Caldwell started using his hands to describe the situation. "So, I dart down the dirt road, but the little blonde bitch gets squirmy. I tell her to calm down. I can hear her talk to the other one…they must be sisters or something. So, I stop the car and turn the lights off and checked if the Tahoe was following me…and then the bitch just ran!"

"Who ran?"

"The fucking blonde! She takes off running," Caldwell looked back down at the floor, this time with remorse so great Kidd could feel it. "I took out my gun and shot the two in the back seat…" Caldwell's head went to his knees and Kidd could see the drops of tears hit the floor in a very tight pattern. "They were fucking babies! Fuck Carlos for making me do that shit!"

Kidd let Caldwell vent and even encouraged it. He was so disgusted with his actions he had to put some of the blame for his employers, and maybe rightfully so. A good interviewer knows to give the interviewee an out, or a scapegoat to dissipate the guilt. Guilt can be a powerful tool for a confession, but it can also cause a silence due to fear. "What happened next, Trey?"

"I chased down the blonde, but she fought. I hit her pretty hard in the head…knocked her clean out."

"And the car?"

"Set it on fire."

"How'd you and the blonde get out?"

"I called Lena…she came and picked us up and we went back to Laredo."

"With the girl?"

"Yeah, she was hurt bad…I had to hit her. Lena said that she would take care of the girl. I had to square things with Carlos. That's when the shit went bad. I ain't a rat…but I had no choice."

"You made the only choice," Kidd got up and left Caldwell sitting in the plastic chair still shackled. As he closed the door he met Flynt on the other side.

"Made a call to Lansford," he said holstering his phone. "He picked up some Laredo PD guys and they're looking for Lena Davis."

Kidd pulled out the Radio Shack pocket digital recorder from his breast pocket, "Got the confession right here." It was a habit taught to him by his deceased partner, Keith Spearman, from Albuquerque PD. If it wasn't recorded...it never happened. Kidd heard that on a daily basis, and it served him well throughout his career so far.

"Should we take it to the Feds, see if they want to try and use him for info, maybe lessen his charges?"

"Listen to the tape," Kidd tossed the recorder to his partner. "I'd let Texas decide what to do with him.

*

She wasn't allowed in the temple because she wasn't old enough or 'endowed' yet. In fact, the temple is so sacred that there is a guard posted to make sure only the worthy, only those with a temple recommend can enter. Well, it really wasn't a guard, more like an old guy sitting at a desk, but it was still restricted. To all Mormon Sects, the temple is the center of worship, the heart of doctrine, and the very soul of the religion. It was a place where a man could literally communicate with God and Joseph Smith said so. So, imagine Sariah's surprise when the door was simply unlocked at 3:00 AM in the morning. Of course, the Bishop would have had no idea Sariah wanted in, but it wasn't as if she followed his instructions in the past. The break in wasn't about religion, it was about records. Her father told her that all of the sealings and family arrangements have a paper trail and that trail ends in the temple. She entered through he unlocked door into a large, very plush carpeted room. There was a white, wooden alter in the front of the room with a maroon velvet material on the top. The rumor circulating through the sect's kids, that the brethren consummated the marriages with the young girls on that very alter.

Sariah began a methodical search through the temple for what appeared to be an eternity. Since she had never been inside she felt blind. She suddenly felt stupid as she walked down the hall and saw the door with 'office' printed in bold letters on the outside. *Fuck me*, she thought as she checked the door finding it unlocked as well. It was a damn good thing that Inspireds were so trusting of one another or she would be screwed. A modest desk with several filing cabinets made up the contents of the room. The famous portrait of Joseph Smith being visited by God the Father and Jesus Christ was the only decoration that adorned the walls of the office but it was so commonly used that Sariah seldom thought of its significance or accuracy; it was just in her face since birth. It showed the back of a young man, on his knees being hovered over by two, White heavenly beings that were identical. That such a simple concept spawned such a convoluted theology was amazing.

Sariah furiously looked through the drawers on the desk with absolutely no results. She had been told by her father that every sealing performed by the Inspired Church of Jesus Christ of Latter-day Saints had an accompanying certificate and all certificates were stored in the Temple. So even if the sealings were performed in Utah, they would send the certificates to Texas to store in the temple. She noticed the file cabinet drawers were labeled alphabetically. She looked into 'S' files and found one listed as Smoot/Johnson unions. She pulled the file out of the drawer and thumbed through it. There was no paperwork that showed either Amanda or Ruth's marriages. *Could it be because they haven't filed the paperwork yet?*

There was only one real way to get to find out about any relationship between the Johnson and Smoot families. Sariah took out her cellular phone and began to text message Marshal Lansford. Sariah was a typical teenager and thought talking was a complete waste of time since text messaging was invented, she also thought a phone call at this hour in the morning would anger him. Her purpose was simple; she wanted the Federal Government to pay for her ticket to Salt Lake City. The trip would be short, but she needed to talk to the Smoots, or someone who knew of them. Even though she feared the worst, she just had to know.

*

Chuco and Juan passed the Port of Entry into Mexico and proceeded South on Libramiento Sur. They had no trouble entering the country and the sticker on the van, a local restaurant, signified that the van belonged to the Negras. The Negras ran the entire city, so there was security in knowing that. The two men were given GPS coordinates and instructed to pick up the panel van that was parked very conspicuously, unlocked, with the keys in the visor. The Negras were nothing if not regimented. A Nokia throw phone with the coordinates was in the glove box, just as instructed. Traffic in Mexico could be far more intense than even the most metropolitan American city. The dark SUV that casually drove behind them wasn't even noticed. As they drove further from the congested areas, Chuco had to avoid the terrible disrepair of the road itself instead of worrying about the other crazy drivers.

As they drove, a gray Dodge farm pickup pulled in front of them suddenly causing Chuco to slam on the brakes and come to a complete stop in the middle of the road. He looked up into the rearview mirror and saw the three *sicarios* exit the SUV, all carrying submachine guns, and all wearing masks.

"Chinga tu Madre!" Chuco yelled as he reached for his weapon. He attempted to get a shot off out of the window but was drilled two times by an H&K MP5 causing him to slump over the wheel in a bloody mess. Juan sat frozen in fear as the passenger window was broken out and an AR-15 was put to his head. It wasn't that his life was flashing before his eyes; it was that he knew his life was over and if he somehow cooperated his end would be more tolerable. This was Mexico. If a man is confronted by Mexican *sicarios* with masks and weapons there was never a positive outcome. The gunman finally spoke softly to the once hardened Tango, with an intense voice and accent.

"No se mueva."

*

Kidd and Flynt walk in to Eagle Pass reception area and were greeted by his receptionist, a very pleasant and attractive middle aged, Hispanic woman behind the desk. She smiled at the Rangers as they walked in. Her nameplate on her desk read 'Maria.'

"Well hello Maria," Flynt said in his most charming voice.

"Well hello gentlemen," Maria smiled huge. "How can we help the Texas Rangers today?"

"Well we're here to see Old Dan if he's available."

"Well…do you have an appointment?" Maria said playfully to the elder Ranger.

"No, but we're old friends," Flynt said matching the playfulness of the receptionist.

"He's mentioned you, Sergeant Flynt," Maria smiled. "And I don't know that I would use the term 'friend.' But don't worry," Maria checked to see if there was anyone else in earshot. "We all hate him." They both laughed. "Besides, he's been in there an hour getting his ass reamed by Sonia Nava."

"The lawyer council woman?"

"The same," Maria smiled. "Apparently she and the other members of the city council got their cars broken into last night during their work session. She came in here breathing fire." Maria's description of Nava was complete with hand gestures and body animation. Maria leaned across desk and got closer to Flynt. "That bitch is scary," She said in a soft but serious voice.

"Let's face it, all you women are a little scary," Flynt's statement caused another burst of controlled laughter from both of them. Kidd just watched with amazement. Women absolutely adored his partner and didn't even notice him. He watched Flynt and Maria continue to talk and eventually exchange phone numbers. Kidd shook his head and smiled. His thought was interrupted when he looked up and saw Gummit escorting Sonia Nava out of his office. Dan Gummit's look reminded him of when he was a child being scolded by his mother. Gummit looked at the floor and kept repeating, 'yes ma'am' to any statement the woman made. He was obviously a special type of man that would subject himself to the most humiliating situations in order to protect his position. Kidd would never stoop to that level, he thought. But then again, he wasn't chief.

"Well hello Sergeant Flynt and Ranger Kidd. How are you?" Nava said with an obvious patronizing smile. Both Rangers noticed her dismissive posture towards Dan Gummit who looked like a whipped, abandoned puppy.

"Well Sonia, I still got just one wife, but I'll call you if I get a few more," Flynt smiled at the council woman who was visibly not amused at the remark or the implications.

"Now come on council woman…that was pretty damn funny," Kidd chimed in, and obviously not helping the situation.

"Good day, gentlemen," Sonia Nava walked out of the front door of the administrative office. All three of the men, and even Maria, took note of her long flowing hair and expensive dress and heels. Bitch or not, the woman was gorgeous.

"Can I help you Richard?" Gummit's tone was that of stress and fatigue. The men entered the office, and everyone sat down around Gummit's desk. Gummit let out a loud sigh when sitting, as if a load of wright was lifted from his shoulders. Kidd could tell Gummit had no desire to deal with him or his partner at this time. "I just got my ass handed to me because of some silly fucking BMV's."

"Well, property crime is extremely important to get a handle on, Dan," Flynt observed in his usual sarcastic, but sincere tone. "Besides, I heard it was at a council meeting."

"Yeah it was!" Gummit was obviously agitated. Mostly from his prior meeting with Nava, but Flynt's sarcasm wasn't helping. "Four fucking units in the area and nine cars were broken into…all councilmen. So, I just took a big ass hit. I'm putting paper on all those officers!"

"Now come on Dan, it probably took minutes to get in those cars. Those patrol officers aren't at fault, no need to write them up" Flynt pled to the chief. He hated to see officers receive reprimands in their files if they didn't deserve them.

"The hell they're not! They work for me," Gummit slammed his fist on the table. "I can't have this shit."

"I'm sure something will come up," Flynt smiled at the distressed chief. "Look, we've come to ask a favor from you."

"What do you need?"

"We need you to move Trey Caldwell to Eagle Pass Jail…"

"The murderer? Richard, you must be out of your mind." News regarding notorious cases travels fast in law enforcement circles.

"Dan, he's got information that could help us with several cases, maybe even shut down the Negras. Now if he stays in Maverick County…he's dead. He's at least got a chance at your jail."

"Why the hell would I expose our jail to that type of civil liability?"

"Goddammit Dan! This man's life is at stake!" Flynt's sudden vocal eruption startled both Kidd and Gummit. Gummit was obviously not used to having other cops raise their voice to him. He also knew that Flynt was not a man to be taken lightly.

"Didn't he kill two girls? Maybe he deserves whatever happens next?"

"He can help us with the Negras."

"I would have to talk it over with the City Council."

"You're the chief of fucking police!" Kidd interrupted. "They hired you to lead police, not ask permission to wipe your ass!"

"You don't know shit Ranger Kidd! And I don't much care for your tone. Remember son, I still know your bosses…"

"And I bet they hate you as much as I do you pathetic Bastard!" Kidd stood up and began to come around the desk at the chief which caused the chief's posture to become noticeably defensive. Flynt instantly stood up and blocked Kidd from getting his hands on the terrified chief. Panicked, Gummit began yelling at the Rangers.

"Get the hell out of my office…now!" Both Flynt and Kidd put their hats on and calmly walked toward the door. Flynt walked through the threshold and turned and faced the still seated chief. Maria was deathly silent and stared fearfully from her desk. She had obviously heard the argument inside the office. Kidd put his hand up and smiled at the receptionist while Flynt stared at Gummit through the doorway.

"This is a cop problem. We need that man alive. Please Dan, whatever our problems are, we are still cops," Flynt was sincere in his request.

"There are no more cops, Richard. We're just servants."

Flynt walked away from the chief, tipped his hat and smiled at Maria as he walked out the door. They walked toward the Crown Vic.

"So, what now?" Kidd asked his senior partner.

"We make our move," Flynt said as he opened the car door. "Oh yeah, we really need to work on your people skills."

"What about Caldwell?"

"He's in God's hands now."

CHAPTER FIFTEEN

Turning

Carlos again walked into the Los Palmos Restaurant. Though the place was charming to all that went in, to him it was a dark reminder of how fragile his life had become. He was brutalized in this place and this time, he was unsure if he'd even make it out alive. As he walked to the back of the room his eyes caught those of the waitress he remembered who witnessed his assault. She smiled at him, but not joyfully. It was one of pity and sorrow. She was beautiful, but somehow Carlos's pain became hers. He stood next to Tio Muniz and Marisella in the normal booth, his water was waiting for him on the table. Tio's two men that were always with him stood over the table with a watchful eye. They were casually quiet upon his arrival, but given their brutal volatility, he wasn't sure that the silence was necessarily a good thing.

"Sit down, Carlos. *Como esta?*" Marisella's voice, though sweet and warm, had an eerie tinge of authority to it.

"Bien…bien," Carlos turned to the older man. "You wanted to see me Tio?" His voice sounded meek, but he did his best to at least exude some type of confidence.

"Yes, Carlos…I just wanted to see how you are doing, that's all."

"Fine Tio, we are picking up the pieces, you know from that *cabron,* Caldwell."

"Excellent, you are picking up the pieces, eh?"

"*Si*, I got Chuco and Juan on the drop right now. When they finish that we got a line on some more merchandise. My boss assured me the future is set."

"Oh, it is set? Because I keep getting calls from my clients from the last time, I need to know what to tell them."

"I'm good for it...you know that. Chuco and Juan will get the girls to your clients and my boss promised me future pick-ups…"

"Well that's just it, Carlos. I need your boss's information. I think that we need to do the pick-ups ourselves."

"But Tio, I already told you, I don't know any names. I get my orders over the net. The money is dropped, and my payment is delivered, cash. I'm a soldier, Tio. That is all."

"But you work for us, Carlos. We are not interested in how you do your business. However, we are interested when our business is not taken care of, *entiendes?*" Tio paused and took a drink. "I need you to get me the information on who pays you. I think we may need another arrangement."

Carlos felt the hair on the back of his neck stand up. He again felt helpless in front of this man. He swallowed before he could utter his next, timid question, "What about me, Tio? Haven't I proved myself before? If I knew who my boss was, believe me I'd tell you."

"Tio's laughter erupted and he slapped the table as if he were watching a professional comedy show. "You're like a scared little duckling, *Mijo!*" Even Marisella was chuckling silently. "Did you think I would just kill you now?" Tio laughed and muttered some unintelligible words off in Spanish to the delight of everyone, except Carlos. Carlos closed his eyes as Tio pulled his .45 from his waistband and laughingly pointed it at Carlos's head. Seeing Carlos terrified, he quickly re-holstered the weapon and laughed some more. "Relax, *Cabron*…you have proven your value, but I'm not so sure about your colleagues."

"They're okay, Tio. They've always done what I've asked so far…"

"But they couldn't solve your problem, *no?*"

"We've had some delays, but they've been trying to help me un-fuck this deal, man. I swear, they're cool."

"Well in that case, go meet with your colleagues and give them my regards, yes?" Tio tossed a small, black handheld GPS tracker to Carlos who caught it with minimal effort.

Carlos's stomach dropped, "What's this, Tio?"

"Please get me your employer's information as soon as possible. And I still expect all deliveries with no more complaints or delays. I expect to hear from you soon."

"But what about this?" Carlos held the GPS tracker in the air.

"Oh that? Why that is your colleagues…we'll be in touch."

*

Sariah smiled when she saw Linda Melton waiting for her in the Salt Lake City International Airport. The two women hugged. The only way to describe her was beautiful and stunning. Her long, flowing blonde hair, tight leggings and fashionable, knee high leather boots were a far cry from her origins as a fifteen-year-old polygamist bride only seven years ago. Sariah remembered Linda's escape from the brethren's grasp. Linda's parents consented to her marriage to an older priesthood holder. On the night of the wedding, Linda snuck out of the house with only the clothes on her back and some money she had saved. The next anyone ever saw of Melton was on television as one of the youngest, most vocal, and filmed voices in the anti-polygamist lobby headquartered in Utah. Sariah reached out to Linda a few years ago. She became a heroine to the disenfranchised girls from polygamist backgrounds. There were mumblings and cursing her name throughout the sect to this day, even threats on her life. Linda offered to help Sariah in any way she could, but Sariah didn't think it would ever be in this capacity.

"You look great, Sariah!" Linda hugged Sariah tightly. There was no way to explain the bond of women raised in polygamy. There was beauty and horror in the shared experiences that was found nowhere else. As they embraced, both women's eyes filled with tears, Sariah for her association with the sect and her frantic search for her friend, and Linda because of the memories of her past and her fear for Sariah's future. "Boyfriend?"

"With the brethren's all-seeing eye and snitches everywhere?" Sariah got a devilish grin on her face, "maybe one or two…but they're not ILDS."

"You slut!" Linda said again hugging Sariah. The two began walking through the courtyard filled with business kiosks. "I checked with all my contacts, Sweetie, no one has ever heard of Amanda and Ruth Johnson coming to Utah."

"Maybe the Smoot's are keeping the marriage on the down low? Maybe they're afraid of the police finding out the old man's marrying some teenagers?"

"I don't know Sariah, you know our people…they can't keep secrets for shit. Besides, you think those old perverted bastards wouldn't be bragging about a marriage with a couple of hot little blonde girls from Texas?"

"Oooh you're right. Damn…no one is talking?"

"Not a one," Linda stopped in front of one of the nicer restaurants. "Are you hungry?"

"I could eat," Sariah replied as the two women walked into the open dining area and were seated promptly. "So, what do we do now?"

"Tomorrow morning I'm taking you to my office. These women I work with know everything about every polygamist sect. If Amanda and Ruth came to Utah, we will find them."

"You get paid for this?"

"Sariah…I get paid to fuck over the brethren. It's the best job ever!" Linda smiled. "Oh and I get paid well."

"Well I have a confession to make myself," Sariah looked at the ground when she spoke.

"Do tell…now I'm listening."

"I broke into the temple and looked at the records."

Linda slammed down her imported, bottled beer and nearly choked. "Holy shit girl! That is so awesome you're a fucking Rock Star!" She finished her drink and raised her hand prompting the waiter to bring her another beer. "What did you find out?"

"I found out the man you ran out on was Bishop Johnson," Sariah's revelation caused Linda to stop her ear to ear smile and put her beer on the table. Sariah all of a sudden felt she might have offended or alienated her friend. "I'm so sorry, Linda…I didn't mean…"

"No, no, Sweetheart, you didn't say anything wrong. I've just been trying to forget that you know," Linda pointed to her drink as if to show Sariah one of her coping mechanisms.

"Every time I hear that man's name I get sick to my stomach. I was fucking fifteen years old, Sariah?" Linda's eyes watered but she was somewhat surprised when Sariah began to cry as well. It was as if Linda could perceive Sariah's thoughts. "He commanded you to marry him too, didn't he?"

Sariah's head hung down in embarrassment. Even with a woman who knew exactly what she was going through in her life, still the thought of God commanding her to marry an old son of a bitch was still hard to face. There was also no way she could admit to Linda that she was living on the compound for a time, and certainly never admit to giving the old pervert oral sex. "It started about two years ago, when I turned sixteen."

"Well, maybe he's turning over a new leaf by waiting till sixteen, huh? How fucking cosmopolitan!" Linda's statement made Sariah chuckle amid her pain.

"I've just been avoiding him like a virus." A necessary lie, Sariah thought.

"What about your parents?"

"My Dad told me it's my decision."

"Wow! Mine sold me out right away. Good for your Dad," Linda took another drink of her beer. "What about your Uncle Moroni LaFey?" Sariah's head snapped up and saw a smirking Linda. "You're not the only one who knows a few secrets."

"How…how did you know we were LaFey's?"

"Sariah, the whole sect knows. Why do you think your dad has never been called to a leadership position? Nephi Josephs is still scared of your uncle."

"Well if he's scared, shouldn't he be kissing my Dad's ass?"

"He knows that your Dad doesn't want to be associated with his family and he's taking advantage of that. There haven't been many assholes made that would rival the Prophet, Seer, Revelator, Nephi Josephs. And Satan himself couldn't conceive Thomas Johnson."

"I guess not," Sariah really didn't want to talk about her family anymore. "Okay so we work tomorrow, but what about tonight?"

Linda raised a bottle of imported beer in the air, "We party!"

*

"All units stand by and wait for contact," Lansford quickly put down the radio and quickly picked up his cellular phone. "Alright Flynt, we're in position."

"How many units do you have?"

"I got a ten-man team, five Marshals and five Laredo PD. Tell me about this girl."

"According to our intel she is just Caldwell's old lady. No weapons charges, a couple of possession charges and a few stints for prostitution."

"We got a no knock. We're just gonna get in there."

"Okay, be safe Brother."

Lansford got out of the vehicle and made a motion for the other members of the task force to converge on the location. They parked the vehicles at a diner that sat adjacent to the motel. The motel was a one story, brick structure that was built at least sixty years ago complete with a partially working neon sign. Like many of the buildings in that part of Laredo, they were the product of decay and crime. When Lansford approached Laredo PD and requested their help, they not only knew the location well, they also knew exactly who Lena Davis was. The layout of the hotel was the traditional horseshoe style, with a central parking lot, a tactical nightmare ensuring that every room had a complete view of the front entry. When the officers committed to the entry, there was no turning back. Lansford watched as two Laredo PD detectives circled to the back of the motel. All the men had their weapons drawn as Lansford approached the door. Lansford leaned his head against the door and could hear the rustling of people and the television. He raised his arm, as if he was a quarterback calling a play.

"Police…search warrant!" almost simultaneously from those words exploding from Lansford's mouth, he put a well-placed kick directly above the door lock causing the door to spring open and splinters from the door jamb hurled inside the room. "U.S. Marshal's…get on the ground!" Lansford entered the room with a 'button-hook' maneuver clearing the blind spot behind the door. The other cops piled in behind him with their weapons at the ready. A very skinny brunette, wearing only a bra and panties, quickly sprung up from the bed and ran towards the bathroom only to be stopped by the Laredo detective that tackled her before she could break the threshold.

"You cocksuckers!" Lena Davis screamed as she was cuffed. Lansford ran to the closet and forced it open, nearly tearing the door off its sliding tracks. He was horrified when he saw an emaciated young, blonde girl curled up in the fetal position on the floor. The girl was clothed only in soiled underwear. She looked at the Marshal, the smell of the urine and feces-soaked linen was overpowering. Her eyes were sunken and blackened with the obvious results of malnutrition. It was as if she was trying to say something to Lansford, but the words just would not come.

"You're safe, Sweetheart," Lansford gently stroked the girl's hair, but she was too weak to respond either way. The other officers finally got Lena Davis to quit spewing profanity laced sentences and calm down. Now she was trying to convince everyone of her innocence, but Lansford could only think about the young girl that lay before him. "What is your name?" The young girl seemed puzzled at his question initially, but finally mustered enough strength to answer in a weak, raspy voice.

"Amanda."

*

Caldwell was brought inside the showers inside the Maverick County Detention Center. It was a routine he was used to. Although the prison showers were stuff of legend in movies and contemporary literature, in reality they were routine and boring. Turns out not much of anything goes on within those walls. He did notice Henry Garcia next to him. Henry was a valued soldier with the Mexican Mafia, *La Eme*, but he and Caldwell went way back. Garcia looked around to see if anyone was looking at either he or Caldwell, "The word's out on you, man. You got to get out of here."

"And go where?" Caldwell answered. I'm looking at two murders." Henry shook his head upon hearing Caldwell's answer and continued to wash his short, stalky body which was covered in tattoo shading. No matter how much soap was used he still looked unclean. His head was closely shaved and bare, with the exception of the tattoos that faded up his neck and into his would-be hairline. His gaze was completed by a filled in tear drop tattoo which signified that he had killed and solidified the look of a man resigned to spend his life and die in an institution. "Why the fuck you back in?" Caldwell asked.

"Got pinched on an armed robbery in Del Rio. They violated my parole on the Murder Charge."

"They gonna drop the armed robbery?"

"Shit, *ese*...they take one look at me, they ain't dropping shit."

"So, what's the fucking word? Why am I marked?"

"Fuck *ese!* Everyone knows the Rangers came to talk with you. Get them to move you. It could buy you some time," Henry looked around again to make sure no one was listening. "Word is the *Negras* got it out for you."

"Yeah, yeah I fucked up a drop on the outside, but listen man, I need to know whose coming?"

"Tangos, the circle, even *La Eme* will come for you for the right price. You don't fuck with the *Negras!*"

"Look motherfucker I didn't know it was the *Negras!* That fucker on the outside never told me."

"Well it fucking was. I'm trying to warn your dumb ass. Reach out to the Law, *ese*. It's going down quick."

"Of course it is," Caldwell smiled. When you are educated within the prison system, there are varying layers of trust. On the one hand, he did a stretch in TDCJ (Texas Department of Criminal Justice) with Henry who always seemed to be a stand-up guy. But Henry was of a Mongrel race loyal only to their kind. The bottom line is that you never give implicit trust to a rival. "So tell me how it's coming."

"Look, *ese*, I know you're into your Nazi bullshit, but you and I got history. When I say it's coming, it's coming."

"And you ain't in on it?"

"If I was, I'd have killed you first thing when we walked in here. What the fuck do I gotta lose?"

Caldwell nodded to Henry as they finished showering. They heard the guard yell for them to get finished. They filed out in a semi-orderly fashion and walked back to the blocks. As Caldwell walked down the hall with the differing cells he casually stepped into door of his cell which was adjacent to the common area of the pod.

"Turn around and put your hands on top of your head, Caldwell. You know the drill." Caldwell complied, although he found it odd that there was a single guard escorting him on this date. They had strict instructions to search him any time he left his cell and upon his return. Perhaps they didn't fear him as they should; something that would need to be remedied. No sooner did his hands go up onto his head, the guard inserted an icepick into the base of Caldwell's skull. Caldwell fell to the floor as if someone turned off a power switch to his life. The guard walked calmly back to the control booth for the pod and re-activated the surveillance cameras as if nothing was wrong at all.

CHAPTER SIXTEEN

Tangos

"I need more, Lena! You're not just looking at State kidnapping charges. Human trafficking falls under Federal jurisdiction now…It's day for day, sweetheart," John Lansford was sitting directly across for Lena Davis, who was wrapped in a blanket and sipping coffee from a Styrofoam cup. The methamphetamine use was obvious upon first glance of the tattered woman. Her skin was so thin and loose from her flesh that it appeared to slip. The fresh, red pick marks indicated recent use of the drug as well. When the Marshals got done searching the room, they could only locate a few personal effects, some drug paraphernalia, and pornography and sex toys. This woman could hardly keep herself alive, much less another human being. "You're only shot at freedom is to help us out."

"It wasn't my idea…I swear! Trey knew I needed money," Lena Davis sat fidgeting in her chair. Lansford knew he had a limited time to speak to her before she crashed and went into full withdrawal. Her hands and legs were moving almost uncontrollably, like a patient with Parkinson's disease. Lena grimaced as she spoke. It was as if talking caused her pain because she desperately needed that fix. "Trey fucked me over!"

"Then its time you tell us everything you know."

"I just know he kept talking about a guy named Carlos a lot."

"Is Carlos hooked in with the Negras?"

"I don't know… he never told me."

"What about the girls? Did he ever mention picking up girls before?"

"Never…he's a dope smuggler. He wasn't into all this other shit. He said Carlos forced him to do it."

"So, who is Carlos, Lena?"

"I don't fucking know, I swear!"

"You better start remembering, Lena! I'm not protecting

your ass if all you can say is 'I don't know'," Lansford got up and stormed out of the interview room, obviously frustrated, leaving Lena Davis wither head in her hands crying. As he poured himself another cup of coffee, hoping to eek out another forty minutes of energy, his cellular phone rings. "Hello?"

"Hey John, it's Flynt. I heard you got Davis?"

"We got her early this morning. Amanda is alive and was taken to Doctor's Hospital in Laredo. I got two Laredo PD officers guarding her. She's in bad shape."

"Does Sariah know?"

"Not yet. Can you call her?"

"Sure. Davis tell you anything?"

"More about this Carlos guy. She's so goddamn strung out I'm lucky to even get that."

"Listen...Caldwell is dead."

"What! Dead? How?"

"I don't know. We're headed there now. Better not tell Lena Davis."

"Copy that. Isn't County on lockdown by now?"

"Helps to know people my friend."

"Is it just me or is this getting more fucked up by the second?"

"Yep. Do you think you can get more out of old Lena?"

"Doubtful, but I'll try."

*

"Thank you for letting us come in Johnny. I know ya'all are locked down, but I certainly appreciate it," Flynt said as he and Kidd walked into the pod where the crime scene was cordoned off. Johnny Rodriguez was a thirty-five-year veteran of the Maverick County Sheriff's Department. He and Flynt's paths crossed on numerous occasions and all were very respectful and cordial. The thin, Hispanic Chief Deputy smiled back at his old friend.

"Shit, what choice do I have Richard? The Sheriff likes you more than me."

"Do you blame him? You're kind of an asshole!" The two

men laughed as Flynt and Kidd observed Caldwell lying lifeless on the floor in his cell. A small, but significant pool of blood was under his head. The rest of the body seemed unremarkable, as if he just laid down to sleep. "M.E. give any info?"

"Single puncture wound to the back of the head. Don't know how deep."

"Deep enough to hit the brain stem," Kidd observed.

"That's what the Doc said," Rodriguez replied. "This isn't the typical shit we get in here. This is clean, almost calculated. Most jail house assaults are vicious and messy. This just doesn't make sense."

"You don't learn something like that in the Detention Officer Academy. To kill a man with a single puncture in the head takes practice and skill," Flynt added.

"They tell me that many of the victims of the *sicarios* are just for practice. I also heard they use pigs sometimes…that's just what I heard," Rodriguez said. *Sicario* was a term used in Mexico for an assassin. What was truly sad was that American Law Enforcement was extremely familiar with the assassins' methods, but the general public had no idea of the sheer horrors transpiring across the border or worse yet, that the brutality spread into the United States. The public continued to use the very product driving these killers ignorant, or simply dismissive of the real consequences.

"What about camera views?" Kidd asked.

"Don't have footage from the cell block during this time." Both Flynt and Kidd looked suspiciously at Rodriguez who acknowledged their concern. "I know…I know. We already thought of that."

"What are your plans for the investigation?" Flynt asked.

"C.I.D. has already round up the guards. They are tossing the cells and the guards' lockers. We can do that since its County property."

"What about the cameras?"

"We got the computer guys looking at it. If we can figure out who was in the booth that would give us a good start."

"Any good witnesses?"

"There's a guy he did time with in Huntsville that got popped on a probation violation. His name is Henry Garcia, last person to see Caldwell alive. He's affiliated with La Eme. Caught an armed robbery case still on parole for a Murder so he's done. He'll have to serve out his original plus what they give him for the robbery."

"Can we talk to him?"

"He's waiting in my office," Rodriguez smiled and escorted the two Rangers back to his office. There, waiting for them, sat Henry calm and collected. Flynt waived at Johnny who left the room closing the door behind him. Henry looked at the two Rangers then down at the floor, though still unmoved by the actions of the day.

"You don't seem so moved that your friend is laying there dead in that cell?" Kidd finally spoke up.

"He wasn't a friend…more like an associate. He was always stand-up to me. This is kinda fucked up."

"You spoke with him recently?"

"Bout twenty minutes before lockdown, in the shower."

"What did you all talk about?"

"I told him to do all he could to get the fuck outta here, but he wouldn't listen. I told him he was marked…"

"Let's cut the shit, Henry, who killed Trey?" Flynt interrupted.

"The fucking guard, ese! Who the fuck else could it have been?" Henry wiped his face with his hands. "There's no one in here that hard core. It was just me and him. They got a few Tangos running around, but their nobodies. Trey would have seen those fuckers try to punk him from a mile away. It was the guard."

"What's the Guard's name?"

"I think its Flores? That's the guy that escorted Trey. We call him 'Red', because of his fucked-up hair. That's who I would talk to if I were you."

"Thank you, Henry," Flynt tipped his hat and walked outside to meet up with Johnny Rodriguez. "You hear all that?"

"I did. His name is Micah Flores. He's been on for about a year. To tell you the truth, he's already the Investigator's number one suspect. He cut out of here early."

"Are they going to pick him up?" Kidd inquired.

"You know how it is, man…The Sheriff is going to want it air tight before he has to go in front of the commissioners and publically admits he hired a killer. This is going to be bad."

"Do you have the guest footage from visitors for the last seventy-two hours?

"Yeah, we got that."

"Could we get a copy before we leave?"

"Absolutely."

*

Sariah was crying when she hung up the phone. The news was like a jolt of joy and sadness all at once. Her friend was alive, but Ranger Flynt's good news was shrouded in a darkness that she could hear in his voice. What happened to Amanda? And where was Ruth? There seemed to be only more questions. She had to get back to Texas and see her friend. She was barely able to wipe the tears from her eyes when Linda Melton and another very attractive brunette walked in the modest, but very nice conference room. The Anti-polygamist lobby apparently had some friends with money. It was in an old building that sat across from the Salt Lake City Temple, the very symbol of Mormonism.

"Hey Sariah, this is Mary Smoot…" Linda's sentence was stopped mid-stream when she realized Sariah had been crying. "Sweetheart are you okay?" There was genuine concern in Linda's voice.

"They found, Amanda," Sariah answered in very positive but reserved voice. Linda and Mary's faces took on a look of surprise and joy as they rushed over and hugged the Sariah still seated.

"Thank God! Where is she?

"Doctor's Hospital in Laredo. I…I have to get back to her."

"Of course you do. But where's Ruth?"

"They didn't say. I'm afraid something bad is going on, Linda." Linda put her arms around Sariah and squeezed her close.

"You need to be happy that she is alive and well. Take comfort in that," Linda squeezed Sariah a bit tighter. Her voice became emotional, "We never asked for our lot in life. We were dealt shit by God, himself. Take joy in the small things, to us, they're really big."

Sariah wiped her eyes and turned and looked at Mary Smoot, "It's nice to meet you Mary."

"Nice to meet you," Mary replied. "Even though I've been forbidden to go near my family, I still have my contacts. Amanda and Ruth Johnson were never meant to have a sealing with the Smoots."

"So, what do you think?"

"I think Bishop Johnson is lying. You need to get back to Texas. Amanda is the key to this." Mary sat on the other side of Sariah and embraced the girl just like Linda.

"I want to see Nephi Josephs. I want to confront him and the brethren…"

"Sariah…Sariah!" Linda interrupted Sariah before she could get herself worked up over the matter. "You're a young woman…you are not a person to that animal."

"What about you guys? I mean, you guys have powerful political allies…"

"Yes, we can battle these bastards in the political world," Mary Smoot said. "But we have no power to influence the hearts and minds of the members of the Inspired Church. Josephs knows this. He knows we will never be a threat to the hearts and minds of his true followers."

Sariah sat back and thought for a moment. She so admired these two women that were willing to leave their families and fight against a tradition and dogma that had suppressed its followers for decades. They were strong, but their feelings of loss and mourning due to being banished from interacting with their loved ones somehow made them even more courageous, perhaps heroic. "You guys are right. I need to get back to Texas." Sariah got out of her chair, preparing to leave the room. "Oh yeah, here's something weird the Texas Ranger said." Both Mary Smoot and Linda Melton turned to Sariah with their attention completely surrendered to the teenager. "He wanted to know about Josiah and Nathan Johnson."

"You mean those two devil children of Bishop Johnson's?" Linda asked, obviously familiar with them.

"Yeah."

"What did he say about them?"

"They said something about AFIS, Fingerprints, and video. Then he just said he was going to pay them a visit."

Linda smiled almost devilishly, "What I wouldn't pay to see that one."

*

Felipe's Hot Dogs wasn't particularly crowded as Flynt and Kidd walked in the door. They found it easy to spot the Johnson brothers. The two simply looked out of place in the restaurant, sort of a social awkwardness no doubt the result of being raised in a polygamist sect. The two seemed suspicious of every person in the room, and their suspicions were only deepened as Flynt and Kidd sat directly next to them at a table. Both Rangers simply stared and smiled at the boys who continued to eat their meals, occasionally glancing at the two with great anxiety.

"So, which one of you is Josiah, and which one is Nathan?" Flynt finally spoke out. Both boys glanced at Flynt, obviously surprised and showing an ever-increasing anxiety, then kept eating occasionally glaring with contempt at the officers. Kidd could see that the two hated police, no doubt because of their upbringing. He and Flynt represented a threat to their traditions. "Ya'all twins are something?" Flynt continued smiling as if it were his birthday, enjoying the fact that he was really getting under Josiah and Nathan's skin. The moments of uncomfortable silence were too much for the boys to take, and just like Flynt had planned, they began to talk.

"I'm Josiah and we've got nothing to say," Josiah finally exclaimed.

"But I got a question for you."

"What question?"

"Why would you two visit Maverick County Jail?"

"Spiritual reasons…we don't have to explain!" Josiah

snarled.

"You wanted to visit Trey Caldwell?"

"I don't remember the name."

"You know what? He's dead."

Nathan Johnson's face went white. "We had nothing to do with that."

"Oh, I believe you…but I think we need a DNA sample from you both."

"DNA?"

"Yes…DNA dumbass! You little inbred fucks ever watch television?" Kidd interrupted the conversation with his usual grace.

"No, we don't cop!" Nathan sneered back at Kidd. "It's full of Gentile shit, like the both of you!" Kidd and Flynt looked at each other with a pleasant surprise at the boy's feistiness, then promptly busted out laughing.

"If you weren't so damn cute, Little Nathan, I'd whoop your ass right here," Kidd continued to laugh. "Now seriously, we need your DNA."

"We're done here," Josiah said as both he and Nathan got up to walk out of the restaurant. Flynt followed the two boys, but Kidd stayed inside the restaurant. As they walked toward the parking lot the Rangers kept talking. The finally stopped walking and the Johnson brothers turned and faced Flynt.

"Are you two even going to ask why we want a DNA sample from you?" Flynt asked. That was usually the first question out of anyone's mouth if they're asked to submit a DNA sample.

"We've been persecuted all of our lives by you Gentiles. Whatever the reason is…we don't care," Josiah sneered.

"Now how have I ever persecuted you, Boy?" Flynt stepped in front of Josiah. His close proximity made the boy nervous, but Josiah remained in front of him still defiant. "I'm a back-row Baptist that attends church bout once a year, much to the chagrin of my dear mother. I don't care about your little religion. You want ten wives? Go get em'. But don't accuse me of persecuting you, you little snot-faced Bastard!" Flynt inched closer to Josiah's face.

"You represent the government…and the government is

evil! Unless you submit to the true prophet of God, you're nothing but a lost sheep with no shepherd! You don't know God…you don't know Christ. You feed off the crumbs of truly great prophets of God without even understanding their words. I testify my father is commissioned by the prophet Nephi Josephs…And we serve him, not you!" Josiah spit as he spoke. "So no…we won't give you any DNA!"

All three turned and saw Kidd walking out of the restaurant with a paper bags each hand. He smiled as he walked to the Crown Vic and gently placed both bags inside the cab of the vehicle. He then pulled two evidence slips from his notebook and walked over to join the conversation in the parking lot, still busy filling out the evidence tags. "Hey all, what did I miss?"

"Well, these boys won't give us a DNA sample, Ranger Kidd," Flynt answered sarcastically.

"Oh yes they did Sergeant…I got both of them. Cups, straws, all that stuff," Kidd smiled and continued to fill out the paperwork meticulously.

"You…you can't do that…" Josiah stammered for words.

"Actually, we can. You see, when you abandon trash, it becomes free game for us," Kidd smiled again. "Does Josiah have just one S?"

"You mother fuckers!" Nathan lunged at Kidd, causing the Ranger to react by shooting a jab directly into the young man's nose with the pen still in his grip. Nathan's head snapped back, and his knees buckled causing him to simply slump to the ground.

"I think you boys better get the fuck outta here," Flynt said very calmly. "You tell that prophet if he has anything to do with these murders, ya'all ain't even seen persecution." The two boys walked away from the two Rangers gingerly, but quickly. Flynt turned to his junior partner. "Must you solve everything by violence? We'll get a call from Sonia Nava now."

"Goddamnit, he came at me! You saw?" Kidd reacted firmly yet still with a grin. "Besides…you think Sonia is pretty and now we have a blood sample."

*

The Church High Council Meeting ran late and the Prophet, Seer, Revelator Nephi Josephs was tired. His office complex South of St. George Utah was simple and unassuming. The Inspired Church of Jesus Christ of Latter-Day Saints preferred not to meet and center their business activities around their temple located near Colorado City, Utah. Instead, it was operated like a business or corporation. The lease on the office space was reasonable and the brethren, with their uniform like black suits simply blended in with the rest of the professionals in the area. It was a form of hiding in plain sight, thus keeping the sect out of the watchful eyes of the anti-polygamist lobby. The other sects could flaunt their cases before the public and the court system, but the Inspireds would simply worship right under the secular public's judgmental noses.

Josephs was not as old as the prophet and apostles of the mainstream Mormons in Salt Lake City. He was in his late forties, six foot one, slender build with graying brown hair. He was often told he looked like the portraits of the prophet Joseph Smith with his prominent nose and chin. Josephs welcomed that comparison with open arms. He sat down in his office chair and gently leaned back. He was sure his wives were waiting on him at home, but his mind was heavy with the burdens of the church. The disputes between the families of the sect grew numerous and the prophet couldn't afford to lose any of the members to other sects. The sect didn't have the growth patterns of the Mormons, or fundamental Christians, that meant that the precious tithes that filled the accounts of the sect had to be protected at all costs; that protection was tiring. He laid his head back on his chair with his eyes dimming with fatigue.

"I see God's work is weighing heavily on your soul Brother Josephs. Perhaps a sabbatical is in order?" Moroni LaFey's voice was like a knife slicing through tender meat. Josephs' neck snapped around to see Moroni sitting leisurely on the office couch. This was the man rumored to have killed his father. He wondered how he never saw LaFey come in. Moroni LaFey was never welcome on church property, and Josephs began to rack his brain wondering why he would be there. He took comfort in the fact if Josephs wanted him dead, he would most likely be dead.

"There are no sabbaticals in the Lord's true church, Brother LaFey. You of all people should know that," Josephs replied with a smile. As frightened as he was of his unexpected visitor, he couldn't show it. "What brings you up so far in the mainland?"

Moroni sat up and smiled back at Josephs, but the smile wasn't cordial. Moroni's look was filled with contempt. Josephs knew of the LaFey's disdain for him, but they generally were submissive to the word of God, but nothing else. "Have you been down to Texas in a while?"

"I'm sorry to say I haven't. Bishop Johnson seems to be running a tight ship…"

"I'm not so sure you're inspired on that subject, Nephi."

"I don't need to be inspired on everything Moroni…I'm not God."

"But you are his Prophet and his mouthpiece on earth, are you not?" Moroni seemed to be becoming more agitated. Now the safe feeling that Josephs once had was fading. "Correct me if I'm wrong, President Josephs, but if we have no prophet, we're no better that the hordes of Gentiles that surround us?"

"Is there a point to this conversation, Moroni? I have no clue where you're going with this."

"Have you been watching the news in Texas?"

"You mean the mass grave…"

"Among other things, but yes," Moroni leaned back onto the couch again. "Why would members think Bishop Johnson is connected to that?"

"Connected? How?"

"You see, that's why I'm down here, Nephi, I thought you could enlighten me."

"That's absurd, Moroni," Josephs shook his head in unbelief. "What possible connection does Thomas have to that gentile mess?"

"Well for starters, the grave is on his land."

Josephs became speechless never hearing about this until now. Surely a Bishop that he appointed would have given him a fair warning concerning a potential publicity meltdown for the small sect. The Mormon Church in Salt Lake employed a battalion of lawyers that were prepared to fight for just such an occasion. The Inspired Church of Jesus Christ of Latter-day Saints was much smaller. This was potentially devastating. "That is church land," Josephs corrected Moroni LaFey.

"Does that make it better, President?" Moroni made a valid point. But Johnson was Josephs' man. He had to stand by him and trust that he was acting in accordance with his calling and church policy.

"It does not. But the church has vast amounts of land down there, and I'm sure there is no connection to this awful crime."

"Are you willing to stake your authority on that, Nephi?"

"I'm not quite sure what you mean by that?"

"I mean are you willing to face the consequences if it turns out Johnson somehow is involved with this thing?"

"I am the Prophet, Moroni…I answer to God alone!" Josephs' voice rose with indigence, but a clod rush soon came over his body as Moroni rose to his feet and with cat-like quickness crossed the room into the Prophet's personal space.

"Don't forget your history, Nephi. Though God hasn't called me as his prophet, he has given me abilities and gifts. And with those gifts, I will protect his church, with or without a prophet!" Moroni sneered as Nephi felt his warm, moist breath across his face. "You know what I am capable of."

Nephi was frozen with fear, as Moroni drew away from him. He finally was able to muster up the courage to speak again. "I will go down and speak with Thomas. I will assure you, and the entire LaFey family, that there is absolutely nothing to worry about."

Moroni smiled as he walked towards the door, "That's all I wanted, Nephi."

"Wait…who are the members that complained?" Josephs was able to catch Moroni's attention before he was able to exit.

"Only God and I can know that," Moroni replied. "It's the only way to test the honesty of the accused, as well as yours, President." Moroni disappeared. Josephs searched the interior of the building with no sign of him. It was as if he vanished.

Josephs sat down at his desk and called the airline. He needed to get to Texas.

CHAPTER SEVENTEEN

The Fray

"Howdy friend, where's Bob at today?" Flynt said in a semi-jovial tone to a mid-twenties, bald, tattooed man working the front desk at A-1 Bail Bonds. It was inevitable that law enforcement and bondsman have a close working relationship, but it was rare that one was a pure friendship. It was more a relationship out of necessity, but Flynt and Bob Sanchez went way back to his time as a trooper. He stopped by and saw him if ever he was in the area.

"Bob don't work here no more," the young man said rather shortly.

"Well I'm sorry to hear that…he was a friend."

"Well he's gone. Now if there isn't anything else, I'm kind of busy."

"Have I done something to offend you, partner?" When Kidd heard the partner, he knew Flynt was about to jump down this rude punk's throat. To be a policeman, you needed a clean record and to demonstrate at least a hint of moral fiber. To be a bondsman, you didn't.

"No, but I hate cops," The man said flippantly.

"You at least got a name?"

"Johnny."

"Well Johnny, I apologize if we've offended you in any way, but we come here for some information."

"Sorry, I can't help you…"

"We haven't asked you anything yet?"

"Still…unless you got a court order?"

"Well, we been running around so much we haven't had time to stop and get one."

"Well that's too bad then," Johnny smiled at the two men.

"Okay, excuse me for a second," Flynt pulled out his cellular phone and placed it to his ear. Johnny stared at him curiously. Flynt winked at the young man and began speaking to someone. In the meantime, Kidd began to walk around the desks picking up various files and looking at them.

"You can't do that!" Johnny yelled objecting to Kidd's actions.

"And yet I am," Kidd replied continuing his actions. Johnny went to physically approach Kidd but was suddenly and unexpectedly hit in the head with a large, thick accordion file expertly placed on the side of his face. The blow caught Johnny off guard and caused him to fall to the ground. Kidd cuffed Johnny effortlessly and sat him in the desk. "Now that's assault on a Texas Ranger. Who should I call for your bond?"

"What the…"

"One more word and I'll club you so hard in your goddamn head you'll forget next football season you disrespectful little shit!"

Flynt casually walked over to Johnny who sat dazed and upset and placed his cell phone next to the young man's ear. "Johnny, talk to your boss, Mr. Williams, please?" Johnny stared at Flynt with fear and confusion. He then started to speak frantically into the phone.

"Okay, okay…I'm sorry, Sir…I didn't realize they were your friends," the look on Johnny's face clearly showed he was being scolded. "Yes Sir, I will get them what they need…" Johnny handed the phone back to Flynt and bowed his head. Kidd un-cuffed the man.

"Yeah Rich, I'll get with you when I get up to Austin…thank you my friend, I owe you," Flynt ended the call and put the phone back into his pocket. "Now Johnny, can we start over?" Flynt leaned over to get up close to Johnny's face. "Your Boss and I play a little golf every once and a while. If I were you, I'd start being a little kinder."

"Yes, Sir," Johnny muttered humbly.

"Well goddamn Flynt I like this new Johnny!" Kidd said boisterously patting the humbled young man on the back. "Can we see your file on Nathan and Josiah Johnson, please?"

Johnny retrieved the file in a cabinet. Kidd couldn't get over the archaic file cabinet system still used in the office. While most of America was going paperless, Kidd counted a dozen filing cabinets at A-1 Bail Bonds. Sometimes traditional is better he thought. "They've been handled by Eagle Pass PD several times."

"What like drugs?"

"No says here Josiah got popped for an indecent exposure and Nathan for Public Lewdness."

"No shit…anything else?" Flynt asked.

"Couple of traffic related shit," Johnny paused. "Hold on…they got an assault case too."

"You got all the bond info in those files?" Flynt asked.

"Yep."

"You think you could get us a copy of those files?"

"Yes Sir." Johnny turned and began diligently began copying the files. As the pages were turning out, Kidd decided to take a few pages and read. He held up one particular page and showed it to Flynt. Flynt smiled and nodded his head in affirmation. The trip had proven fruitful.

"Now you see Johnny, this is called cooperation," Flynt smiled. "You got their fingerprint cards?

*

The plane ride was long and boring. Sariah had to fly into Laredo from Salt Lake City on the late flight due to the U.S. Government being so cheap, according to Marshal Lansford. The drive from Laredo to Eagle Pass was even worse. It was the early hours of the morning when she pulled into her driveway. Surely the family would be asleep by now. It would feel nice to sleep in her own bed, she thought. She wouldn't be returning to the Johnson Compound now. It was far too dangerous. She stealthily opened the door with her key and walked through the living room.

"Why didn't you tell me you were going to Utah, young lady?" Jeremiah's voice cut through the dark like a searing knife. Sariah's heart sank to her stomach with anticipation.

"I couldn't tell you…"

"Sariah listen to me. It hurts me you run off and not tell me, I've been worried sick!" The lecture Sariah had been dreading was finally here. "Your mother is beside herself!"

"I'm sorry, Daddy!" Sariah said truly apologetic. "How did you know I left?"

"Kaye Johnson called when she didn't see you on the compound."

"Did she tell Bishop Johnson?" Sariah was suddenly struck with fear.

"Not a chance," Jeremiah said casually and didn't even seem concerned about the question.

"How do you know? She's his wife."

"There are some ties that are deeper than marriage."

"Like what?"

"Kaye is a LaFey, Sariah. She's my cousin. I simply told her the family was looking into something and needed it to remain a secret," Jeremiah could see the befuddlement of her daughter. "You and Amanda are related."

"But I thought the LaFey's hated the Johnsons?"

"They do, but you remember your history?" Jeremiah waited for Sariah's nod that she understood. "Marriages are sometimes arranged for strategy. There's a LaFey somewhere in every family of this sect."

"You think Kaye will keep a secret because of that?"

"I do. I instructed her to tell Johnson you were back at home," Jeremiah smiled. "Make no mistake, sweet daughter, a marriage does not make a family…remember that. Blood is the key to life. It's the only one."

"How did you know I was back in Texas?"

Jeremiah looked at his daughter with partial disgust, "You don't think I have my eyes?" Jeremiah got up and looked out the front window. "How is Linda Melton?"

Sariah was now officially freaked out now. She was beginning to understand why the LaFey's were so feared. "She is good. You should see her…she does well and looks great."

"She was always a beautiful girl."

"She told me there was no sealing the Smoots and Johnsons."

"I know."

"Well shit, Dad! You could've told me…"

"You never asked," Jeremiah replied calmly even

coldly. "And watch your language."

"Well, I wanted to talk to President Josephs, but he apparently won't speak to women."

"He doesn't, but he'll speak to your Uncle Moroni."

"Will Uncle Moroni help?"

"He already has." Jeremiah hugged his daughter. It calmed his fears.

"Can I ask you a question, Daddy?"

"Yes, my love," Jeremiah smiled. He loved it when she called him Daddy.

"Do you really believe all this stuff the brethren teach?"

Jeremiah thought about his answer. Sariah was unsure if he would even answer the question. "No Sweetheart, I never have." The answer stunned the young woman so that she was speechless and simply stared at her father. "I truly love your mothers, and this is the religion of my fathers. So I stay."

"I…I could never do that," Sariah muttered still in somewhat of a state of shock.

"I know, Sariah."

*

The GPS coordinates lead Carlos to a farm road Southeast of Eagle Pass across the river from Perez. The road seemed to bend forever through thick brush and trees. There was no radio playing in the car, Carlos was left to his thoughts which were racing through his uncertain mind. The road washed out in a natural arroyo with the last few miles being accompanied by the shrieking sounds of limbs scraping against the metal of the vehicle. Carlos glances at his GPS machine. He was there.

He stepped out of the vehicle and looked around. The dark of the night hindered his sight, but it was his stomach that gave him the gravest of feelings. Whatever happened next in this washed out, Texas gulley, he would be changed forever. As he looked around in the darkness, he thought about his next move. Carlos spent his life in service of those whose names would never be known. He served only people not willing to place their name willingly in the public eye. That simply made him expendable. He was the fall guy for those who benefited from his labors, taking no risk, and seizing the lion share of the reward. He felt sentenced to death; if not a literal one. As the wind current shifted, Carlos could smell in the air the reality he already knew. He began to walk upwind toward the distinct scent. He shined his flashlight to the ground and observed the discoloration in the sand. It was no doubt coagulated blood commonly seen in Texas with hunting and all. He slowly continued walking up the dry wash. A feeling came over him causing Carlos to take out a 9mm pistol from his waistband.

As he rounded a bend, he raised the weapon seeing a silhouette in the night luminance. He crouched to the ground gripped in such fear that his heart was literally pounding out of his chest cavity. As he watched, the image remained motionless. Carlos got closer to the ground in a low crawl position and began to squirm to a position in which he could see better the image that was before him. His stomach was still in his throat as he stood up and carefully walked towards the silhouette. He calmly put the pistol back into his waistband.

He walked towards the two stakes sticking up vertically from the ground. Juan and Chuco's heads stood prominently on the end of each stake. The assassins took great care into preserving the faces of Carlos's friends, so there would be no doubt of their identity. The heads were precisely severed mid-neck. Their bodies were nowhere to be found. He sat down in the course sand of the wash and began to cry. He never expected to things to turn out this way. He cursed Caldwell and Tio as he sat under the decaying heads of his friends. The silence of the night was suddenly interrupted by the irreverent ring tone of Carlos's cellular phone. When he saw the number, he answered it, but didn't say a word.

"Carlos, you knew we could not let this go, eh?" The voice was unmistakably Tio Muniz. Hatred for this man seethed in the soul of Carlos. He clenched his teeth in anticipation of talking to this monster. He wanted nothing more than to tear this man's heart from his body, but it was reality finally grounded Carlos's senses.

"This was senseless…it didn't need to happen," Carlos's

tone was collected but firm.

"Sometimes this is what is necessary. It maintains order within the organization."

"Now what?"

"No entiendeo?"

"What becomes of me? The business?"

The disgusting sound of Tio's laughter was beginning to wear on Carlos. *"You are still my man, Carlos, and we have several accounts to get settled."*

"The border is locked because of all the killings. There's too much heat right now. Plus, I don't have any guys!"

"Another problem you must solve, Carlos," Tio said in gest. Carlos held his tongue as Tio joked with him. There were few times in life where Carlos felt this helpless. There was no good way out in any direction. Carlos was correct in thinking tonight was a turning point in his life, however short it may be.

"Just answer me one question, Tio?" Carlos finally muttered coldly.

"Yes, Carlos…I think you have at least earned that."

"Who gave the order?" Carlos's question was met with silence on the other end of the phone. Could it be that the great Tio Muniz was not confident in his answer? "Was it *El Patron?*"

"El Patron cannot be bothered in these matters," Tio finally answered after several awkward moments of silence. *"I gave the order. The decision was mine."*

"Very well, Tio…you're the boss. What should I tell Chuco and Juan's families?"

"Tell them nothing Carlos and you are right…I am the Boss," Tio's phone disconnected much more discreetly than it rang leaving Carlos once again to the Texas night and his dead friends. A million thoughts went through his head, but the most prominent one was that he would be dead soon. If Tio proved nothing else, he would kill anyone. Carlos knew that he was replaceable and Tio could fill his spot anytime. If desperate times called for desperate measures, then Carlos had nothing to lose. He raised his cellular phone to his ear, *"Puedo hablar con El Patron?"*

*

"Remind me of what I'm looking for again?" Deb Nichols placed her flashlight on the ground and got her head close to the ground to see that refractive light reveal the secrets of the floor. It was an old crime scene technique she was taught as a rookie by an old Texas Ranger. Rangers were trained extensively in crime scene searches, even today, but with the complex nature of today's litigation and legal precedence, they decided that specialized training and units was the wave of the future. Deb Nichols was among the first wave of recruits. Though her personal life suffered immensely, she couldn't have been happier with her choice of professions. Even when it meant she had to search on the nasty floor of a Texas State Prison. She received a call from Kidd and Flynt requesting she help them re-search the cell of Trey Caldwell.

"Well now Deb, you're a trained professional and we just don't want to miss anything," Flynt smiled as he answered.

"Wasn't he killed by the guard?"

"So, it seems, but we ain't necessarily worried about that case."

"So again…what are we looking for?"

"That's just it, Deb, we don't know. That's why you're here," Kidd admitted, he himself looking furiously around the small cell.

Deb looked at the small desk inside the cell that appeared to have a piece of stationary with doodling drawings all over it. Next to the drawing was an envelope. "You guys see this?" Deb looked closer at the drawing. "Doesn't that look like a building?"

Flynt walked to the desk to take a closer look at the drawing. His eyebrows raised when he saw it. "Kidd look at this. Look familiar?"

Kidd took one glance at the drawing, "Sure as hell does."

"Can you guys let me in on this?" Deb sated curiously, you somewhat annoyed.

"It's the Johnson compound. That building is the Inspired

LDS Temple."

"The polygamist group?"

"Yep."

"So, the girl the Marshal's rescued?"

"It's Amanda Johnson, a daughter of a polygamist, but she hasn't said anything yet."

"The polygamists are involved in this shitstorm?"

"So, it would seem," Flynt said casually, obviously deep in thought. "On a related note, did you test the buccal swabs we sent from the Marshals?"

"I did," Deb answered, though her suspicions were raised. "And what do you mean related?"

"Wait, tell us the results first," Kidd smiled at the annoyed Crime Scene Investigator.

"We ran the mitochondrial and YSTR DNA and discovered the donor of the hairbrush is related to one of the burn victims," Deb looked at the Rangers curiously. "Now start talking!"

"That hairbrush belongs to the girl in the hospital…Amanda, we think," Flynt replied. "It's a theory that we been working, but until now, it's been a lot of smoke."

"I'd say there's a goddamn fire now," Kidd observed.

"I'd say," Deb concurred. "How'd you all figure the polygamists in this?"

"Didn't at first, till this little young lady came along and filled us in," Flynt said. "She's Amanda's best friend."

"What's her name?"

"Sariah."

"Then you need to get Sariah to talk to Amanda."

"Why?"

"A young girl isn't going to open up to two old, ornery men. She will open up to her best friend."

"You think?"

"I know?" Deb squeezed Flynt's cheeks together playfully as she spoke. "What about the girl's parents?"

"Hospital has her as a Jane Doe. We're waiting for confirmation on her identity to tell them. Don't want the parents to know just yet…don't know if they're involved."

"You know if the hospital finds out first, they will notify

them with or without you, right?"

Kidd thought about Deb's comments and knew she was right. If Johnson got to Amanda before they were able to speak with her, she would never cooperate with police. He looked over at Flynt; he knew Flynt was thinking the same thing. They had to get a hold of Sariah and get her to the hospital. Kidd once again looked around the cell and noticed a wadded piece of paper covered in dust and lint. It appeared the paper had been in Caldwell's pockets and survived time and maybe a washing or two. "What do you make of that Richard?"

Flynt reached down and picked up the paper with his gloved hand and carefully began to unfold it without damaging it further. Flynt immediately recognized the spreadsheet.

CHAPTER EIGHTEEN

The Question

President Nephi Josephs smiled as he addressed the Celestial Room in the Inspired Temple on the Johnson Compound. President Josephs observed the small gathering seated, all in their white robes, green aprons, and baker caps. The women wore white vails. The robes represented the robes of the priesthood of God, while the aprons symbolized Adam's struggle after being exiled from the Garden of Eden. Today, however, was Brother Benson's Second Anointing Ceremony, a ceremony reserved only for the very faithful. If differed from the normal temple ceremonies for members in that the Second Anointing made one's calling and election made sure. In short, it guaranteed them a spot in the Celestial Kingdom with Elohim, God the Father, as a joint heir with Jesus Christ.

The ceremony started like the normal endowment ceremony by washing and anointing. Brother Benson and his wives removed their clothing and a cloth 'shield' or sheet was placed over them for modesty. The officiator, President Josephs, then pronounced a blessing while symbolically washing them with water, and then anointing them with oil. He Blessed Brother Benson's family with wealth and promised that they would see the return of Jesus Christ. The next part of the ceremony involved President Josephs washing the feet of Brother Benson. Brother Benson and his four wives were then escorted into the sealing room together. While inside, the wives blessed Brother Benson by laying their hands on his head. It was the most sacred ordinance in the Inspired Church of Jesus Christ of Latter-day Saints and it always reinforced the faith of the prophet, seer, revelator, Nephi Josephs. But Nephi had another purpose today as well. He scheduled an appointment with Bishop Johnson. They were to speak in the Holy of Holies, the most sacred room inside the temple where only the prophet and his designees could dwell. It was thought that Jesus Christ himself would visit the prophet in that very room by the members of the sect, but truth be known, Jesus only appeared to President Josephs in his heart; that would have to be good enough for the faithful. The group gradually filed out of the temple and President Josephs and Bishop Johnson made their way into the small eight-foot by eight-foot room. It was sparsely furnished with a few ornate chairs and a marble alter in the center. The two knelt at the alter and asked God for his spirit to be with them during their meeting. President Josephs was sure that Bishop Johnson thought this was merely a personal priesthood interview, or PPI, as it's known, when one high ranking priesthood holder interviews the other. But this was different, and the stakes were much higher.

"How are things going, Thomas?" President Josephs smiled, trying to personalize the conversation.

"Very well, President Josephs," Bishop Johnson replied. It was an unwritten rule that the ranking priesthood holder, especially a prophet, was always referred to by his formal title. If they were not, it was seen as robbing them of the title given to them by God. "We struggle, just as any congregation, but in all we are good."

"I had a very disturbing visit recently."

"From who?"

"Moroni LaFey," President Josephs watched Bishop Johnson's reaction. It was one of concern, anger, and fear. All appropriate, President Josephs thought.

"I thought he agreed to never come to the states?"

"Moroni LaFey has his own rules," President Josephs stated after clearing his throat. "He brought up a concern about how the sect is being run."

"Specifically?"

"He mentioned that some members had suspicions about possible involvement with that awful mass grave found on your land."

"I can assure you, President Josephs, neither I, nor my family had any involvement with that awful crime," It was Bishop Johnson's turn to clear his throat. "Who gave him such a ridiculous notion?"

"He didn't say."

Bishop Johnson laughed out loud, but reverently and nervously, given their holy surroundings. "It had to be Sariah Larsen! She's a silly, confused girl that doesn't even heed to your counsel, President Josephs!"

"Silly and confused girls can still be a problem, Thomas."

"You know I have never had a good relationship with, Sariah's father, Jeremiah, or his brother, Moroni." Bishop Johnsons' comment caught President Josephs off guard. He realized that his entire flock knew Jeremiah's secret, but he'd never heard it mentioned out loud, until now. Bishop Johnson could see the prophet's shock. "He's a pariah to the sect. He and his wives have little regard for yours, or any of the brethren's counsel. Besides, the Lord commanded me to take Sariah as a wife,"

"I was not aware of this, Thomas. A revelation?"

"Yes, after a long night in prayer.

"How did she receive the revelation when you told her?"

"Not very well, I'm afraid. No doubt because of her father."

"So, it seems."

"She rejects the words of the prophets, President Josephs, even yours."

"Thomas…I did not receive this revelation that you should marry Sariah Larsen. Are you sure that it was a sanctified revelation from our Heavenly Father?"

"As sure as I sit before you."

President Josephs stared at the bishop for quite some time. It was the burden of the leader to know the hearts of his subjects. As the prophet of the church, Nephi Josephs couldn't rely on the Lord's help in judging this bishop that sat before him. As of right now, he saw a faithful follower, man that dedicated his life and wealth to further the cause of the Lord's plan on earth. So how could President Josephs trust the word of an admitted murderer and blasphemer? But he still had at least one question for the bishop. "Thomas…when you told Sariah of the revelation, did you tell her the commandment came from me?"

Bishop Johnson's smile wasn't completely lost when President Josephs' question was asked, but the luster certainly was. "Why no, President Josephs, I would not say such a thing."

"Certainly not Thomas," President Josephs smiled. It was not a smile of relief, more of smile of intrigue. "I certainly do not need to remind you, Thomas, of the consequences if you are not telling me the absolute truth?"

"President Josephs…I have lived and devoted myself to the law of the Gospel, I know full well the consequences."

*

Amanda could barely open her eyes when the social worker came in to see her. She never spoke to Gentiles. The girl was Hispanic, slightly overweight but attractive just the same. She could smell the lady's perfume and loved her outfit. It was pretty and modest; all of the things the brethren always preached. The woman smiled big at Amanda, who didn't have the strength to respond.

"Are we going to speak today, Sweetheart?" The woman's face was so friendly and inviting, Amanda could not resist.

"Yes…Yes, ma'am," The words literally hurt to speak. Her throat was so raw and dry that she wondered if the woman could understand her.

"What is your name?"

"Amanda Johnson."

"Where do you live?"

"I…I don't know," Amanda's answer seemed to confuse the kind woman who stopped writing on her clip board. "I used to live in Eagle Pass."

"Any family there now?"

"My father and mothers."

The woman's face wrinkled with confusion. "Tell you what, just give me your father's information," the woman handed Amanda the clipboard which she simply stared at. She began to fill it out as the tears streamed down her face. What would her father think of her now?

*

"I don't understand why I can't just go see her?" Sariah pled with the two Rangers outside of Doctor's Hospital. Kidd and Flynt insisted the young girl speak to them before she visited Amanda. "Please!"

"Listen to me young lady," Flynt was firm but still warm. "We need you to get her to talk. I mean, she needs to tell us everything she remembers."

"You don't think I know that?"

"I don't think you realize how important this is. She hasn't spoken a word to the Marshals after telling them who she was."

"And she won't, Sergeant Flynt" Sariah retorted. "She hates Gentiles worse than I did. She would never betray the brethren."

"All the more reason to get us all the necessary information before her family gets to her."

"All the more reason to let me go now then?" Sariah pointed out. They gave her a digital pocket recorder. Sariah pulled out her cellular phone, "Excuse me…I just need to make a quick call."

"We're burning daylight, c'mon kiddo!" Kidd barked.

"It will only be a second," Both Rangers nodded at the girl. Sariah walked a few steps over and appeared to be sending a text message and quickly covered up the keyboard. As she walked back to the Rangers' Crown Vic and got into the vehicle. Kidd helped her into the vehicle reminiscent of his days on patrol making sure suspects didn't hurt themselves getting into squad cars, or worse, getting hurt by other officers. As she bent over she handed her belongings to Kidd so she could bend and contort herself into the small back seat. They quickly drove away to make good time to the hospital. It was a race against time at this point.

*

"Jeremiah…what brings you out this way?" Bishop Johnson greeted Jeremiah at his office with a superficial smile and some suspicion given his recent interaction with the prophet. Jeremiah shook his hand and entered the small office without so much as a smile. "Please sit down, this is quite unexpected."

"Thank you for seeing me, Bishop," Jeremiah's voice was cordial, but somewhat firm. He stared at the Bishop. Before him stood a man called by a prophet, but not a man Jeremiah would think God would deal with. In fact, if God was actually the being that he has been taught about since his youth, then Bishop Johnson would be the last servant called. But then again, God's ways are not man's, and Jeremiah definitely did not understand God's ways. "I'm not sure how to ask this, but I've heard some troubling information."

"Like that I had something to do with this awful mess in the news?"

"Partly," Jeremiah answered suspiciously.

"President Josephs already spoke to me," Johnson stared at Jeremiah. "Seems Sariah has been spreading rumors about me?"

"No rumors Bishop…simple concerns."

"And you couldn't come directly to me?"

"You and I have never really had an amicable relationship, Bishop," Jeremiah responded. "I am only approaching you now out of necessity. I want to hear your answers from you."

"So, you got the prophet involved in this?"

"No, I did not."

"Your family?"

Jeremiah sat back and smirked at the Bishop. What kind of man is simply worried about accusations and innuendo if he had nothing to hide? "Do you mean the LaFeys?"

"You said it," Johnson smiled back as if his knowledge of Jeremiah's background was an advantage in this situation. "I know about your background, Jeremiah. Your family has a colorful history. I should think the authorities would be interested in it as well."

"You say you know my family's history, Bishop?" Jeremiah looked at the Bishop and waited for the affirmative nod. "Then you should know the United States Government has been investigating them for years. I should also think that they perhaps know a little about you. Our family has no loyalty to man…only to God"

"You say that, Jeremiah, but you don't heed to the counsel

of his servants. 'whether it be by my voice, or the voice of my servants, it is the same,' that is our mission in life, Jeremiah."

"I know the scriptures, Bishop. How have we not heeded his counsel?"

"Your daughter has refused a commandment from the prophet! And what's worse, she spreads vicious lies about her own bishop."

"The prophet's commandment or the bishop's commandment?"

"It is the same!"

"It isn't," Jeremiah snapped back which clearly unsettled Bishop Johnson. "There's a big difference."

"I'm still unsure why you're even here, Jeremiah?"

"I want to hear it from you, Bishop," Jeremiah glared. "Did you have anything to do with this mess on the news…the mass grave?"

"Absolutely not!"

"What about Amanda and Ruth's marriage to the Smoots?"

The question made Johnson pause, it was clear he did want to answer the question. "That is complicated, Jeremiah."

"How so Bishop?" Jeremiah sat back in his chair obviously interested in Johnson's explanation. "Seems to me either you had an arrangement with the Smoots or you didn't."

Johnson cleared his throat as if his explanation was to be the authoritative end all to the conversation. "There was an arrangement, Jeremiah. But a tragedy occurred."

"What tragedy?"

"Amanda and Ruth were kidnapped," Johnson looked embarrassed and humbled.

"My God! Why didn't you tell anyone?"

"Who would I tell?" Johnson's face was like stone. "I'm like you… there is no one in this country that will help people like us, Jeremiah."

"You have us, Bishop…"

"It's more complicated than that."

"Please enlighten me? Are we not commanded to lighten one another's burdens? To bear one another's cross? It seems you need another scripture lesson, Bishop, or perhaps you don't heed to the scriptures?" Jeremiah looked at the Bishop in part with sympathy, and in part disgust. "What about the girls, what is going on now?"

"I have reached out to various associates to keep their ears to the ground; some Gentile, some members. I have the Smoots help of course."

"My sources tell me the Smoots know nothing of any arrangement."

"Perhaps you should check your sources. Brother Smoot is a true ally."

"What do you mean ally?"

"He does not question the word of God, Jeremiah."

"Neither do I, only the vessels that relay the word," Jeremiah stood up to leave the small office. "You said you knew my family?"

"I know of them, yes."

"Then you should know what they're capable of."

"Is that a threat, Jeremiah?"

"Not at all, Bishop," Jeremiah said casually as he walked toward the door. "But you should know the LaFeys take special exception to those that are called, but not serving the Lord in their full capacity. Moroni especially, he's particularly pious in that respect…but I'm off." Jeremiah continued towards the door and turned around right before completely leaving the office. "Oh, I thought you should know something."

"What's that?" Johnson stared at Jeremiah with anger and disgust.

"Amanda is at Doctor's Hospital in Laredo…thought you should hear that from us and not the Gentiles," Jeremiah saw the color drain out of Johnson's face, turning the anger to fear and uncertainty. It was very telling to Jeremiah as he walked from the office.

*

Sariah couldn't help but cry as she sat by her best friend's bed. The once voluptuous, energetic, and beautiful Amanda lay there with leads and oxygen hooked into her like tentacles on a sea creature. She was at least thirty pounds lighter and the gaunt look on her face was accentuated by the darkness around her eyes. The teen looked as if she was approaching middle age instead of the prime of her life. She hadn't even said a word, but Sariah could tell that the sweetest soul she had ever met in her life was changed forever. Sariah knew Amanda would recover physically, but it was her spiritual welfare that was of concern. If their friendship was to suffer it would be more than Sariah could bear.

"Sariah?" Amanda's voice was so weak it was hardly audible. Her voice so deep and cracked, she sounded like a fifty- year smoker.

"I'm here Sweetheart," Sariah grabbed Amanda's cold hands that felt lifeless. She hung onto Amanda's hand as if she were about to leave again. "You're safe now…"

"Everyone keeps saying that, but I don't feel safe."

"Well you are," Sariah fought hard to hold back the tears. "You are."

"My Dad is coming…the nice social worker girl told me."

Sariah didn't know what to say to her best friend. Does she tell her about her father's suspicious behavior or lies, or about her rapist brothers? Or perhaps she would simply bury those facts and memories and enjoy the fact her friend is alive? After all, she had been raised in a sect that buried deep, dark historical secrets so effortlessly it was commonplace. At that moment, the latter was the better choice, Sariah thought. "That's great, Amanda!" Sariah's pseudo-excitement was accompanied by a gentle kiss on her friend's hand.

"I don't want to see him," Amanda cried humbly and softly.

"Why not?" Sariah could think of a thousand reasons, but she wanted to hear Amanda's.

"I couldn't protect Ruth!" Amanda closed her eyes and looked away from her friend in shame.

It was Sariah's turn to cry, "You did everything you could…you hear me? Those people are monsters!"

"I should've done more."

"Tell me what happened, Amanda?"

Amanda continued to cry but did her best to compose

herself. Sariah kept rubbing her hand softly. "Nathan and Josiah took us to Laredo to the bus stop…"

"Bus stop? Your dad makes millions…"

"Sariah…it's less hassle for two polygamist girls to get a bus ticket. You need solid identification to fly," There was a tad bit of disgust in her voice and justifiably so Sariah thought. Families in the sect don't like the scrutiny of airport security. "So Ruth and I went to get some Chinese food at that place off of San Bernardo Avenue."

"Yeah… China Border."

"Yes," Amanda's throat became parched prompting Sariah to hold a cup of water with a straw to her friend's mouth. Amanda drank gently before continuing. "We go in and sit down to eat and a really handsome man sits at the table next to us."

"Where were Nathan and Josiah?"

"At the bus station with our luggage, I guess. I really don't know…Ruth and I wanted to be alone."

"What was the guy's name?"

"He said Carlos…he was really handsome," Amanda replied with a look of shame. "We all talked and flirted. He even told us how beautiful we were and that we were too young to get married."

"He was coming onto you?"

"Yeah, sort of… I mean…I didn't see anything wrong with flirting. It wasn't like anything was going to happen, right?"

"What happened next?"

"That's the weird thing…I don't know. The next thing I remember, I'm lying next to Ruth on a bed in some motel room. It was gross and smelled like mildew. We were half naked and Ruth looked very sick. Then we were in a car and I ran…I just can't remember everything!"

"Was Carlos there?"

"No, this other guy was. He was big and White and covered in tattoos. He was awful…he swore at us and was just filthy."

"Was anyone else there?"

"We had been there for some time and they brought another girl in the room. She was young, and really pretty. She didn't speak English. She kept saying she wanted her mother in Spanish. Either they didn't know Spanish, or they didn't care."

"You keep saying they? Besides the tattoo guy, who else was there?"

"A woman," Amanda closed her eyes and really cried for an uncomfortable moment. "She hated Ruth, Sariah! She wouldn't give her any food and called her terrible names."

"A woman did that?"

"Yes, she beat on her…I begged her to quit!"

Sariah stroked the forehead of her friend as her tone became more serious, "Did they rape you Sweetheart?"

Amanda cried and couldn't even speak. She nodded her head in the affirmative confirming Sariah's suspicions. "Over and over… I convinced the guy that I was way better than Ruth, so he would leave her alone. I think it worked, but I think he raped her in the beginning too." She stopped for a moment attempting to conceal her embarrassment. "They said I have gonorrhea and human papillomavirus. The gonorrhea will go away but the HPV never will. I guess to the brethren, I really am unclean now, huh?"

"Don't you ever say that, Amanda!" Sariah barked angrily. She could not stand to hear the sweetest girl she ever met degrade herself. Amanda kept talking about her experiences. Sariah was absolutely horrified hearing the details of her dear friend's brutal captivity. Sariah knew she had to be strong for Amanda, but the sickness inside her stomach almost manifest itself physically more than once. It was almost more than the young girl could handle; Sariah almost wished it was her that had to experience the horror and not her best friend. "What happened to Ruth?"

"I don't know…I tried to get away when we were in the car…but when I woke up in the motel with the mean girl…she was gone."

"Do you remember anything else?"

"No," Amanda buried her head into her friend's shoulder. Sariah was speechless. She peered at the digital recorder to make sure it was recording. She could feel her friend get tired and decided Amanda needed rest.

"You need to rest, Sweetheart."

"Sariah?"

"Yes?"

"Do you have a blade I could borrow?"

The question took Amanda back. She had never known Amanda to even touch a weapon, much less request one. "You're safe, Honey?"

"I thought I was safe before, too…turns out I was wrong. Besides, the policemen that were guarding me are gone now."

Sariah scanned the area for nurses, then secretly handed Sariah a spare butterfly knife she kept in the side pocket of her purse. Amanda accepted the knife secretly placing it under the mattress of hospital bed. Sariah embraced her friend one last time before getting up to walk out of the room.

"Sariah?" Amanda called. Sariah stopped at the sound of her friend's voice.

"Yes, Sweetheart."

"I love you," Amanda said with tears in her eyes. The statement brought tears to Sariah's eyes as well.

"I love you, too."

CHAPTER NINETEEN

Realizations

The scene had already been released, but Kidd and Flynt entered the residence anyway. The tape and barricades were gone, but the smell of death remained. It was a combination of mildew, must, and a tinge of rot, but it's a scent familiar to every investigator. It did help that Texas Don was at least clean. The scene was largely untouched except for paramedic's gloves and leads left by first responders. The events over the last days began to weigh heavily on the Rangers and the investigation took on a new turn. Some investigations are sprints, the motives and methods are so obvious that the solvability is never an issue. This case was different; it was a marathon. This meant that the investigation was scorched earth, nothing was to be overlooked and no stone unturned. The reason the Rangers still had interest in Texas Don wasn't the real question. The real question was who exactly was Texas Don? If they could find that out, the case was solved; at least his murder. As to the big picture…that still remained unclear. Kidd walked into the master bedroom and looked on the floor of the closet.

"Got something," he called out to Flynt still lurking around in the kitchen.

"I'm coming," Flynt replied making his way across the modest home. "What do ya got?"

"Floor safe," Kidd called out manipulating the lever and pulling the door open. It amazed him that so many people went to the trouble of buying and installing safes only to leave them unlocked regularly. "It's open."

"Never fails."

"Yep."

"What's in there?"

"Shitload of docs, just like you figured."

"Sack em' up."

"Shouldn't we get another warrant?"

"We're just borrowing them?" Flynt smiled. "Tell you what,

if someone wants them back, we'll give em back." The statement made Kidd chuckle. Texas Don had no family to speak of, so no one would be looking for his belongings. However, there was the legal question when and if these documents would be entered into evidence at a trial.

"What about the trial old man?"

Flynt smiled as he thumbed through the mountain of documents Texas Don collected. "These documents ain't never going to make it in a trial."

"Why not?"

"It's time I teach you something about Texas politics, son," Flynt looked at his younger partner. "Now listen good…there are two classes of people here in Texas, connected and unconnected. Now the unconnected, like you and me, we're the ones that get prosecuted. The connected don't…they plea." Flynt continued to thumb briskly through the paperwork but stopped when one particular document struck his interest. He casually folded it and placed it inside his pocket. "The other thing you got to know about connected people…" Flynt paused staring more intently at his partner but remaining silent.

"Did you forget old man? What?"

"They circle the wagons and protect the other connected people if they're in trouble, even if they don't like em. It's how they stay connected."

"How can you say you're not connected? You're in with the Governor, Senators, some of the brass…"

"You seriously think I'm their friend, son?" Flynt laughed.

"You're not?"

"I'm useful to them…I serve their purpose."

"That's pretty damned cynical."

"As soon as I don't serve a purpose to them…they'll throw me out with the trash. Now that's the goddamn cynical part," Flynt gently put the rest of the documents in a paper evidence sack. "We got what we need. Let's roll."

*

"There's my beautiful daughter," Bishop Johnson walked

248

into the hospital room smiling as his daughter lay in the bed, still weak from her experiences. He wore his signature black suit, white shirt and tie that seemed to be standard issue for every male associated with Mormonism in any way. Though he touched her shoulder, he never hugged, kissed, or showed the affection of a normal father. Amanda managed to force a smile back, but inside was scared out of her mind.

"Hi Father," she managed to say in a low, soft voice.

"Are they treating you well?"

"Yes, Father. They said I'm improving every day and that if my strength continues to improve, I can go home within a few days. How's Mother?"

"Worried sick, she hasn't slept much since Josiah and Nathan told us you and Ruth were missing."

The mention of Ruth's name triggered a strong emotional response from Amanda and the tears began to flow from her face yet again, she wondered how she could even have any tears left. "Father…I really tried to help Ruth…they were too strong. You gotta believe me."

"Oh. I do," Johnson smiled and stroked the freshly washed hair of his daughter. Amanda didn't feel the love of her father, but the judgmental eyes of a church leader. She didn't feel the warmth of family, but the coldness of dogma and doctrine. She felt more alone with him present than when he was away. "But what happened… happened, and it is the will of God."

"Surely God would not approve of what happened?"

"Oh, but he does allow men to make mistakes… even young ladies."

"What mistake did I make?"

"Before you were taken, did you speak to any Gentiles?"

Amanda closed her eyes and thought about Carlos, the handsome gentile that flirted with her and Ruth. She knew she would have to confess her sin of flirting to her father and it didn't make it any easier that it was a gentile. "We just spoke to him, Father. His name was Carlos…"

"What have I told you about the Gentiles?"

"I know, Father, but it was just talking in a restaurant…"

"It does not matter, it displeases the Lord…and his wrath is great."

"But I can repent, Father...right?"

Bishop Johnson smiled, "Of course...the blood of the lamb is for all, but there are real consequences of sin in this life, Amanda." Johnson watched his daughter bow her head in shame. "The nurse told me about your diseases."

"I'm sorry, Father...I ...I kept telling them no, but they wouldn't listen," Amanda explained franticly. "It's not my fault!"

"Of course, it isn't my dear, but again...if you hadn't spoken to that Gentile, this would not have happened."

"But I don't know what happened, Father...I must have been drugged!"

"Drugged or not, it is Heavenly Father's will that you have to live with this situation."

"What does that mean?"

"It means that most likely none of the brethren, including the Smoots, will have you as their wife."

"But I need a husband to get into the Celestial Kingdom..."

"Don't worry, perhaps one of the elders need another wife," Johnson tried to console the girl, but was obviously failing due to the tears streaming down her face. "A servant maybe?" Sariah knew her eternal salvation, in part, was based on the faithfulness of her husband and the priesthood officer he held. An elder was an essential part of the church, but she wanted more and had been taught to expect more ever since she was a young girl. "Okay sweetheart?"

"Okay...but do I have any other options?" Amanda asked in an increasing empty voice. Bishop Johnson smiled in an almost sympathetic, yet condescending manner. "There are always options, Amanda. You know from the teachings of the prophets that are always options."

"I know everything is the Lord's will, Father," Amanda acknowledged in a humble manner. "And I know that his will shall be done."

"I have always known that you were a special child. The Lord spoke that to me before you were born. May he welcome you always, dear daughter," Johnson got up and walked towards the door, again no display of affection towards his daughter. In fact, his body language didn't even show that Amanda was even related. He buttoned up his suit coat as he got up.

"Father?" Amanda cried as Bishop Johnson walked towards the door. He stopped and turned his head in acknowledgement.

"Yes Dear?"

"Can I see Mother?"

Bishop Johnson stared at the girl with his normal stoic look, "I don't think that would be a good idea. It would only hurt her more."

Amanda shook her heard in acknowledgment and continued to cry. As she watched her father leave she decided that there was no reason to delay the inevitable. She buzzed the nurse in and sat up in bed. A petite, attractive nurse walked into the room and smiled at Amanda.

"What can I do for you, Sweetheart?"

"I wanted to see if it was okay that I took a walk?" Amanda answered with a cheerful face, as if nothing was wrong in her life. "I just wanted to get some air and you know…to get stronger."

"Well girl that makes me so happy! You have been so down lately?"

"I know, but I'm alive and I need to start living again."

"Good for you, but I really should go with you…"

"No," Amanda laughed to reassure her nurse. "You're so busy…besides, where would I go?"

"I guess that's true," the sweet nurse replied. "Let me get those leads off you." The nurse carefully removed the leads from Sariah but leaving the pads in place so that they could be easily hooked back up. "You're all set, just call me when you get back and I'll hook you up with some food."

"Okay, thank you," Amanda said cheerfully. She got up to walk and discovered how weak legs can be if they're immobile for too long. She soldiered on and put on another gown to cover her exposed body. She slipped her hand underneath the mattress and retrieved the butterfly knife. As she got up to walk out she found herself only able to limp as her right leg was badly bruised from her ordeal. As she made her way past the nurse's station and waived invoking several smiles and waves back from all of the staff. She casually walked into the stairwell undetected and made her way up to the top floor of the structure. She found the entrance to the reyser room unlocked and crawled up the ladder to the roof. She had a little trouble with the steel ladder but managed to navigate it nonetheless to find the roof access door unlocked. She struggled to get the clunky door opened and crawled outside. As she made her way towards the ledge of the building she felt the cold air and the bite of the wind on her bare legs. She looked at the sky, the moon, and the stars on the clear night. She knew she was doing the will of her Heavenly Father as she was no longer worthy of a priesthood holder's love. No worthy man would want a disease laden woman, she thought. Since the whole point to her life was gone…she had only one option to regain her favor in the eyes of God. As she looked over the ledge, she knew the fall wouldn't kill her. She carefully unfolded the knife in her right hand.

"Heavenly Father…into your loving hands I commend my spirit to serve thee in the eternities. Forgive me of my sins as I spill my blood for Thee!" She raised the knife in the air as to show it to the invisible God. She then brought the knife underneath her chin and thrust it into her neck puncturing the vital carotid artery. Amanda could feel the immediate coldness from the blood flowing out of her body. As her eyes closed for the last time her body fell over the side of the building towards the ground and eternities.

*

"Como Estas, El Patron?" Moroni stepped onto the Crime Lord's front patio to a warm handshake from the boss himself. The multiple armed guards treated the visitor with a respect not afforded to other men. In fact, it was almost a fearful respect when the fundamentalist stepped onto the property with full welcome and blessing from their notorious boss.

"Muey Bien! And how is my old friend?" El Patron and hugged Moroni.

"The Lord has blessed me and my family…what can I say?" Moroni smiled back.

"Excellente!" The two men made small talk or several minutes, mostly reminiscing about the good old days as they remembered. But there was a tension in the air and it was very obvious that there was an issue with their friendship and it had to be dealt with.

"You got my message?"

"I did…I am greatly concerned and disappointed."

"I trust you will handle things on your end?"

"As always my friend," El Patron smiled again. "I would offer you a drink, Amigo, but I know you will not take it." The two men sat down for lunch on the patio.

*

Ranger Kidd hugged Sariah as she stepped into the café and sat down. It was a little quieter in Bolillos Café in Laredo than most restaurants in the area. They sat in a corner booth and Sariah smiled as she sat down. She looked so happy. Kidd tried to smile but somehow he couldn't manage to be as jovial as the young girl. The news that he had to tell her would crush Sariah and he didn't know if he could bear to see her heart broken.

"You look good, Kiddo," Kidd managed to smile at the young girl.

"I know this whole thing is a tragedy and all, but I just can't help but feel relieved Amanda is back. I mean…I know she's got to go back to the Johnson Compound which is like…hell on earth, but at least she's back," Sariah smiled at Kidd which made him feel sick to his stomach.

"That's kind of why I called you here, Sariah," Kidd said very softly. "It's about Amanda."

"I don't understand?"

"Late last night she took her life…"

"No!" Sariah began to sob uncontrollably in a sudden fit of anger induced sadness. "What! How?"

"She put a butterfly knife into carotid artery then dove off the roof of the hospital."

Sariah stopped breathing for an uncomfortable period of time. She got up and sprinted to the bathroom inside the restaurant quickly into a handicap stall. She barely got her head over the toilet bowl as the vomit purged from her body and her muscles contorted. Her eyes were bloodshot and tearful as the reality set in that it was Sariah's own blade that was the instrument of her best friend's death. How could she do this? Sariah knew exactly why, which ate at her very soul. She walked to the sink, cleaned herself and composed her face. She calmly walked out into the dining area to a standing Ranger Kidd.

"Are you okay, Sariah?"

"No, but I'll make it," Her tears and sobs were on the brink of reappearing, but the strong young woman was able to hold them in allowing her anger to appear.

"Do you know why she would do something like that?"

"Yes…it was Bishop Johnson. It was that son of a bitch…"

"Sariah, it was clearly a suicide…"

"He made her do it…you can believe that."

"How?"

"She was raped, that means she is not good enough for the brethren," Sariah answered in a resentful tone. "Don't you see? He convinced her that she was a sinner and could never be redeemable in this life."

"Blood atonement?"

"Exactly…the only way she can make herself worthy for God is to spill her own blood."

Kidd had heard of this belief that was not unique to Mormonism, but was a principle taught by Joseph Smith and Brigham Young. It was also included in the Mormon Church's original endowment ceremonies within the temple until the early Nineteen Nineties. At that time, Mormon General Authorities, bowing to popular pressure, changed the endowment ceremony and removed the references to blood atonement. Kidd had no idea that fundamentalist Mormons still believed in the archaic doctrine. "His own daughter?" Kidd was sickened by the thought.

"Do I even have to answer that?"

"Did he give her the knife?"

"I did…"

"What the fuck?!" Kidd looked around to see whether or not anyone saw his outburst. "What the hell were you thinking, little girl?"

"She asked for protection! She just got raped and brutalized by fucking degenerates who killed her sister… what was I supposed to do?"

Kidd put his coffee down on the table and thought. The girl had a point. She felt she was helping her friend, she couldn't have known Amanda would use the blade in that manner. "Is it traceable to you?"

"No, I picked it up in Coahuila."

"You think the Johnson's already know?"

"Bet on it."

"Listen, I want you to go home to your family…steer clear of those crazy bastards…"

"Nathan and Josiah set her up, Ranger Kidd…you know it!"

"Listen, this case is far from over and we just lost our star-fucking witness. We need to regroup and press forward."

"What does that mean for me?"

"You lay low for now."

"I can't do that!"

"You have to!" Kidd said firmly. "There's a storm coming, and I don't want you in on it."

"I'm already in on it."

"Yeah…and that haunts me every day," Kidd finished his coffee, stood up and put his Stetson on his head. "Now please go back to your family."

"I will," Sariah answered unconvincingly. "I just need to make one stop."

*

Sariah crept into the barn and listened while remaining hidden. The Johnson property had several barns, including the one where she hung out with Amanda. Amanda used to tell her that Nathan and Josiah would hide out in this particular barn and watch porno movies. Of course, the girls laughed at the creepiness of two brothers sitting together watching pornos, still seeing was believing. As she approached the barn she could hear the screams, grunts, and moans of hardcore pornography. But she could hear something else as she approached as well. It wasn't just the two brothers watching movies, or even masturbating. Sariah stood in the shadows and watched as Nathan sodomize Josiah vigorously, she even recorded it with her cellular phone. As he performed, Josiah screamed out scriptures calling both Jew and Gentile to repentance while being ravaged. The two were oblivious to the teenage girl that watched them. It wasn't the act itself that bothered Sariah, unlike the members of her sect, and Mormonism in general, she subscribed to the genetic explanation of homosexuality and didn't look upon it as a carnal sin that guaranteed a spot in hell. But this wasn't homosexuality she was witnessing. It was the act of two sick men brutalizing each other for sport. It was no secret around the sect that the two brothers molested young girls and even sister-wives, what was unknown was their using each other to train for their brutality; till now.

"Well I thought you two were sick and twisted, but I never imagined this," Sariah said with a devilish grin as she stepped out of the shadows. Both Josiah and Nathan scrambled to try and cover themselves obviously extremely shocked. Nathan quickly closed the laptop screen. "Easy there guys, we don't want a repeat do we?" Both men could see that flash of what little light was allowed into the barn reflect off the blade in her hand. "Don't bother covering up, boys…I've seen it all."

"What the fuck are you doing here?!" Josiah spit in anger, while Nathan stood in silence and embarrassment.

"I want to talk to you about Amanda."

"We are grieving for our dear sister," Nathan finally responded in an unconvincing manner as far as Sariah was concerned.

"Grieving huh? Why did you set her up?"

"We don't answer to you, Gentile…we serve the prophet Nephi Josephs!" Josiah answered.

"I just want to know why you would send your own sister to

her death?"

"Now hold on Sariah…" Nathan attempted to interrupt.

"No both you listen! She was my best friend and my sister. She deserves more respect than to die a whore's death!"

"Maybe she was a whore?" Josiah answered prompting Sariah to lift the blade into the air in an aggressive manner. Josiah responded by picking up a piece of rebar and taking a defensive stance. "C'mon you fucking cunt!" He barely got the words from his mouth when he saw the barrel of Sariah's nine-millimeter directly in his face. The barrel of the small pistol must have look enormous to the two boys who were not used to being victimized.

"Whoa…whoa, Sariah! Please calm down!" Nathan pled.

"Oh I'm calm. Looks like you boys need to sit your asses down…now!" Sariah's voice was confident, sinister, and firm. Josiah dropped the rebar and both he and Nathan sat on the cold, dirty wood floor. "I want the truth, so start talking."

"Here is the truth, Sariah…we serve the prophet and the brethren," Nathan answered in a humble, yet reserved manner. "We believe that if it is from the mouth of his servants…it is the same as God's word. Therefore, we cannot betray the brethren…even if it means our lives would be lost."

Sariah lost it and rapidly closed the distance between her and Nathan. She reared back and struck him in the face rendering him almost unconscious. "Really, motherfucker?!" she screamed. Josiah shrieked in fear and attempted to scoot back on the floor away from the angry girl. Sariah quickly placed a precision kick to his exposed groin causing him to scream and double over in pain. "Your sister is dead and all you can say is 'follow the prophet'?" She felt liberated pointing the weapon at the two monsters. In fact, she knew that if she pulled the trigger, no one would hear the shot because this barn was so far out which is why Nathan and Josiah chose this location to perform their nasty deeds. She gritted her teeth and began to feel the slack in the trigger as she pointed the gun directly at Josiah's head. The lust to kill this man flowed through her very body like the thirst of a dying man. Her hands began to shake with anticipation, but there was an unexplained restraint within her. "Both of you…on your hands and knees!" Both Nathan Josiah got on their hands and knees with their posteriors exposed to Sariah. Sariah took out her switchblade, bent down and thrust it into the meaty part of Josiah's buttocks. The young man screamed in pain as his body went fully to the floor.

"Awww! You fucking bitch!" he yelled. Sariah quickly turned his attention to Nathan who was still on his hands and knees staring back at her. She thrust the blade into his ass as well, causing a similar reaction as his brother. She calmly took out the DNA kit she bought online and very carefully collected blood from each brother's wound. She reveled in their terrified faces shrieking in fear of her sudden power. Although her demeanor was calm, she felt so empowered shoving that knife in their flesh. She put them into two separate cartons and into their respective bags secured in her purse.

"The Rangers already got our DNA, Sariah!" Nathan observed, still in pain.

"Well I guess they'll have two samples then," Sariah smiled walking toward the door, leaving both boys laying there naked and wounded. The sound of their whimpering and cries were the only sound being made which brought a slight smile to her face. "Relax…I just stuck it in the fleshy part." Before she left however, she took out her cellular phone. She took several photos of the two monsters, naked, ass up, bleeding and crying. This didn't satisfy her need for vengeance for the loss of her friend, but it did help.

*

Michael Cordova was shocked when he opened the door to his house and saw Sergeant Richard Flynt of the Texas Rangers. The Ranger stood with a manila folder filled with paperwork. Their last conversation was not exactly cordial and the look of bewilderment and confusion were evident in the councilman's face. Flynt just smiled his warm, welcoming grin he was known for.

"Evenin' councilmen, mind if I come in?"

"S…Sergeant Flynt…I thought I told you to go through my

attorney from now on…" Cordova was stammering in his speech obviously nervous. But there was also an element of obvious curiosity, so his communication was at least cordial.

"I think you're gonna want to hear what I have to say, Sir. You always sounded like a reasonable man," Flynt continued to smile at Cordova who simply stared back at the imposing Ranger. Cordova finally made a silent motion for Flynt to come inside the residence and sit on his fine leather couch.

"Can I get you something to drink, Sergeant Flynt?"

"No thank you, Sir. I won't be long."

"Where is your partner?"

"Had some other business. We have been burnin' that candle at both ends lately…ain't enough time in the day I guess."

"I completely understand," Cordova smiled, "What can I help you with?"

"Let me tell you a story, Sir," Flynt sat back on the couch and made himself more comfortable. "When we came down here to work this mess we were contacted by a crazy blogger named Texas Don."

"Yes…the man was crazy, full of stories…"

"You realize he's dead, right councilman?"

Cordova's face turned suspiciously stoic, "Yes…yes, may God rest his soul."

"Turns out Don wasn't as crazy as he came across," Flynt tossed the folder down on Cordova's stone coffee table. Cordova stared at the paperwork as if it was carrying an infectious disease.

"What's that?"

"Enough evidence to convict the whole bunch of you."

"Listen, Sergeant Flynt…I will not be threatened…"

Flynt raised his hand to signal the councilman to be silent, "You will, and you will listen to me carefully." Cordova immediately went silent and stared at the floor. "The fact is you know exactly what that paperwork is, don't you?" Cordova remained motionless and silent. It was as good as a written confession in Flynt's mind.

"What are your plans?" Cordova muttered silently.

"Ain't you gonna look at em'?" Flynt smiled. "Well, I guess I'll tell you then." Flynt shuffled the paperwork, taking out two specific papers. "Here are the City of Eagle Pass's deposits of Federal Highway funds going to into the Coahuila Highway project. Here are the actual funds released by the State of Texas to be deposited." Flynt stared at the Councilman whose head remained aimed at the floor. "You know they don't add up, don't you?"

There was a long, uncomfortable pause of silence between the two men. Cordova finally decided to speak. "It just spiraled out of control…all of it."

"Which councilmen were in on it?" Flynt asked the councilmen but was getting no response. "You…the Mayor?"

"It's been going on for years Sergeant," Cordova said in a defeated voice. "It started way before I got into office. The Negras have been influencing policy and economic development for years."

"That sounds like an excuse, Councilman…"

"No excuses, Ranger. When I got elected, I wanted to do good…change the world. And then reality set in and I was no better than anyone else."

"Soto in on it?"

"He knew. We all knew," Cordova sighed.

"What do you do for them?"

"Nothing."

"I don't understand Councilman?"

"Nothing…nothing! We simply allow everyone to live, Sergeant! *Entiendes?* All of us." The frustration in Cordova's voice was unmistakable. It was the voice of a man that was caught; a man exposed for his deeds. Flynt knew what he meant by nothing. It meant that the Negras could operate and the elected officials, sworn to uphold the law, simply looked the other way. If information concerning illegal activities were to surface, it was immediately quashed. The Negras didn't want someone actively working for them. They simply wanted the powers that be to look the other way. Cordova stared at the Ranger, "So what now?"

Flynt chuckled in more of a disgusted manner.

"Councilman, I've been doin this for close to forty years. This may be hard for you to believe, but my focus is to solve murders. Politics is never clean…is it?" Flynt smiled at Cordova who finally managed to force something of a grin in response to the observation. "It's the Negras down here, but it's the Tech industry up in Austin and Dallas. It's oil down in Houston. Those folks just ain't as violent as the Negras. I know ya'all are crooked as the day is long and I know you ain't no different than anyone else. Hell, I golf with folks with dirtier hands than yours." Flynt sat down and looked Cordova directly in the eyes. "But there were innocents murdered, Councilman, and that I will not look the other way."

"We had nothing to do with that."

"But you do have information," Flynt could tell he hit a nerve in the nervous politician. "And that's your payment to me. I want information…"

"But I don't…"

Flynt held his hand in the air to signal the politician to quit talking. "You have one shot at this Mr. Cordova." Cordova again signaled that he understood the Ranger simply by the expression in his face. "What was Soto's role in this?"

"Soto was a crusader…he wanted it both ways."

"I don't follow."

"The Negras money was good when it supported his causes, but when it didn't, they were the evil Cartel."

"Like the highway project?"

"Exactly, Sergeant. The homeless shelter, the alternative school, and the recreation center were all built by Negras money…we all looked the other way. But when the highway was being talked about, Soto objected. He opened his mouth."

"The Negras kill him?"

"I really don't think so. Don't get me wrong, they will take care of business on American soil, but I don't think they'd bat an eyelash at a mouthy councilman…especially one in their pocket."

"So who did?"

"I don't know, but I'd say they are home grown."

Flynt sat back in his chair and stared at the councilman. Was he honest and forthright? No, but he was probably just like other criminal. They never tell one hundred percent of the truth, that was the only surety in investigation. "I need more, Councilman."

"Like what?"

"The Negras can't operate in this country without couriers and soldiers."

Cordova's nervousness appeared to be re-emerging with the Ranger's questions, "It's all done electronically. Look I don't…"

"Mr. Cordova there has to be someone or something that gets the money from point A to point B. Someone has got to facilitate that…now you're gonna tell me who that is!"

"Sergeant Flynt…I…" As Cordova stammered, Flynt quickly moved to a position on the couch right next to him. It was an investigative tool to invade the subject's personal space to create a subconscious discomfort. Flynt could tell it was bothering the councilman.

"Now Councilman…I need you to think real hard about your next answer, cause it will determine how things will go from here," Flynt's voice was calm but firm. Cordova knew the Ranger was not bluffing. "I need a name."

"There is a guy that delivers messages and gets all the necessary account numbers," Cordova sighed with relief as if he was confessing a mortal sin to a priest.

"Name?!" Flynt barked impatiently.

"Carlos Estancia…here's a phone number. That's all I know" Cordova watched Flynt write it down.

"Well I doubt that, but I'll go with what you told me for now." Flynt stood up from the couch.

"Sergeant Flynt?" Cordova asked causing the imposing Ranger to look down on him. "What about all this?" Cordova pointed to the paperwork left on his coffee table. "What now?"

"That's yours to keep, Councilman," Flynt smiled. "When and if the public or Feds begin to ask more questions, I guess you'll have a problem, huh?" Flynt walked to the front door and casually let himself out of the residence. He walked to the Crown Vic, unlocked the door and sat down. As he drove away he took out his cellular phone and dialed.

"This is Lansford."

"John...this is Flynt."

"Hey Richard...what's up?"

"Got a name, may be our ghost we been huntin'."

"Well praise the Lord! Give it to me, Brother."

"Carlos Estancia...that name ever come up on any deal with ya'all or DEA?"

"Doesn't ring a bell, but as you say, he may be our ghost."

"The AUSA get the files I sent?" AUSA's or Assistant District Attorneys of the United States worked in assigned districts handled all Federal cases submitted by law enforcement.

"She got them. You sure you don't want Texas in on this?"

"Johnny Boy...I love my state, but political sticky fingers ain't a priority if you catch my drift."

"Caught it."

"Does she know to hold this information till we can get this shit sorted out?"

"If there's one thing an AUSA can do really well, it's sit on shit... believe me," Lansford's response caused both men to laugh. *"Does your councilman know how much shit they're gonna be in when this thing hits?"*

"I'm gonna say no. My guess is they never thought that silver spoon in their mouths was gonna be shoved up their ass." The two men continued to laugh and chat as friends, but the conversation ended on a more serious note. "You ready for the next phase?"

"Say the word."

CHAPTER TWENTY

Reckoning

"I got the targets going into the store now," the radio cracked. Lansford glances down at his watch. It was like clockwork, the information Sariah gave them was gold. He received the call from Flynt that two murder warrants were issued for Nathan and Josiah Johnson. They also mentioned these two subjects were involved with human trafficking. That's really all Lansford needed to know. His specialty was the pursuit and capture, not the investigation. So, to get a call from State law enforcement requesting the capture of a violent felon was an everyday occurrence in his world, but this case was different. The images of the burned bodies in the car were burned into his conscious and would never be removed. He struggled to forget the suffering and agony those little girls in that car must have endured and the very loss of their dignity being left to rot. The murder warrants were a means to an end. Although their warrant was for the dead councilman, if these two subjects were involved in trafficking, Lansford wanted to get them. He turned to his favorite informant, Sariah, and she was all too happy to give the two boys up.

"We set?" Lansford replied over the air. Two team members were in the rear of the store, one inside and two in the front. Lansford sat alone in his government issued Tahoe. He generally had to stay away from the scene. He had been asking his bosses for a more covert vehicle, but they insisted that as a team leader that he drive a government approved vehicle. Unfortunately, every hook with eyes can spot a G-vehicle from a mile away.

"We're set, come on in, Top."

Lansford casually drove to the front of store and got out of the vehicle. Customers stared at the former-NFL player with a Glock on his hip as he walked into the convenience store. Three other team members converged on the store as well. Lansford walked over to Nathan and Josiah who were limping up to the counter with soft drinks. "You boys need some help? Looks like you're injured?"

"Who the fuck are you, Cop?" Josiah spit at the Marshall's direction. Lansford had to admire the intestinal fortitude on the kid since Lansford was literally three times his size.

"I know ya'all got your asses whooped by a girl." Both boys looked at the Marshal with a sudden suspicion.

"You know what I know, Cop?" Josiah replied. "You were a less valiant spirit in the pre-existence which caused God to curse you with a skin of blackness!"

"Well I'll be damned! That's what happened?"

"Yeah…maybe you can be my servant in the afterlife, seed of Cain!" Josiah never saw Lansford's right-hand land on his jaw causing him to fall to the ground as if he were a sack of garbage.

"Oh yeah…stop resisting, Sir!" Lansford looked at his team members. "Ya'all saw that right?" Each member held their thumbs up acknowledging that Lansford's use of force was both necessary and appropriate. Even the scared shop-keeper put his thumb up causing the officers to chuckle. Lansford then turned to Nathan.

"That's not right, I'm going to complain," Nathan protested, though much more soft and cordial than his brother.

"I'm a highly decorated Black, Federal Marshal," Lansford smiled. "You're an over-privileged, polygamist White boy with a murder warrant…batter-up, Bitch!" Lansford spun the boy around and placed the handcuffs on him with literally no resistance at all. The rest of the team scooped up a still incoherent Josiah. Lansford took out his phone and dialed Flynt. He waited patiently for the answer.

"Got some good news, Fed?"

"I like my whiskey from Kentucky. We got em' both."

*

The Prophet Nephi Josephs was tired when he walked into

the hotel suite. He laid his suitcase into the cutout closet and hung his suits on the rack. His suit coat was removed and he laid it neatly on the back of the plain wood chair at the table. As he loosened his tie he sensed something was wrong. "How did you get in here?"

Moroni LaFey emerged from the corner of the room. "I told you…I work for the Almighty God." The two men stared at each other distrustfully for a few awkward moments. "I'm curious, President, did you get a chance to speak with Bishop Johnson?"

"I did. He denies any involvement in this horrible matter."

"Have you heard about his daughter Amanda?"

"I heard she committed suicide."

"I'll say," Moroni started to pace. "After she stuck a blade into her own carotid artery, she dove of the roof of Doctor's Hospital." Moroni looked at the prophet and studied his reaction. "That's quite a suicide, don't you think President?"

"What are you saying, Moroni?"

"Do you believe Bishop Johnson?"

"He is a priesthood holder…"

"He is a man!" Moroni snapped back. "What do you think?!"

"There is an order in the church, Moroni!" Josephs said in desperation. "The brethren are infallible…even when they are not."

Moroni smiled. He knew what the Prophet would say and he knew the Prophet could never turn on the brethren. He continued to pace the comfortably large hotel suite. "I'm sure you heard the story of the internal struggle of my family?"

President Josephs as well as every polygamist sect knew about the LaFey family war. When Moroni's father, Bernard LaFey, passed away, there was a dispute between the two older brothers, Charles and John, as to who would inherit the keys to the Colonia LaFey. They both started a feud that at times turned violent. It was no secret that the third son, Moroni, thought the feud was an abomination unto the Lord. Moroni was the more pious of the brothers and had a sizeable militia he formed to protect the colony. All of the militia, including himself, were former military. All were either family or close associates. One cold December Morning, both Charles and John, along with all their wives, were found murdered in their homes. The surviving children were scattered among the remaining members of the family and colony. The rumor was that it was Moroni ordered the executions. Moroni never publically denied this allegation, but always stated that it was the Lord's will that such tragedies be a part of life.

"I do know about your family, Moroni," Josephs answered cautiously.

Moroni walked right up to the Prophet who was sitting on the edge of one of the hotel beds and kneeled next to him. As if it were already uncomfortable enough, Josephs noticed the blackened, tactical knife in Moroni's right hand. Josephs felt his stomach literally touch his throat in fear. Moroni leaned in so his mouth was right next to the Prophet's ear. "I didn't just order my brothers' deaths, I did it myself." Moroni's voice sounded so soft, but terrifying at the same time. "You know what I did while I watched my men execute my brother Charle's second wife? I warmed up some of my sister-in-law's casserole and ate." Moroni leaned back out and stood up. "It was delicious." Moroni smiled. "The Lord is no respecter of men and I serve him." Moroni stared at Josephs who was collecting himself. Moroni tossed an envelope filled with affidavits to the Prophet. "You need to look at it."

"Is this information from the Gentiles?"

"Nope, it's from Kaye Johnson and a few of the other wives," Moroni replied. He then disappeared from the room as the Prophet's eyes fixed on the paperwork.

*

Nathan Johnson sat in the chair with face in his hands. The eldest of the Johnson brothers had never experienced an interrogation or even seen this side of the law in his life. He watched as his brother was carted away, screaming scriptures and curses incoherently. Kidd could see that Nathan was the smarter one. Unlike his brother, Nathan was weighing his options in his head. Kidd knew from his experience, this was a sign that a suspect was bargaining with himself and deciding just how much truth would be rendered. A confession was forthcoming, but the value of the confession to the case would still be in question. Flynt told Kidd to interview the brothers solo. There was no taking to Josiah, but he did a masterful job interviewing Nathan. As Kidd's mentor and deceased partner, Keith Spearman, once said, 'It's always easier to interview someone with a conscience.'

"Nathan?" Kidd addressed the boy using his name to personalize the conversation. "You need to go ahead and tell us the truth now. We know you killed Councilman Soto, all we need to know is why?"

"Do you believe in God, Ranger Kidd?"

The question threw Kidd for a loop. He grew up Baptist but joined the LDS Church when he got married. Church was something that was never that significant to him, other than the fact it spurned his curiosity about the origins of Christianity and why it had such a hold in the world. Why people, such as his partner, one of the most intelligent men he's known, chose to live a life based on the belief? After discovering the historical problems of the Mormon Church, Kidd didn't stop there. He looked into the history of the Bible and of Christianity itself and discovered the true historical accounts differed greatly from the narratives taught on Sunday. So, Nathan Johnson's question was more than a simple yes or no, but Kidd wasn't concerned about the greater implication of religion; he just wanted a confession. "Of course, I do, son."

"Do you believe that if he tells you to do something, you should do it?"

"I gotta be honest with you Nathan, God's never asked me to do anything that I know of?"

"Well he speaks to me through his prophets…and I have to obey."

Kidd saw an opening in the line of questioning. "Well I suppose if a bona fide prophet talked to me, I'd listen."

"Then you see my problem?"

"I do, but I still don't know where you're going with this?"

"The politician had to die…thus sayeth the Lord," Nathan looked away from the Ranger. It was a sign that he felt some remorse for his actions, even though he could never say such a thing in front of God or witnesses.

"Who commanded it? God?"

"Yes."

"Was Nephi Josephs involved?" Kidd inquired. Nathan's eyes snapped back at Kidd. He was surprised to hear the Gentile mention the Prophet Nephi Josephs. "I told you I know more than you think."

"It was Josiah and I that climbed through the window of the house!" Nathan snapped, obviously wanting the subject changed. "That man was a sodomite…we watched him for days. We saw the unspeakable acts he committed."

"Now Nathan…it's a bit unfair to criticize the dead man's sexuality. I heard you and Josiah were involved in some dablin' of your own in the barn?"

Nathan smirked, "You spoke to that Gentile bitch, Sariah?"

"Now that's unkind, son."

"Josiah and I act to make one another pure."

"Pure?"

"The Lord commanded us to be pure and to do what's necessary to keep our eyes single to the glory! We cleanse ourselves sexually so that we won't be tempted in life by Gentiles."

"Good answer, ain't never heard of that before," Kidd knew that this kid was gone. He was the perfect killing machine. All someone would have to do was utter an order in the name of God and this kid and his brother would execute it. It was a good explanation as to the mindset of a killer, but Kidd knew that this fact would complicate a prosecution. Any lawyer worth his weight in salt would ask for an insanity plea. "Tell me more about the house…did you go in more than once?"

"We broke in several times the alarm was never set."

"You watched him?"

"For several nights. We watched him defile his body and the bodies of other sodomites."

"That why there's so many prints in the house?"

"We entered the through dog door, windows, and other ways…it was easy."

"What then?"

"The Lord finally told us to kill him."

"Which one of you did it?"

"The Lord was clear that both of us needed to spill his blood."

"And ya'all raped him?"

"Nathan smirked and glared at the Texas Ranger, "You have the DNA Ranger."

"Why brutalize him?"

"It is not enough that he simply dies…the Lord wants an example made out of him."

"Explain?"

"Mr. Soto's sins were grievous in the eyes of the Lord. His death and mutilation is simply a warning to all mankind that every knee shall bow to the Almighty God. Homosexuality is among the most grievous sins. It was better that the sodomite was killed than to continue his aggressions against the Lord."

"But why death? I'm trying to distinguish what Jaime did to what you and Josiah do? Shouldn't you be merciful? I mean…am I missing something?"

"What Josiah and I do is not homosexuality…we are definitely not sodomites. Sometimes I just need to release the sinful lusts of my body, and so does he."

"Damn, you're full of good shit today, Nathan!" Kidd exclaimed half sarcastically and half out of genuine disgust, anger, and fear. "So, all of the theatrics surrounding Jaime's murder was for our benefit? Meaning us Gentiles?"

"Precisely."

"So how exactly did God tell you to kill Mr. Soto?" Kidd watched closely as Nathan began to squirm again. "Was it Nephi Josephs?"

"I already told you…no!"

"What about your Dad, the Bishop?" Kidd paused. "Did he tell you to do it?"

"I told you, Ranger, the Lord told me…"

"But you said yourself that the Lord speaks through his

270

prophets? Right?"

"Exactly."

"So, your Dad must not be a prophet," Kidd knew he was starting to press Nathan's buttons, but he had to push the interview.

"My Father speaks to God!"

"Apparently not…"

"He communes with the Almighty Father…the Lord of Hosts!"

"Well tell me what God tells him?! What the hell does God even sound like? You and I both know that your father, Bishop Johnson received a revelation that you and Josiah kill Jaime Soto! We know that don't we Nathan!" Kidd's voice was raised slightly. Nathan looked at the ground. Though he wasn't speaking, Nathan's non-verbal communication was acknowledging allegation the Ranger made. "I just want to know what God said?"

"God spoke and I obeyed…can we talk about something else?"

"How about your sister, Amanda?"

"I think I need a lawyer."

*

"Sit down, Sweetheart," Flynt's hand was placed gently on Sariah's shoulder as he guided her into the booth at the café. Flynt felt he had grown on the young girl and finally earned her much sought after trust. She smiled back at the older Ranger.

"Nathan and Josiah are going down for Murder," the Ranger smiled. "Nathan gave up the Soto killing."

"What about Ruth's murder and Amanda's kidnapping?" Sariah inquired.

"We still got some work to do on the case. Seems they're hesitant to give up they're Bishop."

"So, they may never face charges for Amanda?"

"Now I didn't say that, Sariah…"

"I knew they wouldn't give up the brethren…I knew it."

"Sometimes, Sariah, justice isn't served by the law."

"Oh, don't tell me you believe God will get them in the end? I've been taught that my entire life and I just can't buy the God thing anymore…"

"Ain't about God, young lady," Flynt said in a stern voice. "What's about to happen I'm sure God wants no part of."

*

"How'd she take it?" Kidd asked his partner as they drove across the border into Coahuila. He knew Sariah would not like the fact Nathan and Josiah would not give a full confession of their wrongdoings. Even though they would spend their natural lives in a Texas Prison, most people simply believed that if an individual commits a crime, that individual pays the price for said crime. But reality was that if law enforcement is able to put any viable charge on an individual to keep them in jail, they will.

"Not too well, but can't say I blame her," Flynt replied, but was obviously distracted. He drove the Crown Vic with a stare that indicated he was deep in thought.

"What's wrong?"

Flynt look at his younger partner but did not give his typical smile. It was a look Kidd had never seen, a look of sadness and just shy of despair. "I'm afraid."

"Hey Brother…I got your six…"

"I'm not afraid for me, I'm afraid for you."

"I've been in deeper shit than this…"

"It's not your safety, Darren!" Flynt interrupted in a firm tone. "There are worse things than death."

"Like life? Kidd replied. Kidd knew exactly what his partner's concerns were.

"I don't know if we can ever be the same after this," Flynt said. "I wanted to be a cop to help people, to arrest bad guys, and tell stories. I never would have guessed I'd be picking through the bodies of mutilated girls for scrap evidence. I'd have to look these guys in the face, helpless with this badge. Fact is that little piece of metal made me powerless." Flynt took a long pause staring at the empty border landscape. "I've spent forty years working the system to get results that's led me to this. When I stand before my maker, I can't say I'm a better man for it…guess I'm scared for you."

"I ever tell you about Somalia?" Kidd stared at his grieving partner. "We got intel a local chief was in the area. Battalion told us to go in and extract him. I was an E-5 and squad leader. We were the entry element that was supposed to hit the house." Kidd's voice began to crack ever so slightly. "We hit the front door…I was behind point. There was blood and shit everywhere…bout five kids and two women."

"What happened?"

"Simple…the chief didn't want his family to be used as leverage and killed them. Ain't complicated…kind of smart actually…just brutal."

"That's war, Darren…"

"No, it's not, Richard," Kidd interrupted abruptly. "I held Keith in my arms while he died…for what? Because a two-bit politician wanted some extra money and hated his gay son…that's all." Flynt listened intently. Kidd hardly ever talked about his old partner from Albuquerque. Flynt knew Keith Spearman as well and worked with him several times. "That wasn't war…that was just life." The car was filled with a thick silence that though it was only moments, seemed endless. "There's no truth, justice, and law that guides mankind, Partner…it's good people trying to get by. Make no mistake…I ain't proud of what we're doing." Kidd paused again, "As far as my maker's concerned…God left me in Albuquerque, so there ain't no reason for him to come to Texas."

Flynt smirked in acknowledgement, "Let's end this evil."

CHAPTER TWENTY-ONE

Benediction

The Cantina Vallejos on Periferico Road outside Piedras Negras was certainly not the image of the old and dilapidated bar that was portrayed in movies and literature. The brick structure was updated and well maintained. The interior was decorated in shiny, clean Mexican tile accented with dark wood furnishings. There didn't seem to be any chair or table with any defect whatsoever. It was rumored that the Negras' boss, El Patron, would never frequent a dirty, unhygienic facility. The ten thousand square foot facility was meticulously clean. Kidd and Flynt sat in a dark corner. It was an operation unlike any they had ever been on. This particular mission was not authorized by the Department, or the Federal Government for that matter, but it was necessary closure even if it wasn't by legal means. The child killings had to stop. The Rangers watched across the room as Carlos entered and sat down amongst a group of chairs that were seemingly set up for a large meeting.

Shortly after Carlos sat down, Sonia Nava came inside the cantina and hugged El Patron. Carlos stood up and greeted the woman as if she was royalty. She dismissively greeted him as if she was angry or inconvenienced and sat down. There was silence between the two parties. Upon closer examination, the Rangers could see the woman; the final piece to their investigation. The door opened again. Marisella and Tio Muniz walked through the door, into the gathering area. Kidd and Flynt watched as all of the parties stared at one another suspiciously while everyone sat down. No sooner did they sit down, a Hispanic man entered the room with four armed, hooded men. Each of the hooded men carried H&K MP-5's and took positions in the room to dominate the space, much like military close quarter combat techniques.

Flynt looked at his younger partner, "Here we go." They watched as the Hispanic man motioned for them to come forward. The Rangers emerged from the darkness much to the surprise of the parties that were sitting there. Tio Muniz began to rise from his chair.

"Tranquillo, Tio, sienta se por favor," El Patron smiled. "These men are my guests." He stood six-foot-tall and dressed in jeans and a sport coat. His outfit was neatly pressed, and his hair was flawless. He did not resemble the popularized colorful loud shirt, black cowboy hat version of a cartel boss. Both Rangers knew he would be a formidable adversary to any man. He spoke with a soft, direct and sophisticated voice, however when his voice was heard, it was obvious people listened. "Thank you all for coming today and I do hope we can straighten this mess out." As he spoke, Moroni LaFey appeared from the shadows as well. "Please welcome my good friend Moroni from *Colonia LaFey*."

"I don't understand, Patron…" Tio questioned.

"Please be patient, Tio. Everything will be explained," El Patron looked at the two Rangers. "Do we need introductions?"

"Allow me, El Patron," Flynt smiled and looked at the parties involved. Though everything seemed cordial at that point, looks of distrust and tension filled that room. "This is Carlos Estancia. That is his boss in the States, Sonia Nava, a councilwoman with Eagle Pass, Texas…"

"What is this, El Patron? Why are we here?" Sonia Nava was obviously flustered and nervous.

"Please Sonia, it's very rude to interrupt…continue Sergeant Flynt."

"That is Marisella Campos and Tio Muniz. Both of them belong to you I believe, Sir?"

"Technically, they all belong to me, Sergeant," El Patron retorted causing he and the Rangers to chuckle. The rest of the parties remained silent. But it was a fact; they were all told to be there. When a man with the power of El Patron tells you to do something, you do it. "And you know this man?" El Patron pointed to Moroni LaFey.

"That's Moroni LaFey. I can't say I know him, we had a phone conversation. I've grown to love and admire his niece, Sariah." Flynt's comments received a head nod and slight smile from Moroni who appeared to be focusing all of his attention on

Sonia Nava.

"Impressive."

"We Texas Rangers are full of tricks, Sir."

Tio Muniz abruptly interrupted the conversation, "El Patron...we can kill these men right here. They are here illegally and they are liars!"

"Well now Tio, I ain't said a damn thing?" Flynt protested. "Besides, that's rich coming from the likes of you."

"Then I will kill them myself..." Tio attempted to rise from his chair.

Flynt held up a Motorolla hand-held police radio causing Tio to freeze with curiosity. El Patron seemed to be attentive as well. "Give me a SIT-REP," Flynt called over the airwaves.

"Two on the roof. Two SUV's with six total. Two standing outside the door. Four inside the premises," John Lansford's voice was unmistakable even over the radio. But it was obvious both Tio and El Patron understood that the Rangers had the tactical advantage.

"What's your strength?" Flynt called out again."

"Twenty on the ground, two eyes, and the Bitch."

El Patron smiled, obviously impressed with the Ranger's preparation and readiness right under their noses. He knew that twenty trained men would be hard to subdue. He also knew that the police term for sniper was 'eyes.' "I'm curious Sergeant Flynt...what is the Bitch?"

Flynt took out his cellular phone and displayed a picture of the very secretive Texas Department of Public Safety Apache Helicopter, complete with mini-guns minus the Hellfire missiles. Flynt showed the picture in front of all of the parties present. "Ladies and Gentlemen...the Bitch."

"So, the rumors are true?" El Patron smiled.

"Can't confirm or deny, El Patron," Flynt smiled back. "There's an old saying about walking softly and carrying big sticks. They obviously didn't have a Bitch. Besides, ya'all know we Texans like big guns?" Flynt looked at Tio Muniz, "Mr. Muniz, you even sneeze, you son of a bitch, I'll cut you and your men to shit."

"There will be no violence...I called everyone here to talk,

276

now let's talk," El Patron's voice was surprisingly calming and reassuring for the leader of such a brutal organization.

"I agree, El Patron. We came in peace and God willing, we will leave that a way," The older Ranger smiled. "Tell you what…how do you want me to proceed?"

"I want to hear about this case of yours. The one with the dead little girls," El Patron looked directly at his seated guests. It was clear that fear was in the air.

"Of course, Sir," Flynt began pacing, reminiscent of the great detectives in literature like Hercule Piorot and Sherlock Holmes. Since prosecution was unlikely at this point, he was anxious to expound on the investigation to anyone who would listen, but even more than that, he wanted all of the parties involved to know that their nefarious schemes, actions, and deeds were discovered. It was like cleansing his soul of a deep filth. Kidd stood by his side tactically watching all parties in the room. "Let's start with the highway fund. The money that you pay to distribute inside Texas is through Sonia's organization."

"Yes, Sonia and I have had dealings for years."

"You know this woman?" Tio inquired.

"Tio, I have forgotten far more than you will ever know."

"We'll get to you Mr. Muniz," Flynt shut the side conversation down. "Sonia was laundering the money through the Coahuila Highway Project…pretty ingenious actually."

El Patron nodded to Sonia, *"Esta Bien."*

"It all went South when Sonia's worker, Carlos, met up with Marisella there."

"How so?"

"Tio and Marisella started the human trafficking operation which is the reason we are even here…"

"That's a lie, El Patron! It was Tio's idea…" Marisella began to protest.

"Silencio," El Patron's voice remained silent yet more firm. "Please Sergeant, continue."

"Well, whoever's idea it was, Tio, Marisella, or whoever, a side deal was cut. Sonia and Carlos provided the girls for Tio and Marisella's sick bastard clients," Flynt turned to El Patron, whose normal stoic face showed a slight hint of emotion. "I'm assuming you had no idea?"

El Patron shook his head that he did not, "Where did these girls come from?"

"Most come from poor families in Piedras Negras and Laredo," Flynt answered. "And several were taken from a polygamist sect in Eagle Pass...The Inspired Church of Jesus Christ of Latter-day Saints."

El Patron looked at Moroni LaFey, who was staring deeply at Sonia Nava. Moroni nodded to the affirmative at the Cartel Boss who closed his eyes in shame and embarrassment. "How old were these girls?"

"Ranging from twelve to seventeen."

"Babies, *no?*"

"Yes Sir."

El Patron turned to Tio Muniz, "Is this true, Tio?" Tio Muniz sat and stared at the ground. His silence was more than an indictment. El Patron walked over and stood in front of Muniz. "Have I not paid you well?" Tio nodded to the affirmative. In an instant, El Patron removed a .45 from his waistband and fired a round into Tio's skull before anyone knew what was happening. Tio's body jerked violently and slumped lifelessly in the chair. Kidd reacted by going to his sidearm, but Flynt's left hand covered Kidd's shooting hand to cease any sudden reaction.

"Stand down! Repeat...stand down!" Flynt's voice was loud but meant to instruct the men outside that surely heard the gunfire. "Everything is 10-4."

El Patron calmly stood up, took out a handkerchief and wiped the blowback blood spatter from the pistol and his hand. "I apologize, Sergeant, guests, I lost my temper." Marisella, Carlos, and Sonia sat glued to their seats and frozen with fear. Marisella even had high velocity spatter on her custom outfit, but she dare not protest; she sat silently, shaking in her seat. Tio's body remained present as a symbol of El Patron's sovereignty.

"Um, El Patron?" It was Kidd who addressed the Cartel Boss this time.

"Yes…um…Ranger Kidd is it?"

"Yes, Sir," Kidd was obviously choosing his words carefully. "While I think you did humanity a favor for executing that piece of shit, could ya kind of give us a 'heads up' next time?"

"Very well, Sir," El Patron smiled. "Please continue Sergeant Flynt."

All of the guests, minus Moroni were visibly shaken. Flynt too had to gather his thoughts after witnessing the execution, but both he and Kidd knew they would face a situation unlike any they'd ever seen; and they were right. Flynt continued, "Sonia here developed a working relationship with Bishop Thomas Johnson of the polygamist sect. She did lots of legal work for him. Johnson would mark various girls within the sect that could be sold to Tio and Marisella, he even included his own daughters."

"Madre de Dios," El Patron whispered audibly.

"Carlos here took the orders from Tio and Marisella and passed them up his chain to Sonia. Sonia would give her answer and give instructions back to Carlos on which girls to collect, or kidnap really, if we're being honest," Flynt paused.

"So, what happened?"

"Well, several things. First, a highway crew discovered the mass grave during their excavating. They were all young girls, Local police blamed ya'all for the murders, but some of us didn't believe it," Flynt stopped to check his next sentences extremely carefully. "You see most the people ya'all 'eliminate' are adults with ties to business. A hole full of babies didn't seem like the Negras' modus operandi."

"It is certainly not and thank you for at least giving my organization that much credit," El Patron answered in an exasperated tone. "Who killed and buried the girls?"

"That's the part that's still unclear. Bishop Johnson has two sons. The evidence points to them for disposing of the girls. But in all honesty, El Patron, it was most likely them and the clients that killed those babies. We may never know." The two Rangers again witnessed the Boss close his eyes in disgust.

"What about the burned girls in the car?" El Patron finally

279

asked.

"Ya see, this is where the deal between these folks unravels," Flynt replied pointing to Marisella and Sonia. "Carlos here hired an ex-con, Nazi Low-rider piece a shit, Trey Caldwell, to transport these girls back and forth across the border. Caldwell gets spooked one night thinking the task-force is on his trail and panics. He kills two of the three girls but leaves one alive. He then burned the vehicle with the girls inside. One of those girls was Bishop Johnson's daughter."

"What about the one that lived?"

"Also Bishop Johnson's daughter, the task force rescued her in Laredo."

"She is okay then?"

Flynt went silent not even wanting to answer the question. Kidd could see his reluctance and stepped in, "Her father visited her at the hospital. Shortly after, she committed suicide…"

Kidd's statement was abruptly interrupted when El Patron's fist slammed hard on the table. "Once again, I apologize. What happened to this Caldwell character?"

"Tio had your boys kill him in county lock up," Flynt replied.

"Finally, some good news…*Chinga!*" El Patron exclaimed as a relief. "Just as well…at least that *cabron* did something right, no?"

"You see, Tio was upset with Carlos because the girls that were promised his clients never showed. So Tio not only killed Caldwell, but two of Carlos's other hired hands. What Tio never found out was that Carlos worked for Sonia, your longtime associate."

"What about this murdered city councilman?"

"Bishop Johnson's boys killed Jaime Soto, on Sonia's orders of course," Kidd couldn't help but chime into the conversation.

"That's a lie Ranger Kidd!" Sonia snarled at the younger Ranger.

Kidd turned to Sonia, "You sent the Johnson boys to Maverick County Jail to get a message to Trey Caldwell...we saw them in the surveillance footage. You were going to pretend to represent him and then have him killed, but what you didn't know, was that Tio already had someone inside. The Johnson boys wrote out confessions...they're done." Kidd smiled at the council woman. "But we also have God, video, fingerprints, and DNA as well, so those boys won't go anywhere, cept maybe a Texas Death Chamber."

"You can be sure they won't," El Patron's statement was eerily understood by everyone in the room. "But why kill a city councilman?"

"He was threatening to leak that the highway fund was full of Negras money. She couldn't allow that. She went to Johnson and made a deal to kill off Soto. Johnson used his two sons, simple as that," Flynt explained.

"When did you connect the highway fund to Negras money? Someone confess?"

"That's the most interesting part of the story," Flynt smiled. "There was a nobody political writer that had a blog, virtually nobody read. That man was known as Texas Don. Somehow, Don was able to mirror city hard drives and developed some snitches that worked for the city."

"This man figured out Sonia's scheme?"

"No, he just figured out money was being laundered. He thought it was some grand political conspiracy. It was Ranger Kidd and I that figured out it was Negras money."

"More tricks eh?"

"We're just full of em."

"Where is this Don now?"

"Well, Sir...Sonia killed him herself..."

"I've had enough! I'm leaving," Sonia Nava stood up to leave and had four MP-5's pointed directly at her.

"Sienta se, Sonia...ahora!" There was no questioning El Patron's anger at this point. "What proof do you have of this accusation Rangers?"

"We recovered the GPS from her vehicle. The night of the incident she had Texas Don's address programed in fifteen minutes before he was shot. She was able to figure out he knew about the scheme."

"You broke into my car, Sergeant Flynt?!" Sonia cried expressing her displeasure that it was two Texas Rangers that burglarized her vehicle the night of the council meeting and not some common thieves.

"Well he did," Flynt replied pointing to Kidd.

"Well goddamn…drop the dime on me partner…"

"I'm just keeping it real…I'll take a report for ya, Ms. Nava…"

"Shut up!" Sonia yelled at the Rangers. "El Patron…please let me speak," she pleaded.

"Any objections?" El Patron asked the Rangers.

"Nope…I want to hear this," Flynt answered.

"They could never convict me in court with this evidence. They illegally broke into my car and stole my property. They have hearsay on Soto's death and I can't be connected to these girls' unfortunate deaths. No court in America would consider that evidence. They have no case," Sonia said smugly. "I can fix this, but I need these two disposed of."

"Sonia your killing of the writer is the least of your worries," El Patron replied casually. "Your indifference to the lives of those young girls ought to worry you at this point."

"They wouldn't be missed, El Patron! We made sure of it."

"Everybody has those that love them, Sonia…shame on you."

"We knew we couldn't convict you for the murder, Sonia," Flynt interrupted. "Hell, you'd only do about two to four for the money laundering. We made contact with El Patron through Moroni there. Your wickedness had to end somehow, so we were hoping to settle out of court." Sonia sat back in her chair in silence.

"How did you discover Carlos's involvement?" El Patron asked.

"Carlos left more clues than Hitler," Flynt answered. "Councilman Cordova gave him up. Trey Caldwell and his girlfriend gave him up as well. Hell, he and his boys were even spotted. As soon as we got his information, it was easy to track his movements." The room fell silent. It appears that all parties were contemplating the information they had just heard.

"What now, El Patron?" Marisella finally spoke up.

"I will dismiss you to my men. They can do what they like

with you. Maybe they need more whores downtown, or maybe they kill you…it makes no difference to me. The blood of those babies should haunt you for your last remaining breaths, however few there are," El Patron paused. "Just tell me why, Marisella? I gave you more power and position than any other woman. I don't understand?"

Marisella answered with her head still to the ground, "I was the Boss, El Patron. It was mine."

No sooner did she finish her sentence than three large men entered the area and grabbed Marisella who began kicking and screaming in protest. Her fight subsided quickly with a right cross to her jaw. She was dragged by her hair out of the building and out of sight. Both Kidd and Flynt couldn't help but flinch as the older woman was abused. Though they knew they would witness such brutality, still they were emotionally unprepared. They perspired greatly and heart rates skyrocketed as they witnessed this woman pulled to her most certain demise. "Moroni?"

"Yes, El Patron?" LaFey finally spoke.

"Ms. Nava is yours," El Patron replied. Sonia got up to run, but was intercepted by two White men, obviously LaFey's men. "What about this Bishop?"

"I want to talk to Bishop Johnson! He speaks for your prophet, Nephi Josephs!" Sonia protested as she was subdued physically by LaFey's men.

"Ms. Nava," Moroni smiled. "Bishop Johnson should have told you he may speak for God, but I smite people for him." Moroni turned to El Patron, "The Bishop is in the hands of God." LaFey and his men, with Sonia in tow screaming, exited the building through the rear and were gone.

Both Kidd and Flynt, still shaken but stoic, stood alone in the room with El Patron and his men. Though their host had shown great courtesy, both Rangers still didn't trust the man. "What about Carlos here?" Flynt asked.

"Carlos will come with me…that is my decision."

"If he comes to Texas, we will get him, Sir."

"Agreed…Carlos will never set foot inside the U.S. That is my promise."

"Then we're done here?"

"Unless you have any other issues," El Patron smiled. "I hope to never cross paths again Sergeant Flynt and Ranger Kidd, but I do admire you both. What will you do now?"

"We got a few loose ends in the states to tie up."

CHAPTER TWENTY-TWO

Atonement

The song *'Ye Elders of Israel'* always began the General Priesthood Session of the Inspired Church of Jesus Christ of Latter-day Saints. Typically, any male who held the Melchizedek Priesthood, along with his sons, was to attend. It was very similar to the mainstream Church of Jesus Christ of Latter-day Saints. But this year was different. This year, the Texas families would be honored with the Prophet himself, Nephi Josephs, would be presiding this meeting. The sanctuary was packed with brethren waiting to hear the words of the very man that speaks to God. It was a belief common to every LDS sect that their leader, the prophet, seer, and revelator spoke to God. In recent years, the mainstream Salt Lake Church began to downplay the popular belief due to increased member scrutiny over the church's sorted history and theology most of which now was available over the internet. But the Fundamentalist sects had the luxury of a less cosmopolitan and information savvy congregation. The result was a firm and strict adherence to the Lord's anointed. They came today to hear their Prophet.

Bishop Johnson ended his talk on faith and obedience. It failed to move the brethren spiritually, but Johnson was an earner, not a speaker. He smiled at the brethren, who filled the Temple Sanctuary to capacity. "I turn the time over to President Nephi Josephs." The excitement for the brethren seated inside the sanctuary would have manifested itself with huge applause but clapping and all other forms of audible adoration was forbidden within the Lord's house. As the Prophet rose to get to the podium, three figures appeared in the back of the room, Moroni LaFey, Jeremiah Larsen, and Sariah. Josephs acknowledged them with a look as he began his talk. Sariah shrunk between her uncle and father in an effort not to be seen by the congregation. Women were not allowed in the Priesthood Sessions so she felt wildly out of place.

"Brethren, it is so good to be with you today. As Heavenly Father's covenant people, what a blessing it is to gather as Saints in Southern Zion, or Texas as we know it," Nephi Josephs smiled as the gathering laughed at his 'Southern Zion' comment. Josephs went on to pontificate for what seemed like an eternity on how enlightened the brethren were because of their obedience to the laws and ordinances of the gospel; the gospel of the Inspired's that is. Sariah literally felt ill as she heard her 'prophet' pump this crowd up with rhetoric every bit as dynamic as a football coach before a game, delivered in a pretentious, reverent tone. She watched the smiles and nods of belief from the audience. It was at that point, she knew after this ended, she would need to go.

"Please come up to the podium Bishop Johnson," Josephs finally requested. Sariah watched as Bishop Johnson stepped to the prophet's side, his smile beaming as if an award was about to be bestowed upon him. "We'd like to release with a vote of thanks, Bishop Thomas Johnson as Bishop and spiritual leader in the Texas Stake of Zion…" Bishop Johnson's countenance changed as quickly as Sariah had ever seen. His pasty white face became flush with fear and embarrassment. He appeared bewildered like a lost child.

"President Josephs…please…may we discuss this in front of the brethren?" Johnson was pleading desperately. His priesthood mantle was stripped there on the spot and he was not taking it very well. The crowd went silent. The meeting went from a normal meeting to something memorable. The anxiety and tension in the room could be cut with a knife and all were on the edge of their seats.

"Absolutely Brother Johnson," Josephs smiled as he used the term 'Brother' to describe Johnson.

"What is the reason for my release?"

"You have to ask?" Josephs turned from the jovial prophet to spiritual examiner in an instant. "Your daughters are dead, victims of an evil plot. Your sons are charged with the murder of a councilman and only the Lord knows what will become of them." Josephs began to pace along the stand obviously playing to his crowd of adorers. "You lied and said it was my revelation to give Sariah Larsen to you!"

Brother Johnson's head was hung in shame. "President…"

"Your own daughters, Thomas?" Nephi Josephs threw the affidavits down in front of Johnson, who recognized what they were immediately. "An evil has come before our people and you're right in the middle!"

"These are Gentile lies…"

"Those affidavits are from your wives…but let's talk about the Gentiles," Josephs smiled. "I agree they made this mess, but answer me this, Thomas?"

"Anything President Josephs," Johnson answered pathetically.

"As the leader of the sect in this area, you are commissioned by God to lead, correct?"

"Yes, President Josephs."

"So, you were either blinded by ignorance or slothfulness to observe what was going on inside your family, or you were complicit in the evil plot? Which is it?"

"I…"

"Leadership can be trying Thomas," Josephs tone turned soft and understanding. His gaze upon Johnson became patronizing. "Sometimes we as leaders make mistakes." Josephs leaned toward the ex-Bishop's ear, "Did you make a mistake, Thomas?" Johnson bowed his head in shame. His silence was an answer to the affirmative. "You know what must be done?"

"What about my family?"

"They will be given to another for the remainder of their earthly life but will be reunited in the eternities."

"Yes President."

"Are you strong enough, or is help needed?"

"I need help," Johnson was in tears at this point.

"Kneel before Heavenly Father."

Johnson knelt on the elevated platform facing the brethren and the crowd. Not a sound could be heard, but an eerie silence that deafened all who were present. Nephi Josephs waived his hand to the crowd, and the crowd began to sing *'We Thank Thee O God For A Prophet'*, a popular LDS tune. Nephi Josephs approached Johnson from behind and innocently put his hand on Johnson's shoulder. He began to speak loudly as the crowd continued to sing.

"Paul says in 1st Corinthians Chapter 5, Verse 5, *'To deliver such a one unto Satan, for the destruction of the flesh that the spirit may be saved in the day of the Lord Jesus.'* Simply put, brethren, if we fall prey to Satan on earth, our loving God provides us a way to return to his glory and exaltation. But it does require sacrifice," Josephs looked like a supreme leader and Johnson his subject kneeling at his feet. "The sacrifice is our flesh. This is the law of the prophets. This is the law given with the restored Gospel of Jesus Christ, and Thomas accepts it." The crowd, still mesmerized as they sang. In an instant, a dagger appeared in Josephs' hand that was presumably secreted in his suit pocket. Josephs clumsily attempted to slice Johnson's throat but his inexperience could not complete the task. Johnson was bleeding and in agony but only squirmed in pain on the ground, never actively resisting his fate. Josephs finally straddled Johnson on the ground and thrust the blade in the former Bishop's neck several times. The passive struggle suddenly ended almost as fast as it started. Johnson's last sound was the whispering gurgle of his own exsanguination.

The Prophet stood to his feet, his white shirt stained with the blood of Thomas Johnson. The crowd finished the song, some with tears, some with sadness or indifference, but all in dead silence. He collected himself and his thoughts. Sariah looked at her father and uncle which stood looking on with complete contempt for the deceased. It was as if they merely witnessed a bug's death. Her feelings, however, were different than she imagined. She expected to cheer the death of such a monstrous man, but instead she was horrified by what she witnessed. Tears appeared as more of her innocence was lost at that meeting, but even worse, her belief in any God suffered due to the Prophet's spiritual justification of such brutality. She pitied Johnson. A lifetime of service to a misogynist, vengeful God left him slumped in a bloody mess with nothing to show. His wives, his company, and position would go to another. Her attention once again focused on the Prophet who stepped in front of the podium, bloodied and tattered from the night's activities.

"I say these things in the name of Jesus Christ...amen."

"Maria, we got to speak with Dan," Flynt said as he and Kidd walked directly towards Dan Gummit's office door.

"I...I haven't seen him in two days, Rangers," Maria said in a worrying manner. "His wife and family are calling too. I don't know what to tell them."

"Have you been inside his office?"

"No, Sir...Chief Gummit said he'd fire anyone that went in his office without his permission."

"Where are the keys?" Flynt asked in an expedient voice.

"I don't have any."

Kid approached the door in preparation for a door kick. Maria watched in an alarming manner. Flynt turned to the frightened receptionist and smiled, "Don't worry, we're professionals." Kidd gave a healthy kick forcing the office door to slam into the wall behind it. There the two Rangers discovered Dan Gummit dead, still sitting behind his desk. His head lay back appearing as if the deceased chief were staring at the ceiling. There was a bottle of whiskey and a half full glass on the desk. The deceased chief was shirtless, the Rangers noticed as they approached cautiously. It looked as if Dan Gummit had been dead at least 24 hours. *Why shirtless?* Kidd thought as they carefully continued towards the desk to take a better look without disturbing any evidence. A shriek from Maria at the doorway startled the Rangers, causing them both to jump. They turned to see a horrified woman standing at the entryway.

"Maria, darling," Flynt said. "Call in to Company D of the Rangers. Tell them that I am requesting a Ranger investigate a police chief's death. Then please take the day off."

Maria nodded in agreement with tears in her eyes. She disappeared from the doorway and the Rangers continued to search. Kidd took out his Stinger flashlight and shined it on the body.

"Richard?" Kidd addressed his senior partner.

"Yes?"

"Look at his side," Kidd shined the flashlight on the side of

Gummit's torso. Four clear patches were seen stuck to his body. The Rangers recognized the patches immediately; they were Fentanyl Patches. Both Rangers had worked several cases where those particular patches, made for the most extreme pain relief, were misused with fatal results. "Recommended dosage is one patch every forty-eight hours. He had enough to kill a horse. Wonder where he got em?"

"That's Company D's problem now," Flynt answered. He shook his head. "He knew we were coming for him. He even died a coward." Flynt looked at the paperwork on his desk. A certain spreadsheet caught his eye. "Kidd?" he called out.

"Yeah?"

"Look familiar?"

Kidd looked at the spreadsheet. He immediately recognized it as the same one seen at Trey Caldwell's residence. "Holy shit!" Kidd exclaimed and looked at the document more closely. "Richard, that's a Department of Public Safety document?"

"It is," Flynt responded. Flynt calmly folded the paper and placed it in the packet of his sport coat. Both Rangers looked up and saw several Eagle Pass PD officers in the doorway. "I need ya'all to set up a perimeter and start a case log. Company D will be down here shortly." They watched as the officers went into work mode; no emotion was observed at all.

"How'd he know we were coming?"

"Writing was on the wall. My guess is he heard about Mexico and Texas Don's findings, couldn't face the fallout."

"We done then?"

"Nope, afraid not," Flynt replied sadly. "We have one more stop."

POSTSCRIPT

The bumpy road that led to Jim Foster's house was familiar and long, but somehow this anticipation of seeing his friend did not seem as welcoming this trip. Flynt could not hide his look of anguish and he knew his younger partner saw it. Flynt turned to his junior partner as he parked the Crown Vic, "You mind staying in the car, Darren?"

"You sure you don't want me with you?"

"Yeah, I need to do this alone."

"Okay, I'll be right here."

Flynt got out of the vehicle and walked up the steps to the front door. As he approached, he heard a voice yell from the back patio.

"Come on in, Richard! I'm on the back patio!" Jim Foster's voice was unmistakable.

Flynt couldn't help but look at Jim's family pictures hanging on the wall and all of his awards from his days as a celebrated Texas Ranger. The smiles in the pictures were an outward sign of happiness and accomplishment which made Flynt's visit that much more difficult. He walked outside to the elevated patio and saw Jim Foster sitting at the far end of the table. He was wearing his Ranger Stetson and a formal shirt. A glass of whiskey sat right next to a stainless Colt .45 on the table. Flynt recognized the pistol as the one Jim received at his retirement, stainless steel with custom wood grips.

"I been expecting you, Richard," Jim said with slight smile. It was clear to Flynt that he was drinking by his mannerisms, and not necessarily by the half bottle of whiskey on the table.

"I suppose you have," Flynt smiled back. The two men stared at each other for a couple of very uncomfortable moments.

"Well sit down...let's talk."

Flynt sat down at the table opposite of his longtime friend. It was hard to muster the words to say but somehow he managed, "How long did you supply Gummit with the checkpoints to the Human Trafficking Task Force?"

"Richard…"

"We found the spreadsheet in a man by the name of Trey Caldwell's possession. Caldwell smuggled the girls across the border for a couple of Cartel connected folks. We saw the same spreadsheet in Gummit's office."

"Gummit's still connected…"

"No Jim, local law enforcement was prohibited from knowing the locations of the task force," Flynt interrupted Foster. "Those spreadsheets came from an internal DPS email."

"You know me, Richard, I hate emails and texts and such," Foster attempted to smile to lighten the mood.

"I know you hate them," Flynt's voice was turning more serious. "That's why you wouldn't have known that you can trace the source of emails to an IP number."

"IP number?"

"Basically, we can tell where the emails come from." Richard stared at Jim Foster, whose expression never changed. "The email was sent from DPS headquarters to you. You then sent them to Dan Gummit." Flynt continued to watch Foster. There was a long pause in the conversation. Eventually, Jim Foster broke the silence.

"When Nita passed, she left me with some pretty hefty bills that stretched my pension…"

"You could've called…"

"Now listen damnit!" Foster was becoming frustrated. "I don't want no help. That ain't the kind of guy I am." Foster's eyes appeared watery as he conveyed his feelings "Dan came to me and said I could earn a few bucks and help law enforcement out."

"You believed him?"

"The man was a snake…but I was in a bind," Foster replied. Jim Foster put his hand on the .45 on the table. Flynt stared at Ranger. As fast as Flynt was, Jim was faster, even at his advanced age. Flynt watched the torment in his former idol's eyes. He also knew that a desperate man with nothing to lose was the most dangerous of them all.

"You going to shoot me, Jim?"

"Considered it," Jim Foster no sooner got the words out when both he and Flynt heard the distinctive sound of the selector switch of an AR-15 switching from safe to fire.

"Tell you what I considered," Ranger Darren Kidd's voice was strong and distinctive. Foster turned to see the young Ranger pointing the rifle directly at his head. "Being the man that kills a so-called legend. No matter how fast you are, I can goddamn guarantee you this trigger finger is faster." Foster stared at Kidd for a considerable amount of time. He appeared to be sizing him up again. He eventually turned back to Flynt.

"I like this kid, Richard." Foster smiled as he pushed the weapon toward Richard who promptly unloaded it and set it back on the table. Kidd lowered the rifle to the low ready position.

"Yeah he's got his strong points," Flynt smiled back at his mentor.

Jim took another swig of whiskey. "How long do I got?"

"Company D's dumping Dan's computers. They're going to take them to the lab in McAllen. I'd say three weeks."

Jim smiled, "They might not catch it?"

"Might not...but we did," Flynt observed. "I don't know what to say, Jim."

"Ain't nothing you can say," Jim looked at the ground. "Give me a week to get things situated with the family?"

"Of course," Flynt's sadness was coming out in his demeanor. "I'll take care of this mess, Jim. I promise."

"I appreciate it," Jim Foster finally smiled. He looked at both Rangers, "Drink?"

"Not today, Jim," Flynt replied indifferently. "We gotta go." Flynt got up from his seat and took the .45 round out he kept in his chest pocket and set it on the table, bullet up. Flynt and Foster looked at one another in that moment, both understanding the inevitable future. It was death before dishonor. Flynt walked down the outdoor patio stairs to meet Kidd in the back yard. They never looked back as they walked from the legend's house.

*

Both Rangers got up from their seats when Sariah came into the restaurant, they could see Sariah smile as she crossed the busy dining room. There was something eerily different about her. She wasn't the confused angry girl that they initially met; she was beautiful, mature, and wise. Kidd couldn't help but feel some sadness, he knew what it was like to lose a belief system and feel unguided in a large world. But he also knew that Sariah was strong and that she would be successful and overcome this episode in her life. But he was also not naïve enough to believe there would be no scars.

"Hey guys!" Sariah gave both men a big, sincere hug on her approach. She sat down jovially.

"Hungry," Flynt asked.

"No, just coffee."

"We're going to report you!" Kidd smiled with the obvious coffee reference.

"Really?" she smiled and made a sarcastic, disgusted face. "Besides, there's no bishop to report to." Both Rangers chuckled at Sariah's dark humor. "Too soon?"

"Um…yeah," Flynt responded sarcastically. Both had heard about what took place at the priesthood meeting. They looked at this young, beautiful woman who had witnessed more brutality in her short life than anyone should. "You want to talk about that?"

"Nope," the young lady smiled. "Anyways, I wanted to thank you guys."

"For what?" Flynt asked curiously.

"Getting me the DPS Scholarship for one. And you know…for everything."

"Not bad for a couple a godless Gentiles, eh?"

Sariah again looked sarcastically at the men, "Okay, whatever. Anyway, I'm headed to the University of Utah. Linda Melton also offered me a job with the Anti-polygamy lobby."

"Bet that went over well at the home front?"

"Well, I just managed to piss off two of the three sister-wives," Sariah's statement caused an outbreak of laughter at the table.

"Dad?" Kidd inquired.

"Didn't jump for joy…a bit disappointed, but good I think," Sariah smiled. "I just really can't thank you guys enough." The young girl's eyes began to tear. She felt the arms of both Rangers wrap around her in a sudden display of warmth. "One question though?"

Both Rangers looked at the young lady with anticipation. Flynt finally responded, "Sure, Dear?"

"How did you guys get Uncle Moroni's contact information?"

Kidd cleared his throat, "When I was being a gentlemen and helping you in the vehicle…I kind of saw your phone contact list and copied it."

"Before I went to see Amanda?"

"Yep."

Sariah smiled, "You crafty sons of bitches!" Sariah grabbed both men around the neck again and started to cry. "Thank you."

"Thank you," Flynt whispered to the young girl. It went without saying that perhaps this wayward daughter of a polygamist touched both Kidd and Flynt a lot more than even they realized. The three sat at the table and talked for two hours. For that time, they had no care in the world, just friends forging ties and building memories. It was the first taste of happiness that each had felt in a long while.

*

Flynt and Kidd stepped out from under the funeral tent into the bright setting sun which was setting in the West, carefully placing their Stetsons atop their heads. Jim Foster's funeral precession was massive. Seemingly every agency in Texas sent squad cars to participate in the ceremony. The lights of the hundreds of squad cars remained on, even during the service. There were two straight hours of speeches, from the Director of the Agency down to some lowly Troopers that lamented the passing of their idol. The stories of valor, bravery, and courage filled the speeches and the collective tears from the gallery seemed endless. But the real question pondered by the attendants was why such a highly decorated and celebrated Ranger would take his own life.

The investigation was clear to the County Deputies. Foster was found in his favorite chair with his .45 pistol still in his hand. Dead from a single gunshot wound to the head. There was no formal note, but his will and instructions to the family were laid out on the floor for all to see. Investigators also discovered that the pistol was empty. Meaning only one round was ever loaded in the gun's chamber.

"You think he knew?" Kidd's question broke the silence. It also reminded both Rangers of the dark cloud that lingered over what was supposed to be a solemn occasion. Kidd still was very careful when he referred to his partner's fallen idol, Jim Foster.

"He knew," Flynt replied expressionless, staring at the horizon.

"And Gummit? He know about those girls dying cause of all this greed?"

"He did." Flynt sighed. "I think the only person that didn't know about this deal was El Patron. How's that for irony?"

"Then explain how a multi-millionaire, spiritual leader could sell his own daughters into sexual slavery? I mean…that money would be peanuts compared to what he's worth…"

"You know it was never about money, Darren," Flynt abruptly interrupted his younger partner. He put his head towards the floor. "It's about the sickness."

Kidd immediately understood his partner. There were no theories, or experts that could explain human actions. The depravity and indifference shown by mankind towards its own would never be quantified or even understood. His partner called it a sickness; perhaps it was. Or perhaps humanity's expectations for itself were simply unrealistic and naïve. "We done here?" Kidd asked in an indifferent tone.

"Yep," Flynt just kept staring in the direction of the sunset. "You know the bad thing about being the only people that know a secret…is the secret itself. I guess we carry it till death."

"I guess," Kidd too looked to the dimming sunset, for no

particular reason. "You were right."

"About?" Flynt asked.

"I was taught growing up God can't give us anything we can't handle. I since found out life can."

"Mexico?"

"I thought it would be easy, ya know. Those bastards killed little girls for Christ's sake," Kidd paused. There was an emotion that could be appeared suddenly in his voice. There were no tears or sobs, just a voice that his partner heard only a few times before from the hardened investigator. "All I hear are those women's screams in that cantina. I...I just don't feel the satisfaction I should." He felt a gentle pat on the back from his partner.

"You were right," the elder Ranger said.

"Come again?"

"This is life. I been going to church all these years, prayin', worshiping and such. I hear about all the beauty and love in the world," Flynt shook his head at the sun. "But when I go to work I see none of that. Hell, I can sometimes see the beauty, like that Texas sunset out yonder...but I'll be damned if I can find the love. And God? Hell, best I can say is maybe the Good Lord saved my ass a few times."

Kidd finally cracked a smile to try and lighten the mood. "That's beautiful ain't it?'

Flynt smiled at Kidd, "Guess it'll have to be. Seemed ugly at the time, I guess." The two men turned and watched as Deputy Director G.W. Cahill approached them from behind. He wore a simple black funeral suit foregoing the popular police formal uniform.

"You alright, Richard?" Cahill's accent was thick with Texas, but formal reflecting his formal education. "I expected you to say something? You knew him best out of all of us."

"I guess I got nothing to say today, G.W." Flynt replied coldly, watching Cahill nod his head in agreement. It was apparent that G.W. understood his longtime friend's mood. He must have also recognized the hurt and pain in his two subordinates.

"Then I guess I need to come clean," Cahill stated

remorsefully.

"You mean about sending the task force schedules to Jim?" Flynt looked at Cahill who was hanging his head in shame and embarrassment. "G.W., there ain't nothing to be sorry for."

"He said he had some connections to help out. Hell, Richard…it was Jim?"

"G.W. I probably would've done the same thing…I guess we were all fools."

"What now?"

Flynt turned to his boss; probably one of the few people that have made sure Richard Flynt even had a job over the years. "The Johnson boys are in jail for the murdered councilman. Nobody cares about Texas Don or Trey Caldwell. Ain't no one going to miss Sonia Nava and the Feds are digging up the records at Eagle Pass. Hell, the polygamists are always quiet."

"What about the mass grave?"

"Everyone thinks it was the Mexicans…I suppose we let em." Flynt's face was absent of any feeling. "The issues are resolved. Let's not speak of em again."

"And Mexico?"

Flynt gave the Deputy Director a look of finality that was understood. He knew Cahill was too smart not to figure out that there was more to the unorthodox resolution to the matter. But Cahill had been around long enough to know that complex situations required similar solutions and the less the public knew of the specifics, the better. As far as the justice system was concerned the matter was resolved, but the price and cost to the men tasked to resolve such matters was always much higher than anticipated. "It's finished."

G.W. stared at his longtime friend and could sense the anguish. "You know when I started this job forty years ago…I planned on changing the world. I was going to clean up all this shit and bring policing into a civilized age," Cahill looked again at the ground. "Ain't nothin civil ever come about. It's just as brutal as it ever was. I suppose the less people know the better. We'll let folks sleep at night." Cahill turned to walk back toward the crowd, "Look, Richard, why don't you and Darren come up to Austin and stay with me and Katy for a week or so?

Plan on going down to the Blanco for some fishing."

"Sir, we can't impose on ya'all," Kidd interjected.

"Nonsense, I insist. You both are coming and that's an order. It's fully paid, you don't have to burn any vacation at work," G.W. smiled and walked away. "See you soon." The Rangers watched as the Deputy Director walked back into the throngs of mourners. Flynt looked at his younger partner and they both laughed. The human toll they had witnessed, the carnage and misery seen over the proceeding days seemed to culminate in a brief, humorous moment. Flynt smiled.

"Looks like we're fishin."

*

"Look at you…you, Gentile whore!" Linda Melton threw her arms around Sariah as they stood on North Temple Street, overlooking the Salt Lake City Temple of the Church of Jesus Christ of Latter-day Saints. The stone edifice cast its shadows on throngs of visitors that flocked to it daily. Linda looked fashionable and sexy as always sporting tights and knee-high leather boots. Sariah now looked to be her twin. A smile came over her face not seen since her parting with Rangers Flynt and Kidd.

"Well…I'm here," Sariah replied to her friend. Her journey to Utah was indirect. For the first time in her life she didn't have a direct purpose. She stopped in cities along the way, Dallas, Albuquerque, Santa Fe, and others just for the experience. There was no more anguish about whether or not her words or deed would anger an unseen, fickle God. But moreover, she discovered she was okay with not knowing what life or the eternities had in store for her. She would just have to be pleasantly surprised along the way. It was life before death, not after.

"I'm so glad," Linda beamed. "How'd your folks take the departure?"

"How do you think?"

"Yeah, dumbass question," they both laughed.

"So, what will my job be?"

"We're going after someone big and we need your connections."

"You're not talking about the LaFeys?"

"Oh God no!" Linda exclaimed. "You think I want that crazy family of yours to raise my head on a stake?"

"Very funny."

"Besides, they're Mexico's problem…why they would never come into the United States, right?" Linda's sarcastic look and tone made them both laugh again.

"Then who's the target?" Sariah asked. Linda held up a glossy picture of the Prophet Nephi Josephs to her face. An internal excitement that was difficult to contain came over her. "I get to go after Nephi Josephs?"

"He's been flying under the radar. The lobby's been focused on Warren Jeffs and the Allred Group for so long, we forgot how much of a dirty fuck Nephi Josephs is. Most of the women here know the Utah polygamists, but hardly anyone knows about what goes on in Texas," Linda observed. A wry smile came over her face. "Did you really stab the Johnson boys in the ass?"

Sariah showed Linda the cell phone photos of Josiah and Nathan naked, wounded, and whimpering in the barn. "I can't describe how good that felt."

"You are my fucking hero!" Linda jumped for joy, smiling again at Sariah, "So what do you say, can you get some dirt on old Nephi?" Sariah smiled back and took the picture out of her friend's hand and tossed it on the ground flagrantly. The two young women grasped hands and began walking up the street with no real destination in mind.

"The son of a bitch, pervert won't know what hit him."

ABOUT THE AUTHOR

David R. Waters is a relative newcomer in the crime fiction genre. David lives with his wife, Marti, in Dallas, Texas enjoying the newfound freedom as empty-nesters. He's a twenty-year veteran of a metro area Police Department specializing in crimes against persons and crime scene investigation. His books focus on the visceral reality of crime and the moral effects on both the victims and those that enforce the law, often taking the reader through exciting twists and dark places without sacrificing literary style.

Printed in Germany
by Amazon Distribution
GmbH, Leipzig